Drama in the
Church Saga

Drama in the Church Saga

Dynah Zale

www.urbanbooks.net

Urban Books, LLC
300 Farmingdale Road, NY-Route 109
Farmingdale, NY 11735

Drama in the Church Saga

ISBN 13: 978-1-62286-532-1
ISBN 10: 1-62286-532-4

First Mass Market Printing September 2017
First Trade Paperback Printing February 2015
Printed in the United States of America

10 9 8 7 6 5 4 3 2 1

Distributed by Kensington Publishing Corp.
Submit Orders to:
Customer Service
400 Hahn Road
Westminster, MD 21157-4627
Phone: 1-800-733-3000
Fax: 1-800-659-2436

Drama in the Church Saga

a novel by

Dynah Zale

Dedication

To my mother, Lorraine Evans.
Your support of my dreams has shown me just
how blessed I am.
You've been more than a mother, but my best
friend.
You encourage me, stand by me, and love me.
I thank God for you every day.
Love, your daughter.

Acknowledgments

To my loving Father in Heaven, Your word has been a lifeline for me throughout the conception of this book, and I pray that every person who reads this will recognize that **ALL THINGS** come from you.

To my BIG brother, Michael Holmes, you have exceeded my expectations of what a big brother is supposed to represent. I love you, not because of what you do, but because of who you are. Your kindness, compassion, and generosity is what places you above all the rest.

To my FIRST brother, Kalee Evans, biology tells us that we're only cousins, but because of our close relationship, you feel more like a brother. We fight and argue like siblings, but I'm glad to say you are one person I can count on. You are there when I call for help and ready to lend a helping hand. You never forget about me, and for that, I love you.

Roxanne Evans, you have been a shining example to me of what a prayer-driven life looks like. You have passed your Godly wisdom down to me and now I'm trying to share that with the world.

Thanks for caring, thanks for driving me to all those church conference meetings, and, most of all, thanks for praying for me.

Shantece, Courtney, and Michael Jr., you three are all a part of me. Your spirit and words are kept in my heart and that pushes me to succeed. Auntie loves you XOXO.

I have to shout out my Philly connection. Special thanks go out to Shelly, Gwen, Kathy, and Dana for being true friends. You ladies don't realize how much a simple phone call or letter from each one of you has meant to me. You have kept my spirits up with your words of encouragement, and I truly appreciate every single word.

Macdonald Taylor, you should be a motivational speaker because I can't count the number of times you've called at just the right time to remind me that I CAN DO ALL THINGS THROUGH CHRIST.

A special shout out to my friends down in the ATL: LeKisa Blackmon, Dajuan Boyd, Kimberly Flagg, Alfred Giavance, and Tamiko Young/Miller. Holla at your girl. DramaInTheChurch@hotmail.com. Lil Little, I am thankful to have you as a friend, confidant, and sister in Christ.

Special recognition goes to Tatiana Cody, Monica Fauntleroy, Maurice Lomax, and the entire Evans family. Tatiana's lighthearted wit and humorous critique of the book cover was priceless advice that I couldn't do without. Maurice and

Monica, I appreciate your invaluable time that you disposed to me at my convenience. Thanks to my entire family for your support and encouragement. (Janae Gilbert thanks for being my little helper) Hugs and kisses go out to my cousin Leah Long for reading the first three chapters of the book and wanting to read more. I guess I need to put an APB out on Margo Lane Muse because that will be the only way I can get the girl to get in touch with a sistah. (You know I love you from the bottom of my heart.)

To Deborah Mathis, a special friend who extended her help, advice, and expertise. Thank you so much and I hope to work with you again one day.

To Mr. Kenny Johnson, a solider who is overseas defending this country. Stay in prayer, read your bible, and have faith, and before you know it God will be sending you back home to all those who care and love you. You are in my prayers. Love ya.

I need to thank the entire Q-Boro family; from each and every single individual who has read, edited, and touched my book. To those individuals I will be working with in the future. Thanks.

Candace, I once heard a pastor say that angels come to earth as friends and they will bless you at a time when no one else can. I see you as being one of those angels. . . . I'm a firm believer that everything happens for a reason. Our connection was not a chance meeting, but definitely a well-orchestrated plan. Without you, none of this would have been possible. Thanks again.

Last, but definitely not least, Mr. Mark Anthony. You have blessed me with an opportunity that most people only dream of. Thanks for recognizing my talent and being such a versatile visionary that you saw a place for Christian fiction at Q-Boro.

Chapter 1

JUNE 2003

Valencia Benson, a twenty-year-old, mocha-brown knockout—which was how most guys referred to her—stood five feet three inches tall with a small body frame and ample 38D breasts. Her large bust size drew a lot of attention, which at times could be a problem. Guys would approach her just to stare at her chest. She had seriously considered undergoing a breast reduction, but when it came time for her to meet with the doctor, she lost the nerve. Her bust was probably the only part of her body she wanted to change. Val's body closely resembled an Olympic athlete's; her stomach was tight, her thighs were strong, and her booty was firm. She worked out often and drank plenty of water to keep her body fit.

Val tossed her shoulder-length weave over her shoulder and gazed up at the wooden cross illuminated by light hanging above the pulpit and whispered a silent prayer. *That cross held so much power*, she thought to herself. She had knelt in front of it a zillion times since she was old enough to walk. The cross was a reminder to her that God was her foundation and nothing would break the promise He made to walk with her through life. She often looked to the cross when she was going through bad times, but she was glad to know that God was also there during the good times.

"Here you go, dear. Enjoy the service," came a soft voice.

A startled Val looked up to see Ms. Young handing her a Sunday program. Ms. Young was a member of the prestigious Seniors Club. There were only a few senior members left in the church. All of the others had gone on to see the Savior, but Ms. Young was still biding her time here on Earth. She was a dedicated member who walked a mile to church every Sunday. She never allowed a foot of snow or a deadly hurricane stand in her way of serving the Lord. Val admired Ms. Young's commitment and love for Jesus.

Val loved being a member of First Nazareth A.M.E. Church, where the congregation felt like family. Every Sunday she was always welcomed with a huge smile and a warm hello. Once she entered the church, the Spirit took over and all she could do was sit back and enjoy the ride. The choir shouted praises to the Lord and Reverend Simms jumped for joy at the teachings of God's word.

Although First Nazareth was a small church with less than seventy-five members listed on its church roster, it still ranked high on the list of lying, scheming, backstabbing, and deception that played out among its members.

Mrs. Simms, the pastor's wife, interrupted Val's thoughts when she began to speak before the congregation. "The time has come for us to bring our burdens to the Lord," she said. "We use this time to tell God what's in our hearts and minds. It's also a time for us to repent to the Lord for the wrong things we've done by thought, word, or deed." She motioned for Olivia to come to the front of the church.

"Church, our dear, sweet Olivia has an announcement to make." Mrs. Simms held Olivia's shaking hand tightly. Silence filled the church. All eyes settled on Olivia, waiting on her to speak. Finally, words began to drift from Olivia's mouth.

"Church, I'm a s-s-sinner," she stammered. "I'm pregnant."

The announcement stunned Val. She stared at her cousin and tried to understand what she was doing. Val thought everyone in the church was a sinner, so for Olivia to make a public announcement was extreme. The congregation replied with disapproving stares and whispers.

The women in the church ran to her, poured oil over her head, and began to speak in tongues. Others caught the Holy Spirit and ran around the church. The remaining members formed a circle around her and held hands while they prayed.

They acted as if they were performing an exorcism on her. Val wanted to console her very passive cousin, but Mrs. Simms lovingly placed her arms around Olivia's shoulders.

"I've spoken to Reverend and Mrs. Simms, and they have shown me the error of my ways," Olivia continued. "I have repented to the Lord, and I want to apologize to the church for any shame or embarrassment I may have caused." Olivia wiped her eyes as tears fell down her face.

"Church," Mrs. Simms yelled above the commotion. "I have assured Olivia that the Lord loves her and no one here would ever judge her. Isn't that right, church?" she asked. Suddenly, amens and hallelujahs exploded throughout the sanctuary. Olivia's announcement had really moved the congregation. The pianist began to play, and members stomped their feet.

Val felt like the church was treating Olivia's confession as a black stain on a pure white wedding dress—like it was something she was supposed to hide or be ashamed of. When Val looked at Olivia she saw that innocence she had possessed since they were kids. Her light brown hair was pulled back in a ponytail that cascaded down her back. Most people would describe Olivia as plain looking, if not homely. She never wore make-up or any type of revealing clothing that showed off her curves. The only distinctive features she had were her light, hazel eyes and round, full lips.

Val was older than Olivia by seven months, and it was still hard for Val to accept that Olivia was no longer her little cousin. Val remembered the many times she had to fight girls on the playground because Olivia wouldn't stick up for herself. She was always very quiet and kept to herself.

Bryant, whom Val had met a few times, was Olivia's very first boyfriend. Olivia never dated much, so when Olivia began often talking about the things she and Bryant had done together, Val knew he must have been something special. Val was eager to get to know him better, but every time she suggested they go out together, Bryant was always working out of town. It was a surprise for Val to find out that Olivia was having sex. She had always assumed that she would be the first one to have a baby.

The church settled down and refocused its attention on Mrs. Simms and Olivia.

"Olivia has decided to keep the baby," Mrs. Simms announced. "And the church is going to support her in any way we can."

Another series of amens and hallelujahs stirred the church. Mrs. Simms hugged Olivia one more time before Olivia returned to her seat next to Val.

Val immediately pounced on her. "Olivia!"

"Val, don't say anything to me. You're going to make me cry." Olivia took a tissue out of her purse and wiped her eyes.

"Olivia, how could you not share this kind of information with me?" Val whispered.

"I was going to tell you. I could never find the right time."

"But you found the time to tell the entire church?" Val asked, astonished by her cousin's last comment.

"Val, can we discuss this later?"

"Hell no!"

"Val, we're in church!" Olivia said. She looked over her shoulder to make sure no one had heard her cousin's foul mouth.

"How could you let them coax you into doing that?"

"What . . . what did they do?"

Val hated it when Olivia acted so naïve. She was always trying to please somebody instead of doing what was right for her. Val knew that Olivia was blind to many things that went on around her, but she thought the girl would know when someone was trying to manipulate her.

"They had you crucify yourself as the sacrificial lamb. You put your flaws on public display, when not one of them is any better than you. They ain't nothin' but a bunch of hypocrites."

"Val, stop it! I won't have you speaking against the church."

"Olivia, you know I'm telling the truth. Remember how Desiree Carter stole the Sunday School Superintendent position from you?"

"She didn't steal it! The elders appointed her to the position."

"Yeah, right. She played you for months, stealing all your ideas for the Sunday School." Val laid her hand down on the Bible. "You told her all the plans you had, and she pretended to be your friend, telling you that you would be perfect as Sunday School Superintendent. Then when the announcement was made, Desiree acted surprised when her name was called.

"Her husband made a three thousand dollar donation to help the church get a new roof," Val continued. "Then the following week an announcement was made that she had accepted the position of Sunday School Superintendent. They never even held the required elections like they were supposed to."

Olivia tried to ignore Val by opening her Bible.

"Val, what does that have to do with anything?" she asked anxiously.

"It bothers me that you told the entire congregation personal information, when you couldn't even tell me, and we're cousins."

"Val, I needed to talk to someone. I spoke with Mrs. Simms about it and she suggested I tell the church. She said I would feel a lot better if I confessed my sins."

"Yeah, confess your sins to the Lord, not to the whole damn church!"

"Val, stop cursing in church!"

"I can't help it. I'm so mad. I don't believe they did this." Val tried to calm down.

Focusing back on the service, the pastor asked everyone to open their Bibles to John 8:7. "My sermon this morning is entitled, 'Let thee without sin, cast the first stone.'"

"What a coincidence," Val sarcastically mumbled.

Elise, Val's Bible Study facilitator and mentor, walked through the church gathering Bibles. Val followed behind her ranting and raving about what had happened to Olivia on Sunday. Elise believed in giving direction and spiritual guidance to each one of the young adults in her Bible Study class. She listened to their problems and gave advice on how to lead a righteous life, but it wasn't always easy trying to nurture a young adult's mind.

"Elise, are you listening to me?"

"Val, I'm listening to you. I was there."

"I know. That's why I don't understand why you didn't do anything." Val took the Bibles out of her hand.

"What was I supposed to do?" Elise ran her fingers through her Halle Berry haircut.

"They used her!" Val said boldly.

"Are you cold?" Elise asked, trying to change the subject. She walked over to the thermostat. "They didn't use her. They just helped her realize the wrong she had done," Elise finally commented.

"So, you agree with what they did?"

"Val, Olivia committed a major sin. This sin is going to follow her for the rest of her life. Perhaps Mrs. Simms thought that if Olivia acknowledged her sin then others wouldn't make the same mistake. The pastor's wife did say that the church was going to support her in any way they could."

"Elise, you were the one who taught us that a sin is a sin, that it doesn't matter how big or small you may think it is. It's all sin," Val said.

Again, Val stared at the wooden cross that hung in the front of the church. She was determined to get her point across. "Listen to this." She sat in one of the pews. "Olivia never actually admitted to doing anything wrong. She just announced she was pregnant."

"The last time I checked, sex outside of marriage was a sin," Elise replied.

"Yeah, but pregnancy outside of marriage isn't."

Elise looked at her strangely. "Val, what are you talking about?"

"The Virgin Mary wasn't married when she got pregnant with Jesus. She wasn't considered a sinner, so why should Olivia?" Val replied with a smirk on her face.

"You always have to have the last word, don't you?"

Val smiled brighter.

Suddenly, the church doors swung open and Julian Pennington, Val's boyfriend, strolled down the church aisle flashing his pearly whites.

Val and Julian had been together since their freshman year in high school. They had endured their share of ups and downs like every couple, but their love for one another always pulled them through.

Most of the girls at Philly High School described Julian as a pretty boy with a baby face. He was often told he resembled the R&B singer, Usher. Julian was considered a good catch, not just because of his handsome good looks, but also because of his determination to be successful.

Obsessed with the dream of one day becoming a basketball star, Julian perfected his basketball skills by spending all his spare time in the gym. Ultimately, it paid off, securing him a spot on the varsity team. The coach recognized his talent and appointed him co-captain of the team his freshman year.

Despite Julian's arrogant attitude and boastful behavior, Val's love for Julian was rare. He was her first love and she dedicated her life to making him happy. She would do just about anything he asked. Whether she had to stay up all night writing a paper for him or finishing his homework before her next class, Val was the kind of woman who stood by her man through the good and the bad.

Julian's feelings were mutual for her. He knew how lucky he was to have Val in his life. The love they shared was special and hard to describe. Their bond was strong and they refused to let outsiders interfere with their love. Their decision to wait until after marriage to have sex seemed to strengthen their relationship.

Julian finished his sophomore year at the University of Kentucky, and after several debates with his parents, he decided to forfeit the remaining two years of his scholarship and enter the National Basketball Association.

With his six feet, two inch, 210-pound frame, Julian bent down to kiss Val on her lips. "Valencia, I hope I wasn't interrupting anything." Julian always used Val's full name. He loved the way her name rolled off his lips.

Elise shot Val a look that asked the question, "Were we finished?"

"No, honey you didn't interrupt anything," Val responded. "Where have you been?"

"I went to get a haircut and then I went to the gym." He thrust his arms into the air and bulged his biceps, mimicking Popeye. "I'm trying to get in shape. Is it working?"

"Yeah, baby, it's working," Val replied sarcastically.

The next person to arrive for Bible Study was Montrese Cox, whom they called Tressie.

"Hey, Tressie." Elise greeted her with open arms. "We missed you in church on Sunday. Where were you?"

"I overslept," Tressie responded. She took a seat in the pew directly in front of Val and Julian.

Elise stood up. "While we wait on Danyelle and Olivia, I thought maybe—"

"Danyelle is outside," Tressie said, interrupting Elise mid-sentence. "She's outside smoking a joint." Tressie made a loud cracking sound with her gum.

Elise walked to the church doors and stuck her head outside. "Danyelle, what did I tell you about smoking marijuana in front of the church? If the police catch you they're going to arrest you."

Danyelle took one long last drag of her joint and threw it on the ground. She walked up the church steps. "I'll just tell them that it's a European cigarette."

"I'm sure they can tell the difference," Elise said.

"Jesus loves me," Danyelle sang as she entered the church. Her high-pitched voice went to a screeching high that made everyone in the church stop and look at her.

"Yes, Jesus loves me," she sang out again. She laughed because she was used to getting strange looks because of her odd behavior at times.

Danyelle was a hefty girl and nobody would ever make the mistake of calling her petite. Her body had lots of curves. Her hips were wide and her huge bust size was a genetic trait that had been passed down in her family from generation to generation.

Danyelle smoked morning, noon, and night. She claimed that marijuana was her motivation to get out of bed in the morning. Before inhaling her first puff, she would always kiss it up to God first and say a silent prayer. She prayed that the Lord would bless her experience, so she would get the most out of her high. She believed that God made weed as a natural herb, and it was there for everyone to enjoy.

"For the Bible tells me so." Danyelle finished her song. Julian laughed at her.

Elise walked in after picking up the joint Danyelle threw on the ground. "Danyelle, why must you do that every time you enter the church?"

Danyelle knew she was referring to her singing, "I'm just letting the Lord know that I've arrived."

"I'm sure the Lord could never miss you. Where's Olivia?" Elise asked Danyelle.

"She said she wasn't feeling well and decided to stay home."

Val gently cleared her throat to signal to Elise that Olivia was embarrassed by what happened on Sunday.

Elise spoke up. "Today, I would like to talk about the power of prayer. It is so important for us to maintain a close and intimate relationship with the Father." She clasped her hands.

"The only way to do that is through prayer. God wants us to tell Him about any burdens that we are carrying. He also wants us to tell Him about the amazingly good things that happen in our lives. We can only do that by going to Him in prayer. I challenge everyone in here to double the amount of time they spend in prayer. If you pray for five minutes a day, double it to ten minutes. If you pray for an hour a day, double it to two hours a day. Prayer is going to be our focal point for the next few weeks. We will have a more in-depth conversation on prayer next week. Does anyone have any questions?"

Julian raised his hand. "Is it all right that I pray about which team I prefer to get drafted to?"

Elise laughed at his question. "Yes, Julian, if you want something specific, you need to be specific in your prayer. If you desire something and it's in God's plan for you to have it, you will receive it. God wants to bless you. All you have to do is ask."

"Can I pray for a man?" Tressie asked.

"Sure."

"Can I pray that the Lord send me Nasir Jones?"

"Who is Nasir Jones?" Elise asked.

"Nasir Jones is this rapper who's already engaged to Kelis," Val spoke up.

"Tressie, I'm pretty sure God isn't going to give you someone else's fiancé, so you need to change your prayer request."

Elise fielded the other attendees' questions and they all sang a few hymns.

Elise concluded her lesson by saying, "For the first week everyone should pray for one thing. Next week, when we gather again, we'll discuss whether or not God answered your prayer. Is that all right with everyone?"

Everyone in the room nodded.

"I'll close out in prayer."

Everyone held hands while Elise prayed.

"Heavenly Father, I want to thank you for once again bringing us safely together. I ask that you bless each and every heart here, and that they increase their prayer life to get closer to you. Through prayer they will realize and experience that you have control over all things great and small. Amen."

In unison everyone responded, "Amen."

Chapter 2

The following day, Olivia walked into the apartment she shared with her sister, Danyelle, and was welcomed by a cloud of smoke. She waved her hand in front of her face to see what was causing the entire apartment to be engulfed in smoke. She found Bryant and Danyelle sitting in the living room with what appeared to be a pound of marijuana lying on the coffee table.

"Why can't you two smoke outside?" Olivia asked, annoyed. This was not the first time she had asked them not to smoke in the house.

"Hey Livie," Bryant said. "How was your doctor's appointment?"

Olivia looked at him, surprised that he had even asked. After her first doctor's appointment, weeks had passed before he asked her how it went. Lately, he had lost interest in the baby, which concerned her because when she first told him, he was so excited. Olivia badly wanted Bryant to participate more in her pregnancy.

Ever since Olivia was a little girl she had wanted to be a mother, and the idea of her soon becoming one brought joy to her heart. She looked forward to the monthly doctor visits and midnight food cravings.

Her only regret was that she and Bryant weren't married. She never thought she would be having a baby out of wedlock, but she knew there wasn't too much she could do about it now. Bryant had made it clear that he was not going to marry her just because she had gotten pregnant.

"Well the doctor said that . . ." Olivia began.

"Hold up, baby." Bryant held up his finger. He turned toward Danyelle. "Yo, where you going with that?" Danyelle had gotten up from the couch and started to retreat to her bedroom, taking the smoking joint and the ashtray with her.

"Oh!" She looked back at Olivia. "I was going to my room. I wanted to give you and Livie some privacy."

"Yeah right, you were trying to smoke the whole joint by yourself."

Danyelle pointed back at Bryant. "Negro, you've got five joints rolled up in front of you that we haven't even touched." Then she pointed over in the corner. "Not to mention the bundle we haven't even opened."

Olivia looked over at the cube of marijuana securely wrapped in clear plastic wrap lying on the floor.

"No need to get hostile. I forgot. My fault!" He turned back to Olivia. "Sorry, honey. Now what did the doctor say?"

"Forget it!" Annoyed, Olivia stormed toward her bedroom. She was tired of Bryant putting his marijuana habit before their baby.

"Where are you going?" Bryant yelled out.

Olivia closed the door and cried. She felt like her life was falling apart. She wanted the baby to come into the world feeling that it was loved by both its parents, but Bryant acted so selfish at times she wondered if that was possible.

She wished her mother were there to fix the problems in her life. She remembered the last conversation she had with her. Olivia was in her bedroom getting ready for bed when her mother walked in.

"Livie, can I speak with you for a minute?"

"Sure, Mommy." Olivia jumped into bed and pulled the comforter over her legs.

Her mother smiled and took a deep breath. "Olivia, I don't like to ask you to promise me anything because I know you're only nine years old and you have a lot of growing up to do, but I have to ask that you make me this one promise."

Olivia's soft eyes asked, What is it, Mommy?

"Promise me that no matter what happens in life, you will always keep the word of God close to your heart. Being obedient to God will carry you through the roughest times in your life. Trust him. He will never leave you."

Olivia held her mother's final words close to her heart. Later that night her mother had a heart attack in her sleep and died instantly.

Since then Olivia had kept her promise to her mother and was a devoted Christian who read her Bible regularly. She tried to live the life of a righteous woman, but lately she struggled in her Christian walk. It all started with Bryant.

From the beginning, Olivia was very up front with Bryant. She told him she was a virgin and explained how important it was for her to remain one until her wedding day. Olivia knew how most men felt about being in a celibate relationship, and she had prepared herself for the possibility of him walking out of her life forever. Surprisingly, he wasn't angry nor did he walk out on her. In fact, he told her that he respected her values and her desire to wait.

Three months later, he suddenly had a change of heart and started pressing her to have sex with him. Every time they went out he would beg her to make love to him, but Olivia was strong and held on to her vow. Before long, arguments arose and he threatened to end their relationship. Olivia panicked. She didn't want to lose him. He was her first boyfriend and the only man she ever cared about besides her father. She felt cornered, and after careful consideration, she gave in to his demands, but only under one condition: that they always use a condom.

The first time they made love Bryant made her feel like he was the one she had been saving herself for. He was gentle and compassionate. She couldn't help but fall in love with him. Being in his arms and sharing her body made her happy. There was nothing she wanted more than to be with him. After they made love, they realized the condom had broken. She missed her period, and then the morning sickness began. She bought a home pregnancy test and that's when her greatest fears were confirmed. She was pregnant.

Depression set in fast and Olivia isolated herself from friends and family. Val often questioned Olivia's strange behavior. Olivia reassured her that the stress from working long hours at the bank was making her tired, but Val wasn't buying it. Bryant was also concerned about her. Unsure of what to do, he asked her if she wanted to have an abortion. *An abortion?* The baby growing inside of her was so unexpected. And then to suddenly get rid of it? Would that be another sin? She needed somebody to talk to. She usually confided her problems to Val, but this was different. Val and Olivia had made a pact to remain virgins until marriage, and now Olivia was embarrassed to admit she had broken their vow to one another. For weeks Olivia prayed that the whole situation would just go away. Finally, the burden of hiding her secret became unbearable. That's when she went to see the pastor's wife.

Mrs. Simms always encouraged members of her husband's congregation to come and pray with her if they had problems that were too much for them to bear alone. Mrs. Simms and Olivia prayed for over an hour. Afterwards they discussed the pros and cons of her pregnancy. Mrs. Simms pointed out that terminating her pregnancy wouldn't erase the sin that had already been committed, but ultimately Olivia would have final say on the fate of her baby. Olivia pushed her fears aside and decided to give her baby a chance at life.

Mrs. Simms asked a lot of questions about Bryant. Where was he from? Did he have any ties to the community? What did his parents do?

Olivia couldn't answer any of her questions. She didn't know too much about Bryant's background because he never talked about family or friends. One time he did tell her that he was raised by an elderly aunt in North Carolina. He described himself as a drifter who never stayed in one place for too long. Bryant worked for Amtrak as a conductor, which required him to travel a lot. That was how they met.

Anxious to get back to Philly after a long, uneventful visit with her Aunt Gretchen in Chicago, Olivia ran through the train station trying not to miss her train. She was already late because her aunt tried to get her to stay another week, but one week of playing bridge with the old woman in her retirement community and watching reruns of *The Golden Girls* was more than Olivia could bear.

She couldn't figure out why her aunt never invited Val or Danyelle to come visit her. Olivia had been branded with the term 'Favorite Niece'. Olivia hated going out to visit her aunt every year, but because her aunt didn't have any of her own children and she was Olivia's mother's only sister, she felt she couldn't refuse her offer.

She looked at her watch as the whistle blew, giving the signal for the final call. People ran past and around her. Olivia made it just in time. She lifted her foot to climb on board when her foot missed the first step. Just before she hit the ground, Bryant came out of nowhere and caught her mid-air.

"You have to be careful. These steps are tricky," he told her.

"Thank you." Olivia was embarrassed by her clumsiness, but she was more embarrassed that the handsome conductor witnessed it firsthand. Olivia gathered her things and occupied the first empty seat she could find. Soon after, the same handsome conductor who broke her fall walked through the train collecting tickets. When he approached her aisle he asked her again, "Are you sure you're all right?"

Olivia wished he would forget her small but humiliating accident. "I'm fine," she replied.

"Good. Now that I know you're all right, would you mind going to dinner with me?"

Excited by his invitation, she gladly accepted. Over time they began to spend more time together and eventually their friendship developed into a relationship. When Olivia found out she was pregnant, Bryant asked if he could move in with her so they could be a real family.

Olivia looked at her growing belly in the mirror. The baby was getting bigger every day and her clothes were getting tighter around the waist. It wouldn't be long before she would have to start shopping for maternity clothes. Olivia grabbed her baby book and plunged into the first chapter when the phone rang.

"Hey mommy-to-be! What's up with you?" Val screamed into Olivia's ear.

"Nothing much. I just came from the doctor's office."

"How's the baby?" Val asked.

"The doctor said the baby is fine. I should have a healthy baby in six more months," Olivia nonchalantly responded.

"Why do you sound so down? This should be one of the happiest times in your life."

"I *am* happy," Olivia unconvincingly replied.

Val heard concern in Olivia's voice and she wondered what was bothering her, but instead of asking, Val decided on a different approach.

"Why don't you come to the mall with me? I need to pick up some things for Julian's party tonight."

"I don't know. I'm really tired."

Val acted like she didn't hear her cousin's response. "I'll be there to pick you up in ten minutes."

"I would like to see those three rings," Val pointed to three platinum diamond rings displayed in the glass showcase. The saleswoman laid them before Val and Olivia on a black velvet cloth. Val slipped a ring on her finger. "What do you think?" she asked, holding up the ring for Olivia to see.

"Nice," Olivia replied

"But do you think it's me? I don't want something too big, but it has to be classy."

Olivia looked at the rings more closely. "They're all nice."

"I think I like that one." Val looked at a fourth ring sitting inside the display case. The saleswoman retrieved the ring and handed it to Val. "Yes, I really do like this ring." Val stared at the large marquise diamond.

"I thought you said you didn't want anything too big," Olivia said.

"I don't, but this ring is beautiful. This is the one I want!"

The sales lady beamed. Val could see her brain calculate how much her commission would be on such an expensive purchase.

"Thank you." Val handed the ring back to the saleswoman, and the pleasant expression on her face turned sour.

"She thought she was getting that sale," Olivia whispered.

"She should have known better than that. What woman purchases her own engagement ring, except for Britney Spears?"

Olivia chuckled at the thought. They strolled through the mall and window-shopped.

"So, you and Julian are really going to get married?" Olivia asked.

"Yes. We've been talking about it more and more now that the draft is here. I think he's going to propose any day now. He doesn't want to get married his first year in the league because he wants to concentrate on the team and the role he's going to play with that team. He's really worried about his performance and how well he'll compete against different players. Playing in the NBA is so different from playing at the collegiate level. He wants to be able to go in and defend Kobe Bryant or block Kevin Garnett's shots. I keep telling him not to worry so much about proving himself to the other players. If he concentrates on his game, the respect he wants will follow."

Olivia pretended she was interested in what Val was saying, but she couldn't help thinking about Bryant and the baby.

"Do you want to eat here?" Val asked. They stopped in front of a small lunch café called Kaffe Crossing.

"Sure. I am hungry."

They entered the café and squeezed through the crowd of patrons to grab an empty table in the corner. Val and Olivia were regulars there. They loved the quiet, serene atmosphere that was provided by the dim lights and burning incense, in addition to the great food.

"What would you ladies like?"

Val heard a male voice behind her that was laced with the softness that accompanied a woman's voice. She turned and looked into the eyes of man built like a sculpture. He wore a black tee shirt that outlined his well-defined pecs and revealed the bulging muscles in his arms.

"I'll have a glass of lemonade and a chicken Caesar salad," Val told the waiter. "What about you, Livie?"

"I'm starving. Can I get the Angus cheeseburger with cheese fries, and a pickle? I'll also have a lemonade."

"Darn Livie, you really are pregnant. I've never seen you eat so much food."

The waiter scribbled their orders down on his pad and switched away.

"Do you believe that?" Olivia pointed to the waiter. "He is fine. He should be a model."

"A lot of male models are gay. They just don't advertise it. He apparently does," Val responded.

"Whoever his man is, he's lucky." Olivia stared in his direction.

"Livie, you could try to change him." Val laughed. "Seduce him back over to the loving arms of a woman."

The waiter walked back over to the table and placed their food and drinks in front of them. Before he had a chance to walk away, Val stopped him. "Excuse me."

He paused, turned, put his hands on his hips and looked at Val with attitude.

"Can I have some French salad dressing?" she asked.

Being overly theatrical, he acted as if Val's request was a nuisance. He snatched a bottle of salad dressing from the table next to theirs and slammed it down on their table.

"Is that all?" he asked.

"No," she replied. "What's your name?"

"Derrick!" he replied.

"Derrick, I love that name," Val said. Derrick responded with a blank stare.

Val continued. "Derrick, when did you start here? I come here often and this is my first time seeing you."

His body language expressed how unhappy he was with Val's question. "Well, Lois Lane, if you must know, I don't work here. I'm friends with the owner and his waitress called out, so I'm helping him for the day."

"Oh, okay. I was just wondering. I didn't mean to upset you."

He sucked his teeth and switched away.

"He acts just like I do when I'm on my period," Olivia said.

"Forget him. Back to what I was saying. I've been thinking about the wedding. I decided that I want something intimate. No press and no media. Also, I've decided not to hold the ceremony at the church."

"Well, where else would you get married?" Olivia asked.

"I have been thinking about getting married atop the Bellevue Tower. Julian and I went to visit their ballroom the other day and the place is exquisite. It would be romantic to get married by candlelight."

"That sounds beautiful."

"I want a six o'clock wedding." Val paused. "Livie, will you be my maid of honor?"

Olivia's heart was softened by Val's request. "I would love to be your maid of honor."

"Great, so you're going to help me with everything?"

"Yes, I'll help with whatever you need."

Olivia was happy about Val's pending nuptials, but she couldn't help but feel a little jealous. Val had a great boyfriend who not only loved her, but showed her how much he loved her. He always bought her little presents or would leave small notes reminding her of how much he loved her. She wished Bryant could be more like Julian.

Val knew there was something on Olivia's mind, and she was dying to find out what was bothering her. She hoped that if she kept talking, Olivia would eventually open up.

"Julian went to training camp with a lot of different teams, but he thinks that the teams most interested in him were the Miami Heat, Seattle Supersonics, and Milwaukee Bucks. I hope he doesn't get picked by Milwaukee. Girl, I can't imagine myself living in Wisconsin. There isn't anything there but cheese. I would go crazy."

"Val, you'll adjust."

"What school would I transfer to, the University of Wisconsin? Wouldn't it be exciting if he went to Miami with the warm sunshine, celebrities, and the parties? I heard that they party in Miami twenty-four hours a day. It would be great, but I'm not going to complain. Wherever my man goes, I will follow."

They sat for a brief moment not saying a word before Val finally broke the silence.

"Livie, what's up? You've been blue all day long. Is everything all right?"

Olivia flashed Val a phony smile, scared that if she said too much she would burst into tears.

"Is the baby all right?"

"The baby is fine."

"It's the church, isn't it?" Val concluded with a hint of menace in her voice.

Unable to hold back the tears any longer, the burdens and concerns Olivia had held in for so long poured forth.

"I knew it was the church," Val said, her teeth clenched. "I am so mad at what they did to you, Livie. But don't worry, I will handle everything. I will give them a piece of my mind. They will be sorry they ever messed with you."

"No, don't do that, Val!"

"Girl, I'm so sick of that church taking advantage of you. I think it's disgraceful how those members sit in church every Sunday and call themselves children of God when they treat people so badly."

Val paused to take a forkful of her salad. "The church is where people go for acceptance and church people are the most judgmental. I attend First Nazareth because Pastor Simms knows his Bible and he preaches the word, but outside of that I can't support that church."

"Don't condemn the church like that, Val. They're not bad people."

"No, they're not bad people, but they are not without sin either. So who are they to point out someone else's faults when they have their own?"

Olivia thought for a moment. Val did have a point, but she didn't want to talk about the church. "Val, it's not the church. It's Bryant and the baby."

"Oh, honey, I'm sorry." Val didn't know what to say. "What's wrong with you and Bryant?"

Val never thought to think that Olivia might be having problems with her boyfriend. Since Olivia barely spoke about him, Val often forgot he even existed.

Olivia told Val about how Bryant and Danyelle smoked marijuana in the apartment, even after she had asked both of them not to. She was concerned about how the smoke could affect the baby's health. She also described Bryant's distant behavior toward the baby.

"Olivia, you know that you have got to be positive and stress-free," Val said, stroking her cousin's arm. "Don't worry about tomorrow, for tomorrow will worry about itself. You and the baby are going to be perfectly fine. Bryant will come around. Maybe it just hasn't hit him yet. You really aren't showing yet, but as you get bigger and he realizes that there is a part of him inside of you, he'll be just as excited as you are. So just enjoy the time you have now, because once that baby gets here, you'll have no time for yourself."

Olivia smiled a genuine smile for the first time that day. She was glad Val was not only her cousin, but also her best friend.

"Are you coming to the party tonight?" Val asked.

"I don't know. I've been really tired lately."

Julian's mother was throwing a draft party that night in honor of her son. She had invited all of Julian's friends and family. Julian opted not to go to New York for the draft ceremonies because he preferred to watch it from home.

"Please come. It's going to be such a big night for Julian. And I would like for you to bring Bryant. I really don't know Bryant that well, but tonight would be the perfect time for me to get to know him better."

"All right. We'll be there."

When Olivia and Bryant walked into Julian's mother's house, it was crowded with people. Olivia recognized a few of Julian's family members and a couple of his teammates from Kentucky. She waved hello to Tressie who was standing in the corner talking to a very tall basketball player.

Julian's mother walked by carrying a tray of hot wings. Olivia thought Mrs. McCormick looked stunning every time she saw her. She had her hair pulled up into a ponytail and wore a thin layer of golden-brown gloss on her lips. Her low-rise jeans flattered her petite figure. Mrs. McCormick was often mistaken for a college student. Julian's mother looked much younger than her thirty-seven years. She gave birth to Julian when she was seventeen. Julian never knew his biological father; he was killed in a car accident two days before Julian's birth.

"Hello, Mrs. McCormick."

"Hello, Olivia." She reached over and gave Olivia a hug. "Congratulations. I heard about the baby."

"Thanks," Olivia responded, a little embarrassed that Julian's mother knew about her pregnancy.

"This must be the baby's father," Mrs. McCormick commented while looking in Bryant's direction.

"Yes. Mrs. McCormick, this is Bryant." They exchanged greetings as Bryant reached to shake her hand.

"Val told me you two were coming tonight. Bryant, why don't you come with me? I'll take you in the living room with the rest of the guys. Olivia, you can go see Val. She's in the kitchen."

"Val's in the kitchen?" Olivia asked, not sure if she heard the woman correctly.

"Yes, that child is in my kitchen. Please check in on her before she burns something."

Olivia walked into the kitchen to find Val walking around with an apron on. "Hey cuz, whatcha doin'?" Olivia asked.

Val pulled a tray out of the oven and almost dropped a pan of honey-roasted wings on the floor. "Girl, you scared me. If I had dropped these wings Mrs. McCormick would have my head."

"I was surprised to hear that you were in the kitchen. Of all the rooms in the house, the kitchen is the last place I would expect to find you."

"Yes, I know, but I felt bad. Mrs. McCormick cooked all the food for the party by herself, so I offered to help. I only offered because I thought she was going to turn me down. She hates for me to be in her kitchen."

Olivia laughed so hard she had to hold her stomach. It was weird seeing Val wearing an apron. Olivia pulled out a stool to sit on.

"No girl, don't sit down. Come into the living room with the rest of us. The guys have turned on the draft and my kitchen duty is over." Val took off her apron and threw it on the counter.

"Where's Bryant?" Val asked, looking around the living room.

"I'm not sure. He was supposed to be in here with Julian and his friends."

Val pushed her way to a seat next to Julian, and Olivia sat in a chair not too far away from her cousin. Olivia wondered where Bryant was. *Maybe he went to the bathroom.*

Julian was mesmerized by the pre-draft commentaries being aired by ESPN. A few analysts were sharing their opinions of where various draft hopefuls would wind up by the end of the night. His face was expressionless and his mind was preoccupied with his future.

"Honey," she called out to him. His eyes stayed glued to the television.

"Julian." She pulled his face toward hers and away from the television. "No matter what happens tonight, everything is going to be all right because we'll still be together."

Julian smiled and kissed her lightly on the lips.

"That's why I love you, because you're always by my side."

NBA Commissioner David Stern began the opening ceremony for the NBA Draft by making a short speech about the history of the NBA and the high standards the league holds each one of its players to.

The room fell silent as the celebrants waited to hear the first name called from Mr. Stern's mouth.

"With the first pick for the 2003 NBA Draft, the Cleveland Cavaliers select LeBron James." Julian's head dropped. *The wait and anticipation were taking a toll on him,* Val thought. She massaged the back of his neck to help relieve the pressure. Val watched LeBron hug his mother and walk across the stage to shake the commissioner's hand. They showed a quick interview with LeBron before they moved on to the next draft pick.

"With the second pick for the 2003 NBA draft, the Detroit Pistons select Darko Milicic."

The commissioner repeated his routine until he finally called Julian's name. All of the guests were gathered in the living room listening to every word the commissioner said, "The Seattle SuperSonics select Julian Pennington."

The whole house erupted into a roar. Val jumped up and hugged Julian. His mother pushed through the crowd to congratulate her son. Soon Julian was surrounded by well wishers.

After the commotion settled down, Julian yelled through the crowd, "Valencia! Where is Valencia?"

Val emerged from the crowd and stood beside her man.

"I want to make an announcement while everyone is here," Julian screamed over the crowd of people.

"First, I want to thank everyone for coming tonight. I appreciate all the love my family and friends have shown me, not just today, but throughout the years." He looked toward his mom and stepfather, Jerald. "Thanks for all your love and support, Mom and Dad. Through the years both of you have struggled to provide the best for me, and I appreciate all the things you've done for me." Julian walked over and gave his mom and stepfather a hug. The crowd applauded Julian's kind words.

He walked back to Val and grabbed her hand. "Now, I would like to thank my queen." He looked deep into her eyes. "You have stood by me since the ninth grade. You cheered me on at every high school game. You encouraged me when I lost faith in myself, and I know you will continue to support me in Seattle." Val blushed. "That's why I want to ask you . . ." He bent down on one knee. "Will you be my wife?" Julian pulled a small, burgundy velvet box from his pocket. Inside was a three-carat, pear-shaped solitaire diamond engagement ring.

The surprised expression on Val's face showed that the proposal was totally unexpected. She hugged him and tried to hide her tears from the host of people watching them. Julian pulled her back from out of his arms and looked into her face. "Should I assume that your answer is yes?" he asked her.

"Yes," she replied and again the house erupted into a thunderous roar.

Olivia watched her cousin accept Julian's marriage proposal. She thought it was so romantic how Julian surprised Val. She knew that Val's lifelong dream was coming true. Once again she wished Bryant looked at her the same way Julian looked at Val. Olivia looked around the room for Bryant, but did not see him. She walked into the kitchen, but he wasn't there either. She walked to the back door and found him talking on his cell phone.

"I'll guarantee delivery by the end of the year. Trust me, you'll have your package," Bryant said into the phone. Bryant had his back toward the door, not realizing that Olivia was standing behind him.

Olivia never heard him talk like that before. She wondered what he was talking about and whom he was talking to. *Was Bryant dealing drugs?*

"Bryant!" Olivia opened the door and walked onto the back patio.

Bryant turned around. "I'll have to call you back," he said into the phone.

He walked over to her with his arms wide open. "Hey, baby, did I miss anything? Did Julian get picked yet?"

"Yeah, he was just selected by Seattle."

"That's great. I can't wait to congratulate him. Come on, let's go back inside."

"Wait a minute. Who were you talking to on the phone?"

"Oh, that was nobody. It was an old friend from down south. He wanted to know if I could get him a few cases of shrimp. I work with a guy from Baltimore who can get cases of shrimp at a cheap price."

Olivia looked at him, unsure if she should believe his story.

He noticed the worried look on her face. He gave her hug and said, "Don't worry, it was nothing."

Chapter 3

Elise stumbled into the house with a purse, briefcase, and a Bible all in one hand. She planted her feet firmly on the ground and tried to regain her balance. She laid her Bible down on the small vestibule table and walked across the marble floor that expanded throughout the front foyer. The clickity-clack of her high heel shoes echoed throughout the empty room. She walked into the kitchen, expecting to find her husband slaving over the stove, but to her surprise, he wasn't there. She walked over and opened the oven door. Inside was a pot roast with potatoes. The aroma drifted past her nose, provoking her stomach to growl. From the den, Elise heard the sound of clacking computer keys. She followed the sound and there was her husband, with his eyes glued to the computer screen.

"Hey, baby!" Elise said in an attempt to grab her husband's attention. Preoccupied with the article he was reading online, he lifted his hand and casually waved to his wife. She walked across the room, sat on his lap, and peered at the screen to see what had him so absorbed. The title of the article was, "Is Impotency Hereditary?"

Elise's temperature immediately rose. Unable to control her anger, she jumped off his lap and stormed into the kitchen. Miles could sense an impending argument. He got up and followed her.

"Elise, I'm trying to find answers to what's wrong with me."

"Miles, you've been tested and your results came back fine. Why do you insist there's something medically wrong with you? The doctor told you to relax."

Uncontrollably, Miles's ears began to twitch, a sure sign that he was frustrated over a situation he couldn't control. She walked over and held his ears in her hands. She looked into her husband's eyes through his glasses. Her husband was not the best looking man, but his ordinary looks were appealing to her. He wasn't stylish nor was he athletic, but he was a man who loved the Lord, and that was so much more attractive than a man who worshipped himself or the material things around him.

"I've been relaxing. I took a month off from work and I haven't done anything, but . . ."

"Sit at the computer and search for medical reasons why you can't keep an erection," Elise said, finishing his sentence for him.

He looked at her strangely. This was the first time they had acknowledged his problem out loud.

"We've been married for six years, and I never had a problem until we decided to have a family."

Elise pulled two plates down from the top cabinet. "Well, you've been seeing a therapist. What does she say?"

"I told Dr. Johnson how I witnessed my father rape and beat my mother repeatedly. She thought my sexual deficiencies had something to do with what I saw as a child. She said that I might be suppressing my feelings of how scared I am of becoming a parent. That traumatic experience could be causing my body to react in a negative way, subconsciously, resulting in my inability to . . . you know."

"I didn't realize that experience affected you so deeply."

"Neither did I. Now I just have to find a way to live with it, because no matter what happens, I can't erase my past. I'm more concerned about the children we were planning. I know how excited you are to start a family."

"We just have to be patient. One day the Lord is going to bless us with a house full of kids. If we continue to pray, God will answer our prayers."

"I've been praying and he hasn't answered them yet."

"He will. Just remember, it's all in his time, not ours."

Elise fixed their plates to eat. They sat down at the dining room table in silence until Miles couldn't suppress his feelings any longer. "Elise, what are we going to do if my condition becomes permanent?" Miles blurted out. "I've been having problems for the past three months. How long can I expect you to wait for me?"

Elise never thought about what would happen if Miles's condition never improved. She realized that sex was a very important part of any marriage. She thought for a moment, *I can do without sex for a while.* But what would she do if he never got better? She looked over at her husband and saw the worried look on his face.

"Elise, I have a responsibility as a man to satisfy you. What's going to happen to our marriage if I can't please you? I can't expect you to live the rest of your life celibate because I have a sexual affliction."

He pulled his chair closer to her and grabbed her hand. "Maybe we should start thinking about what we're going to do if this condition persists."

"I haven't really thought that far ahead," Elise replied.

"First, I need you to know that my number one aspiration in life is to make you happy. You should never be sad, mad, or lonely." He held his head not sure if he should tell her what he had been thinking. "What would you think if I suggested that we explore an open marriage?"

"Open marriage! What is that?"

"It's kind of like having an affair, except you have your spouse's permission to see other people."

"Miles, you can't be serious!" she yelled.

"Hear me out. I know it sounds unorthodox, but it can work. I wouldn't ask you any questions about where you've been or who you've been with.

The only thing I would ask is that you choose someone I didn't know."

Elise got up and walked over to the refrigerator. She filled her glass with ice. "Miles, a marriage is not based on sex. It's based on our commitment to one another. This is a battle we have to fight together. I love you and only you." She walked over and kissed him on the lips. "'Til death do us part."

He smiled, relieved that she wanted to fight for their marriage. He pulled Elise down on his lap and wrapped his arms around her.

"I love you," Elise said. "Sex is about sharing yourself with someone you love. I love the way you wrap your arms around me at night. I love the way our bodies come together as one. If I have to wait a lifetime, that's what I'll do. I'll wait out this impotency thing, and God will fix everything."

She took a deep breath before finishing her thoughts. "If our situation doesn't change by the end of the year, we can begin to think about getting a surrogate or possibly doing in vitro. Whatever it takes, we will have a baby together."

Miles kissed Elise passionately on the lips.

***

"Elise, I hate going to these conference meetings."

"Tressie, yesterday you said you were looking forward to going," Elise shot back.

Elise and Tressie were on their way to Harrisburg, Pennsylvania. The youth of the A.M.E. Church were holding their quarterly meeting, where they collectively discussed ways to promote Christ and reach out to the community. In the past they had food drives, charity events, and church carnivals.

This year the conference president, Payne Boyd, said he wanted the church to "take things to the next level." Tressie wasn't exactly sure what that meant, but she did know from past experience that when Payne had a vision he would drive himself and those around him insane until he achieved his desired goal.

His last project, "Renaissance Children," focused on getting children reacquainted with Christ. He was determined to increase Sunday School attendance across the state of Pennsylvania by at least fifty percent. The project required that Tressie, as the conference secretary, travel with Payne to different churches to promote his campaign. Having to deal with Payne's bossy, pushy, and rude attitude was torture for Tressie. They argued all the time and never agreed on anything.

They arrived at the A.M.E. District Diamond Center just in time for the start of morning church services. Tressie took her place behind the podium as the morning emcee. A lot of different A.M.E. churches throughout the state attended the conference meeting, so the huge sanctuary was crowded and allowed for standing room only.

"I would like to welcome everyone here this morning and thank you for attending the third quarter conference meeting." The congregation applauded. "First, I would like to introduce our conference president, Payne Boyd. He is going to deliver the official welcome."

Tressie stepped down as Payne stood up and straightened his suit. On his way to the podium he gave Tressie a snide grin. As Payne addressed the congregation, Tressie had thoughts of pushing him out of the pulpit and into the audience. She mouthed a silent prayer: "Lord, forgive me for the mischievous things that just ran through my head."

After the morning service concluded, Payne called a meeting with all cabinet members. Tressie followed Payne into the back office, took a seat, and pulled out a pen and a pad of paper to take notes.

"First, I would like to address the attendance issue. I need for all members who hold office positions to be present at all quarterly meetings. If there is an . . ."

"Excuse me," Tressie interrupted. "Wouldn't it be wise if we opened with prayer first?"

"Of course. I was going to say a prayer after I addressed the attendance issue, but if you'd like for us to pray first, we will."

After prayer he again addressed the issue of attendance. During his speech there was a knock at the door.

"Come in," Payne commanded.

When the door opened Tressie looked up and locked eyes with the man of her dreams. The handsome stranger stared back at her. An electric current drew them both into a trance that neither could break.

"Payce, you wanted something?" Payne asked his twin brother.

"Um, yeah. I came in here to tell you that Daddy has made arrangements for you to catch a ride home with Deacon Law."

"All right, thanks," Payne replied.

Before Payce closed the door behind him, he winked at Tressie, planting a smile on her face that lasted for the remainder of the meeting.

After the meeting concluded, Mariah, the treasurer, walked over to speak with Tressie. "Hey, girl!"

"Hey, Mariah. What's up with you?"

"Nothing much. What about you?" Mariah grinned. "I saw you checking out Payne's brother."

The smile dropped from Tressie's face. "Payne's brother? Where?"

"The guy who interrupted our meeting, Payne's twin."

"Twin!"

"Yes. You didn't notice?" Mariah asked.

"No!"

"That's probably because he had a wave cap on his head. They look exactly alike. He's been locked up for the past year for selling drugs. Since his release, I heard he has been trying to get his life together."

"I bet that's really hard with a brother like Payne."

They laughed together and walked out of the office.

"Girl, give me a call. Maybe we can hang out sometime." Tressie waved good-bye to Mariah and went to track down Elise.

On the ride home Tressie was so excited about her brief encounter with Payce. She couldn't wait to fill Elise in. "Elise, we had a connection. He looked deep into my eyes and I looked into his. That is going to be my new man. I've got to find him."

"Tressie, slow down. You just met the guy."

"Elise, he is what I've been praying for. I prayed for a thug. He is the man I'm supposed to marry."

"Tressie, you didn't even speak to him."

"I didn't have to. We spoke through our eyes," she explained.

Elise laughed, thinking Tressie really had lost it.

"Listen, I prayed to the Lord for a thug. You should have seen him." She began counting off her fingers. "He had a wave cap on his head, a white T-shirt, a pair of baggy shorts, and Timberland boots."

"Well, for someone who only saw him for less than a minute, you sure did get a good look at his wardrobe."

"I know." She rattled on. "I was so mesmerized by his eyes that I didn't even notice that he resembled Payne. I didn't even notice they were twins until Mariah told me. Imagine me having to spend my entire life looking into Payne's face—the person I despise the most."

Elise laughed.

The following morning Elise decided to go for an early morning jog. Running was a stress reliever for her. It helped to clear her mind of the most recent burdens that were testing her faith. Her biggest concern was Miles and the sex that hadn't existed in their marriage for months. She had to admit, it was hard for her to go from having sex just about every day to three months of consecutive celibacy. She was frustrated and unsure of what to do.

Elise stretched her legs in preparation for her run. Each time she ran the three-mile perimeter around the park, she compared it to running the race of life. She believed that Christians who crossed life's finish line by enduring trials and tribulations would receive an abundance of blessings at the end. But not everyone will finish the race. Some people choose to spend their lives taking shortcuts and following their own plans that lead them off God's desired course. Over time, they get tired of trying to make it to the finish line and quit the race. Unfortunately, a lot of people miss out on what God has to offer them.

Elise took a deep breath and started around the park. The intake of fresh air into her lungs invigorated her. Jogging along the path, she tried to think of alternative ways she could satisfy her sexual desires without committing adultery. *I should invest in a vibrator*, she thought. Although she had never used one before, she had heard they could be quite helpful. She knew that they came in different sizes, but she didn't know what size she would need. She hoped they came with a user's manual. She didn't want to injure herself.

She was quickly approaching the end of the trail. Determined to finish the three-mile trail, she picked up her pace and circled the lake at high speed. Her legs were shaky and her joints ached. Ahead of her, she could see the marker where she started. Two steps from crossing the finish line, she was knocked to the ground with an intense pain that paralyzed her leg. She held her leg while a stream of blood flowed from the gash.

A strange man came and rushed to her side. "I am so sorry, ma'am." She looked up into the stranger's handsome face and was stunned by how handsome he was. His lips caught her attention first. He had a perfect set of full lips with a small mustache above his upper lip. Her sudden fascination with his lips scared her.

He asked her a series of questions, but Elise could not respond. Her sudden attraction to him left her speechless. Without warning, another shot of pain went up her leg.

"Ma'am, are you all right?" the stranger asked.

Elise nodded her head yes.

"I am so sorry."

Elise found the strength to utter the words, "I'm okay."

"I'm so sorry. You came from out of nowhere. I should have been more careful riding my bike."

"No, I should have been looking at where I was going."

"Can I take a look at that?" he asked, pointing to her leg. She slowly moved her hand so he could look at her wound more closely.

"That cut looks pretty deep. You may need stitches."

"You think so?" Elise had a tremendous fear of hospitals. Her Nana died during surgery when she was eleven, and the mere sight of a hospital gave her the chills.

"Can you stand up?" He helped her to her feet, but she couldn't put pressure on her leg. He made a suggestion. "How about you stay here and I'll go get my car? Then I'll take you to the hospital."

"No, you don't have to do that." She looked at her leg. "I don't think it's that bad. I don't need to go to the hospital."

"Let's just get a doctor's opinion." He knelt down and looked at her nasty wound.

Elise became hysterical. Her hands began to sweat and a look of horror came over her face. "No, please. I'm terrified of hospitals. I don't want to go. Please don't ask me to go." Elise grabbed hold of his hand and tried to keep him from going to his car.

He knew she needed medical attention. "Relax; I'm not going to leave you. I promise. You're going to be all right, but you need to have a doctor look at your leg."

"I don't want to go!" she screamed.

Surprised by her outburst, he tried to calm her. "Everything is going to be all right. You have to trust me. I'm going to pull my car around to the trail so you won't have to walk far. Stay right here. I'll be right back. Okay?" he asked.

Elise looked at him and nodded. The stranger ran away and Elise leaned back against a nearby tree. She hoped she wouldn't regret agreeing to go to the hospital.

***

Sheridan sat in the hospital waiting room watching reruns of *Three's Company* and looking at the hands on the clock move slowly around the dial. He was angry with himself for being so negligent. *How could I have hit someone with my bike? Please, God, let her be alright.* He was tired of waiting. They had been there for hours and the nurses wouldn't give him an update about her condition. When they arrived at the hospital he had attempted to go into the emergency room with her, but the hospital staff stopped him. They said that if he was needed, they would call him. He held her hand the entire ride to the hospital, but when he had to let go, she looked terrified. She even cried out for him. He felt bad. He had broken his promise not to leave her side.

Sheridan's intention that morning was to get in a little exercise by riding his bicycle through the park before he went to his friend Kyle's barbecue. He had been looking forward to the get-together all year long. He and a few of his buddies played cards, drank beer, and ate crabs—a party strictly for the guys.

He looked at the clock again. He had already missed the first three hours and he still needed to go home, shower, and change clothes. He decided to stop a nurse and try again to get some information. "Excuse me, could you give me an update on the woman I brought in?"

"I can't tell you anything, but I'll have a doctor come talk with you," the nurse replied.

Sheridan sat back down. He hoped he wouldn't have to wait much longer. All he wanted to do was get her stitched up and back to her car, and be on his way to the barbecue.

"Mr. Reed." A doctor invited him to walk down the hospital corridor. "Mr. Reed, your wife is ready to go. She just needed a few stitches. She did get a little hysterical when she saw the needle we used to give her a tetanus shot. I guess she's a little scared of hospitals, huh?"

Sheridan looked at the doctor strangely when he referred to Elise as his wife. He guessed the nurses had assumed she was his wife when he informed them that he would be paying for her hospital bill. After all, he was the reason she was in the hospital.

"Oh, yeah! She hates hospitals." Sheridan remembered how she reacted in the park when he suggested that she go to the hospital.

"I gave her a light sedative. She'll sleep 'til morning. You can take her home now."

The doctor pulled the curtain that surrounded the emergency cubicle. Elise lay on the bed sleeping soundly. Sheridan had to admit, she was a very attractive woman. Her slightly tousled hair lay over her left eye. Her beauty branded his heart, leaving a lasting impression.

"Here's a prescription for the pain." The physician handed Sheridan a piece of paper. "The nurse will bring you her discharge papers."

What am I going to do with her now that she is asleep? Sheridan wondered. "Damn, I'm going to miss that barbecue," he said out loud.

Elise focused her eyes on a photograph that hung against the wall across from her. The photo captured the innocence of a twelve-year-old boy dribbling a basketball. The photo and the boy were both unfamiliar to her, so she closed her eyes again, thinking it was all a dream. She turned over and pulled the covers over her head. *This bed seems awfully hard,* she thought. *It's usually much softer.* She smelled the scent of the sheets and that too was unfamiliar. These sheets didn't smell like Gain laundry detergent. She lifted her head and stared around the room. This wasn't her bedroom. The walls were a dull blue color. The far wall was devoted to baseball caps of various shapes and sizes, and trophies were crammed onto a small shelf in the corner.

Not exactly sure where she was, she listened to the noise coming from the other room. She could hear someone cooking in the kitchen. Elise attempted to swing her legs off the side of the bed, but a surge of pain shot up her leg. She grabbed her leg, hoping to stop the burning sensation.

She looked up and the stranger from the park was watching her. He stood in the doorway holding a bowl. He wore a Dajuan Wagner basketball jersey with a pair of black, oversized basketball shorts. His muscular, tattooed arms exposed the fact that he worked out daily.

"Good morning. Are you hungry?" he asked. Elise watched the words slide off his lips. His lips invited her to come closer. For a split second she wondered what it would feel like to have those lips pressed against her lips, neck, and breasts.

"Do you remember what happened yesterday?" he asked.

The last thing she remembered was being in the hospital and being poked with a needle.

"You may still be a little incoherent from yesterday. The hospital gave you a sedative. They said you were pretty upset about getting a needle." He flashed a devilish smile that looked like Denzel Washington's.

The throbbing pain from her leg was becoming a little too much for her to bear. The stranger noticed her holding her leg. "Your prescription pain pills are sitting on the nightstand next to you."

She turned and grabbed the bottle of pills. "Thanks," she replied.

"I'm making breakfast. Would you like something to eat?"

She glanced over at the clock sitting on the nightstand. "Oh my goodness! It's eight o'clock in the morning? I spent the night here?" Elise thought about how worried Miles would be. "I have got to get out of here!" She jumped off the bed and the immediate pressure she applied to her leg caused her to stumble. Sheridan ran over to catch her before she fell to the floor. They looked into each other eyes and the attraction between them multiplied by ten. Elise pulled away from him.

"Where's my cell phone? I can't believe my phone didn't ring all night."

"Ma'am, you didn't have a cell phone on you," Sheridan informed her.

"I must have left it in my car. You kept me here all night? I don't even know you. Did you ever think I could be married? What am I going to tell my husband? He has probably called the police and reported me missing." Elise yelled a series of questions at him. She pushed his hand away from her and leaned against the wall to regain her balance.

"I'm really sorry. I didn't mean to cause you any problems. When I took you to the hospital, they assumed I was your husband. You didn't have any identification on you or a cell phone, so I had no choice but to bring you to my house. The sedative they gave you put you in a deep sleep. I couldn't ask you where you lived." Sheridan's voice got higher and higher. He tried to defend his actions to her.

Elise felt bad for lashing out at him the way she did. "I'm sorry. It's not your fault. You don't know my husband. If I'm ten minutes late coming back from the supermarket, he gets worried. Can you take me back to my car?"

He walked out of the room upset by her accusations. *How dare she get mad at me for helping her out? I could have left her at the hospital and they would have labeled her a Jane Doe. I messed up my plans trying to be a Good Samaritan.* He grabbed his keys from the key holder hanging by the front door. He looked at her, rolled his eyes, and walked out, leaving the front door wide open. She followed behind him, limping.

Sheridan hated for a woman to be upset with him. Although he knew that he had done no wrong, he didn't want her to leave upset. "I really didn't expect for you to sleep through the night. I thought you were going to wake up in an hour or two and go home. Is everything going to be all right at home?" he asked.

"Everything will be fine," she replied.

He pulled up next to her car.

"Do you have a pen and a piece of paper?" she asked.

"In the glove compartment."

Elise pulled out a small notepad and pen. She scribbled her name and address on the sheet of paper, tore it off, and handed it to him. "I assume the hospital is going to send my hospital bill to your address."

"Yeah, I did give them my address."

"When you get the bill, can you send it to me?"

"No." He pushed the paper away. "I'll take care of the bill. I am the one responsible for your accident."

"No, I insist. Please send me the bill and I will have my insurance company take care of it."

"Okay," he replied reluctantly, taking the slip of paper.

Thirty minutes later, Elise opened her front door and came face to face with Miles. He sat on the bottom step of their winding staircase with his head in his hands. He lifted his head and Elise saw the worry in his eyes.

He saw the bandage wrapped around her leg and he ran over to her. He lightly brushed his hand over the gauze covering her leg. "Elise, what happened? I was so worried about you! I've been calling you all night. Where have you been?"

"I got in a minor accident in the park."

"In a car accident? Are you all right?" he asked and pulled her over to sit on the steps.

"No, not in a car accident." She carefully sat down on the steps, trying her hardest not to move her leg any more than she had to. "Some guy ran into me on his bike in the park yesterday. I was bleeding badly, so he took me to the hospital and they gave me stitches."

"You went to the hospital?" he asked, surprised.

"They gave me a tetanus shot. I completely lost it when I saw the needle. They had to give me a sedative to calm me down. So I spent the night at the hospital." This was the first time she had ever lied to her husband. She felt it would be best if she spared him the truth. The truth would only add to the problems they already had.

"The hospital! I didn't even think to call there."

"I left my identification and cell phone in the car, and the man who took me to the hospital didn't know my name. So they had no idea how to contact my family."

"Who is the guy who took you to the hospital?"

"I'm not sure. I didn't get his name."

"You never saw him before at the park?"

"No!" She wondered if he believed her story. "I caught a cab from the hospital back to my car this morning."

"Honey, I was so worried about you. I had so many terrible thoughts running through my mind. I wasn't sure if I should call the police. I thought . . ." He stopped mid sentence.

"You thought what?"

"I thought you left me. Maybe the problems we've been having was too much for you to bear." Her heart crumpled. She hated to hear him talk like that.

"You have no reason to think that way. I told you I'd never leave you."

"I panicked. I couldn't reach you and I thought the worst."

"I love you!" She leaned over and kissed her husband on the lips. "Can you help me up the stairs? I need to take a shower."

Chapter 4

The hands on the clock approached the eleven o'clock hour. Sunday school teachers were bringing their lessons to a close while members of the congregation arrived for Sunday morning service.

"Can someone volunteer to close us out in prayer?" Tressie asked her Sunday school class.

A group of seven-year-olds waved their hands, begging to be picked. Tressie looked out among them and chose Dontonio, who was hiding behind his sister. "Dontonio, why don't you close us out in prayer?" she asked.

"Awwwww man, why you pick me?"

"'Cause you were trying to hide from me, that's why. I'm sure the Lord would love to hear from you. Please close us out in prayer." The children gathered around, held hands, and formed a circle.

"Dear Lord, I want to thank you for waking me up this morning," the boy said. "Bless my mother, my father, and my sister. Amen. Oh! And bless Ms. Tressie, too."

Tressie looked up and smiled at Dontonio. "Thank you for including me. I'll see you next week, all right?"

"Yes, Ms. Tressie."

Tressie straightened up the church pews as the children gathered their things to go home. She grabbed a stack of Bibles and returned them to their place on the back of the church pews.

"Ms. Tressie?" Ta'Lena, one of her Sunday School students, called out her name. "This man was outside looking for you." Ta'Lena pulled a man by his hand into the sanctuary.

Tressie turned around and looked straight into those eyes. Those captivating eyes that held her completely hypnotized before; long, perfectly curled eyelashes above almond-shaped eyes. It was him. He was here. A wave of heat suddenly passed through her body like a storm. Except this storm held her like a hurricane that kept circling around inside of her.

"Hello," Tressie greeted him.

"Hi," Payce responded. Ta'Lena instinctively let go of his hand and ran back outside with the other children.

"Nice to see you again. What brings you here this morning?" Tressie asked.

"I came here to see you," Payce answered.

Before she could respond, Reverend Kane, the associate pastor, came up to her with the morning service program. "Tressie, I need for you to make a few announcements at the start of the morning service, and I want to change the scripture reading."

Tressie stood and listened to the adjustments Reverend Kane wanted for the program. Before the pastor had a chance to walk away, Tressie stopped her.

"Reverend Kane, this is a friend of mine, Payce."

The minister turned and reached for Payce's hand. "Hello, Payce." She greeted him with a huge smile and shook his hand. "I'm glad you came to worship with us this morning." She turned back to Tressie. "Thanks again for those changes, Tressie."

The organist began to play the opening hymn, giving the signal that service was about to begin. Tressie excused herself and took her seat in the pulpit next to Reverend Simms, the senior pastor. After the opening hymn concluded, Tressie led the church in prayer. As she bowed her head, she glanced over in Payce's direction. He winked his eye at her and she replied with a smile. *He is so cute*, she thought to herself.

Reverend Simms stood before the congregation and delivered a soul-wrenching sermon. "Church!" Reverend Simms screamed. "Beware of wolves that disguise themselves in sheep's clothing. Everything ain't what it seems. I Peter 5:8 tells us to be careful and watch out for attacks from the devil; for the devil prowls around like a roaring lion looking for victims to devour." Tressie absorbed the words of wisdom spoken by Reverend Simms.

After church, Payce waited around to speak with Tressie.

"I was so surprised to see you today," she said to him.

"I remember seeing you in Harrisburg, and my brother mentioned that you lived in Philly. Finally, after a lot of harassment and putting myself in debt by promising to get his car washed every week for the next three months, he told me your name and what church you attended."

"I'm flattered that you went through so much trouble."

"On my way over here I hoped that you would be worth all this fuss. Now that I'm here, I can see that you are."

Payce's compliments left Tressie speechless. She silently thanked the Lord for answering her prayers. He was what she had prayed for. She asked the Lord to send her a man who knew the Lord, but also knew the streets. She didn't want an uptight church boy who always followed the rules. She needed a man who broke at least some of the rules and created his own. It looked like Payce was that man.

"Would you like to go get something to eat?" he asked.

"Sure. There's a diner around the corner we could walk to."

They arrived at the diner and were immediately seated. Tressie had been to the diner at least one hundred times before, so she already knew what she wanted to order.

"Pastor Kane looks very familiar to me. Has she been with your church very long?" Payce asked.

"She's been a part of our church for probably five or six years now."

"She looks so familiar. I've probably seen her at one of the conferences or meetings that my father has, but I don't want to talk about the church. I want to find out more about Montrese Cox."

Tressie looked over at him. He was casually dressed in a blue-striped button up Sean John shirt with a pair of matching blue khakis. She loved his style. She could definitely fall for him.

"There's not much to tell. I'm a full time student at Temple University. I'm majoring in psychology. I lead a boring life."

"Well, it can't be that boring if they voted you in to hold a position with the church state conference, along with my brother."

"Oh yes, your brother. I had no idea your brother had a twin."

"Well, he wouldn't tell anybody. I'm the bad boy of the family."

Luckily I like bad boys, Tressie thought.

"I heard that you were away for a little while," she replied.

"Yeah, I did some stupid things that got me locked up, but I'm home now and I'm determined to do better. I just need a good woman by my side to keep me out of trouble."

"I'll say a prayer that you'll find that woman."

He looked into her eyes. "I think I already have."

"I did it! I prayed without ceasing! I took my troubles to the Lord and he answered my prayers!" Tressie screamed as she danced her way into the church.

Everyone was gathered together going over their current Bible Study lesson when Tressie burst in with her testimony.

"Did everyone see my man in church Sunday?" Tressie asked.

Olivia was glad to see Tressie so happy. It had been a long time since she had smiled so much. She had seen Tressie and Payce together in church and thought they looked like a cute couple.

"I was surprised to see him here!" Elise replied.

"So was I, but he tracked me down and he came there specifically to see me," Tressie rejoiced. She sat down in the pew smiling. She was obviously in a cheerful mood.

"I just want to testify that God does answer prayer. When Elise told us to increase our prayer time, I did. I began praying in the morning before my first class and in the afternoon. Plus, I prayed on the train after my final class ended. Elise said that we could pray for anything we wanted, so I prayed for a man, and I was very specific about the man I prayed for. I did ask God not to send me anyone who would remind me of Payne Boyd."

"But, isn't that exactly what he sent you?" Elise asked.

Tressie started laughing. "Yes. Payne's twin brother, but he is the total opposite of his brother. They may look alike, but that is where the similarities end."

"Wait a minute, you're dating Bishop Boyd's son?" Olivia asked.

Tressie nodded. "Let me finish telling you about my blessing. I began praying to the Lord telling him I wanted a man who believed in God, but I didn't want a corny church guy. I told God that I wanted him to be fine and respect me, and Payce is all those things. He's different from the kinds of guys I've dated in the past, I wanted a change."

Tressie's past boyfriends were at one time all residents of the county jail. Everyone attracted to her had a criminal record, cornrows in their hair, and Timberlands on their feet. It was hard not to confuse them with one another because their matching tan khaki outfits made them look like they were still imprisoned in the penitentiary prison yard. This stereotype included her former, longtime boyfriend, Jabril. Jabril was currently serving a fifteen-year sentence for drug trafficking.

Tressie had plenty of life-threatening stories involving Jabril. They had been stuck up, shot at, and even car-jacked together, but none of this stopped her from standing by her man.

Jabril was a big time drug dealer from Camden, New Jersey who made a lot of money and bought Tressie whatever she wanted. A drug deal gone bad made him a fugitive. He was apprehended by the police on Christmas Day, and his arrest was televised on the eleven o'clock nightly news. Before he was transported to the county jail from the police station, he stopped to give a statement to the press.

"I'd like to thank each and every one of you for coming here tonight to report on my arrest and the pending charges against me. First I want to declare my innocence. I have done nothing wrong. Secondly, I'd like to give a message to my girlfriend, Tressie." Jabril abruptly snatched the microphone from the reporter. "Tressie, I love you, and if you ever leave me or if I catch you with another nigga, I'll kill you."

The police pushed him into the waiting police transport and closed the door. Tressie watched the local affiliate stations air that statement for two days straight. Tressie feared for her life. She knew what Jabril could do to her, even from behind prison walls. During his trial, television stations replayed the threat against her life.

Jabril was found guilty and sentenced to fifteen years, plus an additional eighteen months was added to his time for the televised threat he made on Tressie's life. Some time had passed before Tressie felt safe enough to date again.

"When I first laid eyes on Payce, I knew he was the one," Tressie continued. "I just wanted to share my story with everyone here so that you would continue to pray."

"Thank you," Elise said to Tressie. "It is important to pray without ceasing. Pray to the Lord about the things you want and continue to pray for them until he answers your prayer. But keep in mind that the things you pray for must be in accordance with the will of God. Don't ask the Lord to give you someone else's husband because that is not going to happen. Don't ask the Lord to successfully see you through on robbing a bank because it's not going to happen. God is not going to give you or put things in your life that are going to harm you, so if you're praying about something, and he doesn't answer, then perhaps the Lord doesn't want you to have it. Some things were not meant to be."

Olivia thought about herself and Bryant. She had prayed to the Lord every day about them getting married, but she was beginning to think it was useless. She had brought up the subject of marriage to him the other day, and he quickly changed the subject. Perhaps Elise was right. Maybe some things were not meant to be.

MID OCTOBER 2003

Val hung up the telephone as Julian walked into the kitchen.

"Olivia said to tell you hello."

"How is she doing?" he asked.

"She's doing well. She said she's getting bigger and bigger every day."

"I bet she looks funny with her big belly and skinny body," Julian replied.

Val smiled at the thought of her cousin being pregnant. "Julian, where are you going?" Val asked as he kissed her and grabbed his keys.

"Oh, I have a meeting with the general manager."

"What time will you be back?" she asked.

"I'm not sure, but don't wait up."

"Julian, you have gone out every night this week. You said you were going to take me out last night and you couldn't because practice ran late. When are you going to be able to spend some time with me? I sit in this house night after night, alone."

"Valencia, please don't complain. I try the best I can to get home to you at a decent hour. I'm sorry I couldn't take you out last night, but you know how important it is for me to grow with this team.

I have to learn everything I can in order to adapt to this new environment. I have to learn new plays, get accustomed to how the other players make advances on the court, and on top of all that, the general manager has asked me to attend a few important meetings concerning the team's future. That's a lot of responsibility for the rookie of the team." Julian took her hand in his. "I promise you that when things settle down I'll spend all my extra time with you. All right?"

Val watched through the living room window as Julian pulled out of their driveway. She was not looking forward to sitting in that big house by herself, again. Is this what she had to look forward to once they got married? Val and Julian had moved to Seattle the first week in September. Julian bought a large house in an exclusive section of suburban Seattle. The five-bedroom house had everything: a swimming pool, two car garage, home theater room, and state-of-the-art kitchen, but even with all those luxuries, she was still lonely.

Before their move out west, Val had been accepted to the University of Washington. She planned on continuing her education so she could graduate on time, but Julian suggested she take a year off. He thought it would be good for her to begin their wedding plans. She reluctantly agreed, but lately every time she mentioned the wedding to Julian, he changed the subject or insisted that they talk about it later.

Val had only been in Seattle a short time, but she already missed the familiar sounds of Philadelphia. She missed the cheese steaks sold at Jim's on South Street, the familiar sound of Carter n' Sanborn on the radio, and the unity of brotherly love that the city represented. She especially missed Olivia. Olivia was going to have her first child in a couple of months and it hurt Val, because she knew she wouldn't be around to watch the baby grow. Val had thought about going for a visit, but she couldn't leave now. The season home opener was next week and she had to be there, plus she was looking forward to attending a party that the owner of the SuperSonics was throwing. The party would give her the opportunity to get better acquainted with the other players' wives and possibly make some new friends.

NOVEMBER 2003

Olivia and Bryant lay in her bedroom watching a Bruce Lee movie. Bryant had rented six of them and they were only on the third one. Tired from reading subtitles, Olivia turned over. The baby kept moving and she couldn't find a comfortable position. Bryant noticed her restless behavior and snuggled in closer to her. Olivia enjoyed her time alone with Bryant. He seemed to change into a different person when they were by themselves—more kind and considerate. For the past few months Bryant had been traveling out of town a lot, working in different cities, but now that her due date was quickly approaching, he had promised to stay close to home.

She lay against his chest as he rubbed her stomach. He pulled up her shirt to glorify the roundness of her belly. "Look at all this baby," he said proudly.

The extra weight was beginning to wear her down. "The baby is getting so big. I wish he would hurry up and come."

The soft kisses Bryant planted on her neck suggested he wanted more than a simple kiss. His hands gradually moved down around her hips and slid off her panties. Olivia sat up and straddled him, allowing the baby to rest on him.

"By the size of your stomach, he should be a ten-pounder," Bryant said.

Bryant slid out of his boxers and into her. Olivia frowned as he entered her.

"Are you all right?" He asked.

"Yeah, I'm all right. Just a little uncomfortable."

"Am I hurting you?"

"No, I'm okay."

Bryant grabbed her hips and took things really slowly. He didn't want to hurt her or the baby. He looked up into her face and her frown had been replaced with a smile.

He was glad she was enjoying herself. It was the first time in a long time Olivia had allowed Bryant to touch her. Any attempts he made to initiate sex were refused. She always claimed she wasn't feeling well. But just because she refused to give him any, didn't mean he went without. When working out of town, Bryant always managed to meet female companions who were willing to share their love with him.

Over the past year Bryant had enjoyed spending time with Olivia. There was definitely something special about her. Usually, Bryant wasn't attracted to churchgoing women. The women he usually dated drank all day and had sex all night. He was used to the fast, ghetto girls, but Olivia possessed a soft, quiet demeanor and beautiful, subtle looks that could easily be overlooked if one didn't pay close attention. Those qualities were probably what attracted him to her, but what made him continue dating her was her kind, compassionate, and unselfish nature. She was the first girl he had ever met who cared about him unconditionally. Bryant was used to girls trying to use him to pay their rent or pay for daycare. Not Olivia. She asked him how his day was and was sincerely interested in his job and the work he did. He loved those attributes and if he ever decided to settle down he wanted to find a girl just like her. Unfortunately, now was a bad time. There was no place in his world for Olivia.

He refused to allow his feelings to interfere with business. Like his uncle always said, "Money first, pussy second."

It felt so good being inside of her that Bryant couldn't hold back any longer. He exploded inside of her. Exhausted and tired, he still wanted more, but Olivia had other things in mind. She immediately climbed off him and fell fast asleep. He knew that if he attempted to wake her up, it would be in vain, but maybe later he would be able to entice her into a second round.

Bryant turned over and tried to get some sleep. He tossed in bed until the clock read five a.m. Not able to endure any more restless sleep, he surrendered to his insomnia and got up to cook breakfast.

He walked down the hall into the kitchen and looked in the refrigerator. Inside was a carton of eggs, bacon, and orange juice. Placing them on the kitchen table, Bryant looked around for a frying pan. He opened one cabinet and found drinking glasses. He pulled one out to pour himself a glass of orange juice. After making several more attempts, he finally found a frying pan.

He threw some bacon into the pan. He watched the bacon slowly turn brown and the sizzling sound drew him into a trance. Getting hot from the stove, Bryant walked over and opened the sliding glass door allowing the autumn breeze to cool off the apartment. He looked out into the forest of trees that expanded across the back of their apartment complex. Thoughts of Daneesha drifted through his mind. She had been calling him, leaving several messages on his voice mail. He knew he needed to go see her soon, but he couldn't leave Olivia right now. She was so close to her due date.

"A penny for your thoughts," came a voice from behind him.

Bryant turned around. Olivia was standing in the doorway holding her stomach.

"Are you feeling okay?" he asked.

"I think I'm having contractions. About twenty minutes ago I had a sharp pain go up my back."

Suddenly she grabbed her belly and motioned for the chair. "Bryant, these pains are getting more intense."

"Do you want to go to the hospital?"

"No, my doctor said that I should try to hold out for as long as possible. Lots of new mothers are sent home from the hospital several times before they are actually admitted."

"Maybe we shouldn't have made love last night."

She responded with a look that said *maybe you're right*. She sat in the chair, breathing heavily as if it took all her strength to walk over to that chair.

"Can I get you a glass of orange juice?" he asked.

She nodded. He poured her a glass and placed it in front of her.

"It sure smells good in here. I'm surprised Danyelle hasn't rushed out here yet. Let me go ask her if she's hungry."

As she attempted to get up from the table, she let out a piercing scream. Bryant turned around. Olivia was frozen with fear. She stared down at the kitchen floor. Her water had broken.

Bryant rushed to her side. "Livie, everything is going to be all right. Do you have a hospital bag ready?"

"It's behind my bedroom door," she answered breathlessly.

He ran into the bedroom and grabbed the small yellow suitcase. He raced back to her side. "Come on, I'll help you to the car."

As they were leaving, Danyelle came out of her room. "What's going on? I heard someone scream."

"Olivia's water broke and I'm taking her to the hospital." Bryant said. "Danyelle, call the doctor and tell him to meet us at the hospital. His number is next to the telephone in the living room."

"Bryant, watch out for the—" Bryant came to a screeching halt just before hitting the back of a trash truck. Olivia held one hand to her heart and the other on the dashboard. She felt another contraction. "Oh no! Here comes another one." Olivia reached out for Bryant's hand.

"Breathe," Bryant instructed her. "Breathe out through your mouth."

"Bryant, this hurts." She gripped his hand a little tighter. "Can you get me to the hospital—now?" Olivia demanded through clinched teeth.

Bryant put the car in reverse, pulled around the trash truck, and sped off toward the hospital. Ten minutes later they arrived. A nurse wheeled Olivia away in a wheelchair while Bryant was left with the admitting clerk, providing Olivia's information.

Bryant eventually tracked Olivia down in the maternity ward. Her belly was hooked up to a monitor. She was immersed in an episode of Maury Povich. Bryant looked up at the television screen. The caption read, "I'm a man trapped in a woman's body."

"You appear to be doing better," Bryant commented.

"I do feel a little better, but I'm still in pain. They gave me some ice chips to chew on." Olivia pointed to the bowl sitting beside her. "I'd rather have a cheese steak."

He laughed. "Sweetheart, I'll be right back. I'm going to give Danyelle a call. I want to keep her updated on your progress." Bryant walked toward the door.

"Hurry back," she cried out.

Bryant walked out of her room and down the hall to the waiting area. He pulled out his cell phone and dialed her number.

"Hello."

"Hello, beautiful," Bryant said into the phone.

"Bryant, where have you been? I have been calling you leaving messages and you haven't returned any of my phone calls."

"Daneesha, I've been busy. I told you I had a lot of business to attend to."

"Yeah, well while you've been out there taking care of business, I got Marquise and Marquita's fathers to relinquish their parental rights. Now, all you have to do is come and sign these papers and you can adopt my kids."

"That's great. I should be there in two weeks to come sign the papers."

"Two weeks? I thought we were supposed to be getting married? I haven't spoken to you once to discuss one detail about our nuptials. "

"I thought we decided to wait until after the baby was born. That would give me some time to make some money to support my new family."

"Well, what about the children? You're the one who said you wanted to adopt my kids, but you're never here to spend any time with them. You act just like their real daddies."

"Daneesha, I'll be there in two weeks."

"Marquise, stop hitting your sister!" Daneesha screamed at the children.

Bryant looked up to see Olivia's doctor walking in his direction.

"Listen baby, I have to go, but I'll call you later, I promise." He hung up before she had a chance to protest.

"Hello, I'm Doctor Purtell. Are you the father of Ms. Benson's baby?"

"Yes, I am. Is everything all right?"

"Yes, everything is fine. Olivia is coming along beautifully. I just examined her and she is dilating quickly. You should have a new baby within a couple of hours. I just wanted to keep you informed of what was going on."

"Thanks a lot, Doc."

Bryant turned and pulled out his cell phone again. "Unc, I'm at University of Penn. I just finished talking with the doctor. He said the baby should be born within the next few hours. Can you get that business together? I want to hurry up and deliver that package and get this over with. Thanks a lot. Call me back when you get a chance."

Bryant hung up the phone and rushed back to Olivia.

"Push, Push!" Bryant yelled.

"Olivia, give me one big push and I promise you we'll be done," the doctor pleaded from between her legs.

They had been in the labor room for over an hour. Olivia was pushing and pushing to birth her son, and finally one more push delivered him.

"Here he is," Dr. Purtell announced. The doctor cleared the baby's nasal passages and passed him to his parents.

"Hello, Bryce Robert Winters," Olivia cooed as she was handed the baby. She held him as he stretched and squirmed. "Look at our son. Isn't he beautiful?"

Bryant smiled at his son. "He came into the world screaming; yelling just like his momma." Olivia looked at Bryant and smiled.

Chapter 5

DECEMBER 2003

". . . and Lord I ask that you watch out for my cousin Val and Julian while they make crazy dollars out in Seattle. Amen."

"Amen," everyone said in unison.

"Thank you, Danyelle, for opening the meeting in prayer," Elise said, then directed her attention toward the remaining members of their Bible Study group. "Can I get a show of hands of individuals who doubled their prayer time since the last time we met?"

No one raised their hands.

"Okay, who has increased their prayer time by at least twenty-five percent?" Elise asked.

Again, no one raised their hands.

"No one here has increased their prayer time?" Elise asked, astonished.

Olivia spoke up first. "Elise, I've been so busy with the baby. I haven't had time to sit down and pray."

"Olivia, since you brought it up, let's discuss 'not having enough time to pray.' I realize that everyone here has a life outside of church. Olivia, you're a new mother. Danyelle, you work. And Tressie, you attend college. All of you have very busy schedules, which can leave you with little time to pray."

"Elise, I always plan on saying a prayer in the morning or right before I go to bed, but the baby wakes me up at four-thirty every morning. That's the start of my day. I feed him and get him washed and dressed. Then I try to clean the house, and by noon, I'm tired. All I want to do is sleep."

"Olivia, I understand that your days are long. I'm sure everyone here wishes there were more hours in each day to carry out all their responsibilities."

"I sure do," Tressie commented.

"Time management is essential to having a successful relationship with God. Designate private time to commune with God. Keep in mind that you don't have to kneel down to pray. You can talk to God anywhere—in your car, on the train, or at your desk before the workday begins. The important thing is that you take the time to speak with God. Thank him for the things he has done for you and tell him about the different things going on in your life. He loves to hear from his children," Elise pointed out.

"I have set up my cell phone to remind me to pray, but I've found that life is too unexpected to stick to a daily schedule," Danyelle responded.

"I'm constantly being interrupted with different things which make it hard to maintain a constant prayer life. To pray every day is a lot. Isn't it enough to just pray at Bible Study and church? Do we have to pray every day?"

"Danyelle, what if God said 'I'm only accepting prayer requests on Sundays and Wednesdays?' Do you realize how chaotic the world would be? Prayers from parents with sick children and people starving in third world countries—their prayers would go unheard. God wants to hear from us every day."

"I agree with Danyelle," Olivia commented. "Too many unexpected things can happen during a day to throw you off track."

"What about you, Tressie? Do you feel the same as Olivia and Danyelle?" Elise asked.

"I did increase my prayer time when you first asked us to. But since then I have slacked off. With school and spending so much time with Payce, I find it difficult to stay committed to my prayer time. It's been a few days since the last time I prayed," Tressie admitted.

"Ladies, I know it's hard. Satan will do what he has to do to prevent you from speaking with God. His job is to put distance between you and the Lord. If he manages to squeeze a wedge between you and God, things will start happening in your life that will force you to pray. Just keep that in mind."

***

A chauffeured limousine pulled up in front of their house at precisely six-thirty. Val and Julian were attending a party hosted by the owners of the Seattle SuperSonics. The entire Sonics organization would be in attendance that night—the owner, the general manager, the president, all the players, and their spouses.

Since the season began, Val had only been able to attend one game, and that was the season opener. She was excited to see Julian play in his first professional game. The entire Sonics team ran out onto the court in single file. Julian wore the number three proudly pasted across his back. He stretched with the team at half court. He didn't start the game, but the coach did put him in at the start of the second quarter. He was only in the game for ten minutes, but he scored nine points by making three three-pointers. Val could see the excitement in his face over his spectacular performance. The SuperSonics won the game ninety-nine to ninety-seven.

During the game Val realized how lonely she really was. In Philly, Olivia had always attended Julian's games with her, but in Seattle she was alone. She had been looking forward to attending that night's game, not just to see Julian play, but to possibly make some new friends.

When Val arrived at the Key Arena, an usher escorted her to Julian's reserved seats. Val was well aware of the fact that the women who had seats around hers were either married or dating some of the other players, so she wanted to take the opportunity to get more acquainted with those women. When Val sat down in her seat she flashed a friendly smile to the two women sitting to the right of her, but both responded by rolling their eyes and turning their heads. Surprised by their response, she introduced herself to the women sitting to her left and they too turned their noses up at her. Val was disappointed, but she wasn't going to allow their cold attitude to discourage her from wanting to make friends. She would think of a different way to make friends with them.

They pulled up in front of the Hotel Monaco. The parking lot attendant opened Val's door and helped her step out into the brisk Seattle night air. Julian came up behind her and placed his hand on the small of her back. He led her up the front steps and into the lobby.

Once they were in the elevator the attendant asked, "What floor, sir?"

"We're attending the Sonics party," Julian replied.

The attendant punched the seventy-sixth floor. Val looked stunning in a gold Cynthia Rowley strapless dress, while her fiancé redefined the term debonair in a black suit made by Marc Jacobs.

Julian pulled at his collar. "I wish we didn't have to dress up."

"It doesn't hurt to wear a suit every once in a while," Val responded.

The elevator attendant announced, "Penthouse floor." The elevator doors opened and they stepped into the breathtaking entrance of the banquet hall.

Val was speechless. Her wide eyes studied the unforgettable Seattle skyline from two walls made entirely of glass. A staircase that resembled the one in *Gone With The Wind* led to an outside balcony.

The room was full of people, leading Val to think she and Julian were the last ones to arrive. The first person to greet them was Mr. Haas, the owner of the team. "Hello, Julian. I've been looking for you all night."

"Hello, Mr. Haas," Julian replied, shaking his boss's hand. "How are you doing?"

"I'm doing so much better now that you're here, our star player. There are a dozen people I want to introduce you to." He noticed Val standing next to Julian. "Oh, I'm sorry. Where are my manners? This must be the beautiful bride-to-be, Valencia."

Val reached out to shake his hand.

"You look lovely," Mr. Haas said to Val. He wrapped Val's arm around his. "Please follow me?" For the next two hours Theodore Haas introduced Val and Julian to every employee of the basketball organization. They met everyone from the president to the towel boys. By the middle of the night Val was tired.

Val and Julian had stopped mingling to speak with Carlos and Pilar Torres. Carlos Torres was the only Latino player on the team, and also one of the few Latino players in the entire league. Julian and Carlos entered an intense debate over the future of the team, while Pilar initiated a conversation with Val. "I remember seeing you at the season home opener on Tuesday."

"Yes, I was there. I don't remember seeing you."

"Oh no, I don't sit in the players' reserved seats. I usually watch the game from the luxury suites."

Pilar was a beautiful twenty-eight-year-old mother of three. That did not include the one she was so elegantly carrying in her womb. Her long, black hair was pulled back in a classic 1930s style bun. She wore a form-fitting maroon dress by Nicole Miller that flowed nicely over her growing belly.

Val swallowed the last of her glass of wine. "Could you walk me over to the bar?" Val asked Pilar. "Do you fellas want another drink? I'm heading over to the bar," Val said.

"No, we're okay," Julian replied.

The two women walked over to the bar where Val ordered herself another glass of wine.

"Carlos is so excited about Julian joining the team. He really thinks they have a chance at winning the championship this year." Pilar enunciated her words as slowly as possible. Her thick Spanish accent was hard to understand at times.

"Well, they are off to a good start. If they continue to play like they did on Tuesday, they have a good chance of bringing the trophy to Seattle," Val said.

"Are you from Seattle?" Pilar asked.

"No, we're both from Philadelphia."

"So you're not familiar with Seattle at all?"

"No, not really."

"How about one day next week we have lunch together? We can go shopping and I'll show you around the city."

"I would really like that. Since I've been here I haven't really had a chance to get out and meet anyone yet."

"So you've been sitting in the house by yourself while Julian goes to team meetings and practice," Pilar guessed.

Val nodded her head yes and took a sip from her glass.

"Yes, it was that way for me too when Carlos and I first moved here. But after a while I got accustomed to him not being home. It gets kind of lonely, so I occupy my time with our children." She leaned her arm against the bar. "Sometimes I have to be both parents to our children. A lot of the time he's on the road, at practice, or out with the fellows."

"Yes, Julian has not spent a lot of time with me. But I have tried to be understanding. I realize that he's just entering the league and it's going to take him a while to get accustomed to handling the responsibilities of work and home. Once his rookie year is over, we'll get married and things will get better."

"You don't think that the money and fame will change him? He signed an awfully large contract."

"I know Julian. Money will never change him."

"Can I offer you some advice?" Pilar asked while gently placing her hand on Val's arm. Val looked at her suspiciously, waiting on her to continue. "If you want to keep Julian, make him realize that home is with you."

"What do you mean by that?" Val asked.

"What I mean is that Julian's financial situation has probably multiplied ten times since he's entered the league and the money only gets better each year. A lot of people, namely home wreckers, will be jealous of what you and him have. They will try their hardest to take what's yours. I suggest you do whatever you think is necessary to keep him from leaving you."

"Oh, I'm not worried. Julian loves me," Val said with a spark of innocence in her eyes.

"Love doesn't have anything to do with sex," Pilar replied.

Val glanced over in Julian's direction. She saw a woman across the room licking her lips at him. Julian smiled back at the woman and continued his conversation with Carlos.

Pilar watched the scene unfold between Julian and the stranger. "Just keep in mind, the Sonics organization keeps plenty of women available for the players to play with in their spare time."

"Tressie, I promise you I'll call you when I get in." Payce unlocked the passenger side door for his friend, Darshon. "Tressie, I don't know what time I'm going to get in. We're just going out to the club. I have to go. I'll call you later." He hung up his phone.

"What's going on, player?" Darshon yelled out. Payce held out his fist and Darshon responded back with a pound.

"I was on the phone with my girl. She's asking me a million questions. Where am I going? Who am I going with? When will I be home? You would think we were married."

"She acts like that because that's what she wants. That's what they all want. They want the man to willingly put on the handcuffs and walk down the aisle of matrimony."

Payce laughed at his friend.

"Is that the girl you met at your father's church conference?"

Payce nodded his head.

"You've been seeing her for a while. Be careful, man. Church women are the worst. Women already think they're right about everything, but a church woman will pull out her Bible and recite scripture to prove she's right."

Payce laughed at Darshon. For once he did have a point. "Man, why did you have me pick you up at the corner? Is there something wrong at home?"

"I was looking out for you," Darshon replied.

"Why? What's up?"

"Lisa heard you were home."

"Ah, man. That girl. Is she still up to the same ole thing?"

"Yeah, she hasn't changed a bit. She kept asking me, 'Where's Payce? When is Payce coming around?' I told her you don't roll with her kind, but she swears she can turn you out."

Payce laughed at the thought of her trying to track him down. "She thought I was joking when I told her that if we were to get busy, I'd have to play the part of the man. She's not strapping nothing on and doing me."

Darshon laughed. "Man, I don't know. Lisa must have something lethal. She has all these girls calling my mom's house for her. They buy her clothes and jewelry. One even offered to buy her a car. She makes me wonder what she's doing that I'm not."

"She must be digging those girls out."

"Man, I'm about to pay her to give me some lessons. If I had women catering to me the way she has all those chicken heads, I wouldn't have any problems."

Payce drove to Center City, Philadelphia where Darshon directed him to a small street off Market Street.

"Man, pull into this parking lot," Darshon directed.

"Give these to the attendant." Darshon pulled out two small metal squares that closely resembled a pair of cuff links and gave them to Payce. The attendant took the pieces of metal, walked over to the garage door, and inserted them into the wall. The huge metal garage door that faced them rose up and a ramp platform was lowered to the ground. Payce stared at the ultramodern device.

"Go ahead, man. Enter," Darshon urged him.

"Darshon, where are you taking me?"

"I told you—someplace we haven't been before."

"Yeah, but this seems like some underground shit. Something where you have to have a membership to get in."

"Relax, you're going to enjoy yourself," Darshon reassured him.

They parked the car, walked to the elevator, and rode to the top floor in silence. Payce was skeptical of what Darshon was up to. They had been best friends since the fifth grade, and since then, Darshon always found the freakiest places for them to hang out. For Payce's eighteenth birthday, Darshon told him that they were going to an exclusive resort in Florida. It was a nudist colony.

Payce could never forget the time Darshon got them on a cruise ship that was filming the sequel to the *Girls Gone Wild* movie. *Nothing could top that weekend*, Payce thought.

The elevator stopped and the doors opened. Payce followed Darshon down a long hallway until they stopped in front of a pair of glass doors. Payce read the words printed on the door. "The Dollhouse Spa."

"A spa?" Payce stopped in his tracks. "Man, I'm not going into a woman's spa. Are you crazy? What happened to you while I was locked up? You've been hanging around your sister too much."

Darshon pulled him to the side. "Man, I promise you, this is not what you think. Would I ever steer you wrong?"

"Yes, everything you do is wrong."

"I'm the one who took you to your first strip club, I'm the one who got you your first threesome, and I'm the one who has always had your back. Now trust me on this one. It's all right!"

Everything he said was true. Payce reluctantly let his defenses down and walked into the spa with him.

A girl with long, sandy blond hair greeted them at the door. She wore a T-shirt three sizes too small. On it were the words "sugar and spice."

"Hi, remember me? I'm Darshon."

The girl looked at him closely. "Oh yeah, I remember you. The last time you were here you came with your sister," she replied.

"Your sister." Payce chuckled.

Darshon hit him to shut up. "Yeah, that's right. This time I brought my friend with me. This is Payce. This is his first time here and he is also a very good friend of my sister's. So can you make sure he receives the VIP treatment?"

"Of course," she replied. "Any friend of Lisa's is a friend of ours."

She grabbed Payce's hand and led him down the hall. Darshon followed them to a small white room with no furniture. A robe hanging from a hook on the wall was the only thing in the room.

"Take off all your clothes and change into the robe. I'll be back to get you," she instructed Payce.

"Payce, I'll meet you in the massage room," Darshon yelled out before the receptionist closed the door.

"Darshon better not be playing games," Payce said.

After he changed into the robe, the receptionist led him to a room where Darshon was getting a massage by two Japanese women. Payce was surprised to see the women massaging him in the nude.

Darshon lay there as if he were a king. "It's about time you made it."

One of the Japanese women gestured for Payce to lie down on the table next to Darshon.

"Man, what is this place and how did you find out about it?" Payce asked.

"My sister turned me on to this place."

"Oh, now I understand. This is one of her lesbian hangouts."

"Yeah, but not only lesbians work here. So do bisexuals. Man, just lay down and enjoy your massage. The night has just begun," Darshon told him.

They enjoyed the soothing massage with oils being rubbed into their backs and therapeutic candles burning around them.

Darshon ordered them each a shot of Hennessy and a Corona. "Payce, everything here is free—the drinks, the massages."

"How did you manage to work that out?"

"I told you Lisa hangs out here all the time. She is a really good customer, so she gets a lot of fringe benefits."

Darshon held up his glass of Hennessy. "Man, welcome home."

"Thanks. Glad to be home. I'm never going back to jail."

They tapped their glasses together. The sound from their glasses caused a curtain in the room to draw open. A large glass window revealed three women engaging in a threesome.

Darshon smiled at the performance as Payce watched in amazement. Payce was jealous. He wished he could join them.

"Man, you knew this was going to happen?" Payce asked.

"I had it all planned. And you were ready to fight me outside." He pointed to the window. "This is what they do here. They provide you with enjoyment and entertainment."

Payce was amazed. He studied the expressions on their faces. He could tell each one of the ladies was enjoying their time together.

The two Asian women masseuses turned Payce and Darshon over onto their backs and gave them each a full body massage. The feel of the women's hands allowed a low moan to escape from Payce; acknowledging how good it felt.

After the women were done Darshon sat up and wrapped a towel around his waist. "Come on, player. I have another surprise for you."

They walked down the hall together and stopped in front of a white door.

"This is where we part ways. I'll meet you back in the massage room later." He patted Payce on the back and walked down the hall to enter through another white door.

Payce slowly opened the door and three Amazon women attacked him. They pushed him down onto an air mattress and wouldn't allow him to move. Fortunately, this was one time he didn't mind being vulnerable to a group of women. They tossed his towel to the side and gave him a time he would never forget. Payce felt like he was the star of his own porn video. He was used to watching porn, but he had never acted it out.

One woman kissed him passionately and spoke to him in French. He thought this was very sexy as she said things to him he couldn't understand. Each woman kept grabbing at him.

One woman pointed her long finger at him, beckoning him to sit up. Payce was mesmerized by her wild make-up and big hair. The woman's eyes were painted with lots of green and pink paint. She wore a green mini skirt with a matching green halter.

He sat up and the woman went to him; satisfying Payce's sexual desires.

After she was done, each woman wanted a turn, and Payce turned no one away. Two hours later, Payce lay on his back, exhausted. A soft bell rang and instantly the girls untangled themselves from their twist around him and quietly left the room. That was the end of their night together.

"I never thought this night would end like this," he whispered.

After he had a chance to catch his breath, he retreated back to the massage room. He found his clothes lying on the table. As he was buttoning his shirt, he heard a knock at the door.

"Come in," he called.

Darshon entered, smiling like the cat that ate the canary. "How you feel, player?"

"I'm tired."

"I bet you are. Did they work you over?"

Payce smiled as he tied up his boots and looked for his coat. The curtain that covered the huge window was pulled back. Inside, two women were having sex.

"This is a night I will never forget," Payce said out loud.

They watched for a second as the two women pleased one another.

"Man, let's go. I've got to go home and get some sleep. I have to be to work later on tonight," Payce told him.

As they prepared to walk out the door, Darshon yelled, "Hold up man. Let's watch this real quick."

The door inside the window opened and another woman entered. She wore a black leather cat suit with a matching facemask. She held a whip in her hand that she repeatedly swung around. She moved around like she was a cat on the prowl. They watched her gracefully dance around the room. She plotted out a strategy as to which woman she would overcome first. Payce watched as the cat woman pushed one girl to the floor, spread her legs, and before she buried her head down to taste the nectar of the woman, she removed her mask.

At that moment she looked directly into Payce's eyes. "Oh shit." Payce recognized the woman. "What?" Darshon asked. "That's Reverend Kane."

Chapter 6

Elise slammed her office door shut, leaving behind the chaos of yelling clients, tight deadlines, and late building permits. Glad to escape it all, she looked forward to beginning her new workout regimen at the gym.

After the stitches were removed from her leg, she desperately wanted to get back out to the park and continue her regular jogs, but Miles did not approve. He felt it was unsafe for her to go jogging by herself, so he suggested she join a health club.

Elise knew Miles was only trying to help, but she thought gyms were so commercial. Health clubs advertised fitness, but it was a multi-million dollar scam. Over ninety percent of members who frequented the gym regularly never obtained the results they desired. It amused her to watch a 250 pound woman cycle on the bike for thirty minutes while eating an entire box of Krispy Kreme donuts.

She would choose the park over a crowded gym any day.

Elise also didn't want to lose the time she spent in the park talking with God, but that wasn't the only reason she wanted to return to the park. She secretly looked forward to running into the man who rescued her like a damsel in distress. Images of his muscular body flashed in her mind. It was hard for her to concentrate on anything besides him.

Elise arrived at the gym and went straight to the treadmills. She started her workout by doing a light one-mile jog to increase her heart rate. Afterwards she followed a strict cardio routine.

After her strenuous workout, she retreated to the locker room to take a shower. She put her hand underneath the spray of water to test it. It was just right. Before she stepped in she noticed that the complimentary towel rack was barren. Elise knew she could use her own towels, but the club kept their towels heated and she savored the feeling of stepping out of the shower and wrapping her body in a warm towel. She left the water running and ran out to the receptionist's desk.

"Excuse me, could you ask someone to bring some fresh towels into the ladies locker room? We've run out," Elise explained.

"Sure, I'll have someone bring some in right away," the young receptionist replied.

As Elise turned to retreat to her shower, she heard a man call out, "Elise."

She recognized the voice, but hoped that it wasn't who she thought it was. She turned around and it was him—her hero—standing before her eyes.

Embarrassed, her face quickly turned red. Not only had he caught her wearing only a towel, but she also had a stupid shower cap on her head. He walked over to her smiling that handsome, devilish smile.

"Hi," he said, sounding as if he were approaching his high school sweetheart.

"Hello." She flinched at the sight of seeing him. She wanted to run and hide. "What are you doing here?" she asked.

"The fellows and I usually come here to play basketball." He pointed to a group of guys entering the men's locker room. "How's that leg? Are you all better?"

"Yes," Elise flexed her leg in and out. "It's all better. I've been waiting on you to send me the hospital bill."

"I put it in the mail a few days ago. You should have gotten it by now. Don't worry, you'll wish I never sent it once you get a look at it."

"You're probably right about that." She laughed. Elise noticed him staring at her and it made her more uncomfortable. "Well I must be going. I was about to take a shower."

"I'm sorry," he said. "I didn't mean to keep you."

She turned to run back into the locker room.

"Elise, wait a minute," he called out to her. He walked back over to her. "Would you care to join me for a cup of coffee?"

Elise intended to turn down his offer, but her mouth betrayed her. "Sure, I'd like that," she replied.

"Great. I'll wait for you out here."

She walked back into the locker room. *What have I just done?* she thought. *I should have said no. I was supposed to say no.* But the excitement that danced in his eyes while he talked to her changed her mind.

An hour later, Sheridan and Elise sat in Starbucks sipping French vanilla lattes. Sheridan watched Elise as she drank from her coffee cup. He couldn't believe his luck. He thought he was never going to see her again. Since the day of their accidental meeting, his mind had been consumed with thoughts of her. He hadn't spent that much time with her, but what he did know intrigued him. He couldn't figure out what was so alluring about her, or why he asked her out for coffee, but he did know that he couldn't allow her to vanish from his life again. He knew she was married, but it was hard for him to fight the magnetism he felt toward her.

"You know I really shouldn't be drinking coffee. I won't be able to sleep tonight," Elise commented.

"Neither should I, but sometimes I find it's best to stay up and work."

"What do you do?" she asked.

"I'm a sports agent. I represent a lot of the Philadelphia sports figures—McNabb, Iverson, Randy Wolf."

"That must be interesting work."

"It can be. It can also be stressful. It's hard trying to keep my clients on top. I have to always present my clients in a positive light, whether it's to another sports team, or for an endorsement deal. And that's not always easy. When Kobe got into all that legal trouble out in Colorado, he lost a lot of money. Everything an athlete does is scrutinized by the media, so I try to make sure my players stay out of trouble."

"Doesn't your job require you to travel a lot?"

"Yeah, I do travel a lot of the time, but since a majority of my clientele resides in Philadelphia, I'm able to work from home through the use of e-mail and fax machines. What about you? What do you do?"

"I work for the city. I'm director of the Urban Enterprise zoned areas in Philadelphia."

"What does that mean?"

"I'm responsible for strengthening the more impoverished areas of the city economically by recruiting businesses into those areas."

"How do you do that?"

"Well, I contact large retail stores, companies, or businesses that are interested in setting up regional distribution centers in Philadelphia. Ultimately, if they agree to establish their business in the city, they are entitled to certain tax breaks. For instance, all materials needed to build the outside structure or furnish the inside of office buildings can be written off. It's one hundred percent tax-free. Plus businesses receive an additional fifteen hundred dollar tax break for every city resident they employ."

"That's a real bargain," Sheridan said.

"Yeah. A lot of smaller businesses that are trying to grow can benefit from these types of incentives." She took another sip of her coffee. "You know you never told me your name."

Those lips curved into that devilish smile that caused her heart to flutter.

"I was wondering when you were going to ask me my name. It's Sheridan."

"Sheridan. That's different."

"Yeah, it's a really old name. My full name is Sheridan Reed the Fifth. It's a name that has been passed down from my great-great grandfather. It's a tradition, and when I have a son of my own he will be named Sheridan Reed the VI."

"So you don't have any children?"

"No not yet; maybe someday. What about yourself?"

She solemnly replied, "No." It was torture every time someone asked her that question, a painful reminder of the problems she and Miles were having. She quickly changed the subject. "I'm glad you invited me out."

"I'm surprised. I didn't think you were going to accept my offer."

"At first I wasn't."

"What changed your mind?"

"I thought there was no harm in having a cup of coffee. Plus, I wanted to thank you for coming to my rescue in the park."

"It was my fault that accident happened in the first place. I should have been more careful."

Her cell phone rang. She knew it was Miles calling to make sure she was all right. She glanced at the clock. She was usually home by this time. She answered.

"Hey, honey. Is everything all right?" Miles inquired.

"Yes, I'm fine. I ran into an old friend at the gym and we stopped for coffee. I should have called to let you know I'd be late."

"No, that's okay. I'm sorry if I intruded. I just wanted to make sure you were all right. When I didn't hear from you I began to worry. I'll let you get back to your girlfriend. Enjoy yourself. I'll wait up until you get home."

"All right, I shouldn't be much longer." She hung up the phone. Sheridan smiled back at her.

"You are very beautiful," he told her.

"Thank you." His obvious attraction to her sent up warning signs, but she ignored them. She enjoyed his company so much that she didn't want to leave.

"You realize I am attracted to you, right?" he asked her.

"You realize I'm married, right?" she playfully replied.

"Yes, I do realize that and I don't want to interfere with your happy home. I just want to get to know you better. You have been on my mind a lot since you left my house."

Scared of what he might confess to her next, she abruptly announced, "I must be going."

"Let me walk you to your car." He walked over to the trash can to discard their cups. Elise stood at the door and stared at him from behind. *He looks so good in those jeans.* Elise closed her eyes and said a silent prayer. *Lord, please get me out of this.*

"Will I get to see you again?" Sheridan asked as they walked to her car together.

"No, I don't think that would be a good idea."

Disappointed by her response, he said, "I understand you're married. I respect that."

Elise could clearly see the hurt in his eyes. Her heart ached for telling him no.

They stopped in front of her car. "You be careful going home," he told her. He softly kissed her on the cheek and walked away with his head down.

Elise got in her car and sat there for a moment. Contemplating her next move, she lowered her window and yelled out, "How about I meet you here next Wednesday? After my workout we can go for another cup of coffee." *It was just coffee,* she told herself. She could handle being in his presence for an hour or two.

That brought an immediate smile to his lips. "I'll see you then."

"I don't understand how two people can accumulate so much laundry in one week." Val sat in the family room folding two laundry baskets full of clothes while Julian stretched out across the couch with the television remote in his hand.

"Babe, you know I change clothes two to three times a day. I get dressed, go to practice, come home, take a shower, and get changed again."

"I've noticed," she replied sarcastically. "You've been changing clothes and going out so much that I barely see you."

"I told you I'm sorry. I'm going to make it up to you. I promise." Julian pulled on her pants leg and blew her a kiss. She jokingly blew his kiss back at him. "Okay," he said. "Don't come over here later trying to cuddle up next to me because I'm going to remind you of what you just did."

Val folded the last of the laundry and headed upstairs to place his clothes in their bedroom. She opened Julian's dresser drawer and moved aside some white T-shirts. She noticed an envelope marked "Colorado." She opened it, and inside were two airline tickets along with brochures of Aspen. Julian didn't say anything to her about going to Aspen. She quickly retreated back downstairs.

He was laughing at the television when she walked back into the family room. "Julian, what is this?" she demanded.

Caught off guard, Julian looked up and his mouth fell open. "What are you doing with those?" he asked.

"That's the question I ought to be asking you. When were you planning on telling me about Colorado?"

For a moment, Julian was speechless. "I . . . I was going to tell you," he stammered. "I just forgot. The team is going to a health clinic in Colorado to make sure we stay healthy for the season. We're going down during the NBA All Star break."

"What about the brochures to Aspen?"

"The fellas thought it would be nice if we did a little skiing while we were there."

"Oh, OK." She stared at the tickets in her hand. "Well, I'm glad I finally found out because I need to go buy some ski gear." Val turned to leave the room.

"Wait a minute." He stopped her. "For what?"

"Our trip to Aspen. You have two tickets here."

"No, the other ticket is for David Childs. He asked me to pick up his ticket for him. I'm sorry, honey, but this trip is for team players only. No women allowed."

The light that filled her eyes quickly faded away. She couldn't believe he was leaving her again. She had made plans for them to fly home together for a quick visit during NBA All Star week. Now she would have to make the trip alone.

"All right," she replied. She walked back to the bedroom and replaced the tickets. Thoughts of what Pilar had said to her weeks ago filled her mind. She stared at the tickets for two. She hoped Julian wasn't lying to her.

Later that day Pilar and Val were out shopping in downtown Seattle. When Pilar called Val earlier and invited her to go shopping, Val initially declined the invitation. Monday was the only day of the week that Julian didn't have practice or team business to attend to. She liked to reserve Mondays as their special time alone, but when she told Pilar that she'd have to take a rain check, Julian interrupted her and insisted that she go.

"Val, why don't you go? You'll only be gone for a few hours. You're always complaining about how you don't get out the house enough and Pilar was nice enough to invite you to go with her," Julian pointed out.

Val knew he was right. She did complain about how she spent most of her time in the house. "Are you sure? I don't want to leave you alone."

"Go. I'll be fine. I'll be here when you get back."

Persuaded, Val went, unaware that Pilar would buy so many things. Pilar managed to buy herself and her children over fifteen thousand dollars worth of clothes, and that was only in one store.

She had so many bags that store security had to help carry her bags out to her Escalade.

"Thanks for going with me. I really hate going shopping by myself, and I would never bring the children with me," Pilar said to Val as she adjusted her seatbelt. "Every time I bring Alec he has to go to the bathroom every ten minutes. I never get anything done."

"I enjoyed this. Maybe we can go out again sometime next week. I really need to go furniture shopping," Val commented.

"Oh! I know the perfect place. It's called the Fine Furniture Gallery, and everything in there is one of a kind. I bought just about every piece in our home from there. Are you redecorating?"

"No, just decorating. Since we moved into the house we barely have any furniture. The house is so hollow and cold. I've tried to wait on Julian so we could go together, but he's been so busy he told me to go buy whatever I wanted. I need to buy something to give the house a warm feeling."

"I understand. Whenever you want to go, just give me a call," Pilar offered.

All afternoon, Val tried to think of the best way to ask Pilar about Colorado. She needed to know if Carlos had mentioned anything to her about him going. She knew that once she asked her, Pilar would know that Val didn't trust Julian as much as she said she had, but the truth was that she did believe Julian's reasoning behind the two tickets. She just wanted to reassure herself.

"Pilar, did Carlos mention anything to you about going to a rehabilitation clinic in Colorado?" Val asked.

"Oh, yes! The team goes every year," Pilar responded. "Why? Were you worried Julian was up to something?"

"No, I just thought that since both Julian and Carlos would be out of town, that maybe we could do something," Val responded, covering up her real suspicions.

"Oh, that sounds like fun. How about we spend the whole weekend together? We can go to the spa and to the theater."

"Okay," Val replied. Her heart had slowly returned to its normal pace. She had been afraid of what Pilar's answer would be, but as usual she knew she had no reason to doubt her man.

Chapter 7

"Yo, Bryant!" Danyelle yelled as she attempted to shake Bryant from his daydream. Immersed in his own thoughts, Bryant took the blunt that she was passing to him.

"So how does it feel to be a father?" Danyelle asked.

"It doesn't feel any different than before he got here, except we have a whole lot of shitty diapers lying around and midnight feedings," he remarked.

Danyelle noticed Bryant's distant behavior toward his son. Bryant barely fed, played with, or held Bryce. He was completely withdrawn from the parenting experience. The only time she had seen him take any interest in his son was when Olivia took the baby to the doctor. He insisted on going with them. Olivia said that he grilled the doctor about the baby's progress and health. He wanted reassurance that Bryce would grow up to be a normal little boy.

Danyelle hoped the new father did not resent his son. A lot of Olivia's time was being taken up by the baby. Morning, noon, and night, she fed, washed, and cared for her son. It was hard being a first-time mother. She barely had any time for herself.

Olivia stuck her head out into the living room. "Is it safe to come out?" Olivia asked, holding the baby close in her arms.

"Yeah, Livie, it's okay," Danyelle replied.

Danyelle got up and tried to fan away the smoke from the blunt they had just finished smoking. Olivia had hoped that once the baby was born Bryant and Danyelle would stop smoking in the apartment out of respect for the baby, but they didn't care. Bryant didn't see anything wrong with smoking around the baby, and Danyelle claimed that since she paid half the rent she was entitled to smoke anywhere she pleased.

Bryant said Olivia was uptight and she needed to relax more, but she disagreed. She didn't think she was the problem. The problem was that she didn't have enough space. It was hard being confined to her small bedroom with a baby because they refused to smoke outside. Olivia constantly nagged Bryant about getting their own place, but he argued that he didn't make enough money. Olivia knew he was right. They couldn't afford an apartment with the expense of a new baby, but she still wanted to try and find them their own affordable apartment.

Olivia sat on the couch next to Danyelle while the baby slept soundly in her arms. Danyelle could see the dark circles beneath her sister's eyes. The T-shirt she had on had the baby's vomit spattered in different places. Her hair, which was usually neatly pressed straight, was wild and uncombed.

"Pass me the baby, Livie," Danyelle said.

"All right, but don't blow smoke in my baby's face, like you did last time." Olivia handed Bryce over and grabbed the television remote.

"He liked his first hit of weed from Auntie Danyelle. Didn't you?" Danyelle asked the baby.

Olivia ignored her and pointed the remote at the television. She noticed a large brick of marijuana sitting on the floor to the left of the television.

"How many times do I have to ask you two to be more careful where you leave that stuff?" Olivia pointed to the weed. "I do have a baby now," Olivia said huffily. "In a few more months the baby will be crawling and getting into stuff. I don't want my baby eating or playing with marijuana at the age of six months," she complained.

"Sorry, baby, that's my fault," Bryant responded. "A guy I know wanted to buy it from me, but when I took it over to his house, he wasn't there. So I brought it here."

"Oh, so now you're a drug dealer," Olivia said mockingly.

"No, it's not like that."

Olivia could not believe that Bryant was selling drugs. Not wanting to argue in front of Danyelle, she asked Bryant if they could speak in their bedroom.

"Bryant, if you're selling drugs out of this house then I have to ask you to go. I will not have you endangering our son's life."

"I'm not selling drugs." He defended himself. "I just thought that if I sold a few bundles of weed I could make a few extra hundred dollars. Things are kind of tight around here with the baby and you wanting to move into our own place."

Olivia sympathized with what he was trying to do, and realized that he was only trying to provide for his family and keep her happy, but selling drugs was not the answer.

"Bryant, I want us to be a family." She reached out for his hand. "You don't have to sell drugs to take care of us. We'll make it as long as we have each other."

Realizing he was wrong, he replied, "All right, let me go see if this guy is home so I can drop this stuff off to him." He moved over to kiss her on the lips and left. A few seconds later Olivia heard the front door slam shut.

Thirty minutes had passed. Olivia, Danyelle, and the baby sat in the living room watching a movie.

"I wish Mommy and Daddy were here to see how beautiful Bryce is," Olivia said.

"Daddy always wanted a boy. He would have spoiled Bryce rotten," Danyelle replied.

Suddenly, a loud crashing sound came through the front door. Olivia looked up to witness a squad of police run into her living room with guns drawn and pointed directly at them. One officer came

over, pulled the baby from Olivia's arms, and
handed him to another officer. The same officer
then grabbed her aggressively and forced her up
against the wall.

Olivia was paralyzed with fear. She didn't know
what to do.

"Officer, what is going on?" Olivia asked. She
could hear her baby's cries in the distance. "That's
my baby. Can I please get my son? He's scared."

"Sorry ma'am, I can't allow you to do that. We'll
have someone take care of him until we're done
here," the officer replied.

Olivia could see several officers scouring her
house. They appeared to be looking for something.
They searched the closets, kitchen cabinets, and
drawers.

"What is going on?" Danyelle screamed.

Detective Collins walked up behind the girls as
they were being body searched by female officers.
"Can I ask who lives here?" the detective asked.

"I do," Olivia replied. "Me, my sister, my baby,
and my boyfriend."

"Is that your sister?" the detective asked.

"Yes."

"Where is your boyfriend?"

"He was just here. He ran out for a second."

"I can question him later. Ladies, please have a
seat on the couch," the detective instructed. He
knelt in front of them. "Do you know Darnell
'Drake' Duncan?"

Olivia shook her head no.

"We got an anonymous tip that Drake Duncan was selling drugs out of this apartment. Drake is a very dangerous man and is a fugitive who's been on the run for months."

"Officer . . ." Olivia started.

"Detective. My name is Detective Collins."

"I'm sorry. Detective Collins, we don't know any Drake Duncan."

"What is your boyfriend's name?"

"Bryant Winters."

The detective scribbled Bryant's name on a note pad. "Ladies, so far we have confiscated four bundles of marijuana and a few ounces of cocaine. He pointed to the drugs sitting on the table. Olivia didn't realize that those drugs were in the apartment. She had made sure that Bryant took the marijuana sitting next to the television with him.

"Who does the marijuana belong to?" the detective asked.

"I plead the fifth," Danyelle said.

"Detective, I don't know who those drugs belong to. I didn't even know they were in the apartment. Where did you find that?" Olivia began to cry.

"I found it in a closet in the back bedroom underneath the baby's things."

Olivia knew he was referring to her room.

"Ladies, you two could be looking at jail time. We already have the evidence. A year or more of jail time would mean your son would be placed in a foster home until you were released."

The detective looked at Olivia. "If you tell me everything you know I'll let the judge know how cooperative you were with us and he may just give you probation."

Olivia was confused and didn't know what to do. If she confessed that the drugs belonged to Bryant, he could go to jail and her son would lose his father. If she didn't say anything, then she would go to jail and her son would lose his mother. She knew it was better for Bryce to lose his father rather than his mother. Prepared to tell the officer everything she knew, Danyelle interrupted before she could say a word. "Detective, can my sister and I speak privately for a moment?"

"Sure." He got up to leave them alone.

"Livie," she whispered. "Drug possession is not a big thing. This is our first offense. They can't send us to jail over drugs that don't belong to us."

"But what about everything he said?"

"That cop was just playing with your head. Trust me, I know people who were caught with ten times as much as us and all they got was probation. Look, let's go down to the station. Let them arrest us. They'll set our bail. We can call Bryant, have him bail us out, and then we can get a lawyer."

"Danyelle, are you sure?"

"Trust me."

"What about the baby?"

"He'll be put in temporary custody of the state, but when we get in touch with Bryant, we'll tell him to go get the baby first. He's the father. He has rights."

Olivia agreed to go along with Danyelle's decision to remain silent.

Danyelle called the detective back over. "Detective, we're going to ask to speak to a lawyer before we say anything," she said confidently.

The detective shook his head as if they were making a big mistake. "Stiles, read them their rights," he barked.

The officer came over, put the handcuffs on the two sisters, and led them out of the apartment. Once they got to the station, they each made one phone call. Olivia called Bryant on his cell phone, but his voice mail picked up. She left him an urgent message telling him what happened and where she was. She also told him where to get the baby from.

Afterwards, they put Danyelle and Olivia in a holding cell where they sat and stared at the clock, waiting on Bryant to come and bail them out.

The next morning Olivia and Danyelle were taken down to the courthouse and escorted into a small, cold room. Inside was a white guy who looked no older than twenty-five. The officer who escorted them in took the handcuffs off and ordered them to sit down on the hard wooden chairs.

"Good morning, ladies." He smiled at them while looking through their file. "My name is Wilson York and I'm your public defender."

"We don't need any public defender," Danyelle informed him. "We're going to get a lawyer."

"Yes. Well, until you're able to obtain suitable legal counsel the state has assigned your case to me. I'm here to advise you of your rights, make sure you're aware of the charges being brought against you and answer any questions you may have."

"Mr. York," Olivia interrupted. "Did my boyfriend ever come down to the station? He was supposed to come and bail us out last night."

"Oh yes," York said. He opened the file and read off a sheet of paper. "A Mr. Winters. He did come down to the station. He was questioned and released. He gave a statement to the police. He claimed that the drugs belonged to the two of you. He denied any ownership of them."

"There must be a mistake. He wouldn't have said that," Olivia said. She looked at Danyelle, who shrugged her shoulders unknowingly.

"He also stated that he didn't live with the two of you."

"All his stuff is at my house."

"That may be true, but his name is not on the lease, is it?" the young lawyer asked.

"No," Olivia responded softly.

"And because his name is not on the lease, he is not responsible for the drugs found inside the unit."

"Shit!" Danyelle screamed.

"So now what?" Olivia asked.

"Well, we're going to ask the judge to grant you O.R."

"What is that?" Olivia asked.

"O.R. is when the judge releases people who have been accused of crimes on their own recognizance. Basically, he's giving them a free pass to go home, trusting that they will appear back in court on their assigned court date. If you don't show up, a warrant will be issued for your arrest. If he doesn't grant you O.R. today, he will. It may take a few days."

"A few days? I can't sit in jail for a few days. I have a son to care for," Olivia said, tears welling in her eyes.

"Well, you may not have any other choice. I will make a plea to the court on your behalf that you have a child to attend to, but I can't guarantee anything." The lawyer got up and grabbed his briefcase. "So let's go see what the judge has to say."

Several days later Danyelle and Olivia were released on their own recognizance. They immediately went down to the Department of Family Services. Olivia was in a hurry to get Bryce back. She approached the receptionist and explained the reason she was there. After Olivia finished her story, the receptionist picked up the phone and made a call. She turned to Olivia. "You can have a seat in the waiting area and someone will be out to speak with you shortly."

The two women waited approximately ten minutes before a woman came out to greet them. She was a black woman who appeared to be in her mid-fifties.

"Hello, I'm Mrs. Johnson. I was told that you were looking for your baby," the woman said.

"Yes, I was arrested a few days ago and the public defender told me that I would have to put in a petition to get my son back."

"Yes, that is usually how it works, but your son is no longer under our care. The baby's father came down here the same night he was brought to us. He had the baby's birth certificate stating that he was the father, so we had no choice but to release him."

A sharp pain pierced Olivia's heart. She knew that something was not right. She ran out of the office to hurry home. Danyelle thanked the lady for her time and followed Olivia out the door.

They arrived home to find their home in disarray; chairs were knocked over, clothes were thrown everywhere. Olivia walked into her bedroom to look for Bryant and the baby. All his clothes were gone and so were the baby's. Danyelle walked in behind her.

"They're gone. He took my baby and left," Olivia cried.

"Don't worry. We'll find them."

"How?" Olivia screamed. "I don't know where to begin to look. I don't know any of his friends. I've never met any of his family."

"You never asked?"

"Of course I questioned him about his past and his family. He told me he didn't have any family. He said that the baby and I were all the family he had. Now he's taken off with my baby and I don't even know why or where."

Olivia cried while Danyelle hugged her sister. Olivia felt closer to her sister than she ever had. Growing up they had never been close, but when a crisis arose, they were there for one another.

"I think Bryant is the one who set this whole thing up," Danyelle told her. "Who would call the cops and tell them that we had drugs in the apartment? I knew there was something strange about him. Every time we got high together he never spoke a word. He got unusually quiet like he was plotting something."

"You really think Bryant is responsible for sending us to jail? But why? Why would he do this?" She wiped a few tears from her eyes. "I need to call the police to report the baby missing." Olivia went into the kitchen and grabbed the cordless phone off the wall.

"I'm going to look around and see if Bryant left anything behind," Danyelle said as she walked back into Olivia's bedroom.

It wasn't long before a uniformed officer, along with the same detective who had arrested them a few days prior, showed up at their apartment.

"Hello Ms. Benson," the detective uttered when Olivia answered the door.

She was surprised to see him.

"I heard the call come in over the radio and I was in the neighborhood. I wanted to come by and see if there was anything I could do to help. I hope you don't mind?" He smiled back at Olivia.

"No, it's fine. Please come in."

While the uniformed officer sat on the couch and asked Olivia a series of questions, the detective looked around the apartment at photos of Bryant and the baby.

"Can we have this photo?" The detective pointed to a photo of Bryant holding the baby in the park.

"Sure." Olivia replied.

The detective handed the photo to the officer and the officer got up from off the couch.

"Ma'am, I'm done with my report. I'm going to knock on a few of your neighbors' doors and see if anyone heard or saw anything," the officer told Olivia.

"MacKenzie, I'm going to look around here," the detective informed the officer.

"So, Bryant is the baby's father?"

"Yes."

"The same guy I interviewed down at the station and said that the drugs belong to you?"

"Yes."

"Do you think he set this up?"

"My sister does."

"What do you think?" he asked.

"I don't want to believe Bryant would do this, but I don't have any choice."

"Why would he want to falsely accuse you of selling drugs?" the detective asked.

"I don't know," Olivia responded.

"If this was a setup, I promise that I will get to the bottom of it, but I have to be honest with you." Olivia braced herself for the worst, "Bryant has got a huge lead ahead of us. He's probably been gone since the night you were arrested. He could be anywhere in the country. The longer he's gone with the child, the harder it's going to be for us to find him."

Olivia's eyes turned sad.

"As soon as I get back to the station I'm going to contact the National Center for Missing and Exploited children. I'm going to transmit all of Bryce's information and hopefully they can help. They have a whole lot of resources that we don't have. So if Bryant left the state, at least we can alert other police agencies throughout the country."

"Detective Collins, do you think you're going to find my baby?"

"I'm not sure, but I sure hope so." He handed her a card. "Here is the name of a guy who has had a lot of success in finding missing children. A lot of parents invest in hiring private detectives because it's good to have someone looking for your child who can devote their full undivided attention.

Don't think I'm going to stop looking for Bryce, but the Philadelphia Police Department can't put its full manpower on one case."

"Thanks, Detective."

Olivia stared at the card. It read "Desmond Murray, Private Investigator."

Payce sat inside his car and stared at First Nazareth Church. He knew he couldn't sit in the car all morning long, Tressie was expecting him. He promised her that he'd attend Sunday services with her this week, but he wasn't ready to face Reverend Kane.

After seeing Reverend Kane at The Dollhouse, he would never be able to look at her again without being reminded of that night. The woman whose curves nicely filled out that black, leather, cat-woman outfit was not the same woman he met wearing a pastor's robe a few weeks ago. If she approached him, he wouldn't know what to say. He wished he had never gone out with Darshon that night.

Payce got out of the car and walked up the church steps. He placed his hand on the doorknob and quickly let go before opening the door. The courage he had built up inside of him a few minutes before quickly deflated out of him like air from a flat tire.

He stood outside the church wishing he could turn around and go back home, but he couldn't. For three weeks straight he had made up excuses why he couldn't attend services with Tressie. Once he ran out of excuses, he had no choice but to go. He looked at his watch. It was getting late.

He opened the church doors and stepped inside the vestibule. The ushers immediately opened the doors and allowed him to enter. Inside the sanctuary Reverend Simms prayed over a woman. He held his hand over her head. "Lord, fill the emptiness left in Sister Monroe's heart from the loss of her husband," he shouted.

Payce looked around and found Tressie sitting in the last pew. He slid into the seat next to her and gently caressed her hand. As Pastor Simms prayed, Payce looked around the church for Reverend Kane. She wasn't in the pulpit. *Perhaps she missed service today*, he thought. A moment later, Reverend Kane rose from out of one of the pews. Payce watched her walk over to Pastor Simms and also laid hands on Sister Monroe's head. Suddenly Reverend Kane's eyes darted in Payce's direction and he quickly bowed his head. *I hope she didn't see me.* After prayer concluded, Payce hoped that the remainder of the service would go quickly.

"Hey, sweetheart," Tressie greeted Payce after church services ended. "I'm glad you made it." She kissed him lightly on the lips.

"So am I." He grabbed his coat in a hurry to leave. "I'm going outside to heat up the car. I'll wait for you out there."

"Payce, I know you're ready to go, but I need to speak with Danyelle about the Sunday school class she's going to teach for me. Can you wait for me? I won't be long." She quickly walked away.

Payce sat quietly, trying to make himself invisible to everyone around him.

Minutes later, he heard her voice behind him. "Hello, Payce."

He turned around in the pew. "Hey, Reverend Kane." He turned back around.

"How are you doing?" she asked.

"Good," he replied, hoping that his one-word answers would be a subtle hint that he didn't want to be bothered.

She sat down next to Payce in the pew. "Payce, I need to talk with you about what you saw a few weeks ago."

"Reverend Kane, I would like to pretend that didn't even happen," he whispered. "What you do is your business. You won't have to worry about me saying anything to anybody because my lips are sealed."

"Well, I'm glad to hear that, but I figured you wouldn't say anything to anyone about where you saw me because then you would have to explain what you were doing there. But that is not the only thing I want to speak to you about. How about we meet for lunch tomorrow?"

"Reverend Kane, I'm awfully busy. I have a new job and I'm trying to stay focused. I don't know if I'll be able to make it," Payce explained.

"Payce, I just want to talk. I have an offer that might be of interest to you. I just want to run it by you."

"I doubt I'll be interested."

"Payce." She grabbed his hand lovingly. "Please, can you just come to hear me out? It's not going to hurt to hear what I have to offer."

Her sincere and loving tone changed his mind, "Where do you want to meet?"

"There's a place called Caribou Café on Walnut Street. I'll be waiting for you at noon."

Someone called her name from across the room. "See you then," she said and strolled away.

"Payce, I'm ready," Tressie announced from behind him.

A minute too late, Payce thought to himself.

The following day Payce walked into the lunch eatery prepared to cut his meeting with the reverend short.

"Hi," Payce said to the hostess, "I'm looking for a woman in her early thirties. She might have a reservation under . . ."

"Reverend Kane?" she asked.

"Yeah, that's her," he replied.

"She's waiting for you. Follow me, please."

Payce trailed the hostess to a booth in the corner of the restaurant. She placed two menus on the table. "A waitress will be over shortly to take your order," she informed them and walked away.

"Glad to see you could make it," Reverend Kane remarked.

Payce removed his coat and took a seat. "Reverend, what's up? You wanted me here. Now I'm here. What do you want to talk about?"

"First, I want to thank you for not telling your father about my extra-curricular activities. I think that if my secret ever got out it could do nothing but hurt the church."

"Then why do you do it?" he asked.

"It's not my choice to be gay. I'm naturally attracted to women just like you are."

"I don't care that you're gay. I want to know why you work at The Dollhouse."

"I started going there because it was a discreet place to meet other people like myself. It allows me to hide my real identity. When I work at The Dollhouse, Sandy Kane emerges and Reverend Kane suppresses herself." She pointed to herself. "After I started working there, a few customers began asking for me by name. I brought in a lot of revenue, so the owner asked if I would be interested in working full time. Being a minister, I saw a conflict of interest and I confessed to her about who I actually was. That's how we came up with the idea of me wearing a mask to keep my identity concealed just in case someone came in who knew me. Plus, she thought I could act out some of the women's fantasies of making love to Catwoman."

"But you took the mask off."

"I know. That was the first time I've ever done that. It instinctively felt right to expose my identity at that moment."

"Maybe you should think about revealing yourself to more than your customers."

"Maybe you're right," she replied.

A waitress came over and placed a glass of water in front of each of them. "Are you ready to order?" she asked.

"Yes," the reverend replied. "I'll have the chicken salad. What about you, Payce?"

"Nothing for me," he replied.

The waitress retrieved both menus and walked away.

"Payce, the reason I asked you here is because I'm aware of your past. And I've experienced firsthand how hard it is for someone who is just getting out of jail to get a job."

"You've been locked up?" he asked.

"No, but I had a nephew who did time in New Jersey. He was locked up in Trenton State for ten years. When he got out he had a hard time finding a decent job. That is why I wanted to make you a job offer."

"Thanks, but I have a job."

"I heard you got a job parking cars down at the Westin Hotel, but is that enough to support yourself, not to mention your girlfriend? Wouldn't you like to take her out and buy her nice things? Trust me; working at The Dollhouse would eliminate a lot of financial problems."

"The Dollhouse!" he shouted. "That lesbian joint!"

"Would you keep your voice down?"

He looked around to see if anyone was looking. "What am I supposed to do at a lesbian spa? Watch y'all eat each other out?"

"Would you listen to me?" she whispered. "That place is making thousands of dollars every night. There has not been a night that I haven't left there with at least two thousand dollars."

"What does that have to do with me?" he asked.

"The place is making so much money that now they're thinking about expanding."

"I'm not giving no man a massage," Payce thundered.

"And I wouldn't ask you to. Have you ever heard of the term 'swing couples'?"

Payce shook his head no.

"It's when married couples or anyone in a committed relationship has sex with someone outside their relationship. You have sex with their partner while the spouse or mate watches."

"I've never heard of it."

"Well, the owner of The Dollhouse has had lots of requests from customers who are interested in it. She is recruiting men to come and participate in the swinging."

Payce started laughing. "You want me to be a male prostitute?"

"No, it's not prostitution."

"Yes, it is. I'm getting paid for having sex with strangers."

"No, you're getting paid for helping a couple live out their fantasies."

"Reverend Kane, you're sicker than I thought." He got up to leave.

"Payce, they're willing to start you off at fifteen hundred tax-free dollars a night."

Payce froze in his tracks.

"That is just to start. If you do a good job and couples return to see you, they will pay you more."

He sat back down in his seat.

"If you don't like it, you can quit, but I'm telling you it's easy money."

Fifteen hundred dollars, he thought.

"What about Tressie?" he asked.

"Tressie doesn't have to know. I'm not going to say anything to her."

Payce thought about having fifteen hundred dollars cash in his pocket. He hadn't seen that much money since he was hustling on the corner. Reverend Kane waited for Payce to accept her offer.

"Let me think about it and I'll give you a call," he told her.

"Don't make me wait long," she replied.

Chapter 8

LATE FEBRUARY 2004

Miles's facial expression said "I'm sorry." This was another failed attempt by Elise to resuscitate her husband's limp rod back to life. She held his manhood in her hand and wished for a miracle. She prayed that he would have a positive reaction to her touch, but her efforts were unsuccessful. She got up and moved to her side of the bed.

The doctor had prescribed Miles medication to assist with his treatment, but so far they saw no improvements.

They lay in silence and stared at the ceiling. Thoughts of Sheridan drifted through Elise's mind. She wondered how an innocent cup of coffee could turn into nights of hot and heavy sex.

A part of her was ashamed. She was a Christian woman who was responsible for pointing out the sins of others. Now she was the one committing sin. This was an unfamiliar place for her in life, a place she had never thought she would be. An extra-marital affair had been inconceivable, but Sheridan's touch electrified her body. The worst part was that she didn't want it to end. She had fallen in love with him.

It started with Sheridan coming into the gym on Wednesday evenings. He would act as her personal trainer by assisting her with the weight machines and demonstrating different techniques to get the most out of her workouts. Those techniques often required that he touch intimate parts of her body. The feel of his hands made her nervous. She knew that their relationship was getting more personal, but she didn't stop it. She enjoyed the attention he showered on her. Then came the night when their relationship took a dramatic turn.

It was a typical Wednesday night, and Elise was expecting Sheridan to walk into the gym at any second, but he never showed. She thought that he might have been running late, but by the end of her workout there was still no sign of him. Disappointed that he was a no-show, she hated the thought of having to wait another full week before she saw him again.

In no rush to go home, Elise chose to sit in the sauna for a while. The warmth from the sauna wrapped itself around her skin. She sat against the far wall, leaned her head back and closed her eyes and enjoyed the quiet, serene atmosphere. She was alone for a while before someone came in, interrupting her solitude. She kept her eyes closed and tried to block out the presence of someone else in the small-boxed room.

"Is this seat taken?" the stranger asked abruptly.

Elise was startled and wasn't aware that her uninvited guest was so close. She looked up. The steam slowly cleared away from her eyes.

"Sheridan?" she called out.

"Yeah, it's me. I hope I didn't scare you."

"Yes, you did scare me, but how did you know I was in here?"

"I asked the receptionist if she had seen you and she told me that you were in here. I'm sorry I was late. I had to go out of town to Miami unexpectedly and my flight was delayed."

"Miami? That must have been a nice trip. Was it business or pleasure?"

"Business, unfortunately." He sat down next to her. "There's this kid who goes to school down there and he is withdrawing from school early to enter the NFL. My firm is eager to represent him. So they asked me to fly down there to give a quick presentation. He's a good kid, comes from a stable home, and has parents who care. The father is the one who actually contacted us. He wants the kid to be represented by a black sports agency, but I got the impression that the kid had his sights on some of the larger agencies."

"What does the father have to do with anything? Isn't it the kid's decision?"

"Ultimately, yes, it is the kid's decision, but his father played in the pros and has had a lot of regrets for putting his trust in a lot of people who would never understand what it's like to be a black man playing in the NFL. He's just a father who wants to help lead his son in the right direction."

"Well, I hope you get the account," Elise replied.

"So do I." They sat in silence for a moment. She felt uncomfortable sitting next to him with nothing on but a towel. At least when they were at the coffeehouse she did have clothes on. She looked down at the towel wrapped around Sheridan's waist. *What do I do if he touches me or worse, kisses me? Calm down, Elise, the man has made no indication that he would ever hit on you. Every time he's been alone with me he has been a perfect gentleman.*

Another five minutes of silence passed before a throbbing feeling began pulsating between her legs. She glanced over at him. He seemed unaware of what she was thinking. Elise couldn't hold back the desire that burned deep inside her. Lust had taken over her body and she was at its mercy. Throwing all caution to the wind, she quickly climbed on top of Sheridan and ferociously kissed his lips. Sheridan responded to Elise's advances by removing her towel.

The heat from the sauna created tears of sweat on their bodies. The sex was invigorating for both of them. He grabbed her tighter and tighter. He tried not to release his seed inside of her, but he couldn't withstand the feeling. He finally burst like a dam.

Elise leaned her head against his. The realization of what she had just done hit her like a ton of bricks. She had broken her wedding vows and deceived her husband. She got up and sat next to Sheridan. She held her head down and placed her hands on her head. Her remorse filled the room. He could sense her guilt.

"I know you regret what just happened," Sheridan said. "If you say you don't want to see me again, I'll understand."

Elise didn't say a word, nor did she look his way. Sheridan wrapped his towel back around himself and got up to leave.

"Sheridan!" Elise stopped him. She walked over and hugged him. "I'm scared of what's happening to me. I've never done this kind of thing before. I don't know what came over me," she whimpered from the embrace of his arms.

They continued to meet, not only on Wednesday evenings, but also on Monday and Friday evenings. She stopped going to the gym and began having her workouts in Sheridan's bedroom. Fortunately, Miles was not suspicious of her sudden appreciation for going to the gym. He encouraged her increased workouts and wished that he could go with her, but Elise intentionally scheduled her time at the gym during his therapy sessions with Dr. Johnson.

Elise glanced over at her husband. *He is such a good man*. She felt guilty for having thoughts of another man while her husband lay next to her, but there was no way she could stop it. All thoughts started and stopped with Sheridan. She and Sheridan had made plans to get together on Tuesday night before he went out of town on business. It would be their last night together for two whole weeks, and Elise couldn't wait to see him. When she spoke with him on the phone, he hinted that he had a surprise for her.

"Elise, what do you think about us purchasing a few sex toys?" Miles asked. "Honey?" Miles shook his wife lightly, trying to wake her from her daydream.

"I'm sorry, honey. I must have been a million *Miles* away. What were you saying?"

"Are you all right?" he asked. "You seemed so deep in thought."

"I was just thinking about Olivia," she lied. "I hope she's able to find Bryant and the baby."

"Yeah, that must be hard—to be wrongly accused of a crime, go to jail, and then have your baby disappear."

"We'll have to keep her and the baby in our prayers. Now, what were you saying?" she asked.

"What do you think about us getting some sex toys? Do you think they could help out with the problems I've been having?"

"Sweetheart, I'm not sure, but it's worth a try. Before, I forget, on Tuesday after Bible Study I'm going to go over to the gym and work out a little, so I may be a little late getting home."

"Why are you going to the gym on a Tuesday night? That's usually your night off."

"Yeah, I know and I'm going to cut back on my workouts a little, but I want to get in there early this week and then I'll have the rest of the week to spend extra time with you."

Miles was glad that his wife was going to be spending more time at home. Lately, she had been spending so much time at the gym that they barely spent anytime together. Also, he noticed a change in Elise's behavior that worried him. She frequently daydreamed and was unfocused. At first he thought she was having an affair, but he later dismissed that as paranoia.

He mentioned Elise's distant behavior to his therapist, who provided him with several logical reasons why his wife could be behaving oddly. She explained that impotency was not only psychologically damaging to him, but also to his spouse. The best thing he could do was to give her space and allow her to deal with the problem in her own way. If things continued or got worse, he could always suggest Elise talk to a counselor or therapist.

Miles turned to his woman. "Elise, would you like to say a prayer with me?"

Elise wanted to pray with him. Prayer was the one thing in their life that had always brought them closer together, but she just wasn't up for it today. "I'm really tired," she replied. "Maybe we can pray together in the morning."

"No problem," Miles said. He leaned over and gave her a quick kiss on the lips, turned over, and went to sleep.

MARCH 2004

Pilar and Val luxuriated at the spa while they received their weekly beauty regimen of facials and body scrubs. They sat with avocado masks smeared over their faces.

"This feels soooooo good," Pilar said aloud. "I love to get the avocado scrub on my face. When I was pregnant, I looked forward to one of these every week. I love the way it opens my pores."

"Is Carlos glad to be back home?" Val asked.

"Oh yes!" she replied. "Since his return from Colorado he has been so attentive to the children and me. I think he missed us while he was away. He has been spending so much time with the children, and last night he even got up in the middle of the night with the baby."

Val was envious of Pilar and Carlos. They were married and had a family. She wanted that from Julian.

"I can't wait for Julian and me to have a house full of kids."

"Did you start with your wedding plans yet?"

"I started while he was away. I contacted several places in Philadelphia to have our reception, but I haven't had a chance to mention it to him. Since he got back from Colorado he's been away from home more than before he left."

Troubled with doubts of what Julian could be doing while away from home, Val asked, "Pilar, do you think Julian is cheating on me?" she finally asked.

Ever since Pilar warned her about the numerous affairs that go on in the NBA, Val had been very suspicious of Julian's whereabouts.

Every time he went out she questioned where he was going and with whom. She checked his coat pockets for hotel receipts or phone numbers. One night she stayed up until four o'clock in the morning waiting for him to get home. When he finally walked in the door, she pretended to be asleep on the couch. He came in, checked on her, and went to bed. After she thought he had fallen asleep, she snuck out into the garage to search his car. When she didn't find anything, she knew she had reached a point where she didn't trust him, and it had to stop. She had to find out one way or another what he was up to.

"I wouldn't jump to that conclusion," Pilar said. "His time away from home could really have to do with business."

"I've been trying to convince myself that he is actually working, but intuition tells me there's something more," Val replied.

Pilar and Val had finally made it out of the spa and were on their way back home. Before leaving the spa, Pilar insisted on treating herself to a detoxifying body mud wrap. The spa services coordinator told her that it would make her feel twenty years old again.

It was Val's first time sitting in a tub full of mud. The mud didn't make her feel twenty years old, but it sure was relaxing. It relieved so much stress; her back, neck and shoulders were less tense. The strain of worrying about Julian had been temporarily lifted.

Driving home, Pilar pulled into the grocery store parking lot. "Do you mind if we make a quick stop? I have to have something good and hot waiting for my man when he gets home, besides myself," Pilar joked.

Inside the store, Pilar quickly scanned the aisles and found the ingredients she needed for her family's dinner. The two women chatted while waiting in the express checkout line.

"You cannot go to Julian with suspicions about his behavior. You have got to have some evidence to prove he's been unfaithful. Trust me, if there is evidence out there, it will come to you."

"How can you be so sure?"

"Trust me. Right after Carlos and I were married, I got pregnant with our first child. I was so busy decorating the nursery and preparing for our daughter's birth that I missed a few of Carlos's games. At the time he was playing for Chicago, so one night I thought it would be a nice surprise if I unexpectedly attended that night's home game. Only I was the one surprised. I arrived at United Arena and sitting in Carlos's reserved seats was an eighteen-year-old redhead. I thought I was going to lose my mind. I politely asked her who she was and do you know what her reply was? She said, 'You know who I am.' I knew in my heart the young girl had been sleeping around with my husband. I grabbed her by her arm and she shoved me. Carlos saw us arguing from the bench and climbed the stands to defend me. He publicly cursed her for putting her hands on his pregnant wife."

"What happened?" Val asked.

"Well, you know that the media taped everything that happened. It was on the news and in the paper. Carlos was fined for leaving the game and I was ready to leave him. Furious, I went home and packed my bags. He begged me not to go and swore that he would never cheat on me again."

"It must have been painful to come face to face with Carlos's mistress," Val replied.

"It did hurt. I hope no one ever has to go through having their personal lives aired throughout the media like we did," Pilar remarked.

Val noticed the corner of a magazine in the newsstand. She couldn't see the entire cover clearly, but the letters "ian" and "ington" caught her attention. Val held up one finger to Pilar and walked over to the magazine stand. She pulled out a celebrity gossip magazine. On the cover was a full color photo of Julian in a loving embrace with a woman. The headline read "Seattle Sonics star rookie and his snow bunny." A short blurb beneath the photo said, "An unidentified witness told the magazine that Pennington and his new girlfriend were vacationing in Aspen and they looked very much in love."

Pilar glanced at the photo from over Val's shoulder. "Val, don't let this upset you. These types of magazines tell nothing but lies. Do you know how many times Carlos has been in this magazine?"

Val heard Pilar talking, but the words were suppressed in her mind. She couldn't believe Julian would do this to her. Her heart dropped, and so did the glass bottle of olive oil she held in her hand. It shattered on the floor.

She ran out of the store and into the rain. Pilar called out after her. Val got into Pilar's truck and watched the rain fall against the windshield. She was hypnotized. Those photos were the proof she needed to confront Julian, and she needed to confront him. Now.

Pilar climbed into the driver's side.

"Can you take me to the team's practice?" Val asked.

Pilar wanted to comfort her friend, but she thought that maybe the best thing she could do for her right now was to say nothing at all. She knew how devastating it was to find out the man you loved had been unfaithful.

The drive over to the team's practice gave Val time to think about what she was going to say. Her mind spun around in full circles. It was hard for her to accept the fact that Julian had lied to her. The foundation of trust that they had built over the years had crumbled.

They pulled into the parking lot, but before Pilar put her truck in park, Val jumped out and stormed into the auditorium. The team was running drills up and down the court. Val walked straight onto the middle of the court. Julian didn't notice her until she walked over and hit him in his chest.

Tears ran down her face as she screamed, "Who is she, Julian?"

"Valencia, what is wrong with you? You can't come down here causing a scene! I'm in the middle of practice!" He tried to shield himself from her punches.

Coach McGee saw the commotion that was going on at the opposite end of the gym. "Pennington, what the hell is going on down there?" Coach thundered.

"I don't give a damn, you've been cheating on me, and I want to know who she is," Val screamed.

"Pennington, this is practice, not *Dr. Phil!*" Coach screamed across the gymnasium. The rest of the team laughed at Julian's domestic dispute.

"Sorry, Coach, just give us a few minutes." Julian grabbed Val by the arm and pulled her into a small corridor off the gymnasium.

"What is wrong with you?" Julian demanded.

"Did you sleep with her?" Val asked.

"Sleep with who?"

"The girl you took to Aspen."

"Valencia, I don't know what you're talking about."

"Julian, you were caught on camera. The paparazzi took pictures of the two of you together. You and your mistress are on the cover of every tabloid magazine from here to Philadelphia."

Julian's face sank with guilt.

"Valencia, go home," he said. "We can discuss this later." He pointed in the direction of the door.

Val refused to budge. "Did you sleep with her?" she asked again.

Julian turned his back to her. She knew the answer was yes, but she wanted to hear him say it. She wanted him to acknowledge the wrong he had done.

"I slept with her once."

Rage flashed in her eyes.

"You're lying," she said, her teeth clenched. "Why would you take a one night stand to Aspen? You've been seeing her for a while, haven't you? That's why you're hardly home and when I call you don't answer your phone. How long has this been going on behind my back?"

He laid his head against the wall but didn't answer her question.

Val was so angry. She wanted to dig her nails into his skin and hurt him the same way she was hurting. The dark cloud that had been following her around finally poured rain down on her head, clearing her mind so she could see what was going on.

There was nothing more to be said between the two of them. What she thought they had was nothing but a lie. She marched back out into the gymnasium and all eyes settled on her. She could feel their stares. Everyone waited to see if she would lose control again.

Val slowly walked back out to the truck, and Pilar followed. Once they were back on the road, Val broke down in tears. She couldn't hold back her overwhelming sorrow any longer.

"Julian slept with her. He shared his body with a woman he barely even knew. We vowed to wait for each other. I saved myself for him. I feel so stupid." She poured out her heart.

Pilar pulled off to the side of the road. "Val, everything is going to be okay."

"How can everything be okay? I'm three thousand miles away from my friends and family. Julian and I are through. I have nowhere to go."

Tears continued to fall from her eyes. Her breathing became uncontrollable. She couldn't catch her breath. Val opened the door and ran over to a nearby bush just in time for it to catch her vomit. The rain beat down on her back. She grabbed her stomach to stop the pain.

Pilar ran to her side. "Let it all go. Once you let go of all the hurt, you will feel so much better." Pilar wrapped her arms around Val as the rain soaked their clothes. She was not going to leave Val until she was feeling better.

Five minutes had passed before Val could calm herself down. She walked over and leaned against the side of Pilar's truck.

"Val, I'm going to bring you back to my house. You can stay with us tonight," Pilar yelled. The rain had gotten heavier and it was hard for Pilar to see what was in front of her.

Val was too tired to put up any argument. She graciously accepted Pilar's invitation.

It wasn't long before Pilar pulled up into her three-car garage. She parked between a 745 Beamer and a Maybach.

They entered the house through a door from the garage that led straight into Pilar's family room. Val admired the view from the family room. Looking through three large bay windows, Val could see acres of land that had an in-ground swimming pool, a tennis court, and basketball court.

Out of nowhere a cute little toddler ran up to hug Pilar. "Mommy's home," he squealed.

Pilar put her hands out and stopped him. "No Alejandro. Mommy can't hug you right now. I'm wet."

The inquisitive three-year-old stared at his mother. She spoke to her children in Spanish and waved her two oldest daughters over.

"Children, this is Ms. Benson. She will be staying with us for a while, so I expect everyone to be on their best behavior," Pilar said to them. "Valencia, these are my two oldest daughters, Nina and Tia."

Each girl politely shook Val's hand.

"And this is the little man of the house." She pointed to her son. "This is Alejandro, but we call him Alec. Say hello, Alec."

He walked up to her. "*¿Hola, usted querría jugar conmigo?*"

Valencia looked up at Pilar for help. She couldn't speak Spanish.

"Alec, Ms. Benson doesn't speak Spanish. Speak English," she instructed him.

"Hi, would you like to play with me?" he asked Val.

Those innocent words melted her heart, and for the first time since her altercation with Julian, she smiled.

"Alec, Ms. Benson is tired. We can ask her to play a little later, after she's had a chance to rest." Pilar turned to the girls. "Where's the baby?" she asked.

"Mrs. Gonzalez has her," Tia responded. "Mommy, why are you so wet?"

"We got caught out in the rain. I'm on my way upstairs to change now." Pilar turned to Val. "You can meet the baby later. Come on, I'll show you to your room."

"Alec is so cute," Val commented as they climbed the stairs.

"Yes, I love all my children, but he's my favorite. He's a momma's boy."

Pilar led Val to a guest room that was larger than her and Julian's master bedroom. She looked around at the bronze interior room. Circular ceiling lights brightened the room. On the nightstand a crystal vase showcased lilies in bloom. *What an elegantly decorated room*, she thought. Against the far wall hung a full length mirror and a forty-two-inch plasma television was mounted above the fireplace.

"There's a bathroom through that door if you want to take a shower."

"Yes, I would love that."

"While you're in the shower, I'll make you a cup of hot tea and I'll get you one of Carlos's T-shirts to sleep in."

"Thanks for everything, Pilar. I don't know what I would have done without you today."

Pilar smiled.

Val got in the shower and turned the faucet until the water was steaming hot. She loved taking a hot shower. The steam usually cleared her mind, but not today. Today her mind was full of memories of her and Julian. She turned her back to the steady stream of water, allowing it to loosen her back muscles. Taking the washcloth to splash water on her face, she remembered how she and Julian met.

Val and Olivia, both freshmen at Philly High, were excited about the school's first basketball game of the season. It was going to be an exciting game against Dobbins High School, and the entire student body was attending.

Before the start of the game, Julian paraded out onto the court to demonstrate his ability to ignite screams from the female spectators.

"That must be Julian Pennington," Val whispered to Olivia.

"Yeah, that's him. He's cute, isn't he?"

"He's all right."

"Stop lying. That boy isn't just cute—he's K-ute."

K-ute was their private definition of a guy that was a 10 or better.

"Okay, I'll admit he is K-ute, but let's see if he's a real baller." She laughed at her emphasis on baller.

From the time the official tossed up the ball until the very last second ticked away on the game clock, Julian put on a performance for his fans. He broke three school records that one night: the highest number of points in one quarter, the highest number of points in a single game, and the highest number of assists.

"That boy can really play," Val commented.

"They said he's good. A lot of people say he's a shoo-in for the pros."

Val watched Julian celebrate with his team-mates. He is K-ute, she thought, but he probably has girls lined up around the block.

Val and Olivia waited inside the school for Val's father to pick them up. They stood not too far from the boys' locker room where, indeed, a pack of girls had assembled, waiting for Julian. Val watched as Julian walked out of the locker room. The flirtatious and obviously excited females pushed and shoved to get closer to the handsome ball player.

Julian looked up and saw Val standing close by. He broke away from the crowd and stepped to her. *"Hi, what's your name?"*

"Valencia," she replied. "Valencia Benson."

"That is such a beautiful name." He batted his long eyelashes at her flirtatiously. "I saw you in the stands. Did you enjoy the game?"

"Yes, I did. You played very well."

"Thanks." He smiled boldly. "Would you like to get something to eat?"

Val shied away from the handsome young man and pulled Olivia closer to her. "I'm sorry. We're waiting for my father to come pick us up."

"I understand," Julian replied. "Can I get your phone number? Maybe we can go out another time."

"I'm sorry, but my father doesn't allow guys he hasn't met to call the house."

Julian was disappointed. Soon the girls heard a car horn.

"I have to go," Val announced. "It was nice speaking with you, Julian." Val and Olivia rushed out to the car.

Julian watched them get in the car, but before she closed the passenger side door Julian yelled out, "Valencia!"

Val looked in his direction as he ran out to the car and over to her father.

"Hello, Mr. Benson, my name is Julian Pennington. I attend school with your daughter." Julian held out his hand for a handshake. "I was just talking with your daughter and she told me that

*you don't allow guys to call your home whom you
haven't met yet. So I wanted to take this opportunity to introduce myself. I hope that sometime
in the near future you will give me permission to
speak with your daughter on the telephone."*

*Mr. Benson was impressed by Julian's respect-
ful manner, and was amused by how smitten he
was with his daughter.*

*"Val is right. I don't allow boys I haven't met
to call the house, but now that I've met you and I
see that you are a nice young man, I don't have a
problem with Val giving you the house number."
He turned to Valencia. "Baby girl, give him the
house number."*

*Valencia was shocked. She could not believe her
father had been charmed by Julian so quickly.
Her father never gave out their phone numbers to
boys without him first giving them a long lecture
on responsibly dating his daughter. Val was
impressed.*

*She knew anyone who could get past her father
on the first meeting was someone special.*

After being in the shower for nearly an hour, Val
decided that it was time for her to get out.

She walked back into the bedroom and moved
Carlos's shirt that Pilar had placed on the bed. She
lay across the bed in her towel.

Val heard a soft knock at her door. "Come in,"
she said softly.

Pilar walked in carrying a hot cup of tea. She placed it on the nightstand and sat on the edge of the bed.

"Are you feeling better?" she asked.

"A little," Val replied.

"Don't blame yourself for what has happened. I already told you that I went through a similar incident and the entire time I blamed myself. I wondered what I had done wrong to make him want someone else. After a while I realized that I had to stop blaming myself. I couldn't take responsibility for his actions. I made him dinner, took care of the kids, and gave him sex." She snapped her fingers. "On demand." They laughed together. "I knew I was the best wife I could be, but if our marriage was going to survive, he would have to realize that I was second to none, and that our family took precedence over everything. And eventually he did."

"I do feel like this is my fault." Val told Pilar. "If I didn't insist we wait until after we were married to have sex, then this would have never happened."

"Don't think that way, because no matter what you had done, this could have still happened. You can't live your life on the assumption that everything you do or don't do will prevent Julian from stepping outside of your relationship. You have to live your life for yourself."

Val absorbed Pilar's words of wisdom.

"Now it's up to you to decide whether or not you think your relationship is worth fighting for. Remember you said that you and Julian shared something special. If you really believe that, then the two of you can work through this together. You have to remember that just because you two are in love doesn't mean that either of you won't make mistakes. I stayed with Carlos because I knew that I could never love anyone the same way that I love him, but some women can't get past infidelity."

Pilar got up and grabbed Val's clothes from the bathroom. "I'm going to take these downstairs and put them in the washer. If you need anything, just yell. My room is right down the hall."

She was finally left alone. She closed her eyes and thought about Pilar's advice. *Should I forgive Julian? Or will I allow one mistake destroy what we have?*

Chapter 9

"Ladies, I'm going to be completely honest with you," Desmond Murray, the private detective, told Olivia and Danyelle. "You haven't really given me a whole lot of information on Mr. Winters. I'm pretty sure that I can find him, but it may take me a while."

"How long do you think it will take?" Olivia asked.

"I could find him next week, or it may not be until next year. It depends on how careful he's been about leaving a paper trail. It looks like he's done this before, because he left this apartment with no signs of him ever living here. But you did say he worked for Amtrak, correct?"

Olivia nodded her head. "They won't give you any information. I tried," she said. "I called them and all they kept saying was, 'We cannot release any past or present employee information.'" Olivia mimicked the woman she spoke to on the phone.

"Let me try. I may be able to persuade them to help us out," Murray replied. "Give me a call if you happen to find or remember anything that could help me find out his whereabouts, like an old phone bill or pay stub. I'll start by going down to

Amtrak. I'll show his picture around to a few people. Hopefully someone will recognize him."

"Mr. Murray, I just remembered something," Danyelle said. "I'm not sure if this will be of any help to you, but Bryant took a trip over the summer to Chicago for a family emergency."

"Oh, yeah, I had forgotten about that," Olivia added.

"There's not too much more we can tell you. He went to Chicago and returned a few days later," Danyelle said.

"I don't suppose he left a phone number where he could be reached?" Mr. Murray asked.

"He did leave me with a number to the Best Western. I think that's where he was staying."

"Great, let's just pray that he used the phone there or maybe even rented a car. This is a great lead. Olivia, I'll call you in a few weeks and let you know my progress."

Val opened her eyes and was surprised to see Alec on the floor next to her bed playing with a handful of toy soldiers. She smiled at his cuteness. "Good morning, cutie."

"Can you come play with me? My mommy said not to bother you while she was gone, and I was really quiet while you was sleeping."

"Yes, you were very quiet." She looked at the clock. It was past one o'clock in the afternoon. "Wow, I didn't know it was so late." She sat up and stretched her arms. Alec stood up next to her. "Alec, why don't you go to your room and set up a game for us to play while I get dressed? I'll be there in a bit."

The boy gathered his toy soldiers and raced out of the room. Val grabbed her cell phone. It had been a week since she had confronted Julian about his infidelities, and she was surprised that he hadn't once tried to call her to work things out. She knew that Carlos had told Julian she was staying with them, but she still wondered why he hadn't called her.

Sitting on the lounge chair next to her bed was another set of clothes from Pilar. Val had been borrowing clothes from Pilar all week long. She knew she was eventually going to have to go home and get her own clothes, but she was trying to put off facing Julian for as long as possible.

Forty-five minutes later Val walked down the hall and found Alec watching an episode of *Sponge Bob Square Pants*. Stacked high on his bed were Candy Land, Chutes and Ladders, Blue's Clues Room Talking Game, and at least three more games. He noticed Val enter and he ran to greet her.

"You can sit right here," he said, pointing to a small miniature chair.

"Alec, I don't think I'm going to fit in this chair. Why don't I sit on the floor?"

"All right," he replied. He quickly turned his attention back to the television.

Val looked around Alec's brightly colored room. The walls were painted lime green and orange. Stenciled on the walls were different characters from Nickelodeon. Against the far wall was a bookcase full of different books. Closer to the television was a miniature chair and desk set with lots of paper, crayons, markers, and paints. Val admired several drawings hanging from the wall, all done by Alec. She glanced at a few unfinished pictures on his desk when she came across a red paper heart. She opened up the heart and inside were the words "i like u" in a child's handwriting. It brought back memories of her and Julian's first Valentine's Day together.

Julian and Val had attended their school's annual Valentine's Day dance. At the end of the night the DJ announced the last song and Julian asked her to dance. He held her close while Val listened to the beat of his heart. Balloons and miniature confetti hearts fell from the ceiling, covering them and making it a moment she would never forget. Julian made it even more memorable by kneeling down in front of her unexpectedly. She thought he was going to ask her to marry him, but they were only fourteen-years-old. He pulled a box out from his coat pocket and opened it. Inside was a heart locket. "Will you be my Valentine?" he asked her.

She knew that moment marked the beginning of a true love story.

"Alec, where'd you get this?" she asked the child.

He walked over to see what she was referring to. "Some stupid girl at school gave it to me."

"Why you call her stupid?" she giggled.

"Because she bugs me. She is always messing with me and she tries to sit next to me on the bus."

"Maybe she likes you."

"I don't like girls."

"You like me, don't you? And you like your mommy, and we're both girls."

"Yes, I like both of you, but I don't like my sisters. They're always telling me what to do and making fun of me. I don't think they like me." His face turned sad.

"They're your sisters. I'm sure they love you."

"Then why are they so mean?"

"Just because a person does something to hurt you doesn't mean that person doesn't love you." Val was surprised by her choice of words. She paused for a moment. "Let me tell you what you should do. The next time either of them is mean to you, you should be nice to them. They will feel bad for mistreating you, and try to make it up to you by being nice. It's hard being the youngest." Val gave him a hug. "Why don't we play a game?"

Alec walked over to his bed and pulled out Candy Land. They played two rounds and Alec beat her both times. After the second game, he set up the board again.

"Here you are," Pilar said to Val as she walked into Alec's room. "I should have known that Alec would have taken you hostage. How are you feeling today?"

"I'm doing much better. Alec has been keeping me company."

"I hope he hasn't been bothering you."

"No, he's been a good boy. I really enjoyed my time with him. He helped me realize a few important things that I need to apply to my own life."

Pilar sensed that she was referring to her and Julian. "Would you like to use my car?" she offered.

"If you don't mind, that would be great."

"No, go ahead. My keys are downstairs on the kitchen counter," Pilar told her.

Val walked toward the door when Alec called out her name. "Ms. Benson, you're leaving?" he asked.

Val forgot all about Alec and the board game. Fortunately, Pilar intervened on her behalf. "Alec, Mommy will play with you. Ms. Benson has to run out. We will see her when she gets back."

Val shot Pilar a thank you smile and dashed out the door.

***

Val pulled up in front of what used to be her home. It seemed like months had passed since the last time she was there. She felt like an intruder as she inserted her key into the door and entered. Val looked around at the familiar home furnishings. Nothing had changed. She walked into the family room, expecting to find Julian laid out on the couch. Instead, she found a spotless family room. The last time she was here the room was a total mess. Julian used this room as his dining room, bedroom and kitchen. He always left a trail of dirty dishes, newspapers, and clothes lying around. *He must have cleaned up himself after he realized that I wasn't coming home,* Val thought to herself.

She walked toward the stairs, but stopped when she heard a noise coming from the kitchen. She could smell the aroma of tomatoes and cheese drifting from the kitchen.

"Julian?" she called out.

She strolled into the kitchen and was surprised to find a blonde-haired girl pulling out a pan of lasagna from the oven. The young woman was so preoccupied with the phone conversation she was having that she didn't notice Val enter the room.

She turned around and jumped when she saw Val's piercing stare. "Melissa, I'll have to call you back." She hung up the receiver. "Can I help you?"

Val recognized her immediately. She was the girl in the photo with Julian. She was the one he took to Aspen—his mistress. "I'm Valencia," she replied. "Is Julian here?"

"No, he's not here right now." The woman's crystal blue eyes stared right through Val. "He mentioned that you might stop by to pick up your things. He asked me to tell you that they're upstairs."

Val was unprepared for the way the woman addressed her. She treated Val like she was a guest in the house Val had shared with Julian less than a week ago. Unsure of how to react, Val decided it would be best if she gathered her things and waited to speak with Julian later.

Val walked up the stairs. "If you need any help, just yell," Julian's new friend called out. "My name is Caitlyn." Val ignored her and continued up the stairs.

She walked into the bedroom that she used to share with Julian, and into the walk-in closet. She pulled her suitcase down from the top shelf and went toward her side of the closet. Lying in the trash she noticed a shirt she had bought a few years back with both her and Julian's names airbrushed on it. Val kneeled down and lifted up the shirt. *Maybe Julian never did love me.*

Upset, she began pulling things off the hangers and throwing them into her bag. Once she was almost finished packing her things, she looked a little closer at the things she was throwing in her bag. None of these clothes looked familiar to her. "Where are all my clothes?" Val asked out loud.

"They were moved down the hall," Val heard a voice say from behind her.

Leaning against the door was Caitlyn. She sashayed into the master bedroom and sat on the edge of the bed.

"When I moved my things in here, Julian said it would be all right if I moved your things down the hall."

Val's mouth dropped open. "You live here?" Val questioned her.

Caitlyn shook her head yes. "I moved in a few days ago."

Val looked toward the bed and images of Caitlyn and Julian making love flashed in her mind. She quickly turned her head to erase the images from her head. In an attempt to escape Caitlyn's company, Val grabbed her bag and stormed down the hall to the guest bedroom. She quickly found her things and began to pack, slamming skirts and blouses into her suitcase. Val felt a pair of eyes watching her and she didn't have to turn around to know Caitlyn was eyeballing her again.

"Can I help you?" Val asked with her back turned toward Caitlyn.

"I just wanted to make sure you found everything. I wouldn't want you to forget anything."

"I think I can handle packing my things by myself," Val said emphatically.

"You don't remember me, do you?" Caitlyn asked.

Val quickened her pace to hurry up and get her things packed so she could leave. "No, I don't. Should I remember?"

"I attended school in Kentucky with Julian. I ran into you a few times when you were visiting."

"You knew Julian at the University?" Val stopped packing her things. She turned toward Caitlyn. *If he was dating her while he was in school, I'm going to kill him.*

"No, I tried to get to know him better, but he wasn't interested."

"So you decided to give it another try after he got drafted into the NBA. How convenient," Val commented sarcastically.

"No, you don't understand," Caitlyn said, laughing. "My uncle is Theodore Haas, the owner of the Seattle SuperSonics.

Val suddenly remembered the party thrown by the owners of the team earlier in the year. Caitlyn was there. She was the one who was flirting with Julian.

Caitlyn continued. "When I found out Julian was leaving school to enter the draft I—"

"You don't have to finish." Val cut her off mid-sentence. "You wasted no time coming after my man."

"It's not like it was hard. From what I've been told you were too good to satisfy *your* man. So I satisfied him for you."

Val stepped up in Caitlyn's face. "Julian never complained to me."

"What do you expect, Val? He would go out and play ball every night. He'd come home tired and needing to relax and relieve stress. You two shared a bed, but you never shared yourself. You never even touched him—no foreplay, no teasing, nothing. I just gave him what he needed. Trust me, it wasn't hard."

Val looked at her with disgust. How dare an outsider tell her what she did wrong in her relationship? This interloper had no idea what kind of relationship Julian and she shared. It was a special kind of love that allowed them to wait for one another.

Val was about to slap her, but she stopped herself. She knew Caitlyn wasn't worth the effort. Val went back to packing her things.

"Valencia, don't be upset. If I didn't go after him, eventually someone would have and it probably would have been a white girl. The owners provide lots of women for the players to play with when they're on the road. They prefer to see their players with pretty white wives with long, straight hair." She stepped in Val's face and said, "instead of dark-skinned wives with kinky hair."

Val lost all self control. Caitlyn had definitely crossed the line. Val wrapped her hands around Caitlyn's throat and squeezed hard. Val knocked her to the floor, grabbed her hair, and banged her head over and over again. Her anger was so strong; she had the strength of a man and fire in her eyes.

Out of nowhere someone lifted Val up off Caitlyn. "Valencia, what are you doing?" Julian yelled.

Caitlyn held her head as blood seeped into her hand.

Julian walked over to her. "Caitlyn, are you okay?" he asked.

"Is she okay?" Val screamed. She walked up to him and pushed him. "What about me? She verbally attacked me."

"And you physically assaulted her. You didn't have to put your hands on her," he responded.

"You don't know what she said to me," Val cried.

Caitlyn wrapped her arms around Julian. "She attacked me for no reason."

"Julian, is this . . ." she pointed at Caitlyn, " . . . what you want? Did you forget about what we had? What we meant to one another? You're going to end our relationship like this?"

He didn't say anything.

"Did you ever love me?" she yelled.

"Of course. But right now I need a break. I can't explain what's going on with me, but I need some time to sort things out."

"Julian, take your time, because when you do figure things out, I won't be here for you." Val looked over at Caitlyn. "And neither will she." Val grabbed her suitcase and left.

On the way back to Pilar's, she knew it was time for her to go back home, back to Philly. Everything she had done was for Julian. Now it was time she did something for herself.

Chapter 10

Olivia looked at the message indicator on her answering machine. There was one new message. She hit the playback button. "Olivia, I have some news for you." Mr. Murray's deep voice echoed through her apartment.

"Good news, I hope," she said out loud.

"I found the hotel you said Bryant stayed at in Chicago. I managed to get a copy of his phone records and he called a Ms. Daneesha Oaks several times. I also have a North Carolina number, but I haven't tracked down to whom that number belongs yet. I'm going to try to get an address for Ms. Oaks and pay her a visit. I'll try to find out what her relationship with Bryant is. I'll keep you posted with any updates. Talk to you later."

Olivia lay on the couch hoping to soothe her aching head. For the past two weeks she had been nursing a headache that wouldn't go away. The stress from worrying about Bryce had put Olivia in a state of depression. She hadn't slept in days. She had lost her appetite and had isolated herself inside her bedroom.

Aside from her worry about the baby she had also been suspended from her job, pending the criminal charges pressed against her.

"Oh God! What have I done to deserve this pain?" she cried. Elise's words of wisdom filled her mind. . . . *by not maintaining an intimate relationship with God through daily prayer and reading of the Word, distance will grow between you and the Lord, resulting in trials and tribulations.*

"Lord, I'm sorry," Olivia prayed. "I was always too busy with the baby to pray. God, have mercy on me and my baby. You promised that whatever we ask for in prayer, we shall receive. So I ask for the safe return of my son. Bring him safely home to his mother. Amen."

A knock at her front door told her she had a visitor, but Olivia wasn't in the mood to see anyone, so she ignored it. The knocking continued and she soon realized that her unwanted guest was not going away, so she lifted herself up from the couch and answered the door.

A beautiful, tall woman with long, black, silky hair pulled back into a ponytail stared back at her. The pecan color of her skin blended well with the earth tones of her make-up.

She shivered from the cold chill of the air. "Hello," the woman said. "I'm looking for Bryant Winters."

Olivia was surprised by the woman's inquiry. This was the first time anyone had ever come to the house looking for Bryant.

"Bryant?"

"Yes, Bryant Winters."

"You're a friend of his?" Olivia asked.

"No, I'm his wife."

Olivia's heart dropped. She couldn't believe Bryant had a wife and she was standing at her door. She didn't know he had ever been married. She was speechless. It took her a few seconds to regain her composure.

"Would you like to come in?" Olivia said, offering the stranger a seat. "My name is Olivia."

"Hello, I'm Taima."

Olivia sat across from her. "Bryant never told me that he had a wife."

"We've been married for four years," Taima said. She hesitated before she continued. "I've been away for a couple years and I'm trying to get back in touch with him." She looked over her shoulder to make sure no one else was in the room. "If you don't mind me asking, what is your relationship with Bryant?"

Olivia wondered whether she should answer Taima's question truthfully.

"If you're intimately involved with him, it's okay," Taima told her. "We haven't actually been husband and wife for a long time."

"I recently had a son by Bryant," Olivia chose her words carefully. She wasn't sure if she could trust Taima or not. How did she know she was really Bryant's wife? She may be working with Bryant to keep her son away from her.

By the look on Olivia's face, Taima knew there was something wrong. "Did Bryant steal your son away from you?" Taima asked.

"Yes, How did you know?"

"Two years ago he did the same thing to me. Bryant had me committed into a drug rehabilitation clinic in Wisconsin. He drugged me for months by putting Ecstasy in my food. He made sure I was so high that I couldn't tell the difference between reality and fantasy. He filed a petition with the court for full custody of our daughter and had me declared an unfit mother. That's when he had me institutionalized. It took me two years to get clean and get out of there. By the time I returned home, he had taken our daughter, Niya, and left town. I've been searching for them ever since."

Olivia couldn't believe the story she had just heard. Finally, here was someone who actually shared her pain. Olivia could see how visibly upset she was. She handed Taima a tissue to wipe her tears. "How did you get my address?"

"It's a funny thing. I've been searching for him for over a year. I filed a missing persons report, put up flyers, and I even did a little investigation of my own, but nothing I did turned up any leads. A few weeks ago I was searching through the closet for something I had lost and I came across a bunch of old sports magazines Bryant used to subscribe to. I remembered him telling me once that he had been a regular subscriber to that magazine since he was thirteen-years-old. Well, I got an idea and asked a male cousin of mine to call the magazine's customer service number and act like he was Bryant. He told them that he had a new credit card number and needed to change the one they had on file. They immediately took the new number and before he hung up, he asked them to verify his current address." She then held up a copy of the sports magazine that lay on the coffee table. "It's a blessing that Bryant changed his subscription address to here."

"Taima, unfortunately, I don't know where Bryant is. I hired a private investigator and he called today with some leads, but he hasn't found them yet. Did Bryant ever introduce you to any of his friends? Maybe a distant relative? Anyone who could help us find out where he has disappeared to?" Olivia asked.

"No." She slowly shook her head. "When Bryant and I were married, we didn't know each other too well. We had only been dating for five months before he proposed. Everyone who attended our wedding was either a friend or relative of mine. I did ask him about his mother and siblings. He said his mother passed away when he was young and that he didn't have any brothers and sisters. He was a loner in life."

Olivia shook her head, "He pretty much told me the same story. Why don't you leave your name and number with me and the next time the investigator calls to give me an update I can ask him to give you a call. You may be able to give him some information about Bryant that I couldn't."

"No problem."

Payce was tired of working seventy-five hours a week and bringing home less than three hundred dollars. He knew he had to start making some real money. That's why he called Reverend Kane and accepted her offer to work at The Dollhouse. Glad that he had accepted her offer, she immediately arranged for him to interview with the owner, Natasha Brown, the following day.

Payce walked into The Dollhouse. Sitting at the front desk was the same girl who was there when he and Darshon were there.

"Hello, I'm here to see Natasha," Payce said to the young woman.

"I remember you," she said, smiling. "Are you going to be working here?"

"If things go well, I will."

She picked up the phone and dialed a three-digit extension. "What's your name?" she asked.

"Payce Boyd."

"Natasha, Payce Boyd is here to see you." A minute later she hung up the phone. "Follow me."

Payce and the young woman walked through a maze of halls until they stopped in front of a door with "Natasha Brown" written on it. The receptionist knocked before opening the door slightly. She whispered to Payce, "Natasha is really cool and laid back." She took a few steps back toward the receptionist area. "Good luck," she called out.

Payce pushed the door open and walked into the cluttered office. Papers and files were piled high in all four corners of the office. Natasha was entering information into her computer from various papers scattered over her desk.

Payce glanced at Natasha and thought she resembled a black Cher. Her hair was long, silky, and straight. It reached past her butt. Her head was buried so far down into her computer that he couldn't see her face.

"Hello," he said.

"Have a seat," Natasha commanded. She never looked up, and continued to type on her computer. "So you're a friend of Kane's?"

"Yes ma'am."

"Have you ever done this kind of work before?"

"No."

"Another amateur." She sighed. "But that's all right. You'll learn." She immediately went into the details of the job. "The job pays fifteen hundred per session. You can work as long as you want, when you want. You can work once a week if you want, or three sessions a night.

It's up to you. Three sessions equal a total of forty-five hundred dollars. Each session ends at the couple's discretion. One couple may just ask you to have sex with the wife once, and then you're done. Another couple may ask you to stay for eight to twelve hours. It's their prerogative. Sometimes couples enjoy role playing. You may have to dress up like a cop, handcuff the husband, and do the wife. Condoms are provided in all the rooms and I leave it up to the employees on whether or not they want to divulge their names. Since this is a business, I would recommend keeping your identity a secret. You can pick up your money at the end of every session or at the end of the night. The receptionist is responsible for distributing compensation. Any questions?"

Payce shook his head no.

"Good." Natasha got up and walked over to a closet. She pulled out a huge trash bag. "What's your waist size?" she asked.

"Thirty-eight," Payce responded.

When she stood up Payce got a good look at her enormous silicone breasts that toppled out of her baby doll T-shirt.

She grabbed a pair of small, leather shorts. "Here you go." She threw them at him. "The men's locker room is down the hall. Change your clothes, and there is a couple waiting for you in Room 18."

"I start now?" he asked. Payce was surprised that she wanted him to start so soon. He thought he'd have a day or two before he began work.

"In this business you quickly learn that time is money," she replied.

Payce changed into his new work uniform, which was a bit too tight around the ass. He wasn't used to this. He felt really uncomfortable walking around with nothing on but a pair of small leather shorts and his Timberland boots.

He found Room 18 and knocked on the door softly. A woman's voice yelled from inside, "Come in."

He opened the door to find a beautiful woman wearing a sheer, black negligee lying on the bed. *This job might not be so bad*, he thought. She was absolutely stunning. Her hazel eyes and lean body aroused him. Her long legs resembled an athlete's and her abs were perfectly defined. He walked into the room and up to the bed.

"What's up?" he said to her.

"What's going on?" A man's voice startled him from behind. He turned around to see a man sitting in a chair. Her husband—or who Payce thought was her husband—resembled a football player. He had broad shoulders, a huge body, and hands twice the size of Payce's.

"Hey!" Payce replied. He felt awkward knowing that he was supposed to have sex with the man's beautiful wife while he watched. Payce wasn't exactly sure how he was supposed to address the man, so he walked over to him and reached out to shake his hand. The man stared back.

"Man, we both know why you're here. So go ahead and get started."

Payce walked back over to the edge of the bed. Without hesitation, the wife pulled him down on the bed and began taking his shorts off. She touched Payce in places that made him feel so good he wanted to shout, but he was scared that if he did it would make her husband angry. Payce didn't want to have a confrontation with the enormous man, so he closed his eyes to hold back all emotion. The only sounds in the room could be heard from the wife moaning. Payce wondered what the husband was doing. He was awfully quiet. He opened his eyes and snuck a quick look over at the husband who was watching his wife. His expression was cold and hard.

The woman lay back on the bed and Payce went to her. He gave her his all. He looked into her face and pretended that she was his wife. He thought about how much he would enjoy making love to her every night.

"She likes it doggy style," the man said from his chair. Payce looked over at the husband and stopped what he was doing. "Did you say something?" Payce asked.

"I said she likes it doggy style," he bellowed.

Not wanting to upset her husband, he did as told. He turned the woman over on her knees.

Payce thought that this was some weird shit. It was already difficult trying to please another man's wife with the husband in the room watching, but for him to request a specific position was crazy.

"You like that, don't you?" she asked. Payce thought she was talking to him, but when he looked down at her she was talking to her husband.

Payce wasted no time in getting the job done. Afterwards, the three of them stared at one another in silence. The husband got up, laid on the bed, and the wife wrapped herself up in his arms. Payce felt strange watching them enjoy their time together when he was the one who did all the work. He slid into his leather shorts and exited the room. He was exhausted and had enough for the day. He put his clothes back on and stopped by the receptionist's desk to collect his pay. As he was reaching for the door, he turned around to see Reverend Kane dressed in a robe, escorting a red-headed woman into one of the rooms.

Tressie was surprised to see Olivia and Danyelle kneeling at the altar when she walked into the church. With everything that was going on with the baby, she thought Olivia wouldn't want to see anybody. Tressie took a seat in one of the pews and waited for them to finish praying.

Olivia got up with tears in her eyes but a smile spread across her face when she saw Tressie. She walked over and gave her a big hug.

"Hey girl, how are you feeling?" Tressie asked.

"I'm doing okay. I'm taking one day at a time."

"Have you heard anything about the baby?"

"The private detective we hired left a message on my answering machine last week, but I haven't spoken to him. I did leave a message on his voice-mail about Bryant's wife."

"Danyelle told me about that," Tressie replied. Danyelle had been giving Tressie daily updates on what was going on with Olivia, Bryant, and the baby. "Keep your head up. That detective will bring Bryce home to you."

"That's why I'm here. I was home feeling sorry for myself when I finally picked up my Bible. All throughout the New Testament are stories of how Jesus healed people and performed miracles, all because they had faith. There was the woman who believed that all she had to do was touch the hem of his garment and she would be healed. And then there was the blind man whose eyes Jesus touched, and he could see again. These are all things that happened because people believed. So I'm here because I believe. I believe God will send my baby back to me. I prayed that the Lord would send me a clue about Bryant, and seconds later Taima knocked on my door. Don't think I'm not worried about my son, because I am but I trust that the Lord will provide. I just need to continue to pray."

"You have really been blessed," Tressie replied.

"I sure have," Olivia said.

"I wonder where Elise is," Danyelle said.

"She must be running late. She is usually the first one here," Olivia remarked.

Tressie sat and wondered whether or not she should tell them what she had seen. She might have been mistaken. Maybe it wasn't Elise after all.

"Last week Payce took me to see a drive-in movie in Atlantic City," Tressie told them.

"I didn't even know they still had drive-in movies," Danyelle replied.

"Neither did I, but that's not what I wanted to tell you. We were watching the movie and I happened to look over into the next car, and I could have sworn I saw Elise making out with some guy in the backseat."

"Uh!" Danyelle cried. "I need a blunt."

"That's ridiculous!" Olivia replied.

"I'm telling you, it was her."

"Did you talk to her?"

"No."

"Then how do you know it was her?"

"What did you want me to do, get out the car, walk over, and knock on the window? It was her. I would know Elise anywhere."

"Tressie, you know Elise would never cheat on Miles. She loves her husband. I'm not saying you didn't see what you saw, but I'm saying maybe you were mistaken."

"I know what I saw."

"Are you sure you weren't high? Maybe Payce slipped a little something into your soft drink when you weren't looking," Danyelle laughed.

Olivia's cell phone rang.

"Hello?" she answered. "Yes, Elise, we're all here at the church waiting on you." She looked at Tressie. "Oh okay. Is everything all right? Okay, we'll see you next week."

Olivia hung up the phone. "That was Elise. She said that something else came up and she won't be able to make it here tonight. She told us just to say a prayer, and we'll pick up next week."

"Something must be really important for her to miss Bible Study. We all know how she feels about being here every Tuesday night," Tressie added.

Chapter 11

Miles walked into the kitchen with a pile of bills from the mailbox. "Elise!" he bellowed. Miles's voice echoed against the still silence in the house before he quickly remembered it was Tuesday night. *Elise said she was going to the gym tonight.* He thumbed through a few bills: electric bill, credit card bill, credit card bill, another credit card bill. "I have got to remind myself to sit down with Elise and get rid of some of these credit cards," he said out loud. A Victoria's Secret catalog had also arrived for Elise. Aware that his wife liked to browse the catalog and shop online simultaneously, he thought he would do her a favor and place it in the den next to the computer. As he walked into the den he browsed through the pages. The lovely Tyra Banks modeled a few items that he wouldn't mind seeing his wife in. Before he laid the catalog down he looked around for a pen. He wanted to mark a few of the things he liked, just in case Elise decided to surprise him one night. He pulled open a drawer to search for a pen and was surprised to see a bill lying inside the drawer.

After Elise and Miles were married, Miles took on the responsibility of paying all the bills, including

Elise's. Anything that needed to be paid, she usually gave straight to him, so it was unusual for him to find a bill Elise had not mentioned.

He examined it closely. It was a hospital bill that detailed the injuries Elise had incurred from the accident she had at the park a few months ago. He reviewed the bill and noticed the admittance date was November second and the discharge date was also November second. *She told me she stayed overnight at the hospital for observation. If she didn't stay at the hospital, where did she stay?* He turned the bill over. It was addressed to a Mr. Sheridan Reed.

He took the bill and ran out of the house. *Who is Sheridan Reed?* He jumped in his car and drove to the address on the envelope. He was unsure of what he was going to do once he arrived, but he couldn't wait until Elise got home to question her. He needed answers now. Perhaps Sheridan Reed could explain why his wife lied and hid the truth about where she spent the night of November second.

He thought about how Elise's behavior toward him had changed over the past few weeks. When he touched her, she would pull away. When he made suggestions of things they could do to arouse him, she acted as if she didn't want to be bothered. He gave her intense foreplay to stimulate her sexually, but after several minutes she would get up and leave him to lie alone in the bed.

Elise's disinterest left him physically and mentally wounded. He thought that the stress of his impotency was wearing her down.

He pulled up in front of the address and parked his car on the next block. As he walked back toward Sheridan's house he noticed Elise's car parked out front. His heart pounded against his chest. Elise had lied to him, again. She was supposed to be at the health club.

He stared at Elise's car for a moment. He was being irrational. Elise would never intentionally lie to him. There had to be a logical reason why she wasn't at the club. She could have stopped here to drop off a friend, or maybe she worked with Mr. Reed.

He turned around to get back in his car, but something stopped him. He wanted to put his trust back in his wife, but something was telling him to stay. He walked up to the door and listened for a moment. He tried to hear voices, but he couldn't hear anything. He raised his hand to knock on the door, but again he stopped himself. He wasn't ready to face what was on the other side of that door. He stood outside the residence for ten more minutes before he lost his nerve. He couldn't do it. He was too scared about what he might have to face. He decided to wait in his car until she came out, and then he would find out who Sheridan Reed was.

Inside the apartment Elise sat on Sheridan's couch. Since her arrival he had been busy preparing something special for her in the bathroom.

She heard the water running in the tub and him moving things around.

"Just wait one more minute!" he yelled from the bathroom.

It was not unusual for Sheridan to plan something special for their rendezvous together. She always looked forward to a candlelit dinner, a dozen roses, or something pretty and pink from Frederick's of Hollywood. The week before he suggested they go see a drive-in movie together. She was hesitant at first because she feared someone might see them together. Sheridan tried to reassure her that no one would see them, but to ease her mind he took her to a drive-in movie theater in Atlantic City, sixty miles away. It was such a romantic night. He bought popcorn and soft drinks and they even made out in the backseat like high school kids. Elise loved his spontaneous side.

She loved spending time with Sheridan, but the guilt of lying to her husband was beginning to weigh heavily on her conscience. She wasn't sure how much longer she would be able to keep it up.

She wasn't just lying to her husband. This affair had also affected different areas of her life and had led her to do things she wouldn't normally do, like cancel Bible Study. The one constant thing in her life was her Bible Study group, but when Sheridan asked her to skip Bible Study and come straight to his house, she agreed.

"Elise, come here," Sheridan shouted, breaking her from her thoughts.

She walked into the bathroom and was surprised by the number of lit candles that were positioned around the bathtub.

"I would appreciate the pleasure of your company," Sheridan said to her. He was sitting in his oversized bathtub that was big enough for two.

Elise quickly undressed and slipped in with him. She squeezed between his legs and lay back on his chest. The warm bath water was filled with bubbles and rose petals. Various colored candles illuminated the room, while Luther Vandross sang in the background.

Sheridan slowly washed her body. They kissed and the magical moment brought them closer together.

Elise moved her leg to get a little bit more comfortable, and she hit it against something hard. She moved her hands underneath the water to search for the foreign object that was in the water with them.

"Be careful, searching around underneath there. You never know what you'll find," Sheridan commented.

She finally found what she was looking for and revealed a bottle covered in suds.

"What's this?" she asked.

Sheridan shrugged his shoulders in response.

She looked closely at the bottle. Written on the outside of the bottle were the words 'A Message in a Bottle'. She opened the cork and pulled out a scroll. Elise unrolled the paper. It read, "I love you." Her heart sank to the bottom of her stomach.

"I love you, too," she whispered in his ear.

After their romantic bath together, they moved to the bedroom. Still dripping wet with water, Sheridan kissed her neck. He continued to please her, but after a while she stopped him.

"I need you," she told him.

He obeyed and they made love for over an hour.

Afterwards, they lay tangled in his bed sheets. He slowly rubbed her arm.

"That was amazing," Elise said.

"Yeah, I enjoyed it myself," he replied.

Sheridan could sense that there was something on her mind, but he wasn't sure what it was. He hoped she wasn't thinking about her husband. He wanted their time together to only be about them. "What's wrong?" he asked.

"I have something I need to tell you," she confessed. "I hope you don't think I do this kind of thing on the regular."

Sheridan knew from the first time he saw her that she was far too sophisticated to have random affairs with anyone. He also knew that she loved her husband.

"My husband and I have been having problems in our marriage. He's been experiencing temporary episodes of impotency."

"I'm sorry to hear that. Has he gone to see a doctor?" Sheridan asked.

"Yes, the doctor told us that a man his age usually experiences impotency for psychological reasons as opposed to physical. There could be a number of reasons why this is happening to him. We didn't start having these problems until we planned to start a family. He's been seeing a therapist, but so far there has been no change."

Sheridan knew there was a reason why every time they were together she would devour him sexually. Her husband hadn't been able to satisfy her for months. Sheridan felt sorry for her husband, but happy for himself. He knew it must have been upsetting for her husband to have such a beautiful woman at home and not be able to make love to her.

"How are you handling this situation?" he asked.

"I'm not the one with the problem," she replied.

"I realize that, but having your husband shut down on you like that has to have some psychological effect on you."

"When he first began having problems, I felt like it was my fault. I thought maybe he had lost interest in me. If I touched him he would get hard, but just before we were ready to make love, he would go limp. Of course he apologized and insisted that it wasn't my fault, but I didn't believe him. I thought I wasn't being sexy enough, or adventurous enough. For months I wasn't sure if he still loved me. I even thought he might have turned gay. I just didn't know. It was hard for me to get through that time until he went to go see a doctor, and that's when I realized it wasn't me."

"I'm glad you told me," Sheridan said, and hugged her a little tighter.

As Miles walked down the stairs that led from Sheridan's front door he heard a door open. He quickly hid beneath the stairs and immediately recognized Elise's voice.

"I love you," Elise said.

"I love you, too," Sheridan responded.

Miles could hear them kiss. They walked down the stairs together. Sheridan held Elise as if he didn't want to see her go. Miles watched as a stranger lovingly embraced his wife.

"I wish you didn't have to go," Sheridan said to her.

"I'll see you in two weeks," she replied as she gazed into his eyes.

Miles watched the love scene unfold before his eyes. He could see the look of love in his wife's eyes. It tore his heart apart to witness the truth. He didn't want to believe that Elise could betray him. He knew that the love they had for one another was real. How could she throw away what they had?

He took a deep breath and stepped out from behind the stairs. "Elise," he called out.

Elise turned around, shocked to see Miles standing before her. She was terrified, speechless, and her heart beat rapidly. She was scared of what Miles would do. She knew he wasn't a violent man, but she didn't know what he was capable of when finding his wife in the arms of another man. Apologetic tears formed in her eyes.

Miles stared at her. He hadn't planned on confronting her, but a minute ago it seemed like the right thing to do. Now that he stood in front of them he didn't know what to say. "I knew there was something going on, but I thought it was my imagination." Miles spoke in a solemn tone. "I'm not mad. I couldn't expect you to wait for me forever."

"Miles, this is not what you think," Elise told him. Natural instinct told her to deny everything.

"Elise, don't lie to me any longer." The pitch of his voice rose and got deeper. It made him mad to hear her lie to him again. "Elise, I heard you say you loved this man. Is it true? Do you love him?"

She didn't want to hurt him by confessing her feelings for Sheridan.

"Elise, do you love this man?" Miles yelled.

"Yes," she whispered.

Those words hit his heart like a ton of bricks. He grabbed his hand and squeezed tightly. He knew he had to calm himself down before he lashed out at her. Hurting her would make him feel even worse.

"Elise, I don't blame you," he said. "This isn't your fault. I understand why you went looking for satisfaction elsewhere. I can't blame you when I'm the one who failed. It was my responsibility to take care of you."

Elise held her head down in shame. Tears rolled down her face. Sheridan watched in disbelief.

"You didn't fail me," Elise responded. She stepped toward him. "Miles, can we go home and talk about this in private?"

"No, I can't do that. I can't leave here with you thinking that once we get home everything will be okay when I know you're in love with another man. Us going home together is not going to change what has happened here tonight."

A teardrop escaped Miles' eyes and rolled down his cheek.

"Elise, you have to believe that I tried. I wanted so badly to give you the baby you wanted, but for some reason God said I was not the one. Perhaps I'm not the one destined to give you a baby. Maybe it was meant for Sheridan to . . ." He looked in Sheridan's direction. ". . . make your dream a reality."

"Miles," Elise whimpered.

"I'm not going to stand in the way of your happiness. That's why I'm walking away."

"Miles, don't say that. Think about what you're saying before you make irrational decisions."

"I know what I'm saying. I'm saying good-bye."

Elise could not believe what she was hearing. Miles was stepping aside so she could fulfill her dream of having a baby with another man.

"Miles, don't do this. We can fix this," she begged and reached out for him, but he pulled away.

"I love you, Elise. I would give you anything. Even your freedom."

Miles's eyes held a look of determination. Elise knew there was nothing more she could say to change his mind.

Miles held out his hand to Sheridan. Sheridan looked at Miles's shaking hand. He couldn't believe that Miles was giving his wife away to another man. He was skeptical of Miles's true intentions. Scared that at any moment Miles would pull a gun out and kill them all, Sheridan reluctantly shook his hand.

"Make sure she's happy," Miles said to Sheridan, and he turned to leave.

APRIL 2004

Tressie was surprised to see a limousine pull up in front of her house. The chauffeur got out and walked to the front door.

"Hello, I'm here to pick up a Ms. Montrese Cox," the chauffer informed Tressie's father.

"Tressie!" Mr. Cox yelled out.

She hurried from her bedroom and into the living room.

"Mr. Boyd has arranged for me to drive you to your date tonight," the driver announced.

She knew tonight was going to be special when Payce asked her to wear something sophisticated and classy. She spent her entire savings on a black strapless dress by Nicole Miller. She wore a pair of diamond stud earrings her parents had given her for her sixteenth birthday, and she borrowed a single diamond pendant necklace from her mother.

Her parents waved good-bye as the limo pulled away from the curb. On the ride there she wondered what Payce had planned for the night. Payce's choice of mystery impressed her. She knew he went to a lot of trouble to arrange tonight, and that meant a lot to her.

The limo pulled into Penn's Landing. The chauffeur ran around to her side and opened her door.

Payce was waiting curbside for her. "You look beautiful," he declared.

"You look rather nice yourself," she replied.

Payce wore a pair of black dress slacks with a white dress shirt. His gold cufflinks were engraved with his initials.

Payce held out his arm and escorted her to the Spirit of Philadelphia, a dinner boat known for its delicious cuisine and breathtaking view of the Philly skyline from the Delaware River.

They walked onto the boat and Payce gave his name to the hostess. She escorted them to their seats. "The ship will be sailing in a moment. Once we're on the water a waiter will be over to take your order," she informed them.

"Payce," Tressie whispered once the hostess walked away. "Are you selling drugs again?"

"Why would you ask me that?" he asked with a confused look on his face.

"You have been spending a lot of money lately. You don't make that much money parking cars at the Westin. Every time I see you, you have on a new pair of sneakers. You traded in that old Chevy for a new Lexus, and now we're having dinner at one of the most expensive and exclusive restaurants in Philadelphia. What's up?"

Payce realized that his lifestyle had improved dramatically since he had started working at The Dollhouse. He knew Tressie was eventually going to wonder where he was getting the money, and he had an answer already prepared for her. "I'm not selling drugs. Before I got locked up I put some money away. I didn't want to come home from jail broke. Since I started working I thought it wouldn't hurt to spend and enjoy a little of my savings."

"I was just concerned, that's all. I don't want you to get locked up again," Tressie demurred.

"Baby, you don't have to worry. I'm never going back there again."

After they finished their meal, Payce asked, "Did I tell you how beautiful you look?"

"Yes, you did. But you can tell me again." She laughed.

Their waiter approached her with a card in his hand. "Excuse me, ma'am. This is for you."

Tressie took the card and wondered what was inside. She opened the card and written inside it said:

> *Tressie,*
> *Since you've walked into my life my heart has been filled with so much love. I never thought I could love someone as much as I love you. With all the wrong things I've done in my life, it's hard to believe that God has blessed me with something so right.*
> *I love you, Payce.*

Payce had never told her he loved her before. She looked over at him with tears in her eyes. He held a jewelry box, and inside was a diamond tennis bracelet.

"It's gorgeous!" she exclaimed.

"This bracelet represents only a tenth of how much I love you."

"Payce, I . . ."

"Don't say it. I don't want you to tell me you love me just because I told you. I want you to tell me when you're ready and when you mean it."

He took the bracelet from her and put it on her wrist. He got up and held out his hand. They walked out together onto the deck and watched the moonlight shine against the water.

"I want to make love to you tonight," he told her. "Can we spend the night together?" She nodded her head yes. After the ship docked, Payce escorted her back to his car and they rented a room at the Hilton Hotel.

"I love you," he told her again.

"I . . ."

"Don't say it." He put his finger to her mouth. "I told you, don't say those words until you really mean it."

Payce slowly undressed her and laid her on the bed. He lovingly admired her body. He took his time with her and kissed every inch of her body before making love to her.

Her body throbbed with pleasure as he kissed her lovingly.

After they made love, she lay in his arms and thought about how many times she had dreamed of making love to Payce. It was better than she had imagined.

"I love you," she finally confessed.

"I love you, too."

Chapter 12

It had taken Murray a while, but he had finally gotten Daneesha's home address. He wasn't sure if the young girl at the supermarket where Daneesha used to work was going to believe his story about him being her long lost uncle. Well, he must be a good storyteller, because it didn't take much convincing for the cashier to give up Daneesha's address.

Murray sat outside Daneesha's home, keeping the house under close surveillance. No one had approached the house all afternoon except for the mailman.

At the start of each new assignment, Murray liked to verify that he was monitoring the right residence because of a mistake he had made three years prior. He had been hired by a wife who suspected her husband was having an affair. After three weeks of watching the husband have one-night stands with different women, he later discovered that he had been trailing the wrong person. He had been following the wife's neighbor, and not his client's husband. That one mistake hurt his business. So he made it routine practice to verify the residence he was watching.

Once the mailman left the block, Murray snuck up to the house. He stepped onto the porch and was startled by the presence of a sleeping dog. Murray was terrified of dogs and he hadn't realized they even had a dog because the mutt hadn't made a sound all afternoon.

The dog woke from his sleep and looked at Murray. Frightened, Murray was about to turn and run when the dog slowly closed his eyes and went back to sleep. Thankful that the beast did not attack, Murray quickly stuck his hand in the mailbox and looked at the envelopes. All bills were addressed to Daneesha Oaks. He quickly replaced the mail and hurried back to his car.

From his car, Murray stared at the small house. The harsh Chicago winters had badly deteriorated the exterior of the home. The blue paint had lost its luster, each window was covered with plastic, and the front screen door was hanging off the hinges. He had also noticed a few floor panels on the porch were missing. It wouldn't be long before the house collapsed.

The sunlight was soon replaced by evening's darkness. It was quitting time for a lot of hard-working people, and he expected Daneesha would be arriving home shortly. He wished to speak with her about Bryant, but doubted she would willingly tell a stranger any information about her relationship with him. He knew he was going to have to watch her for a few days and devise a plan on the best way to approach her.

At exactly six o'clock, a CTA bus stopped a few feet behind Murray's car. A woman and two small children got off and walked toward the Oaks' residence. He watched as they passed by. The young mother struggled with an armful of groceries while trying to keep an eye on her children. The little girl, around three-years-old, held her younger brother's hand tightly as they ran to keep up with their mother. Murray could hear their mother repeatedly yell for them to keep up. The family walked onto the porch and their black Labrador Retriever came alive. The dog stood up and welcomed them home by wagging his tail and licking their faces.

"Hey, Kobe," the little girl sang out.

The mother struggled to get her key in the door. Once she successfully opened the door, she ordered the children to go inside.

As the mother held the door open for her children, Murray could see a front view of her full, round belly. "She's pregnant," he said to himself.

Murray watched the house, hoping Bryant would show up, but no one else entered the home for the remainder of the night.

The following morning, Murray watched as Daneesha and the children left the house. He sat in his car, calculating his next move. He speculated that Daneesha lived alone with the children. He thought about how he could get a pregnant woman to tell him what he needed to know without raising suspicions. He knew he had to think of a subtle way to approach her. *How was he going to do it?* Out of nowhere, an idea popped into his mind that just might work.

Later on that evening Murray knocked on Daneesha's front door. The family dog barked loudly. Murray whispered to the dog, "Calm down, fellow. You don't recognize me? I was here yesterday. I'm not here to harm you."

The dog growled. Murray was surprised at the dog's sudden emergence as a watch dog. He was disguised as a deliveryman and was thankful he had remembered to pack his bag of disguises. He had on a body suit that made him look twenty pounds heavier, and he wore a plain blue uniform. He held a hand truck loaded with a huge box.

The commotion the dog made caused the little girl to run to the door and open it wide.

"Hello, can I speak to your mommy?" Murray asked the child.

"Mommy! Mommy!" she screamed through the house.

Moments later Daneesha appeared at the door. "Yes, can I help you?"

"Good evening, ma'am. I have a delivery here for a Daneesha Oaks."

"That would be me. What is it?"

"Well ma'am, I believe they said it was a crib."

"A crib? I didn't order any crib."

Murray looked at the fictitious paperwork on his clipboard.

"Well my delivery sheet says to deliver this crib to Daneesha Oaks at 19 Holman Way," the man said.

She eyed the unexpected delivery suspiciously. Murray moved the box to the other hand. "Ma'am, if you don't mind, this box is very heavy," he said to her in hopes that she would accept the delivery.

Hesitant to allow him to enter her home, she finally relented. "I'm sorry. Children, move your things from the middle of the living room floor!" Daneesha commanded. She opened the door wide for Murray to bring in the box.

He walked into her home and the interior of her house was worse than the exterior. The kitchen ceiling had several holes, and the wallpaper that lined the walls had turned yellow and was beginning to peel. The children watched a small black and white television that sat on top of a large floor model television. A small wire hanger substituted as the television's antenna to keep its reception.

"Where would you like it?" he asked.

She pointed down the hall. "You can put it in the second room on the right. That's my daughter's room." She rubbed her belly. "This one is going to be a girl, so they might as well share."

Desmond pulled the large box into the room. Daneesha walked in behind him. "Do you have a name of the person who ordered the crib?" she asked.

He looked down at his clipboard. "I'm sorry, ma'am, the office didn't include the buyer's name on my work order."

"That's all right. It was probably my fiancé, Bryant. He likes to surprise the children and me."

"That's a beautiful thing ma'am, a man who loves his family." He pointed to the crib. "This crib is really beautiful. A lot of couples choose this one." Murray began to open the box and pull out the contents.

"You're going to put it together?"

"Yes ma'am. Set up is free of charge when you order one of these cribs."

"Oh! I wasn't aware. Do you need any tools? I'm sure Bryant has some tools lying around here somewhere."

"No, that's all right. I have everything I need right here." He pulled out his tool kit and the directions to assemble the crib. Once he started, he regretted his decision to put it together. He hadn't put a crib together in over twenty years. He had purchased a deluxe crib with the most sophisticated gadgets. It took him a whole hour just to sort out the different pieces.

Daneesha came to check on him. "Are you okay back here?"

"Yeah! I'm all right. It should be done shortly," he responded.

She glanced at the lopsided crib and hoped that it wasn't supposed to sit that way. She stood and watched him for a moment.

He knew that this would be the best time to strike up a conversation with her. "So, when are you due?"

"I'm only six months pregnant. I have three more months."

"I'm sure your fiancé is excited, but he's probably a pro by now since you two have been through this twice before already."

"Actually my two oldest children aren't his. This is his first child, so he is really excited."

"Children really are a joy. My kids are grown, but it seems like just yesterday they were falling asleep in my arms. Kids grow up so fast. Make sure you spend as much time with them as you can."

"My fiancé and I both try to spend as much time with the children as possible, but his job requires him to travel a lot."

"I hope he's going to be around for the baby's birth?" Murray questioned the young mother.

"Oh, yes sir, he should be back home in a few weeks. Once he gets home, he promised me that he wouldn't leave again until after the baby was born."

The phone rang. "Mommy," her daughter screamed. "Grandma wants you."

"Excuse me." Daneesha waddled to the phone.

Murray overheard her telling her mother about the mysterious crib that arrived and how it was a blessing because she could not afford to buy a new crib for the baby to sleep in. By the time she returned back to the bedroom, he had finished the crib.

"I'm all finished."

"It looks good," she responded.

The crib was perfectly assembled after hours of trial and error.

She walked him to the door. "You have a good night, sir."

"You too, ma'am, and make sure you take care of that little one."

"Thank you. I will."

"Player, I'm surprised you could get away tonight. You've been a hard man to catch up with. Every time I call you, I get your voice mail," Darshon said to Payce.

They stood in line at Pinnacle, the liveliest nightclub in the city. They were there to help their friend, T.J. celebrate his birthday.

"I know. I started school and I've been working a lot. Any extra time I have after that is spent with Tressie," Payce responded.

"You still working at the Westin?"

Payce nodded.

"They must be paying really well at the Westin—brand new car, brand new watch," Darshon pointed at Payce's Rolex. "Are you sure you're not hustling on the side?"

"Man, I told you I'm legit this time. Everything I bought, I worked for."

"You wouldn't lie to me, would you, man?"

"Man, I'm not hustling." Payce knew he wasn't being completely honest with Darshon, but he couldn't tell him about working at The Dollhouse. Darshon was his best friend, they had been through everything together, but this was one secret he had to keep to himself. If anyone ever found out what he was doing, he knew he would be jeopardizing his relationship with Tressie and the respect he had earned from his father.

"Well, I'm glad to see you, and I'm sure the fellows will be happy to see you, too."

"You know I couldn't miss T.J.'s birthday."

After a twenty-minute wait, they finally reached the front of the line and paid the admittance fee. Inside the club, lights flashed, music bumped, and the place was crowded with people.

"How are we going to find T.J.?" Payce screamed above the loud music.

"Just follow me," Darshon instructed.

He pulled Payce through the crowd of people. A few girls winked and tried to get Payce's attention as he walked by. *Nothing's changed,* he thought to himself. Darshon led him straight to a table where T.J. sat by himself.

"What's up, player?" Darshon screamed out. He slapped hands with T.J.

"Payce, my man," T.J. yelled. "Welcome home, my nigga. I haven't seen you since you were released."

"I've been trying to stay out of trouble," Payce replied.

"I understand."

"Why are you sitting over here by yourself? I thought you would have sweet talked one of these honeys in here into coming over and helping you celebrate your birthday."

"Me and John just got here. He's already out there on the dance floor with some chicken head. I was just about to order a bottle of Cristal." T.J. pulled out a wad of bills from his pocket. Payce stared as T.J. peeled off a few hundred-dollar bills. He could see that T.J. was still reaping the benefits of a drug dealer's lifestyle.

T.J., Darshon, John, and Payce began selling drugs while in high school. It wasn't long before they realized that they could make more money on the streets than in school. As a result, they all dropped out, except for John. When John told his mom that he was quitting school, she lost it. She grabbed her frying pan and chased him around their house. Scared that he might wake up one day to find his mom standing over him with that black skillet, he decided to finish out his education. He was the only member of the crew who graduated from high school.

Even with John's absence, their pockets got fatter and fatter. Each one of them bought themselves a car, jewelry, and plenty of new clothes.

They called themselves the GT Hustlers. Unfortunately for Payce, that all came to an end two years ago. T.J., Payce, John, and Darshon were at their centralized hub distributing drug packages. The fellas were no longer standing on the street corners. They hired workers to make the money for them. They operated like a legal business. When a worker needed to replenish his drug supply, they dispatched a runner to come and pick up the package. The runner, usually a neighborhood kid between the ages of nine and eleven, was good at transporting drugs from one place to another because of his quick speed and ability to elude the police.

One night a guy called in and said that his runner was sick and he didn't have anyone to pick up his replenishment package for him. He was quickly running out, and he needed someone to bring the drugs to him.

"Fuck that. If he can't get someone to come and get it, then he's going to have to come himself. We ain't no delivery boys," T.J. yelled.

"I'll take it to him," Payce said.

"Man, you know the rules. We don't transport drugs for nobody," T.J. shot back.

"I know, but it's this one time. I'll have a talk with him when I get there." Payce grabbed the package of drugs and jumped into his car. He got no farther than five hundred feet away from the hub when the cops surrounded him and aimed their guns. He was charged with possession, intent to distribute, and carrying a controlled substance in a drug-free school zone.

Since it was his first offense, he got only eighteen months in lockup, but that was enough for him.

"I got it, man." Payce also pulled out his wad of bills.

T.J. looked at the money and put his arm around Payce's shoulder. "My man must have stashed some loot before he went away," he said.

"Yeah, I managed to save a little something." Payce called a waitress over to their table and threw her five one hundred dollar bills. "Cristal, please."

Payce walked over to the balcony and looked out over the mob of dancers on the dance floor. He saw John grinding on some girl. She was shoving her exposed breasts in his face. Payce took a sip from his glass. He watched all the hot girls with their short skirts and low-cut blouses. It had been such a long time since he had been in the club. When he was locked up, he dreamed about hanging out at the club until three o'clock in the morning. He knew he could never take his freedom for granted again.

He was about to walk away when he spotted a girl leaning against the far wall staring at him. At least he thought she was staring at him. He wasn't sure until she waved. He called her over and she slowly made her way through the crowd.

"Hey, shorty, what's your name?"

"Kai," she said. The young woman was dressed in a sequined, backless, pink shirt and a pair of black low-rise pants. Her hair was pulled up into a ponytail.

"Are you here by yourself?" he asked.

"No, my friends are around here somewhere."

"Why were you staring at me?" he asked.

"The way you stood on the ledge watching everyone made you look powerful. That turned me on."

Payce liked her. She was aggressive and she obviously wanted him.

"What are you doing after you leave here?" he asked.

"Probably going home? Why, what's up?"

"I don't know. I thought maybe we could hang out for a while. It's my friend's birthday and he rented a hotel room. I was hoping you and your friends could follow us back there and help us celebrate."

"That sounds like fun."

"Good, meet me out front after the club closes."

She tempted him with her eyes, and left to find her friends.

"Yo, T.J., did you get that hotel room?" he yelled.

"Yeah, what's up?"

"I just invited a few friends over." He smiled.

When Payce walked out of the club he found Kai and her girlfriends waiting for him just like he told her. Payce pulled Kai to the side. "Listen, go get your car and pull up in front of the club. I'm going to go get my car and you can follow me back to the hotel."

T.J. had reserved the penthouse suite at the Marriott, and it was huge. It had three bedrooms and three bathrooms. There was a living room and dining room area and a huge flat-screen television with a wall full of DVDs. Payce was not surprised by T.J.'s expensive taste.

T.J. was known for always reserving only the very best. "Everyone make yourself at home," T.J. yelled from the kitchen.

Payce pulled Kai closer to him. He didn't want anyone pushing up on her. She was his for the night. T.J. came out with glasses full of Hennessy. "What's your name?" he asked one girl.

"Delilah," she replied.

"As in Delilah and Sampson?" T.J. asked.

She smiled and shook her head yes. He looked at her naturally curly, shoulder-length hair. She was pretty. A little shy, but pretty. "Delilah, can you do me a favor and pass out the rest of these drinks? I need to go get some ice."

When T.J. returned, he called Delilah over to him. He whispered in her ear and made her laugh while Darshon and John talked with the remaining two girls.

"So what made you call me over?" Kai asked Payce.

"When I saw you staring at me I thought to myself, that girl is hot."

"Do you still think I'm hot?" she asked. She pressed against his pelvis with her body. His cell phone vibrated against his hip. He pulled it out and looked at the caller ID. It was Tressie. He hit the ignore button and turned his attention back to Kai.

"From what I can see, you are more than hot." He sat his drink down. "Why don't we go into one of the bedrooms for some privacy?"

He grabbed her hand and yelled out to the girls, "Don't worry about her. I'll make sure she gets home in the morning."

Chapter 13

MAY 2004

Elise got up from bed and walked into the kitchen. She quietly poured herself a glass of water and wiped the perspiration from her head. Weeks had passed since Miles had discovered her affair, but her mind kept replaying the scene of Miles stepping from behind the stairs and catching her in Sheridan's arms. She repeatedly heard those words fall from his lips: "Do you love him?"

That night she saw Miles's spirit crumble and his six-foot frame shrink right before her eyes. Ordinarily, her husband's presence dominated any arena, but that night her infidelities left him a weak and defeated man. The man she vowed to love for life walked away from her, his marriage, and their happiness, so she could fulfill her dream of having a family.

Her self-indulgent behavior over the past few months disappointed her. "How did I get here?" she wept.

Awakened by her cries, Sheridan rushed to her side. Hugging her tightly, he said, "Everything is going to be all right. Why don't you go lie down in the bedroom and try to get some sleep?" he offered.

"No, I'm all right," she lied. She broke away from his loving embrace.

He knew her mind held lingering memories of the night Miles had confronted them. Elise had withdrawn from their relationship. Her body was with him, but her mind was with Miles. When they talked she became easily distracted and responded back to him with one word answers. A number of times he had caught her vacantly staring into space.

"Sheridan, I'm all right. I just need to be alone. You can go back to bed."

Unsure if he should abide by her wishes, he hesitated.

She grabbed him by the shoulders and pushed him in the direction of his bedroom. "Really, I'm fine."

Convinced, he slowly went back to bed.

Elise lay on the couch and stared at the ceiling. Lately she had been reminded of the day she married Miles. The church was elegantly decorated in all white. Pink and lavender roses adorned the end of each pew. Her Vera Wang gown, unlike the traditional Cinderella wedding dress, gracefully fell to the ground and cascaded around her feet. That day Miles had surprised her with vows he had written himself.

I promise to always make you happy and never make you sad.

I promise to cherish your love as a gift from God.

And I promise to never allow a day to pass without telling you 'I love you.'

Elise tried to think through the situation in her head. She couldn't understand why or how she had gotten into this predicament. Being an individual who always held high moral standards, was a member of the church, and a woman who never stumbled in her Christian walk, she thought that the sins of the world were beneath her.

But it was becoming clear to her that the same lessons she preached to her Bible Study group were the same lessons she failed to apply to her own life. She often lectured the young adults of First Nazareth on the importance of allowing God to have complete control over your life and not just the parts you want him to have.

Elise was guilty of believing she could withstand the temptations of Satan by herself. Now that her life was spinning out of control, she wanted to call on God. She knew he was the only one who could fix everything.

She wanted to fall to her knees and repent, but she was ashamed and embarrassed to bow before God and admit the wrong she had done.

Elise closed her eyes and dreamt that Miles had found her with Sheridan again. Only this time, he pointed a gun at the two of them. Elise begged him to put the gun down, but before he could the gun went off and the scene turned black. She couldn't see anything. Suddenly a ray of light shone down on Miles in the distance. He lay on the ground, unconscious.

"Miles!" Elise cried. "Wake up." She felt his hand for a pulse but couldn't find one. She searched his body for a gunshot wound, but found nothing.

"Dial 9-1-1!" She screamed from the couch. "Someone please dial 9-1-1."

Sheridan raced in from the bedroom and shook her lightly. "Elise, wake up. You're having a bad dream."

Frightened from her dream, she looked at him, panic-stricken.

Her nightgown was drenched in sweat.

"Here, drink this." Sheridan handed her the glass of water that sat on the coffee table. "You must have been having a nightmare. I heard you screaming," he yelled. "Are you all right?"

She thought about her dream, and instantly she realized the importance of trying to save her marriage. She knew it was not going to be easy, but she had to try. She just hoped that Miles would listen to her once she got there.

"I need to go." Elise grabbed her shoes, purse, and coat.

"Elise, where are you going?" Sheridan asked.

"Home." And she walked out the door.

Elise walked into her house and a cold breeze wrapped itself around her.

"Miles!" she screamed. "Miles?" He did not answer. "He has got to be here. His car is in the garage."

She walked into the dark kitchen and the only noise she heard came from the water left running in the kitchen sink. She moved her way over to the faucet to turn it off. When she turned to her left she discovered blood splattered across the kitchen counter.

"Oh God!" she screamed. "What is going on? Miles!" She yelled. A butcher knife lay in a puddle of blood. She quickly pulled her cell phone out of her purse and attempted to call the police, but before she did her home phone rang. Startled by the ringing sound, she was scared to answer it, but she reluctantly lifted the receiver. "Hello."

"Hi, can I speak with Mrs. Lewis?"

She heard the official tone in the caller's voice. *Please God,* she silently prayed. *Allow my husband to be all right. He is such a good man. He doesn't deserve to be harmed in any way.*

"This is she," she replied.

"Mrs. Lewis, this is Nurse Frazier from Albert Einstein Hospital. Your husband was brought in here a little over an hour ago."

"Is he all right?" she asked.

"Yes, he's going to be fine. He apparently called 9-1-1 and told the operator that he had amputated his penis."

Elise thought for a moment she misunderstood the nurse. "Excuse me, can you repeat that?" she asked.

"Your husband dismembered his own penis," she stated.

Elise looked over at the blood drying on her counter. "I'm on my way."

Elise rushed to the nurse's station. "Hi, I'm looking for a Miles Lewis."

"Are you his wife?" the nurse asked.

"Yes, I am."

"Dr. Bancroft has been waiting for you. He asked me to page him when you arrived. You can have a seat in the waiting room."

Minutes later, Dr. Bancroft approached her. "Mrs. Lewis, thanks for coming so quickly. Before you see your husband I wanted to speak with you about his condition." He took a seat in a chair next to hers. "I don't have to tell you how highly unusual it is for a man to cut off his own penis. The EMT's who brought your husband in this evening managed to find his penis, and I was able to reattach it. In approximately three weeks he should have normal urinary function back and it will probably be a total of seven to eight months before it completely recovers. My biggest concern about your husband's case is his mental state. When he was brought in I had to heavily sedate him. Sometimes under sedation, patients say some crazy things, but he insisted that he did not want his penis. He said it did nothing but cause him heartache."

Elise held her head down in shame.

"Can you explain his behavior? If I'm aware of what's going on, perhaps I can help."

"Doctor, my husband and I have been going through a few problems. He has been experiencing some impotency problems."

The doctor nodded his head to express his understanding. "Has he seen a doctor?"

"Yes, he's been going to a doctor for months. Plus he's been seeing a therapist once a week, but nothing they've suggested has helped."

"If you don't mind, can you give me the name of his therapist? I would like to request that Miles start seeing his therapist five times a week. He needs intense treatment. I want to make sure that this doesn't happen again. The next time he might do something more damaging."

Elise closed her eyes to hold back the tears. Dr. Bancroft stood up. "If you need anything you can contact me here at the hospital," the doctor offered.

"If you'd like to see your husband now, I'll walk you to his room."

Elise watched Miles sleep soundly in his bed. She held on to his hand, praying that once he woke up he would be happy to see her.

Hours later he slowly opened his eyes. "What are you doing here?" he asked groggily, surprised to see Elise sitting at his bedside.

"I was at the house when the hospital called to tell me what had happened."

He turned his head away.

"Did I do this to you?" she asked. "Am I responsible for driving you to do this?"

Tears welled up in his eyes. "Elise, after I left you, I went home to an empty house. Everywhere I looked I saw reminders of you. It drove me insane. I sat in the den and realized the reason this was happening was because I couldn't satisfy you. This impotency has destroyed my life and took the one thing from me worth living for—you. Before I knew it, I had laid it down on the cutting board in the kitchen and picked up the butcher knife. If the doctors couldn't help me, then I knew no one could."

She grabbed Miles's hand. "Listen, you amputating your penis is not going to make things any better. We . . ."

"We?" he interrupted her.

"Yes, *we* are going to battle this together. God brought us together and we can not allow any man or woman . . ." She pointed to herself, ". . . tear us apart." She leaned over and gently kissed him on the lips, " 'Til death do us part." She smiled. "Let's pray, and God will handle the rest."

A Month Later

"Man, she was a freak. I'm telling you. You name it, she did it," Payce told Darshon as he jumped behind the steering wheel of his car. They had just finished shopping at the mall.

"Well, I wish the rest of her girls were like her. Those other two girls wouldn't separate for the world. It was as if they made a pact that night not to leave one another's side. I was better off going home after the club."

Payce's cell phone vibrated. It was Kai, calling him again. She had been calling him nonstop since the night they were together. He sent her call to voicemail. It had been a month since they met, but he didn't want anything serious with her. He had already decided to hit it a couple more times, and then let her go. He couldn't manage to keep both Tressie and Kai.

"The easy girls are always attracted to you. Like this girl Najah you met in the mall," Darshon said, pulling a slip of paper off the dashboard.

"Man, can you put that number away? I have to pick up Tressie. If she sees that number I'll never hear the end of it."

"Sorry, man."

They pulled up to the corner of Broad and Cecil B. Moore. Darshon opened the door for Tressie, and he climbed into the backseat.

"Hey, baby," she said to Payce. She leaned over and gave him a kiss on the mouth. "Guess what I learned in school today?" Without giving him a chance to guess, she continued, "I learned that dogs have the same IQ as a four-year-old child. So do you know what that means?"

He looked interested in what she was saying, but he could feel his phone vibrating on his hip. He didn't want to answer it in front of Tressie because he knew it was Kai. Payce turned up the radio to drown out the vibration sound.

"Why are you turning up the radio when I'm talking?" she asked.

"Sorry, baby. Darshon likes this song."

Tressie turned around to look at Darshon. He was asleep. She turned the volume back down and continued.

"As I was saying, those mutts at your parents' house can fully understand what I'm saying when I tell them to get away from me. Every time I walk in the house they sit in my face and stare."

"Maybe they're mesmerized by your beauty," Payce replied. "You better start being nicer to them or the next time you come over they're going to have you for dinner," he laughed.

Weeks of watching Daneesha's house had finally paid off for Murray. At long last, Bryant had returned to the house. Like a long lost relative he strolled onto the porch and greeted Kobe as if they were old friends. He talked with the black Lab for a moment before entering the home.

Murray thought about calling Olivia and giving her an update, but quickly decided against it. He didn't want to get her hopes up. Just because he had found Bryant didn't mean he was going to find Bryce, especially since Bryant had arrived at Daneesha's alone.

Bryant's first week with Daneesha and the children consisted of many family outings. They dined out, went to the movies, and Bryant even took the kids to see Sesame Street on Ice. Murray tailed Bryant the entire time, never letting him out of his sight.

Murray also paid close attention to Daneesha and Bryant's relationship. It was obvious that she loved Bryant very much. The look in her eyes said forever, but the look in his eyes said never. Every time she grabbed for Bryant's hand, his response to her affection appeared forced and phony. Any displays of public affection initiated by him never seemed sincere.

The funny thing about Bryant was his attitude toward the children. The love and attention he showed toward Marquita and Marquise came straight from the heart. Murray was trained to read people's body language and he could clearly see that Bryant genuinely cared for those children as if they were his own.

One morning Murray pulled up on Daneesha's block and put his new rental car in park. He was still angry about the confusion at the rental car agency, and couldn't get it off his mind. Earlier in the week Murray had made arrangements to exchange his rental car for a different make, model, and color. In his line of business, it was mandatory to change vehicles as much as possible. Using the same car during an investigation was a sure way to tip someone off that they were being followed.

When he arrived to exchange his car they tried to replace it with a bright green Dodge Neon. He knew there was no way he would be able to go unnoticed in that car. He spoke with the salesperson at the ticket counter and she verified that they had made a mistake on his reservation. Unfortunately, they had rented out their entire fleet of cars, and the only vehicle left was the Dodge Neon. After an hour of arguing with the lady at the counter, and with the lot manger, a customer arrived to return their car. Once Murray heard they had another car available, he immediately took the keys and sped off.

Luckily he had arrived back just in time to see Bryant step out of the house wearing a suit. He wore a pair of brown wing-tipped shoes that shined brightly under the mid-morning sun, and he dangled a stogie from his mouth. Bryant's Sunday best caught Murray's attention, and he sat up to get a better look. Normally, this was the time Bryant would leave to take the children to daycare, but today was different. Bryant called for Daneesha and the children to hurry up. The three of them walked out onto the porch looking charming.

Daneesha wore a simple white dress that allowed lots of room for her growing belly. On top of her head she modeled a small, white hat with a veil that partially covered her face. The children were also dressed in outfits that closely resembled Easter attire. Bryant helped Daneesha down the steps while holding her son in his arms.

Murray followed them to City Hall, where he watched a small, intimate wedding ceremony take place from the balcony, presided over by the county judge. The only witnesses were the children and an unidentified woman who stood for Daneesha as her maid of honor. Once the ceremony was over, she hugged Daneesha and wished the newlyweds the best.

Immediately after leaving City Hall, Bryant stopped by a lawyer's office. He quickly ran in carrying a brown envelope, and seconds later he was back in the car. They stopped at a nearby restaurant to have dinner. Murray sat at the bar while they were seated not too far from him. The restaurant was crowded and very noisy, but he could still hear Bryant make a toast.

"I'd like to make a toast to the newest members of the Winters family. My new wife . . ." he leaned over and kissed Daneesha on the lips, "and our children."

"Yeahhhhhh," everyone screamed in unison.

July 2004

A month after they were married, Bryant walked out onto the porch with a small travel bag in his hand. Daneesha followed closely behind him. Bryant said a few final words and kissed her one last time before he got into his car and drove away.

Murray watched the couple say good-bye. He remembered Daneesha telling him that Bryant wouldn't leave her again until after the baby was born. Something important must have come up to make him leave her so close to her due date. He started his car and followed Bryant to the airport.

From a safe distance, Murray watched Bryant return his rental car, take the escalator to the airline terminal ticket counter, check his bag, and walk straight into the Delta terminal.

Wondering where Bryant was going, Murray walked over to the list of flights that were posted on the departure board. There were so many flights leaving that it was going to be hard to determine where Bryant was going. He stared at the list of destinations until one name caught his attention. Greensboro, North Carolina. That flight was scheduled to leave in a little over an hour. Murray rushed over to the ticket counter and purchased a one-way ticket to Greensboro. He quickly went through security and rushed toward his gate number. He looked around, but Bryant wasn't there. Murray thought maybe he had made a mistake and picked the wrong flight. His eyes scanned the area until he spotted Bryant sitting inside a small bar.

Murray strolled into the bar and grabbed a seat right next to Bryant. He ordered himself a beer and watched the Bulls play basketball on TV.

"The Bulls will never be the same without ole' Mike," Murray said to Bryant.

Bryant looked around and realized the old fellow was talking to him.

"When Jordan was playing, everybody was happy," Murray continued. "The city of Chicago was rich, Mike was rich, even I was rich. I own a restaurant located right outside the United Arena. Every night the Bulls played a home game customers would line up around the corner to get something to eat before they went home, but since Jordan retired, business has slacked off considerably." He took a sip of his beer. "That loss of income has affected me and my family."

Bryant nodded his head but kept his attention focused on the game.

Determined to initiate a conversation, Murray continued talking. "So now I'm headed to Greensboro, North Carolina. A friend of mine referred me to a real estate agent who said he has some great properties at a really cheap price. If everything works out, I'm going to relocate down there. Financially that would be the sound thing to do because the cost of living is cheaper."

Bryant turned to face him. "Greensboro. That's where I'm from."

"A country boy?" Murray asked, glad that he had finally said something to get Bryant's attention.

"Yes sir, born and raised. Where's the property located you're going to look at?"

"You know, I'm not sure. But the agent did say that the building was located in a very busy part of town. He mentioned a mall. I can't remember the name right now."

"It must be Four Seasons Mall, and if your property is located outside the mall that is definitely a busy area."

"I'm glad I ran into you. Now I can call my wife and tell her not to worry. You know how women can be."

Bryant nodded his head in agreement.

"Are you married?" Murray asked.

Bryant smiled. "Yes, sir, I've been married for about a month, now."

"So you're a newlywed. Congratulations." Murray signaled for the bartender to refill Bryant's glass. "Where's your wife? Is she accompanying you?" Murray looked around the small establishment.

"No, it's just me. I had some business to take care of. Like you said, I now have a family to provide for."

The bartender placed a drink in front of Bryant just as their gate number was announced over the loud speaker.

"That's me," Bryant said. He downed his drink and gathered his things.

"Me too," Murray replied. The two men got up, left the bar, and walked toward the gate.

"It was nice talking with you, sir. I hope everything works out for you."

"You too, son."

Chapter 14

Once their plane landed in Greensboro, Bryant rushed off. Murray noticed that he repeatedly checked his watch while waiting for the luggage to come through baggage claim. Murray retrieved his bags and went to rent a car. Luckily he had made reservations ahead of time. He just prayed that he wouldn't have the same problems he had in Chicago.

Bryant merged onto Interstate 85 and traveled south. He drove to a small residential community and pulled into the driveway of a blue bi-level house. Murray watched Bryant grab his things from the trunk and knock on the door. He watched carefully as someone opened the door and welcomed him in. Over an hour had passed before Bryant emerged from the house, and he wasn't alone. He carried a baby in his arms. Bryant strapped the infant into the car seat and pulled out of the driveway. Murray's intuition told him that the baby Bryant carried in his arms was Bryce, but he had to be sure.

Before Bryant pulled away, Murray quickly wrote down the license plate number of the car he was driving. Murray waited fifteen minutes before he got out of the car and knocked on the door. An older woman with graying hair answered.

"Hello ma'am," Murray said with a deferential nod. "I'm a friend of Bryant's and he asked me to come back here to see if he left the baby's blanket behind."

"Oh! Come in." She held the door open for him.

She looked around the living room. "I didn't think he left anything. We checked to make sure he had everything before he left. You can have a seat while I go look upstairs."

Murray was unsure of what to expect when he knocked on the door, but he was relieved when a senior citizen answered. The elderly were easier to get information from without them getting suspicious. He looked around her home. Her fireplace mantle held dozens of photos, mostly of Bryant. One photo was taken of Bryant wearing a little league baseball uniform, and another showed Bryant at his prom. He noticed a more recent picture of Bryant holding a little girl. Murray wondered who the child was.

"I'm sorry, but I don't see anything," the old woman reported. She slowly crept back down the stairs.

"Don't worry about it, ma'am. He might have it with him and not know it." Murray stood up to leave. "Did you enjoy your time with Bryce?"

She revealed a mouth full of dentures. "Oh yes. He is such a good baby. I can't wait until he comes back for another visit."

"Is Bryant coming back here tonight?" Murray asked.

"No, he said he had something to take care of and that he needed to get the baby back to his mother. Him and the baby are going to stay the night out by the airport so he can catch his plane in the morning."

"Oh yeah, that's right. We do have an early morning flight to catch. I guess it would just make more sense to stay out by the airport. I'm sorry if I bothered you, ma'am."

"That's no problem. Be sure to give my best to both my nephews."

"No problem, ma'am. And you take care of yourself."

Murray left the home in a hurry. Now that he knew Bryant had Bryce, he had to find out at which hotel they were staying. Once he found that out, he would call the police.

He drove out to the airport and searched all the area hotels for Bryant's rental car. He finally found it parked at the Ramada. Murray walked into the lobby and took a seat. He had followed enough people to know that front desk clerks never gave out guest information. He was certain that if he waited long enough the clues he needed to find

Bryant and Bryce would come to him. He patiently sat for over three hours before he saw Bryant get off the elevators and walk over to the front desk. He watched Bryant say a few words to the clerk and turn back toward the elevators.

"Hey, man," Murray called out.

Bryant abruptly turned around and was surprised to see his old friend from the airport. "Hey man. What's up?" Murray noticed Bryant's jittery behavior.

"I'm surprised to see you here," Murray replied.

"Yeah, the business dealings that I had going on down here are being held at this hotel," Bryant said.

"I was sitting at the bar when I noticed you enter the lobby." The elevator doors opened and they both entered. "What floor you going to?" Murray asked.

"Five," Bryant responded.

Murray pushed the fifth floor button and the eighth floor for himself. "When are you heading back out to Chicago?"

"Sometime tomorrow," Bryant hesitantly replied.

"I have a few more days of business here," Murray replied. "Maybe we can hook up again in Chicago."

Bryant looked at Murray suspiciously. The doors opened for the fifth floor and Bryant stepped off the elevator.

"Yeah man, just leave your name and number down at the front desk and I'll be sure to pick it up before I check out," he shouted just before the elevator doors shut.

Bryant entered his room and watched his great uncle, Mayfield Winters, play with Bryce.

"Look at how handsome this little boy is. He's going to make us a lot of money," the old man said. He held the baby up to get a good look at him. "He is really a cute little boy. He almost looks too good to sell." Bryant grinned at his uncle's compliments about his work.

"He's a strong little fella." Bryce held on to his great-uncle's finger. "Do you have his paperwork?" Mayfield asked.

"Right here." Bryant pulled a brown envelope out of Bryce's diaper bag.

"What about the mother? Did you take care of her?"

"She's not an issue. She won't ever find me or the baby. Right now she should just be getting out of jail, and once she does, she won't know where to begin to look for me or Bryce."

"Good, and I have the adoption papers all drawn up. All we have to do is get the Richardsons to sign off on the contract and give us the check."

There was a knock at the door. "Bryant, take the baby into the bedroom and come back out here. I want you to meet our newest clients," Mayfield said.

When Bryant returned he was shocked by the sight of two men sitting on the couch holding hands.

"This is my nephew, Bryant. Bryant, this is the Perry family—Kendrick and Kyle." Bryant reached out to shake both of their hands.

It surprised Bryant to see a same-sex couple. He and his uncle had provided dozens of babies to a lot of couples, but this was the first time they had ever done business with a gay couple.

Mayfield pulled up a chair from the living room table and handed the couple a pile of papers.

Kendrick spoke up first. "Mr. Winters, I was surprised when you got back to us so soon. I didn't think that you were going to respond at all."

"Well, when I spoke with you on the phone, I appreciated the fact that you were completely honest with us about your situation," Mayfield said. "We did a preliminary background check on both of you and we saw nothing that would indicate a problem with you adopting a child or, in your case, children. That's why I arranged this meeting." He pointed to an envelope. "These are the contracts I need you to look over. I'll give you a week or two to get back to me, and if you want to proceed, give me a call and I will make the final arrangements.

"Is this adoption legal?" Kendrick asked.

"Yes. Is there anything that concerns you?" Mayfield asked.

"Well, the extreme price that you charge for this adoption process. It costs one hundred thousand dollars for one baby. That's a lot of money. Even an overseas adoption costs no more than ten thousand dollars. Why the extremely high price?"

"The reason we charge so much is because we guarantee healthy babies to couples who are usually denied by the standard adoption agencies, couples like yourselves. Everything is kept in the strictest of confidence, and we cater to an exclusive set of people. The process of screening all candidates is costly. I have to make sure that every child we place is going to be cared for properly. I would be deeply hurt if I later found out a child I provided you with was being abused or mistreated."

"I understand," Kendrick said. "Like I told you on the phone, a lot of adoption agencies, both public and private, have denied us the chance to adopt. A few agencies have even tried to discourage us from trying. They thought it was inappropriate for us to force a child into accepting our lifestyle."

"We don't discriminate here," Mayfield replied.

Bryant noticed Kendrick's professional manner, his speech, and his style of dress. It was obvious that Kendrick was not only intelligent, but also powerful.

"Well, I need to have my lawyer look these contracts over and we'll get back to you as soon as possible." He turned to Kyle. "Are you okay?"

"Yes, I'm just delighted. I can't believe we are finally going to have a family of our own," Kyle squealed.

"I invited my nephew here because he knows a little more about the children you are going to adopt," Mayfield explained.

"Well," Bryant spoke up, "right now it's only two children, but the mother is eight months pregnant with a third child. There's a little girl named Marquita, she's three years old, and a boy named Marquise. He's one."

Bryant handed them a picture of the children.

"They are adorable!" Kyle exulted.

Bryant continued, "The third child is also a girl."

Kyle was delighted at the news of three children.

Kendrick grabbed Kyle's knee. "We have always wanted a big family. I know that we do not represent the traditional family structure, but we think the most important thing to give a child is love. I shouldn't be denied the right to be a father just because I choose to share my life with a man instead of a woman." He grabbed Kyle's hand.

"As I said before, our number one priority is to find these children a safe, happy, and stable home environment," Mayfield affirmed. "The mother is young and is having a rough time, so the money that we charge will also be used to help her get herself together, possibly go back to school to make a life for herself."

"Can you provide us with any information about the mother?" Kyle asked.

"I'm sorry, but that information is confidential."

Kyle looked at Kendrick, concerned. "We had discussed the possibility of the children wanting to one day know where they came from, or who their biological parents were. We don't want to deny them that right."

"Well, it is highly unusual for us to allow the birth parents to contact the children after the adoption is final. But if at any time you want to find out who the children's parents are, just give us a call. If the mother allows us to release her identity, then we will gladly provide you with that information."

"Is the birth mother aware of our sexual orientation?"

"No, we just provided her with paperwork from the background investigation. From that she can determine what kind of home her children will be living in, but the names have been concealed."

"Could you please just give her our personal thanks?" Kyle asked. "She is giving us her most prized possessions, and she doesn't have to worry. We will take good care of them."

"Well, it looks like we can wrap things up. I almost forgot," Mayfield said, snapping his fingers. "I need to confirm the final price with you. I believe that I did tell you that the price for all three children, plus the adoption fees, would be three hundred fifty thousand dollars."

Bryant looked at his uncle with a surprised look on his face.

"Yes, Mr. Winters, and that will not be a problem," Kendrick responded.

"All right, well it looks like we've concluded our business here. Please make sure you give me a call when you're ready to proceed."

Mayfield walked them to the door and said a few final words.

"Unc, three hundred fifty thousand dollars!" Bryant exclaimed. "What do they do that they can afford that kind of money?"

"Kendrick is a very successful real estate developer in New York City. Kyle comes from a very influential family. He was born with money."

"Damn, that's a lot of money. The first thing I'm going to do is take a vacation to Maui."

"You did a good job and you deserve it." He quickly reminded Bryant, "Don't forget I need a copy of those adoption papers stating that those kids are legally yours. You did get the mother to sign off on those papers, didn't you?"

"Yes, sir. As soon as I get back to Chicago I'll get in touch with the lawyer to find out if the papers have been filed."

Murray walked around the fifth floor, listening at various doors. He was frustrated because he had no clue which room Bryant was in with the baby. Unsure of what his next move should be, he decided to go back down to the lobby and wait. If he found Bryant, once he'd find him again. As he stood waiting on the elevators, he heard a door open. He hid around a corner and listened closely.

"Mr. Winters, we appreciate you contacting us concerning the adoption and I . . ." Kyle playfully punched Kendrick in the arm, "I mean *we* will be in touch."

Murray watched the two men shake an older man's hand and walk toward the elevators.

"Bryant, I gotcha," Murray whispered. He pulled out his cell phone. "Yes, I would like to report a kidnapping."

"I'm expecting another couple, any minute now. Their names are Albert and Rosa Richardson, an older couple in their late fifties. They will be the ones taking Bryce home."

"What's their background look like?" Bryant asked.

"She's a housewife and he owns a chain of motels across the country. You've heard of Room and Board Motels, haven't you?"

"Yeah, I've stayed at a few of them."

"That's him."

It wasn't long before Bryant got to see what the Richardsons looked like. He thought they looked like a real life replica of George and Weezie

Jefferson. He was a short, balding man, and his wife was a husky woman who towered at least a foot over her husband.

"Mr. and Mrs. Richardson, I'm so glad to see you," Mayfield welcomed them. "Please have a seat." The couple sat down around the dining room table, and Mayfield asked Bryant to get the baby from the adjoining bedroom.

When Bryant returned, he held Bryce up for them to see. Bryant wanted his son to make a good first impression on his new parents, so he had bought him a one-piece, blue striped outfit with a matching baseball cap. Bryce resembled a miniature baseball player.

"He is beautiful!" The wife held out her hands. "Can I hold him?"

"Sure," Mayfield said, nudging Bryant to hand her the baby.

Holding her son for the first time brought tears to her eyes. "I can't believe this is finally happening."

"You can take him home with you tonight," Mayfield replied. "We just need for you to sign a few papers." Mayfield pulled out the contracts and Bryce's medical records. Bryant watched the couple play with his son. Bryce was a friendly baby and took to them immediately. He grabbed at Mrs. Richardson's jewelry and talked to them in his own native baby talk.

"Do you have any other children at home?" Bryant asked.

"No! He will be our first. Does he have a name?"

"Yes ma'am. His name is Bryce."

She screwed up her face. "I don't like that name. Can we change it?" she asked Mayfield.

"Yes ma'am," he replied. "There is a line in the adoption papers for a name change."

"If you don't mind me asking, why did you wait so long to adopt?" Bryant asked.

"I realize that we are considered an older couple," Rosa replied. "My husband worked hard all our lives to make sure that we were financially secure. It wasn't until my fifty-seventh birthday that we realized that we had no children to inherit the business. It was too late for us to try and have children of our own, and that is when we began to look into adoption."

Mr. Richardson looked through the adoption papers and signed off on all the pages. He pointed to the last page. "Is this where we can change his name?"

"Yes," Mayfield replied.

"We've decided to name him Kevin," Rosa announced.

Bryant sat and watched the adoption transaction take place. He had been through this a hundred times before, but today was different. In the past, he had always felt a twinge of guilt for selling his children, but he had really grown to love Bryce. He guessed the reason he felt so close to Bryce is because of how much he cared for his mother. Olivia would always be special to him.

Bryant never had the opportunity to bond with any of his other children like he had with Bryce, except for Niya. Niya was his oldest daughter and the very first child he sold. He could still hear her cries in his sleep. The day he handed her over to her adoptive parents she cried out 'Daddy'.

Before Bryant became a baby broker he had a good life. He was married to a beautiful woman, they had just bought a house, and his wife, Taima, had just given birth to a baby girl named Niya. Life couldn't be better, until Bryant lost his job and the monthly bills starting piling up. He missed several mortgage payments and the bank was threatening to foreclose on their home. Bryant went to his Uncle Mayfield to ask for a loan, but unfortunately his uncle was broke. That's when his uncle mentioned a couple he knew who was willing to pay top dollar for a baby girl. He suggested that Bryant give them Niya.

Hearing his suggestion infuriated Bryant. He couldn't believe his uncle would even think of such a thing. Until he heard that the couple was willing to pay one million dollars. *One million dollars for a baby?* He knew it was wrong, but it seemed to be the only solution.

Bryant agreed and his uncle handled everything. The only other concern Bryant had was Taima. What were they going to do about her? She would never allow Bryant to sell their child. Mayfield convinced Bryant that the only option they had was to drug Taima and sign her into rehab. He didn't want to do it, but he did. He still felt bad about what he did but the money helped make up for it.

"Kevin. That's a nice name," Mayfield replied. "Isn't it, Bryant?"

Bryant slowly nodded his head in agreement.

Mayfield looked through the contracts to make sure everything was signed. "Well, it looks like you have a new addition to your family. Here are his medical records." He handed the documents to Mr. Richardson.

"Here is the adoption fee," Albert Richardson said. He handed Mayfield a cashier's check.

"Thank you, Mr. and Mrs. Richardson. I feel good knowing that Kevin is in your hands." He stood up and they shook hands.

"Wait, let me get you his diaper bag," Bryant piped up. He ran back into the bedroom.

While they waited on Bryant, someone knocked on their door. "Bryant, are you expecting someone?" Mayfield called out.

"No," Bryant shouted back.

"Excuse me for a second." When Mayfield opened the door he came face to face with a Greensboro police detective and two other officers. "Hi, can I help you?" Mayfield asked.

"Yes, I'm Detective Denali. We received a tip that there was a baby who was kidnapped in this room."

"Detective, there is no baby here," Mayfield replied in a whisper.

"Well, if you don't mind, we'd like to take a look around." He tried to push the door open.

Mayfield pushed back against the door. "Officer, I don't mean to be disrespectful, but if you don't have a search warrant, then I can't let you in."

"Sir, you don't own this hotel room. We have the hotel manager's permission to search every room in this hotel if necessary."

The police barged their way into the room and found the Richardson's gathering their things to leave with Brycc.

"Excuse me, sir, is this your baby?" the detective asked Mr. Richardson.

"Yes, this is our son. We just adopted him," Mrs. Richardson interjected.

The detective turned around and asked Murray, "Is this the baby you were hired to find?"

"Yes, it is," Murray said.

Bryant came back out with the baby bag. "What is going on?" He looked at Murray. "What are you doing here?"

"That's him," Murray told the detective.

"Arrest them both," the detective commanded the other officers, pointing to Bryant and his uncle.

The handcuffs were put on Bryant. "What is going on?" he whined.

"You're under arrest for kidnapping a child," the detective informed him.

"I didn't kidnap him. He's my son. I have his birth certificate in the room."

The officer looked at Murray for confirmation.

"Yes, he is the father, but he did not have the mother's permission to leave the state of Pennsylvania with the child."

The detective picked up the adoption papers that lay on the table.

"I assume this was a private adoption?" the detective asked.

"Yes, detective, it was," Mr. Richardson responded.

"How much did you pay?"

Mr. Richardson looked unsure about answering. "I paid one hundred fifteen thousand dollars," he said.

"That's all I needed to hear. Take them away," the detective said. He pulled the baby from Mrs. Richardson's hands and handed him to Murray. "You won't be able to adopt this baby, because the adoption is illegal," he informed the couple.

"What about my money?" Albert Richardson asked.

"You will get your money back. Just come down to the station and provide me with a statement."

The detective walked up to Murray. "I also need for you to come down to the station."

"Sure," Murray said. "I just need to call the mother and let her know I found her baby." He dialed Olivia's number. "Olivia," he said when she answered. "I have some good news for you."

Chapter 15

Monday afternoon Payce dragged himself into work at The Dollhouse. The receptionist stood at her usual post watching an episode of *As the World Turns* on a small television set hidden behind the counter. She raised her eyes slightly and acknowledged his arrival by nodding her head, then turned her attention back toward the television.

Payce walked halfway down the hall before he turned back around. "What is your name?" he asked the receptionist. "I've been working here for weeks and I still don't know your name."

"Simone," she replied.

"Hi, Simone. I'm Payce."

"Oh, I know who you are. Just because you didn't know my name doesn't mean I didn't know yours." She grinned. Payce liked her. Under different circumstances, he would have tried to get her phone number, but dating coworkers was not his thing, especially ones who worked at The Dollhouse.

He attempted to walk down the hall toward the locker rooms when Simone called out his name. "Payce, I forgot to tell you, Natasha wants to see you in her office."

Making a quick U-turn, he commenced walking in the opposite direction. He lightly tapped on his boss's door. "You wanted to see me?" he asked.

Natasha took off her reading glasses and pulled her attention from the magazine article she was reading. "Yes, Payce, come in and shut the door."

He took a seat in front of her desk. "What's up?"

"I have a favor I need to ask of you. Since you've joined our family, my clientele has increased. You have quickly become one of my most requested employees."

"I aim to please," he laughed.

"Saturday night I'm throwing a party. It's an exclusive party extended to wives only. Wives of various celebrities, music artists, athletes, famous politicians—you get the picture. I have already asked a few of the other fellas who work here to help me out that night and I was hoping you would also be interested in working."

"Sure, I'd be glad to help out. Will I be doing the same thing I do here?"

"Yes, except there will be no husbands around to watch you. No husbands are allowed." She stressed her words. "I put this event together because I hear a lot of wives complain about how their husbands are negligent to their sexual needs. Most have never experienced an orgasm. These women are looking for a good time. Give these ladies pleasure, and whatever else they may be looking for."

"No problem," he arrogantly replied.

"I'm calling the party, 'What goes around comes around.' I've got hundreds of responses. Women are bringing their friends and family. This party is going to be huge."

"How much are you paying?"

"I like that! You always have money on the mind." She pulled out two stacks of bills and placed them on the desk in front of him. "I'm willing to pay you in advance. That's how much I trust you. This is fifteen thousand dollars. Is that enough?"

"That is more than enough," he replied while picking up the stacks of money.

Payce pulled up in front of Natasha's home and a valet opened his car door. He grabbed his duffel bag from the backseat. When he stepped out of the car he couldn't help but notice the exquisite landscaping done to her front yard. In the center of the circular driveway a water fountain housed a multitude of gold fish and a row of magnolia trees lined the driveway from the street all the way up to the house. Off to the side, a man-made pond sat underneath a small crosswalk and bright fluorescent lights revealed a path for guests to enjoy the beautiful grounds.

Payce slowly walked up the marble steps that led to the front entrance. A doorman greeted him and invited him inside. Payce passed through the archway and was blinded by a shimmering chandelier that hung from the ceiling. Its reflection gave off so much light that it took a moment for his eyes to adjust to the shine. He glared up at the chandelier when a topless waiter, wearing nothing but a pair of white leather shorts, darted past him carrying a tray of hors d'oeuvres.

"Hello, Payce." Payce turned around just in time to see Reverend Kane coming in his direction.

"Reverend Kane." Payce checked out the dress she was wearing. The midnight blue gown was very tasteful and sophisticated. Her hair was pulled into a single French braid, and the only jewelry she wore was a large sapphire pendant that hung around her neck. "You look nice tonight. Natasha didn't mention you would be here."

"I'm working tonight. Natasha thought it would be good if I was available just in case any of her guests wanted to have the lesbian experience."

Payce hoped that he wouldn't have to do a threesome with her. To watch the Reverend go down on another woman would be embarrassing.

"Payce." Natasha descended her winding staircase in a Valentino original. The white, silk, floor-length dress hugged her curves. "I'm so glad you made it." She hugged him. "I thought you might get lost with all the construction they're doing on the interstate."

"No, you gave good directions."

"I'm glad." She pointed up the stairs. "You can go upstairs to the first bedroom on the left and change your clothes. Once you're ready you can join us in the den."

Before he walked away, Natasha stopped him.

"Payce, let me tell you what to expect tonight." She walked back over to him. "Once you enter the den I want you to walk around, introduce yourself, mingle with the ladies, and get to know everyone. I have provided each woman with a black velvet bag full of small platinum boomerangs. If a woman is interested in your services she will place a boomerang in your hand. If it's a regular boomerang then she is allocated one hour with you, but if the boomerang has a diamond chip inserted in it, then she gets two hours. You can then escort her upstairs to one of the available bedrooms. Do you have any questions?"

He shook his head no.

"Good, I'll see you inside."

Ten minutes later Payce entered the den. Inside were women of every race, nationality, and creed—black women, white women, old women, young women and even a few well-known celebrity women in attendance. The place was swarming with women. It was standing room only. A few guys had three or four women on their arms.

He saw Tariq, one of his coworkers from The Dollhouse, escorting a married pop star upstairs. They acknowledged one another with a nod and Payce walked around the room introducing himself to different ladies.

It wasn't long before a sexy, but mysterious woman approached him with a diamond boomerang in her hand. The way she walked up to him and never said a word, but allowed her eyes to talk to him, was alluring. She placed the boomerang in his hand and led Payce upstairs. He followed and watched her hips sway from side to side in a pair of tight fitting white Capri pants. They entered the room and she sat on the end of the bed. She quickly pulled her sea green blouse over her head. Her eyes beckoned for Payce to come closer to her.

Payce thought the woman looked familiar, but he couldn't remember where he had seen her before. Suddenly, it hit him. She was married to a famous football player who played for the Philadelphia Eagles. She was always seen on television at her husbands' football games, cheering him on. Now he was about to do the man's wife. Payce was so excited he wanted to ask her for an autograph.

He was anxious to get started. She lay back on the bed when the police burst into the room.

"This is a raid! Put your hands against the wall! You are under arrest for prostitution."

Not again, Payce thought. The police pushed him against the wall, put the cuffs on him, and led him away.

AUGUST 2004

A guard escorted Tressie into the visitor's room. She sat for five minutes on one side of a plexiglass partition before Payce walked in, looking shabby. He sat down in front of her wearing an orange jumpsuit, hair uncombed, and the whites of his eyes turned yellow. He gestured for her to pick up the telephone receiver sitting next to her.

"Hey," he said into the receiver. "I'm glad you came. I needed to see you."

"I didn't want to come, but I guess I needed to see for myself that what everyone was saying was true."

"Tressie, don't listen to what people are saying out on the streets. If you have any questions, ask me. I'm right here. I'm the only one who can provide you with the truth."

"The truth? You're the one who has been lying to me for months. You lied to me, your parents, and yourself."

"I'm sorry."

"Sorry!" she screamed. "Payce, you were selling your body for money."

He looked down at the floor in shame.

"I thought we were *one*. Didn't you tell me you loved me? I thought you could tell me anything. Last night all I could think about was how many times you left my bed to go to work. I believed you when you said you were going to the Westin, when the truth was you were going to The Dollhouse to fuck somebody's wife."

"Don't talk like that. You're too much of a lady to talk like that."

"What do you care? You don't want a lady. You want one of those whores who paid you hundreds of dollars to fuck them."

"Tressie, I love you."

"I don't believe you have the audacity to sit in my face and say that. If this glass were not separating us, I'd spit in your face. How do you know one of those women weren't HIV positive?"

"I wore a condom, every time. Tressie, you have got to believe me when I say I'm sorry for what I did and I love you."

"You have a strange way of showing it."

"I know I made some mistakes and there is no way I can take it back, but no matter what you say, we are a part of one another. Like you just reminded me, we are one. Nothing can separate us. Not even these bars."

"What part of *us*," she stressed her words, "thought it was all right to sleep with other women?" she asked softly with tears in her eyes. She loved him so much, and she couldn't understand how he could betray her in such a way.

"Please don't leave me when I need you most," he pleaded.

Tressie hated to abandon him. She did love him and he deserved a second chance. Everyone thought the worst of him. *Maybe he just needed someone to care*, she thought.

"Tressie." He looked into her eyes. "Will you be there for me when I get out?"

"I guess I don't have any choice," she replied.

Tressie knelt at the altar and stared up at the cross. Tears had dried on her face. "King of Kings and Lord of Lords, I'm crying out to you today to watch over Payce. I need you to keep him safe while in jail. Protect him, Lord. I know that he did wrong, but I ask that you look past his mistakes and see what's inside his heart. Jesus, you have given so many of us a second chance—a second chance to serve you, a second chance to praise your name—and I know that if given the opportunity, Payce would take the second chance you give to him and use it to glorify your name. God, I ask that you intervene in our relationship. We cannot and will not last without you. We need your strength and your understanding. We are being faced with obstacles that I can't endure, so I ask that you take the burden from me. Amen."

Tressie stepped away from the altar as Elise walked into the sanctuary.

"Tressie, I heard about what happened with Payce."

"I don't know what to do," Tressie cried. "I love him and I don't want to lose him, but how can I trust him after this? What we had is ruined."

"I understand how you must feel right now, but you did the right thing by coming here to pray. When the Lord answers your prayer, open your heart to accept his answer. It may not be what you want to hear. He may tell you that you and Payce were not meant to be together. Are you prepared to accept that?"

"Elise, how can he not be the one for me? He's the bishop's son."

"Tressie, you know just as well as I do that being the bishop's son doesn't get you into Heaven. You have to be saved, and if I were you, I'd question whether or not Payce was saved by the things that he has done. Don't think I'm here to judge Payce because I'm not. But don't allow Payce's mistakes to be a burden to you. You deserve better than that. Remember II Corinthians 6:14: 'Be ye not unequally yoked with non-believers.'" Elise hugged her. "Just think about what I said. The Spirit will lead you in the right direction."

SEPTEMEBER 2004

Tressie ran out of the university library trying to catch the last bus home. If she missed this bus, the next one wasn't scheduled to come until after four o'clock. She had lost track of time doing research for a paper that was due tomorrow. Her classes were over for the day, but she still had a lot of studying to do. Three different instructors had scheduled exams on the same day, and she was prepared to pull an all-nighter and study until dawn.

Running down the sidewalk, she quickly turned the corner and was suddenly knocked to the ground. Her books scattered over the pavement and her purse slid a few feet away from her. Tressie sat on the pavement, ready to call the scoundrel who ran into her and made her miss her bus every dirty four letter word she could think of, when she looked up and was greeted by a familiar face.

Quinton Briscoe smiled back at her and gallantly rose to his feet. "Tressie, are you all right?" He held out his hand to help her up.

She grabbed his hand and brushed the dirt off her clothes. Onlookers who witnessed the accident asked if they were okay. Quinton reassured them that they were both fine.

Quinton Briscoe was Tressie's first boyfriend, first love, and first heartbreak. Tressie and Quinton dated for several months before he got bored and started dating a girl from New Jersey.

Tressie was hurt, but she hid the pain in her heart and over time she recovered. She later learned that he had been arrested on drug charges and sent away for a few years.

An unexpected hot flash passed through her body, her face turned red, and her palms began to sweat. She couldn't control her body's reaction to seeing Quinton after all these years.

"Quinton, what are you doing here?"

"I came to drop something off to my sister."

Tressie stared at his wavy hair. She wanted to touch it. It looked so soft. "I have seen your sister around campus a few times."

"She forgot one of her books this morning and I promised I would bring it to her." Quinton bent down to pick Tressie's books up from the ground. "Were you late for class? I'm sorry if I stopped you."

"No, I was trying to catch the bus home, but I think I missed it."

"If you need a ride home, I'd be happy to drop you off. My car is parked right around the corner."

"I'd appreciate that," she replied.

Once they were in the car he inquired about her life. "So how is everything for you? Fill me in. Have I missed out on anything exciting? Are you married? Any children?"

"No kids. No husband. Just me. I've been studying a lot, trying to finish school. What about yourself?"

"I got a job in Jersey at a warehouse. They put me on third shift, which I'm not too happy about, but besides that I'm doing all right," he told her. "Just trying to get back what I lost. Being away all those years hurt me, but I'm trying to do right this time." Quinton merged onto the expressway northbound. "I didn't hear you mention anything about a boyfriend."

She thought about Payce and was quickly reminded of the promise she made to wait for him.

"I do have a boyfriend." She cleared her throat. "I'm dating Payce Boyd."

"Payce Boyd," he said out loud. "Payce Boyd, the bishop's son?"

"Yeah, that's him."

"I heard he was arrested for male prostitution."

Tressie slowly nodded her head. Her face turned red from embarrassment. Payce was making it hard for her to stand by his side.

"Tressie, I'm sorry, I shouldn't have said that. He's a lucky man to have you in his corner. I wish I had you when I was locked down."

Quinton pulled up to her house. "How are your parents doing?"

"They're doing well."

"Tell them I said hello."

"I will. I'll see you around."

She quickly got out of his car and rushed into the house. She breathed a sigh of relief when she saw his car pull away. *He still looks as fine as ever.* He had grown from a boy to a man. She walked into the kitchen and poured herself a glass of iced tea. She turned on the fan to cool herself down. "Payce, please hurry up and come home," she said to herself. "If I keep running into Quinton, there's no telling what a girl might do."

Chapter 16

OCTOBER 2004

Tressie sat in the school cafeteria eating her lunch. She had exactly twenty minutes before the start of her next class. She took a huge bite of her sandwich when a familiar voice interrupted her thoughts.

"Excuse me, miss, is this seat taken?" Quinton stood at her table with a bouquet of fresh wildflowers in his hands. She wiped the mayonnaise away from the corners of her mouth.

"Are those for me?" she asked.

"I brought them for the prettiest girl in school."

"Well then, they must be for me." She reached out for them. "They're gorgeous. Thank you, but why did you buy me flowers?"

"I was hoping to get a smile from you," he admitted.

"You didn't have to buy me flowers to get me to smile."

"I thought that my new cologne might do the trick, but I wasn't sure. So I bought the flowers just in case."

They laughed and he pulled up a chair next to hers. "Tressie, I was wondering if you were free this afternoon."

She looked at him strangely. Reluctant to answer his question, she asked him why.

"Don't get any ideas. You already told me you were involved with Payce. I was just hoping we could hang out for a little while this afternoon, like old times. It doesn't have to be anything special. Maybe we could just go for a walk?" he suggested.

He looked so innocent and sincere that she couldn't turn him down. Besides, she didn't see any harm in taking a walk.

"I'll meet you at Broad and Cecil B. Moore at three o'clock," she told him.

"I won't be late." He got up and left.

At exactly three o'clock Quinton pulled up to the corner, and minutes later they were riding rented bicycles in Fairmont Park.

"Slow down, Tressie!" Quinton shouted.

Tressie was attempting to finish the entire eight-mile perimeter without stopping to rest. It was her idea to rent bicycles. She hadn't ridden a bike since she was a kid, and she thought it would be fun. She stopped to allow Quinton to catch up.

He pulled up beside her, out of breath. "Girl, I can see how you managed to stay in shape. Can we walk the bikes for a while? I see a bench over there." He pointed to a corner picnic area.

"If we must," she pouted.

They walked over to the bench and parked their bikes.

"I thought guys were supposed to work out in jail," Tressie said.

"Most do. But I was always in the library studying," he responded.

"Trying to be the good guy?" she asked.

"I remember at one time you used to like good guys."

"I did, but all that changed when I met you."

He laughed. "What would you call Payce?"

"Payce is MINE," she said with confidence.

"Do you love him?"

"I don't just love him, I love everything about him. Even when he does wrong, I love him even more because I know that he is human and is capable of making mistakes."

"Does he love you?"

"I believe he does."

"I hope you're right, because sometimes people confuse love with lust. Being behind those prison walls will make a man say things he really doesn't mean."

"Payce was in love with me before he went to jail, and when he comes home, he'll still be in love with me."

"I don't want to see you get hurt," he replied.

Tressie walked over to look out over the Schuylkill River. Quinton walked up close behind her.

"Didn't you just tell me not to confuse love and lust?" She put some distance between the two of them. "I think you're lusting for me right now."

"I've been lusting for you for five years." He grabbed her and held her close. She didn't make any effort to break away from his embrace. He slowly brushed his soft lips across hers. He looked into her eyes and she quickly turned away. She released herself from his embrace.

"Quinton, what do you want from me?"

"I want you. I don't want anything but you."

"You know that's not possible."

"Why? Because of Payce. He's locked up and I'm right here." He walked up to her and held her hand. "Tressie, all I want is a chance, a chance to show you that we would be good together."

Unsure of what to do or say, Tressie played it safe. "Can you give me some time? I heard everything you've said, but I'm still in love with Payce, and while our relationship has hit some shaky ground, I can't just walk out on him. I need some time to sort out my feelings."

"Okay, I'll give you some space," Quinton responded.

Payce walked to the officer's desk and signed for his personal things. "You never told me who it was that bailed me out," he said to the officer.

"The lady standing behind you," the officer replied.

Payce turned around and saw Reverend Kane standing in the corner. He grumbled a few words under his breath, grabbed his wallet, and walked out of the prison facility.

Reverend Kane followed him outside. "Payce, you could thank me for bailing you out," she yelled.

Payce kept walking and yelled out, "Thanks, Rev."

"No thanks needed," she replied. "Natasha is the one who paid the bail money."

He stopped walking. "I thought she was in jail," he said. Then he realized something else. "Why weren't you arrested?"

"Can we talk in my car? I can give you a ride home." She motioned for him to follow her. He was reluctant to follow, but he knew that she was the only one who could answer his questions.

"When the police raided Natasha's house, I happened to be down in the wine cellar. Someone from the party requested a rare vintage wine, and Natasha asked me if I could go get it for her. That's when I heard the commotion upstairs. I hid out down there until the following morning. The first person I bailed out was Natasha. After she was released, she posted bail for the rest of her employees. You were the last person we had to get out."

"Why was I the last one to get bailed out? She told me I was one of her best employees. I should have been first."

"You are one of her best employees. I asked her to allow me to post your bail. I wanted to be the one to get you out of this mess, since I am the one who got you into it. Payce, I owe you an apology. I never meant for any of this to happen. The last thing I wanted was for you to go back to jail."

Reverend Kane sounded so remorseful that he couldn't allow her to take all the blame. He knew she was only trying to help him out. "Don't worry about it, Rev," Payce said. "I've been in worse situations and I came out of them just fine. Besides, it wasn't entirely your fault. I knew what I was doing was wrong, but again, I allowed money to lead me down the wrong path."

"I still feel guilty," she said. "Plus, I thought you should know I talked with your father."

"What did he have to say?"

"He's disappointed and mad, so be prepared for a long lecture when you get home tonight."

"I guess it's safe to say you didn't tell my father about you working at The Dollhouse."

Reverend Kane shook her head no. "I wanted to. I intended to tell him everything, but I lost the nerve at the last minute."

"Reverend Kane, are you going to continue to hide who you really are?"

"I'm still praying on it, and I know that God will forgive me because he forgives all sinners, but I'm concerned about the church. Will the congregation accept me for who I am, or will they reject me? I love that church too much to up and leave. I love the singing and the glory that is given to God in praise. On Sunday mornings I love to watch the children learn about who Jesus is, and you should see their faces when they realize what God has done for them. If I tell the church who I really am, I have to be ready for the repercussions that may follow."

"Have you ever thought about starting your own church?"

"I have, but it takes a lot to start a church. I need at least one person to support me in an endeavor that large."

"You already have one. You have Jesus."

"Yes, I do." She smiled. "Plus, I've met somebody."

"That's great!" Payce replied. "You didn't meet her at The Dollhouse, did you?"

"No, actually she's been a friend of mine for years. We recently discovered our love for one another."

"That's great. I hope that means you'll stay away from places like The Dollhouse."

"No, I'm not looking to work at anymore lesbian spas. I think I'm going to retire from that line of business." Reverend Kane parked her car a few blocks away from Payce's home.

"I guess this is where we say good-bye," Payce said. "I have to face my father. I'm not looking forward to it, but it's something I have to do."

"Payce, I admire you for facing your problems."

"That is one thing my father has always taught me and my brother—to be responsible for the wrong we've done. Thanks a lot for the ride, Reverend Kane."

Several weeks had passed since that afternoon Tressie shared with Quinton, and since then he had showed her a side of him she didn't know existed. Quinton did everything he could to prove to Tressie that they belonged together. Every week he took her out to the movies, a play, or dinner. His heartfelt generosity was refreshing. He did all the things Payce didn't. He asked about her day, what she did in class, and he was even interested in her involvement at church.

The ultimate surprise came the day he whisked her off to a secluded lake in the suburbs for a picnic and washed her feet in fresh spring water.

Tressie was definitely impressed by how attentive Quinton was to her needs, but as much as she liked Quinton, she was still in love with Payce.

Payce was her soul mate, her gift from God. She refused to end their relationship over a few mistakes.

Payce had called her a few times since his release from jail, but she wasn't ready to see him yet. She was still upset and needed some more time alone. Each time she spoke with him, he sounded so happy. Unfortunately, she couldn't return the enthusiasm. He kept asking to see her, but each time she made up excuses. She knew she couldn't hide forever. She was going to have to see him sooner or later, but in the meantime if Quinton wanted to continue to take her out and spend time with her, she wasn't going to deny herself the opportunity to have him treat her nice.

THREE MONTHS LATER

Payce and Darshon sat in Darshon's living room playing video games. They battled one another on PlayStation 2 for the championship title in *Grand Theft Auto*.

"What did your dad say?" Darshon asked.

"Of course he was ready to put me out, like so many times before. If it wasn't for my mom making such a big fuss about me not having anywhere to go, he would have put my ass on the curb."

"What about Tressie?"

"She said she forgave me, but I still feel the tension between us. When I call to ask her if we can spend some time together, she replies with one-word answers. Then I won't hear from her again until I call her. I have to find a way to make it up to her."

"Make it up to her?" Darshon exclaimed. "Man, I'm still mad at you. You were knocking women off three and four times a day and you didn't tell me. I thought we were tight. Not to mention the fact that you didn't try to share any of the wealth with me. I knew something was up. There was no way you saved that much money before you went away. But I would have never guessed this." He pointed to the front page of *The Philadelphia Inquirer*. The headline read "Madame Natasha Indicted on Twelve Counts."

Like a hurricane, Darshon's sister Lisa stormed through the front door. Her face lit up when she saw Payce sitting in her living room. "Payce, baby! I'm so glad to see you're okay. I was so worried about you." She knelt down at Payce's feet as if he were a king.

Payce laughed at her. "Lisa, would you stop?"

"I was worried about you. Wasn't I, Darshon?" She stroked the back of Payce's head.

"Lisa, leave the man alone," Darshon yelled.

Lisa ignored her brother and focused her attention on Payce. "I should be mad with you. You were working at The Dollhouse, my favorite hang out spot, and you never told me. You should have said something. I would have brought you in lots of business."

"That's all right, Lisa. I had enough clients."

"It never hurts to have more. Plus, we could have finally hooked up. I would have paid top dollar for your fine ass."

"Lisa, he doesn't want your big ass," Darshon screamed at his sister. "Go sit down somewhere. Let the man breathe."

"Sorry, Lisa. I work strictly with heterosexuals, not homosexuals," Payce told her with a smile.

"I would have jumped the fence," she replied. "Only temporarily, of course. Just long enough for me to get a taste of you." She got up and walked away. "Payce, just remember I'm waiting on you." She licked her lips and stuck out her tongue at him.

"That's nasty," Darshon commented.

"Man, reset the game. She broke my concentration," Payce told him. Then his cell phone vibrated on his hip. "Damn!" Payce said out loud. "Can I get in at least one game without any interruptions? He pulled out his cell phone and looked at the caller ID screen. It was Kai. "This girl has been calling me non-stop. She left me a million messages while I was locked up."

He flipped open the phone. "Hello."

"Payce, what's up? I'm glad I finally caught you."

"Look, Kai, I can't talk right now. I have a lot of shit going on right now. I'll have to get back with you when I have some time."

"I read about your problems in the paper, but that's not why I'm calling. I have something important I need to talk to you about and it can't wait."

"What is it, Kai?"

"Can't we meet someplace and I can explain then?"

"No," he replied. "If you want to talk, then do it now while you have me on the line. I don't know when the next time is that I'll be able to speak with you again."

She sighed. "I guess I don't have no choice but to tell you over the phone. I had a baby."

"Congratulations." He wondered why she was telling him that.

"And I think you're the father."

"What?" He jumped from his seat and walked into the kitchen. "How do you think I'm the father? Kai, I haven't seen you in months," he wailed.

"I know. I thought someone else was his father, but the paternity test results said he wasn't the father. The only other person I was with was you."

"You waited all this time to tell me?"

"I've been calling you for weeks. You wouldn't return my calls."

Payce's head began to pound. He couldn't believe this was happening to him now. "What do you want?" he asked.

"I need you to go down to the child support office and take a DNA test."

"Fine, make the arrangements and call me with the details."

Payce slammed his phone shut and sighed deeply.

"What's up?" Darshon asked.

"Man, I might be a father."

Chapter 17

Tressie ran down the subway steps and squeezed through the subway doors just before they closed. She carried her heavy book bag through the crowded train in search of an empty seat. She found a window seat next to a four-year-old boy who was coloring pages in a book.

Tressie sat by the window and watched the scenery turn from row homes to single family homes. The train suddenly made a sharp turn and forced the boy's hand to run straight across the page.

"Damn, I messed up again," he said out loud. Tressie was shocked by the youngster's choice of words.

"Qua, didn't I tell you to color inside the lines?" a teenage girl who sat on the right side of him shouted out. Annoyed, she turned her back toward him and continued her conversation on her cell phone.

"Do you want to see the picture I did today in school?" he asked Tressie.

"I sure do." He pointed to a page in his book and she smiled at the child's creative drawing. "That's beautiful!" she exclaimed. "Are you going home to show your mommy?"

"I am his mother," the young girl shouted at Tressie.

Embarrassed, Tressie criticized herself for assuming the young mother was his sister. Tressie heard her cell phone ringing in her book bag and was grateful for the distraction. She dug around in her bag before she found it. "Hello?"

"Hey, Tressie."

Tressie closed her eyes at the sound of his voice. The person she despised the most was calling her.

"It's Payne," the caller said.

"I know who it is," Tressie snapped. "What do you want, Payne?"

"Why are you being so rude?" he asked.

She realized that she was being short with him. "Forgive me. I'm sorry. What can I do for you?" she asked.

"As I was saying before your rudeness stepped in, I've scheduled a mandatory meeting for Saturday in Harrisburg."

"Since when have meetings with you been mandatory?" she screamed.

"Since I've been conference president," he responded.

"I can't come." She refused to argue with him. "I don't have to attend. You should have listed this on the schedule."

"Tressie, you have to come. I have some important items on my agenda that I need to discuss about the next annual conference meeting. I've been working on changing a few things and I need to assign projects to certain individuals, and that includes you. Tressie, please come."

He had used the word "please." That caught her off guard. She couldn't believe he was actually being polite. This meeting must really be important to him. She hadn't made any plans for the weekend, so she could attend.

"Payne, don't do this again," she berated him. "I'll be there, but don't schedule impromptu meetings and expect everyone to rearrange their schedules to accommodate you."

He sighed heavily into the phone, irritated by her complaints. "The meeting starts at three o'clock. Don't be late." He hung up on her.

She placed her phone back in her bag. She couldn't believe she had agreed to attend an unscheduled mandatory meeting for Payne. Tressie looked around the train for the adolescent mother and her son. They must have reached their stop. Only a small handful of passengers remained on the train. Tressie laid back her head and rested until her stop.

Saturday morning Tressie pulled her car into the First District Diamond Center parking lot. It was five minutes past three and there were no other cars in the lot. She couldn't believe Payne wasn't there. He was such a fanatic about everyone attending his meetings on time. Lateness annoyed him.

Tressie tried calling Mariah before she left Philly to see if they could ride up together, but she couldn't reach her.

"Hello," Tressie called out as she entered the center. Her voice echoed against the hollow walls. "I better not be the only person who showed up. If so, I'm going to personally kill Payne." She walked down the hall to the office where their meetings were usually held. She opened the door. Inside a dozen roses and a card with her name on it lay on the table. She picked up the roses and read the card.

Tressie, this place reminds me of the first time I saw you. I looked at you not with my eyes, but with my heart and with my soul. The red roses represent the world and the single white rose in the center represents how you stand out amongst the world.

Tressie heard someone walk in behind her. She twisted herself around and Payce stood in the doorway.

She ran to him. "This was so sweet. Did your brother tell you I was going to be here?"

"No, I arranged this meeting to get you out of town. I had to pay Payne to call you and arrange this bogus meeting. It wasn't easy asking Payne to do me a favor. He drove me up here early this morning and opened the center for me. He kept reminding me how much I owe him for doing this."

"You did all this for me?" Her eyes danced.

"I knew you were still mad with me for getting arrested. I needed to make things right between us. Do you like the roses?"

"I love them . . . and the card."

"I meant what I said. No one in this world can measure up to you. I don't think I could live my life without you in it." They hugged. "Let's get out of here. I made us reservations at a nearby restaurant."

They left the church conference center and went to a nearby park.

"I thought we were going to eat," she said.

"We are. The restaurant is down that trail. It overlooks the river." They held hands through Riverfront Park, and once they arrived at the restaurant, they were seated in an enclosed balcony that revealed a magnificent view of the sun setting behind the river. The red and yellow colors from the sun sparkled against the water.

Three scented candles provided light for their table. While they waited on their order, Tressie stared at the stars in the sky.

"Oh my! Did you see that shooting star?"

"No, I missed it. Did you make a wish?"

"I wished that you would have told me you were working at The Dollhouse."

"I know I messed up. But I promised myself that I would never hurt you again." He stroked the side of her face. "I should have trusted you enough to tell you the truth. From now on I'm going to be completely honest with you at all times," Payce promised.

They finished their dinner and it was time for them to head back to Philadelphia. Payce sat in the driver's seat and adjusted his seatbelt.

"I love you," Tressie purred.

"I love you, too," Payce replied.

He leaned over to kiss her and just before his lips reached hers, Tressie asked, "What's that?"

"What?" he asked.

"That. Inside your jacket."

"Oh! Nothing. Just something I had to pick up for T.J."

"If it's nothing, then show it to me. Didn't we just get done talking about trust?" she asked.

He reluctantly reached inside his jacket and pulled out a Ziploc bag full of cocaine. Before she could say anything, he tried to explain. "Don't be mad. I told T.J. that I would pick this up for him today while I was out here."

"So this trip wasn't about us. It was about drugs."

"No! I had already made arrangements to meet you when I mentioned it to T.J. He was going to come himself, but since I was already making the trip, he asked me if I would mind doing him a favor."

"And you just couldn't tell him no?"

"Tressie, he's done so many things for me in the past. What was I supposed to do?"

"Tell him no! You are out on bail!" she yelled. "You already have charges pending. What happens if you get caught with that on you?"

"Tressie, ain't nothing going to happen. When I get back to Philly, I'm taking this stuff straight to T.J."

"Didn't you just get done telling me that you would never hurt me again?" she asked.

Payce got quiet and stared straight in front of him.

"When did you have time to pick this stuff up? I've been with you all day."

"I met with the guy earlier this morning."

Tressie held her head to control her anger.

"What do you want me to do?" he asked.

"We don't have any choice but to go home with the drugs. But promise me that as soon as we get back to Philly, you will take those drugs straight to T.J."

"I promise." Payce started the car. "Trust me. We'll be fine."

Payce was on his way to Temple's main campus to pick up Tressie from school like he did every Thursday, but first he had to get rid of Kai and the baby.

"Kai, don't do this no more," he reprimanded her.

"Do what?" she asked innocently.

"You know what. You can't call me last minute and ask me to come pick you and the baby up."

"I had to take Cayden to the doctor's office and I thought that since you had only come to see him once since the paternity results proved you were the father, you'd be anxious to see your son."

"I told you I've been busy."

"Too busy to come and see your son?" she asked with an attitude.

"I told you I'll be over later this week to spend some time with him." He pulled up to the bus stop. "I'll call you tomorrow."

"You're dropping us off at the bus stop?" she screamed.

"That is how you got out here, isn't it?"

"I thought you were taking us home," Kai yelled, not budging from her seat.

"I would have, but you called me last minute. There is someplace I have to be. The next time the baby has a doctor's appointment, make sure you let me know and I will come and get the two of you myself, but today I have something to do," he explained. The baby let out a loud burp. Payce turned around to get a good look at him. He still couldn't believe that the beautiful baby was a part of him.

Payce's cell phone rang.

"I guess that's your someplace calling you," Kai replied.

Payce knew it was Tressie calling to find out where he was. "I have to go," Payce said out loud.

Kai continued to sit in the front seat, pouting.

"What are you waiting on?" he urged.

"I need some money," she shouted. "You haven't even asked me did the baby need anything."

He turned his eyes down in shame. He had forgotten to offer to buy anything.

"I need to get diapers and formula," she screamed at him.

"What happened to WIC? Can't they help you out?" he asked as he dug into his pocket.

"The last time I looked, WIC isn't the one who fathered our son," she replied sarcastically.

"Here." He shoved forty dollars in her face.

"Forty dollars! This isn't going to last long," Kai complained.

"Kai, you know my situation. You know I'm not working. I'll bring you some more money when I come over there later this week."

Kai got out and pulled the baby from the backseat while Payce grabbed the baby's carriage from the trunk.

Meanwhile, Tressie stood on the corner of Broad and Diamond searching for Payce's car. *He's usually never this late*, she thought. She looked at her watch and called him again, but got no answer.

"He must be stuck in traffic," she said out loud. She stood on the corner for another five minutes before a light rain began to fall on her head. She had forgotten to grab her umbrella before she left the house that morning. If Payce didn't show up soon, she would be soaking wet.

The raindrops got heavier and heavier, and Tressie couldn't wait any longer. She hailed down a cab.

"Can you take me to the Gallery Mall, please?" she asked the driver.

She didn't know where Payce was, but once she got to the mall she would call and leave him a message to pick her up there.

Tressie looked out the window at each passing car, hoping she would see Payce's car. The cabbie drove south down Broad Street and stopped at a red light. Waiting for the light to change, Tressie looked out the window and was shocked to see Payce with a girl and her baby. She watched as Payce kissed the baby and handed the baby carrier back to the girl. The light turned green and the cabbie pulled off.

"Wait!" she screamed. "Turn around! You have to turn around."

"You told me you wanted to go to the Gallery." His strong Middle Eastern accent slurred his words.

"I know, but I changed my mind. I need for you to follow that car." She pointed in the opposite direction.

The cabbie made a U-turn in the middle of Broad Street, changing his course from south to north.

"Go faster!" she commanded. "I know you can go faster than this. I've seen you cab drivers drive like you were in the Indy 500."

She looked ahead until she spotted Payce's car. He made a right turn onto Diamond Street. She pointed. "There he goes. Follow that Lexus."

The yellow taxi sped up and trailed Payce's car.

"Blow your horn, flash your lights," she demanded.

The cab driver followed her orders. Payce finally noticed the taxi and pulled over. Tressie jumped out of the back of the taxi and ran over to his side of the car.

"Who were you just with?" she hollered.

"Hey baby, I'm sorry I was late . . ."

"I saw why you were late. I saw you with that girl and her baby. Who is she?" Tressie yelled. The rain poured down on her head. She pulled her wet hair out of her face.

Payce watched black mascara roll down her face. The cab driver pulled up alongside Tressie.

"Ma'am, could you pay me, please?" he asked. Payce got out of his car and paid the fare.

He walked back toward her. "Tressie . . ." He took a deep breath. "We need to talk."

The rain was drenching both of them.

"No! You are going to tell me who she is!"

"Okay, but can you get in the car first?" He tried to reason with her.

She opened the passenger's side door and slammed the door shut. He got into the car and turned toward her.

"There's something I need to tell you," he uttered.

She sat on her side of the car waiting for him to explain. Tressie knew that what he had to tell her was not good.

"That girl . . ." he began, "the baby you saw me kiss . . . he's my son."

"Son?" she shouted.

"Last year, I met his mother and we hooked up for one night. Cayden was the result," he told her softly.

"You cheated on me again?!"

"Tressie, it was only that one time."

"Why should I believe you?" she screamed back at him. Her cell phone rang. She looked at the caller ID and it was Danyelle. Tressie hit the mute button. She didn't want anyone to disturb her conversation with Payce. "You had a baby and never told me."

"She didn't tell me until after I got out of jail. I wanted to tell you but I didn't know how."

Her cell phone started ringing again. It was Danyelle again. "Why do people call at inopportune times? Hello," she answered.

"Did I catch you at a bad time?" Danyelle asked. She could hear that Tressie was upset about something, but what she had to tell her couldn't wait.

"Danyelle, I really can't talk right now."

"Tressie!" she cried. "Don't hang up. I've got something important to tell you about Payce."

Tressie looked in Payce's direction. He pretended to be interested in the falling rain.

"Go ahead," Tressie responded solemnly.

"I was in Southwest Philly today getting high with this girl. We were sitting on her deck in the backyard smoking a blunt when her pregnant next-door neighbor walked out into her backyard. So Loretta, that's the girl I was getting high with, she asked me were you still dating Payce Boyd. So you know me, I'm like, 'yeah.' Well, she goes on to tell me that her neighbor, Najah, claims that she is pregnant by Payce. Girl, when she told me that news I had to put my blunt down. I almost choked on my inhale. That was some startling shit."

Tressie was silent. Danyelle wondered if she was still there. "Hello?" Danyelle called out.

"I'm here," Tressie replied. "Continue."

"Anyway, I asked was she sure and she said 'yeah' and that if I didn't believe her I could ask her myself. So I stood up and asked the girl, and she said she was pregnant by Payce Boyd."

Tressie sat in her seat sniffling, trying to hold back the tears. Danyelle regretted telling her friend this information. "Maybe I should have waited to tell you this."

"No, you did the right thing by calling me. Is he aware of this?" she asked.

Payce turned and looked at her when she asked that question.

"She said Payce knew, and he told her he would take care of his child."

"Thanks. I'll call you later tonight." She hung up with Danyelle and turned toward Payce.

"Payce," Tressie said very calmly.

He turned and looked in her direction. She swung her hand back and slapped him across the face. "You bastard. Who the hell is Najah?"

He stared at her with a blank expression.

She got out of the car and walked toward the bus stop.

"Tressie, where are you going? Get in the car. I'll take you home."

"Fuck you. I'd rather walk!" she screamed.

Chapter 18

Tressie took one last look at herself in the mirror. The strawberry flavored lip gloss she bought at the mall added luster to her lips. She rubbed her lips together and stuck the tube of lip gloss in her purse. She and Quinton were going out and he wouldn't tell her where they were going, but he did promise her it would be a night she would never forget.

The day after Tressie found out about Payce's two children, she ran to Quinton for comfort.

"I hate him," she told Quinton.

"You don't mean that," he responded. "You're just really upset right now."

"You're right. I don't hate him, but he makes me sick and I don't want to see him ever again. I've had enough of being mistreated."

"Does that mean you're a free woman?" Quinton asked.

"Um . . . yeah. I guess it does." It never occurred to her that she was once again a single woman.

"Good, because I was serious when I said I wanted us to be a couple again."

"Quinton, I . . ."

"Before you say no, hear me out," Quinton inter-rupted. "I know you want to clear your head and get Payce out of your mind, but there is no better way to do that than to let me into your life. I can help you forget about Payce. I want a chance to make you happy. You deserve to smile all the time. Plus, if you and I are together, Payce will know that it is really over between the two of you."

Tressie was scared to jump into another rela-tionship so soon after her breakup with Payce, but Quinton did have a point. She needed to show Payce that they were finished, and she knew Quinton would keep his promise to treat her good.

"All right, we can give it a try and see how things work out."

"I promise I will not let you down," he exclaimed.

Tressie heard Quinton's voice downstairs and glanced at her reflection in the mirror one last time. She ran her fingers through her hair and straightened out her skirt over her hourglass figure. "Perfect," she said to herself.

She ran down the stairs. "You look lovely," Quinton said.

"Thanks," she replied. "Are you ready?"

"Yes." He shook her father's hand and said good-night to her mother. He held the door open for her and escorted her out to his car.

"Why are you acting so formal?" she asked. "I'm not used to you acting this way."

He whispered in her ear, "It's strictly for the parents. They want to make sure their only daughter is going out with someone respectable." Quinton turned around and waved good-bye to her parents, who stood in the doorway watching.

"You don't have to put on a show for my parents. You're considered a good catch after some of the other guys I've brought home."

"Well, I don't want them to see me as a good catch. I want them to look at me as their future son-in-law."

She laughed. "You're moving kind of fast, aren't you?"

"Not at all. I already know who I want to spend my life with. I just hope she wants to do the same," he replied.

Tressie felt uncomfortable talking about a future with Quinton when her heart still belonged to Payce. She quickly changed the subject. "Where are you taking me?"

"I told you it was a surprise."

"You can't give me a hint?" she pleaded.

"Don't do that. You make me hot when you do that."

"Pleeeeeeeeease," she whined.

"I can't win," he said. "I'm taking you to see AI."

"Stop playing. Are you for real?"

"Here go the tickets right here." He pulled out a pair of tickets he had stashed under his seat.

"Oh my gosh!" she examined the Sixers tickets. "These are floor seats," she screamed. "I'm going to be so close to Allen that I can see those gorgeous eyes and those pretty lips and . . ."

"Excuse me," Quinton interrupted. "I am the one who is taking you to the game. Please don't forget that you'll be sitting next to your date."

"Oh no, honey! I won't forget about you. But if Allen looks my way, act like you're with the people sitting on the other side of you." She laughed. "I'm just playing. I would never trade you for him."

They arrived at the Wachovia Center just in time to hear the starting lineup for Philadelphia. The Sixers were playing the Pistons and the arena was packed with fans.

"Wow, it looks a whole lot different down here than it does in the nosebleed seats," she screamed.

Music blared from the speakers and the Seventy-Sixers dance team ran onto the court dressed in red and black biker shorts with pom-poms in their hands. The head cheerleader directed the girls to different positions, and they followed her lead.

"That girl looks familiar," Tressie said, referring to the head cheerleader. "Do we know her?"

"She doesn't look familiar to me," Quinton said.

When the girl turned around, Tressie looked closely at her face. "It's Mariah. She's our church conference treasurer. I didn't know she was a dancer," Tressie said.

Mariah led the girls through two dance routines before the buzzer sounded and the girls dashed off the court.

For the entire game, Tressie yelled and cheered Allen Iverson on. AI rebounded, blocked shots, stole the ball, and scored four three-pointers all in one quarter. Quinton was sure Tressie would lose her voice by the end of the game.

The Sixers were down by one and the game clock didn't have much time left. Seconds ticked away. Iverson had the ball. He ran full speed toward the basket. To make the shot before the buzzer sounded, he threw the ball from half court. The fans rose to their feet and watched as the ball swished gracefully through the net just before the buzzer sounded. Iverson had done it again—a last second shot that was the deciding factor in whether this game would go into the win or loss column.

"That was great!" Tressie exclaimed.

"Yeah, that was a good game," Quinton agreed. "I'm glad we came."

"Mariah! Mariah!" Tressie called out to her friend.

Mariah rushed over to the sidelines.

"Hey girl," she said breathlessly. "I saw you over here. I'm surprised to see you here."

"This was a surprise from my boyfriend," Tressie said.

Mariah smiled at Quinton and wondered where Payce was.

"Quinton, this is a friend of mine, Mariah."

They shook hands and greeted one another.

"You are a really talented dancer," he said, complimenting her. "Have you been dancing for long?"

"I've been a part of the basketball dance team for the past three years. I started at the bottom and worked my way up."

"Mariah, why didn't you ever tell me you were a dancer?"

"Because I'm not a dancer. I'm an aspiring dancer, still looking to land my big break. I go on auditions just about every day praying that this will be my chance."

"Girl, keep praying. Your dreams will come true."

"Man, the Sixers killed Detroit." Payce grabbed his coat from his seat. "Detroit lost their defense; both Rasheed and Ben were hurt, allowing the Sixers to walk all over them."

Darshon looked down at the court from the balcony. "Yo, man, isn't that Tressie down there talking to that fine cheerleader?"

Payce turned and saw Tressie holding hands with another guy. He thought his eyes were deceiving him. He stared down at the girl that Darshon pointed to. It really was Tressie.

"Who's the guy she's with?" Darshon asked.

Payce knew that Tressie was mad at him, but he didn't think she would go out with somebody else.

"I didn't know you two had broken up," Darshon said.

"We didn't."

"Well, I think someone oughta tell her that, 'cause it looks like she's on a date with some other dude."

"Come on, man." Payce raced toward the stairs.

"Man, don't start no fight. You can't afford to go back to jail," Darshon yelled.

Payce searched the entire lower level for Tressie and the guy she was with, but saw no sign of them anywhere.

"Payce, look at all these people. You're never going to find her," Darshon screamed above the spectators trying to go home. People pushed past them. "Why don't you just wait until you get home and call her?"

"No, she won't take any of my calls. I just want to talk to her. Wait a minute." He thought for a second. "Mariah. She would know where Tressie went." He ran toward the cheerleaders' locker room and waited outside for Mariah to come out.

Minutes passed before Mariah walked out carrying her gym bag. "Mariah!" Payce screamed.

She jumped at the sound of her name being screamed so loudly. "Payce, what are you doing here?" She was surprised to see him.

"I saw you talking to Tressie," he exclaimed. "Where is she?"

"She was here, but she's probably left by now," Mariah lied.

"Who was that she was with?" Payce asked.

Mariah wasn't going to give Payce any information about Quinton. He would have to ask Tressie about that. "I'm not sure," she replied.

"She didn't introduce you to the guy?"

"She introduced us, but she just said he was a friend of hers." Mariah quickly pretended to look for something in her bag, hoping to hide her dishonesty.

Mariah's body language told Payce she was lying. He wondered what secret she was hiding from him.

"I thought you two broke up," she said.

"Did she say that?" he asked.

"No, I just assumed. Look, Payce, I have to go. The girls from the dance team are waiting on me."

"Payce, come on, let's go," Darshon urged. "She doesn't know anything. You can call Tressie in the morning."

Payce realized he wasn't getting anywhere with Mariah. "Mariah, can you do me a favor? Tell her that I love her," he said sadly.

Mariah felt bad for lying to him. She wished she could tell him that Tressie was waiting in front of the Wachovia Center for her, but she knew it would be best if he left and talked with her later. She watched him walk away with his head down. Once Payce was out of sight, Mariah ran to the side entrance and around to the front of the building. She hoped Payce wouldn't see them on his way out, but once she turned the corner, she saw Payce marching in Quinton and Tressie's direction.

Damn, she thought. *I did everything I could.*

Tressie hugged Quinton tightly. "Thanks for bringing me to the game," she whispered in his ear.

"No problem. You know I would do anything for you."

Tressie blushed. She looked over Quinton's shoulder just in time to see Payce coming their way with Darshon not too far behind him. "Oh no," she softly mumbled.

Quinton saw the worried look on her face and turned to see what had her so concerned.

"Tressie, can I speak to you for a moment?" Payce asked.

"We don't have anything to talk about," she replied.

Payce stared at Quinton as Mariah ran up to the four of them.

"Tressie, I just want to talk to you," Payce said again.

"Talk to me about what?" she screamed.

"I've been trying to apologize, but you won't let me."

"Apologize? Apologize for what? Apologize for conceiving two children outside of our relationship? Apologize for cheating on me? Or apologize for me finding out the truth from someone else?"

Payce tried to move closer to her, but Quinton stepped between them. "Man, she said she doesn't want to talk," Quinton firmly addressed Payce.

Tressie could feel the tension in the air. She didn't want the scene to turn into a fight. "Payce, we're over. I have a new boyfriend." She grabbed Quinton's hand firmly.

"New boyfriend? How could you have a new boyfriend? We haven't broken up," he yelled. Payce slammed his fist into his hand. "Last week we were a couple and this week you're in a new relationship? There is no way you could have found a new man that quick unless . . ." The reality of what was going on suddenly dawned on him. "You were going out with him while I was locked up. You played me."

Tressie was silent.

"You told me you would wait for me." He pointed his finger at her. "You cried about how I lied to you when you were lying to me, too."

"Payce, it wasn't like that," Tressie tried to explain.

"Sure it was. You were spending time with this buster while I was away."

"Man, you don't know me like that," Quinton spoke up.

Darshon pushed in front of Payce. "Player, I suggest you step back. What's going on between my man and his girl is between them. It doesn't concern you."

"Everyone calm down!" Mariah screamed. "If everyone doesn't calm down, the police will be over here. We don't want to give them a reason to drag us down to the precinct."

"Tressie, you betrayed me," Payce said in her face. "You were the one person I thought I could count on."

He turned to walk away, but before he did she jumped in his face.

"Don't you dare try to turn this on me. Betrayal is what you're made of. You have broken my heart over and over again. You've taken my trust in you as a weakness. You think you can do whatever you want to do and I will always take you back because I love you. Not this time."

He knew the words she spit at him were the truth. He turned and stormed away.

After dropping Mariah off, Quinton and Tressie rode in silence, neither sure of what to say.

"Are you all right?" he asked. "I know that was hard for you."

A tear fell from her eye. The pressure of confronting Payce was wearing down on her. She was so mad at Payce for being angry with her that it made her upset.

"I know that you're still in love with Payce. I could see it in your eyes, and I'm sure he could see it, too. That's why it bothered him so much to see you with me."

"I feel so bad. He trusted me and I deceived him. I'm no better than him."

"You shouldn't feel that way. You two are no longer together because of problems he created in your relationship—not you."

"Quinton, I think it was wrong for me to start seeing you so soon after Payce. I'm still unsure about my feelings for him. Seeing him tonight made me think that maybe I was wrong. When I found out about his children, I never gave him a chance to explain. I need to sit down and talk things over with him. If I don't, I will always wonder what the truth was behind our split."

"Sweetheart, I think you're in shock over having to face him so soon after your break up. Once people start seeing us together more often they will begin to accept our relationship, and it will be easier for you to accept us."

"This has nothing to do with me and you. It has to do with Payce and me not ending our relationship the right way," she explained. "You said you wanted my mind, body, heart, and soul, but right now I can only offer you my mind and body. My heart and soul are still with Payce. You deserve to be with someone who can give themselves to you entirely."

Quinton listened to her heart-wrenching words.

"Would you mind if we took a break from seeing each other for a while?"

He didn't want to admit it, but she was right. He did want all of her. He wanted her to look at him the same way she looked at Payce. "I guess I don't have any choice."

"Can I have a kiss to last me until we meet again?" she asked.

He leaned over and kissed her lightly. Tressie cared for Quinton, but the feelings she held for Payce were so much stronger.

Chapter 19

"Tressie, what's up?" Tressie heard Darshon's voice and hoped he was calling her for Payce. She had tried calling Payce every night since the basketball game, but he wouldn't return any of her calls. "Hey Darshon, what's up?"

"I'm sorry for just getting back to you. I know you called me a few weeks ago, but I had forgotten that you called and I just remembered. So what's up?"

She sat for a moment trying to remember why she had called Darshon, "Oh yeah. I did call you. I called because I had planned on throwing a surprise birthday party for Payce, but since he won't speak to me, I'm going to cancel the party."

"Tressie, he was really upset about seeing you with that guy."

"Did he say he was upset?"

"No, but you know how guys are. They never want to show their true feelings. He's my best friend. I know when something is bothering him, but if it helps you to know, I think he misses you."

Tressie was glad to hear that he missed her. That meant he still had feelings for her. "Darshon, let me ask you a question. Do you think if I go

ahead and throw this surprise party for Payce that
he'll forgive me?"

"I don't know, Tressie. He was really mad. I don't
know if a party will make him forget what he saw."

"I know, but I've already reserved the Borgata
Ballroom. I spent all my money to put this party
together, so I really don't have anything to lose.
I'm going to go ahead and still throw the party."

"Wow, this is going to be a nice party. You must
have put out a lot of loot to reserve the Borgata
Ballroom. How are you planning on getting him to
Atlantic City?" Darshon asked.

"I'm going to leave that to you. He trusts you.
Tell him you're taking him to Atlantic City to gam-
ble. I'll need for you to get him there no later than
eleven o'clock. That will allow the guests enough
time to get there before him," she instructed.

"No problem."

"Darshon, are you sure you can get him there?"
she asked a second time.

"Trust me," Darshon replied. "I've already
thought of a plan."

"Payce, would you come on? Man, you take longer than a woman," Darshon yelled up the stairs.
He impatiently sat on the couch next to Payne
and made small talk. "So Payne, what do you have
planned for your birthday?" Darshon asked.

"I have something special planned for my brother and me."

"Cake and ice cream at the church?" Darshon joked.

"No, imbecile," Payne replied. "It's a surprise."

Payce raced down the stairs dressed to the nines. He posed for an imaginary camera in a fancy pair of black dress pants and a solid burgundy button-up dress shirt. This was the only time Payne and Payce had ever dressed alike. The only noticeable difference between the two of them was Payne's pants stopped way above his ankles. Payce walked over to Darshon and gave him a pound. "What's up, man?"

"Man, I hear you're going out with your brother tonight. You two celebrating your birthdays together?"

"Yeah, man. This is the first time since we were kids," Payce responded. "He keeps bragging about how he has something special planned. I can't wait to see what it is."

"I bet it's something out of this world," Darshon snickered. "Can I holla at you outside for a second?" Darshon asked Payce.

"Sure."

They walked toward the front door when Payne jumped in front of them and blocked the exit, preventing them from leaving.

"No!" he shouted. "If you go outside with him, you'll leave, and I'll never see you again."

Darshon laughed. He walked over and put his arm around Payne. "Relax, man. I think you had too much sugar today. I'm not going to kidnap your brother. I just wanna speak with him."

Payne looked at the two of them suspiciously. "All right, but I'll be watching you two."

They moved him out of the way and laughed at his attempt to prevent them from leaving the house.

Once they were outside Darshon spoke quietly. He could see Payne peeping at them through the living room blinds. "Man, I don't know what your brother has planned for tonight, but the fellows and I had something we wanted to do for your birthday."

"It doesn't have anything to do with The Dollhouse, does it?"

"No, it's legit."

"Darshon, I would love to hang with you guys, but I promised my brother that I'd go out with him."

"I understand, but can't you just come out with us for an hour? You can meet up with him later. Payne is probably going to take you to the church for his annual birthday celebration."

"I don't know, man. You saw how he was just acting. He's not going to let me out of his sight."

"Leave it to me," Darshon replied.

"Payne!" Darshon yelled.

Payne hurried outside.

"Payce and I were going to hit the liquor store in Camden. Do you want to ride?"

"Do you really want to go to Camden at this time of night? It is dark outside," he replied. Payce and Darshon both knew that Payne was scared of the small, but edgy city of Camden, New Jersey. Camden was listed as one of the most dangerous cities in the country. Old wives tales circulated throughout Philadelphia about how visitors entered Camden, but never left.

"We're going to pick up some liquor. That's the only place that sells alcohol this time of night. Are you coming or what?" he urged.

Payne was hesitant to accompany them.

"Forget it, Payne. We'll see you when we get back," Darshon told him. He looked at his watch. Tressie had said to be there no later than eleven o'clock. His watch said a little past nine.

"No, wait. I'll ride with you. Let me go grab my jacket," Payne said.

On their way out of the city, Darshon stopped to pick up T.J. and John. The five of them took the Atlantic City Expressway east.

"We passed Camden thirty minutes ago," Payne yelled out.

"Payne, relax," Darshon told him. "You are the one who said you wanted to come."

"I thought we were going to Camden. Darshon has kidnapped us and now we're going to miss my surprise."

"Payne, you really are a pain," Darshon stressed. "Just to let you know, I have my own surprise for Payce."

"What about what I had planned?" Payne whined.

"Payne, forget about the shindig you put together for Payce. You will have a lot more fun with us. What was it you were going to do?"

Payne didn't want to spoil his surprise, but he knew that what he had arranged for the evening was already ruined. "I planned on cake and ice cream."

The car exploded with laughter.

"I told you," Darshon giggled. "Payne, you do the same thing every year, cake and ice cream at the church."

"No, no. This year it wasn't going to be at the church. Reverend Kane offered to hold the festivities at her house."

The car got quiet. Payce had told T.J and John about Reverend Kane. The only person who didn't know about Reverend Kane's double life was Payne.

"Why did everyone get so quiet?" he asked.

"No reason," Payce responded. "No offense, man, but I'm glad we didn't go to Reverend Kane's."

"Why? She told me she likes you."

Payce would never tell his brother Reverend Kane's secret. "You know what?" He put his arm around Payne. "It doesn't matter where we spend our birthday. As long as we're together."

An hour later they pulled up in front of the Borgata Hotel and Casino. They walked in and gazed at a vastly colored sculpture that hung in the front lobby.

"Darshon, you brought us to Satan's den. I'm going to Hell. God is going to punish us all!" Payne exclaimed with his hand in the air.

"Thanks, this is cool," Payce said to Darshon and walked toward the casino entrance.

"Sorry fellas. The casino is not the surprise. Payce's birthday surprise is in the ballroom," Darshon announced.

"I knew this was too good to be true," Payce exclaimed. "Darshon never plans anything without any women."

They followed Darshon down a winding corridor. "Payce, you're right, I wouldn't plan anything without women being involved." The archway opened up to a landing that was immersed in music. "But I didn't plan this."

They approached the balcony and Payce looked down. Dancing away on the dance floor were dozens of couples, young and old, doing the two-step. A banner hung along the wall that said "Happy Birthday, Payce!"

Payce turned to Darshon. "This party is for me?" he asked.

Darshon nodded his head yes.

"Thanks, man. I would have never guessed," Payce said, smiling.

"Don't thank me. Thank Tressie. Tressie is the one who planned it." He pointed down to Tressie who stood among a crowd of people. A wide smile appeared on Payce's face as he rushed to her.

"Happy birthday," she said to him. "You look very debonair." She pulled a single white rose from behind her back. "This white rose represents you, because you stand out from all the rest." He smiled at her choice of words.

"Can I have this dance?" she asked.

"I can't dance," he replied.

"That's all right. I'll teach you."

Payce followed Tressie's lead and matched every step she took. While they danced, a lot of Payce's friends stopped to wish the guest of honor happy birthday. Payce saw T.J., John, and Darshon each trying to step on the dance floor. Even Payne had found himself a dance partner.

Tressie and Payce danced for more than an hour before Payce started sweating. His steps got sluggish and he moved slower and slower.

"Do you want to stop?" she asked him.

"No, no. I'm all right."

Tressie grabbed his hand and led him to a nearby table. "We should stop. I don't want the birthday boy to pass out on me."

"I really appreciate you throwing me this party," Payce said to her.

"I had to do something. You wouldn't return my calls."

"I was mad," he replied.

"So was I. At least I tried to straighten things out."

"How does your boyfriend feel about you throwing me this party?"

"He's not my boyfriend anymore. I asked him if we could take a break until I was able to get over you."

"That's what you want to do? Get over me?" he asked.

"No, I would like for things to work out between the two of us, but I'm not sure if it will ever be the same."

"I wasn't really mad when I found you with that guy. I think I was more surprised. After all the things I've done to you, I had no reason to get upset when you started seeing someone else. I'm the one who messed things up between us."

"Payce, I have to take my share of the responsibility. I knew exactly what I was doing every time I accepted Quinton's invitation to spend time together. I should have kept my promise and waited for you to be released from jail."

"If I would have been a man and been honest and truthful with you from the beginning, none of this would have happened, so I'll take the blame."

Tressie looked at him and smiled. "Okay, if you insist. You can take all the blame."

He laughed. She was definitely the girl he fell in love with.

She laid her head on his shoulder. "You have no idea how disappointed I was to hear you had two children without me. I wanted to be the one to give you your first child. Now you've given that gift to two women you don't even love."

"Tressie, I promise that you and I will have a family of our own. Although I already have two children, I welcome the day when you and I can have our own."

"I love you."

And they sealed their love with a kiss.

Chapter 20

Payce kissed Tressie on the shoulder. "I'm going to miss you."

"I'm going to miss you more," she replied.

They lay in her bed wrapped in nothing but a sheet. They took advantage of Tressie's parents' long weekend getaway by having their own private getaway. This was their last night together before he reported to court the following day. His lawyer forewarned him that his parole would be revoked and he would have to serve out the final three years of his prison sentence.

The hardest thing for him to accept wasn't going back to jail, but leaving Tressie behind. She was the most valuable thing in the world to him. He had never opened up his heart to anyone until he met her. A lot of the girls he met in the past he used as toys, but Tressie was different. She was the kind of woman he dreamed of spending his life with, a woman who would stand by his side no matter the circumstance.

He pulled his arms around her tighter. Their eyes locked and silence seized the moment as their spirits took a hold of one another and wouldn't let go. It seemed as if God had taken the blinders off their eyes and they could see for the first time their destiny as soul mates.

"I need to talk to you about something." Payce broke away from their shared moment. "I'm going to be away for three years and a lot can happen during that time."

"Three years won't stop me from loving you."

"You're familiar with that old saying 'out of sight, out of mind?' The last time I was only away for six days and someone managed to steal you away from me. This time I'll be away for years."

Tressie was embarrassed at how she had allowed a moment of weakness to overcome her.

"If you meet someone, don't hold yourself back because of me. We can use this time as a test. If we were really meant to be, then no one you go out with will be able to come between us. Of course we'll write and I'll call you, but if it is really meant for us to be together, we'll weather this storm. Do you understand?"

She nodded.

"Promise me one thing?"

"Anything," she replied.

"Don't go out with Quinton."

"What's wrong with Quinton?" she asked.

"I don't like him. He's not someone I'd like to see you with."

"Don't be jealous," she responded.

"I'm not jealous. I think that when you two got together he took advantage of the situation. He knew I was locked up and went after you. I don't trust him. Let's change the subject. I don't want to spend my last night with you talking about him. Where is the shoe box of money that I gave to you?" he asked.

"I put it in the bottom of my closet."

"I need you to hold on to that money until I come home."

"That's a lot of money. You trust me with ten thousand dollars in cash?"

"I trust you with my life," he replied.

It warmed her heart to hear him say those words.

"Before I forget, can you leave me your Social Security Number before you leave in the morning?" she asked.

"What do you need that for?"

"I have to check your credit report just in case we ever get married. My mother believes that a man is only as good as his credit. She has always told me that a man who pays his bills on time will always take care of you."

"Well, what does she say about a man who doesn't have any credit because I don't believe I've ever applied for anything before?"

"I don't know what she says about that. I'll have to ask her."

She laid her head against his chest and drifted off to sleep.

At sunrise, Payce got up and dressed. He sat on the side of the bed for a second and watched Tressie sleep. *She is so beautiful*, he thought. He knew he was a really lucky guy to have her by his side. He had put her through hell and she still loved him.

"God," he whispered softly, "watch out for her. She's a good girl who deserves the best. I'm not going to be around, so can you send a few angels to look out for her until I come home? Thanks."

He got up, grabbed his bag, and left a single white rose lying next to her. He kissed her lips. "I love you," he told her one last time and left.

A few hours later Tressie woke up to the sound of her alarm. She turned over, hit the off button, and opened her eyes. She felt around for Payce. He was gone and in his place was a white rose. She held the flower up to her nose to get a whiff of its faint fragrance. *He left without saying good-bye*, she thought. A tear rolled down her cheek. She had hoped to touch his face one more time before he went to jail. The next time she laid eyes on him would be through a glass partition.

She understood why he left the way he did. Neither of them could bear the thought of saying good-bye. She trembled at the thought of what was going to happen later that day in court. She suppressed the urge to throw on her clothes and run down to the courthouse. She envisioned throwing herself at the mercy of the court and begging them to release the only man she'd ever loved. But she knew deep down inside it didn't matter what she did, Payce was still going to have to do the time. She missed him already—his smile, his corny jokes.

She sat up, threw her legs off the side of her bed, and looked out the window. Dark storm clouds lingered above her house. Her first morning class started in forty-five minutes, but she couldn't concentrate on school. All she could think about was Payce. She lay back down in bed and wrapped the blankets around herself.

After watching an afternoon full of talk shows, Tressie got bored and turned on her computer. "I might as well get some school work done," she mumbled. She shook the mouse connected to her computer and knocked over a small piece of scrap paper. She picked it up from off the floor. Written inside was Payce's Social Security number. *He remembered.* In no time, she logged onto the Equifax Web site, entered Payce's Social Security number, and answered a few questions. Within minutes a copy of his credit report appeared on the screen.

She scanned the report carefully. The only debt he owed was to a cellular wireless company. The outstanding balance was a little over two hundred dollars.

"That's not bad. We can handle that," she said.

She scrolled down. Listed at the bottom were two judgments against him for child support. The balance exceeded thirty-five thousand dollars.

"Thirty-five thousand dollars!" she screamed. "For two children under the age of one he owes thirty-five thousand dollars?" She studied the report more carefully. "How in the world did he accumulate a debt this large?"

She remembered her friend Hope who had gotten married last year. Her husband had three children from a previous marriage. He was also behind in his child support payments. Once they got married, anything they tried to get on credit was denied.

Hope told her that there was no way of escaping child support. They couldn't get a house, a car, or a credit card. They couldn't even get approved for an apartment. Currently they were living in a garage apartment atop his momma's house.

Tressie figured that by the time Payce was released, his debt would have tripled. *Another obstacle*, she thought. Every time she and Payce got closer, something was there to tear them apart. Anxiety filled her stomach.

"What am I supposed to do?" she yelled.

The phone rang loudly in her ear. She stared at it for a moment. Not wanting to talk with anyone, she reluctantly answered it. "Hello."

"Hello," a woman called out from the other end. "I have a collect call from Payce. Will you accept the charges?"

"Yes, I will," Tressie replied.

"Hello," Payce screamed into the phone. Tressie could hear cars driving by in the distance.

"Payce, where are you?" she asked suspiciously.

"Tressie, I can't talk right now. I need you to listen. I jumped bail."

"You did what?"

"I couldn't go back to jail. I got scared and ran."

"Honey, we need to sit down and talk this through rationally. If you go down to the courthouse now, things won't be that bad."

"I can't, Tressie. You don't how it is to be locked up. Those cells are cages and the inmates are the animals. Being confined plays with your mind. You're not just physically locked up, but also mentally."

"Payce, I understand what you're saying, but running is not going to solve the problem. Tell me where you are and I'll come and get you."

"Remember when I told you about the safe house that the fellows and I bought out of state for emergencies?"

"Yes, I remember."

"Well that's where I am."

"Okay, just tell me how to get there and I'll be on my way."

"I don't want to say too much over the phone. I have already talked to Darshon. He's on his way to bring you the directions on how to get here. When you get here I want us to get married. I don't want to wait any longer. I want you to be my wife."

"What about my family?" she asked. "My mother will be devastated if she isn't there to see me get married."

"Tressie, we don't have to have a big wedding right now. We can go to the justice of peace. I promise you we will have a big wedding later. All right?"

"I suppose," she replied.

"I'm going to hang up. I'll talk to you later tonight." Before she hung up, he called out her name.

"Yes?" She replied. She thought he had remembered at the last minute to tell her he loved her.

"Don't forget to bring that shoe box full of money," he told her.

"I won't," she replied, disappointed.

She hung up the phone and began to pack her things. She pulled out sneakers, jeans, and sweaters. If Payce needed her, she was going to be there for him. She glanced over at her computer. Payce's credit report was still displayed on the screen.

What am I going to do? Payce wants to get married now. Does it really matter that he owes thirty-five thousand dollars in child support? Will he think I'm being selfish if I tell him I don't want to get married because of his children and the money he owes?

She sat on the side of the bed for a moment to think. *What about all the things that Payce has done to me?* She loved him, but she questioned his love for her. Would anyone else have gone through the things she did to make their love last? He was arrested for prostitution, cheated on her twice, had two children outside of their relationship, and endangered her freedom. Now he had a child support balance of over thirty-five thousand dollars. Elise's words echoed in her mind. *Things happen for a reason. Some things weren't meant to be.*

"God, what am I supposed to do?" she cried out. She needed someone to talk to. She picked up the phone and called the only person she knew who would be honest with her.

An hour later Danyelle sat in Tressie's room.

"What do you think I should do?" Tressie asked.

"Did you pray on it?" Danyelle asked.

"No," Tressie replied.

"Did you look to the Bible for answers?"

"Yes, and I couldn't find anything in there that pertained to Payce and me," Tressie told her.

"That's hard for me to believe. Hand me that Bible please."

Danyelle held a blunt in one hand as she reached for the Bible in the other. She began searching through the Bible.

"What about this—Ephesians 5:25: 'Husbands must love their wives with the same love Christ showed the church. He gave up his life for her.'"

"Payce loves me," Tressie said, defending herself and Payce.

"I didn't say he didn't love you, but to what extent does he love you? Does he love you enough to always put your interests before his? Did he put your interests before his when he picked up that bag full of cocaine in Harrisburg?"

"That was an isolated incident. Danyelle, watch what you're doing. You're burning up the Bible."

Danyelle looked down. She had dropped a few ashes on the pages she was reading from.

"My fault," she wiped away the ashes. "Listen to this. I Corinthians 13:4-5: 'Love is patient and kind. Love is not jealous or boastful or proud or rude. Love does not demand its own way. Love is not irritable, and it keeps no record of when it has been wronged.' Does that describe you and Payce?"

"I think so," Tressie replied.

"Tressie, you can't think, you have got to *know*. We are talking about your future. Do you trust Payce with your future? You know I'm not going to tell you not to be with Payce, because I like him. But if you're thinking about marrying him, you have to be sure he's the one for you. Let's be honest, he has put you through a lot."

"I can't blame him for all the problems we've been having. I did cheat on him with Quinton."

"I wouldn't consider Quinton cheating. Quinton was a test to see if you really loved Payce, and you failed."

"You can't tell me that I don't love Payce just because I made one mistake."

"You have to ask yourself, was Quinton a mistake or were you drawn to him because there was something not quite right in your relationship with Payce? The only reason you and Quinton aren't together right now is because *you* chose to go back to Payce."

Danyelle closed the Bible. "Did Darshon bring over the directions on how to get there?"

"Yeah, they're sitting over there on the desk." She pointed to a sheet of paper. Danyelle went over and glanced at the directions, then placed them back on the desk.

"Take a day or two to sit and pray on it, and if you still feel the need to go to him, go ahead and go. Just call me first and let me know."

Tressie nodded her head okay. Danyelle grabbed her things and left. Once she got into her car, she pulled out her cell phone and made a call.

"Hello, Philadelphia Police Department," a woman answered.

"Yes, I'd like to report the whereabouts of a fugitive on the run," Danyelle informed her.

"Hold, please. I'll connect you to a detective."

Tressie, if you won't remove Payce from your life, then I'll have to do it for you. I just hope that you'll forgive me, Danyelle thought.

Julian watched his plasma flat screen television in the den. Station after station reported the results of his latest drug test. He had tested positive for steroid use.

The NBA was known to perform random drug testing on their players, but this came as a complete surprise to him. On Monday afternoon, the team had just finished practice for the day when the general manager called him into the office. It was then that he learned he had been randomly selected to take an on-the-spot drug test.

Although the league insists they don't know who is going to be selected for drug testing until that day, players were usually warned weeks in advance. One of Julian's teammates later told him that he overheard someone say that Julian's name had been switched with another player's. Suspicion arose in Julian's mind as to why he was singled out for drug testing.

He refilled his glass with Hennessy and stood in front of the television screen. He watched as a reporter interviewed Carlos Torres.

The reporter stuck the microphone in his face and asked, "How do you feel about Julian Pennington's current drug test results?"

"Whatever Julian is going through right now I'm sure he would appreciate the media's cooperation by respecting his privacy," Carlos responded and walked away.

Julian shook his head at the screen. He was glad he had friends like Carlos who didn't judge him.

"Julian?"

He turned around and saw Caitlyn standing in the doorway with a suitcase in her hand.

"Where are you going?" he asked.

"I'm moving back home," she said. "I'm going to go stay with my parents for a few weeks."

"What brought this on?" he brazenly inquired.

"My uncle thought it would be best if I put some distance between us. Not permanently, just until the suspicion of your drug use is straightened out."

He turned his attention back to the television. "You're walking out on me?"

"No!" She ran to him and wrapped her arms around his waist. "I would never walk out on you. We're still going to see each other and if you need me, all you have to do is call." She exhaled. "My uncle is scared that if the press suspects that we're a couple and living together, that they may try to connect your steroid use to the team. He said that the press could say that management coerced your drug use by pressuring you to dominate the court because you were dating the owner's niece. Any negative publicity could affect the entire Sonics organization."

"Caitlyn!" Julian grabbed her hands. "I need you here. Everyone is abandoning me. My family won't return any of my phone calls, I'm suspended from the league, and now you're leaving me!" he shouted. He fell back down on the couch and placed his head in his hands.

"I'm just trying to do what's best for everyone," Caitlyn cried.

"Go!" Julian mumbled. "Go! Leave! I don't want you here. A few nights ago you told me you loved me. Now, at a time in my life when I need you the most, you're going to bail out on me. You never loved me. You loved what I represented. I was a black man with lots of money who could buy you whatever you wanted. That's what you loved."

"That's not true!" she protested. "The only reason I'm leaving is because my family is concerned about me. They thought it would be best if I stayed with them for a while."

"Oh! Now I understand. Your parents are scared that your black boyfriend might lose it from all the drugs he's been using, and hurt their little girl."

"They would never say that."

"They didn't have to say it, because that's what they were thinking. I wonder how they would react if they found out that their baby girl forged a doctor's signature to get me that prescription for steroids."

"Julian, I'm scared!" Caitlyn screamed. "I'm sorry I ever convinced you to take those pills. I was just trying to help. You put so much importance on being named rookie of the year. I knew how badly you wanted to prove yourself to be the best. I thought maybe the steroids would help, but now I realize that I've made things worse, and I may have ruined your career."

Julian stared at her as she cried. He knew it was over between the two of them. She never loved him. She was in love with what he represented, not who he was as a person.

"Good-bye, Caitlyn."

She looked at him and knew that his good-bye was forever. She slowly rose to her feet and grabbed her suitcase.

After she left, silence filled the room. He was completely alone. Never in his entire life had he ever been alone—his mother, his stepfather, Valencia, someone was always around supporting him. Memories of crowds cheering him on, applause from fans in the stands, the sound of his mother's voice giving him praise, classmates holding banners with his name on them, and Valencia sitting in the bleachers beaming with pride filled his mind. Except now there were no fans, no cheers, and no Valencia. He got up and threw the glass he was holding into the fireplace.

Chapter 21

Val, Olivia, Danyelle, and Tressie gathered together at the church for their weekly Bible Study meeting.

Val watched Bryce sleep soundly in her arms. "Look at him. He has no idea of the drama that has surrounded his little life. I still can't believe that Bryant was going to sell his own son."

"And he would have been successful if Mr. Murray hadn't found him in time," Olivia said. "I feel sorry for Taima, though. She still doesn't know where her little girl is. The police are trying to help her locate the couple who adopted her daughter, but it's going to take a while. I'm sure the uncertainty of whether her child is being well cared for is driving her insane." She picked up Bryce's hand and kissed his fingers.

"Do you know how much prison time Bryant could get?" Val asked.

"I'm not sure, but I hope he gets life without parole. The prosecutor's office contacted me and asked if I would testify against Bryant. They let me know that the Greensboro Police did a background check into Bryant's past. This isn't the first time he's done this. They have a list of girls he has pulled this scam on. He not only faces charges here, but also in New Orleans, Phoenix, Minneapolis, and Boston."

"Thank the Lord Bryce was returned safely," Tressie added. "Has anyone heard from Elise? It's getting late. She should have been here by now."

"Oh! I forgot to mention that I heard from her earlier in the week," Olivia replied. "She called to tell me that she wouldn't be able to make it to Bible Study for the next few weeks."

"Did she say why?" Danyelle asked.

"No. The only thing she said was that Miles had been in an accident and was hospitalized."

"Is he all right?" Val asked.

"I'm not sure. She was rather vague over the telephone. She wouldn't answer any of my questions and was in a hurry to hang up with me. She said she'd call me next week. I'm worried about her." Olivia turned to Tressie, "Did you ever find out who tipped the police off to Payce's whereabouts?"

"Livie, maybe you should ask Danyelle that question." Tressie's bitter words shot across the church. "Danyelle, is there something you want to share with the rest of us?" Tressie asked.

Everyone stared at Danyelle, waiting for her to respond to Tressie's question.

"Tressie, I'm sorry," she finally confessed. "I tried to keep quiet, but I could see the pain Payce was causing you. I thought if he went away it would be best for everyone."

"Best for whom? Not me!" she screamed. "Do I look like I'm okay?" Tressie leaned across the church pews and pointed her finger in Danyelle's face, "You had no right to call the cops."

Val leaned over to Olivia, "Aren't you going to do something? It looks like Tressie is going to jump on her at any minute."

"No, they're fine. I think they just need to vent," Olivia said.

"Tressie, you were about to make one of the biggest mistakes of your life. Think about it. You would have not only been married to a fugitive, but you would have been one yourself. You were going to sacrifice your friends, family, and freedom. For what? Payce? Would he have done the same for you?"

"How dare you make decisions about my life? What I do is my business. You had no right to interfere," Tressie roared.

"I said I was sorry," Danyelle replied.

"Sorry is not going to change anything. Payce is locked away for three whole years. He won't speak to me because he thinks I'm the one who sold him out. What am I supposed to do now?" Tressie grabbed her things to leave. "Stay out of my way and out of my life."

The church door slammed shut after Tressie's abrupt exit.

At a loss for words, Olivia spoke up, "Why don't we start the meeting off with prayer? I'll begin."

"Jesus, I praise you and thank you for always acknowledging and answering prayers. When we call out your name, you listen. Lord, touch both Tressie and Danyelle. Touch their hearts that they may listen for your voice in everything they do. Jesus, once again I thank you for bringing my son safely home. Amen."

Danyelle prayed next. "Heavenly Father, I messed up, again. Instead of putting my trust in you, knowing that you are in control of all things, I took matters into my own hands. Now, one of my best friends is angry with me. I ask that you heal her heart from the pain I've caused and that one day she'll be able to forgive me. Amen."

Val was the last person to pray. "Lord, I thank you for providing me with a place to call home. Friends and family are people I have always taken for granted, but not everyone has a family to call their own. I want to thank you for Julian." She paused. "Although we didn't work out the way I had hoped, I know everything was according to your plans. I thank you for carrying me through one of the worst times in my life. I thank you for the memories, the love, and the strength to move on."

Before everyone could say amen in unison, a male's voice spoke up.

"Lord, I want to thank you for placing a woman in my life who loved me unconditionally. She loved me when I had nothing and I took that for granted."

Val lifted her head at the sound of Julian's voice. He stared back at her. She was shocked to see him there.

"Lord, I ask that you forgive me for the way I treated her. I was blinded by your blessings of money and prestige. I mistreated your gifts, and now I realize what really matters. Amen."

"Amen," everyone said in unison.

A surprised Olivia stood up to give him a hug. "Welcome home, stranger. We weren't aware that you were flying in. When did you get here?"

"I flew in yesterday." He spoke to Olivia, but his eyes never left Val. "I needed to see your cousin. I knew she'd be here. I've been calling you at home," he said to Val.

"I got the messages. We said all we needed to say to each other in Seattle."

"Can you just hear me out?" he pleaded. "I traveled all the way across the country to apologize to you. I've admitted that I was wrong in front of all these people. What more do you want from me?" he cried.

"How about the truth? Don't act like the only reason you came home is because of me." She snapped her neck and raised her voice. "Everyone here knows what's going on. It's all over the news.

You tested positive for steroids. You've been suspended from the league for the rest of the season. Julian, how could you do something so stupid?"

"It was the pressure. Everyone expected me to excel, so I had to do something to help me compete." He tried to justify his actions.

"Were you taking steroids when I was out there?" she asked.

He nodded.

"And you never said anything to me? We used to tell each other everything. What happened?"

"I don't know," he replied solemnly. "My whole world just started spinning out of control. I was scared."

"So you chose Caitlyn's arms to run to? Was I not there for you?"

"No, this is entirely my fault. That's why I'm here. I want us to try again," he begged.

Torn between her love for Julian and his betrayal, she didn't know what to do. "Where's Caitlyn?" she asked.

"She left me as soon as the media got word of my steroid use. She said her uncle didn't think it would look good for his niece to be dating a ball player who uses drugs."

Hostility drove her words, "So that's why you're here. She left you, so I'm supposed to take you back."

"Valencia, I love you. You know you are the only person I've ever loved." Remorse filled his words.

"Where was the love in Seattle?" she screamed. Calming herself down, she chose her next words carefully. "I'm sorry, but everyone has choices to make in life and you chose Caitlyn. You allowed another woman and sex to come between what we shared." She pulled her engagement ring off her finger and handed it back to him. "I don't want it and I don't want you."

Silence filled the room and a defeated Julian hung his head down low. Tears welled up in his eyes. He stuck the ring in his pocket and turned to leave.

"Julian, wait a minute." Olivia stopped him. "Val, can I speak to you for a moment outside?" She grabbed Val's hand and pulled her out into the church vestibule.

Once they were alone, Olivia motioned for Val to sit down on a nearby bench. "Val, I'm not trying to get in your business like Danyelle did with Tressie, but maybe you should think about what you're doing?"

"What I'm doing?" she screamed. "What about what he did to me?"

"I'm aware of everything that happened between the two of you, but did you ever think he could really be sorry?"

"Olivia, I don't believe you're going to defend him."

"What he did was wrong, but he deserves a second chance. We all make mistakes; none of us are perfect. You can see he's been beating himself up over what happened. The man apologized."

"His apology is not enough," Val replied.

"Val, the boy is being punished. He's lost basketball, the respect of his friends, family and fans, and now you. Don't you think he's suffered enough?"

Val knew Olivia was right, but she didn't want to admit it.

"You think I should forgive him?" Val asked.

Olivia nodded her head. "Val, think about it. We do things that are unpleasing to God everyday, and after we've fallen on our faces and realized that we were wrong, we drop to our knees and ask for repentance. God readily accepts us back into his loving arms each and every time. So if God can forgive, why can't you? Julian is only human; he is prone to make mistakes. The good thing is that he's realized his mistakes."

"Livie, I'm scared."

"I know, honey, but that's a part of life. Don't think you won't have to endure heartaches just because you found true love."

"When did you get so wise?" Val asked. "I used to be the one who gave advice. This is a switch, you telling me what's best."

"I guess my experience with Bryant and Bryce made me a stronger person spiritually," she replied. "Are you ready to go back inside?" Olivia asked.

They entered back into the church just as Danyelle was wrapping up the saga involving Payce and Tressie. ". . . now Payce is in jail and Tressie is mad at me."

"I sure have missed a lot." Julian replied.

Val sat down next to Julian and turned toward him. "Julian, you hurt me a lot. The trust I had in you is gone, but I'm willing to try again." A smile spread across his face. "Don't think it's going to be easy. It's going to be a long time before I totally trust you again."

"I'll do whatever I have to."

"I should let you know. I'm not going back to Seattle. I'm staying right here and finishing out my education, so if you want to be with me, you have to move back to Philly."

He nodded his head in agreement. "What about the ring?" he asked.

"You keep it. When the time is right, you can slip it back on my finger."

Tressie was pleasantly surprised as she walked into the prison gymnasium. The brightly colored walls and friendly atmosphere was not what she was expecting.

For a few hours every day the prison's gymnasium was turned into visiting hall. Here is where inmates got a chance to spend an hour or two with loved ones.

Tressie sat and patiently waited for Payce. She watched as other visitors—mostly women—entered the prison with their children. Women carrying babies and toddlers seated themselves around her, and it wasn't long before the visiting hall was full of people. She noticed a bunch of guys being escorted into the visiting hall by an armed guard.

Out of nowhere, Payce came and sat down in front of her. Her eyes danced with joy; it had been weeks since she had last seen him.

"Hello, beautiful! Did you miss me?" He leaned forward and kissed her on the cheek.

"Missed you I have," she replied. "I thought you were still mad at me."

He moved over to the chair next to hers and grabbed her hand. "At first I was mad, but after I spoke with Darshon, he told me what happened."

"I'm sorry. I should have never trusted Danyelle."

"It wasn't your fault. Danyelle was only trying to look out for you."

"That's no excuse. I'm still not speaking to her."

"Don't be angry with her. Perhaps what she did was for the best."

Tressie was surprised to hear him say that. She was sure he would have been just as mad as she was.

"When I called and asked you to run away with me I was being selfish and thinking of only myself. What kind of life would that have been for you? You deserve better than that. Being here has helped me to realize I was wrong. Last night, I recognized that this was all God's plan and it worked out just the way he planned. God has been trying to get my attention for a long time, and I would never stop to answer his call. Now that I'm here I have to acknowledge him. I'm here for a reason." He continued, "Tressie, I'm finally getting my life together, and there is nothing here to stop me. I have no distractions. I've enrolled in college, and by the time I'm released I'll be ready to be a productive part of society." He beamed with pride.

Tressie flashed a phony smile.

"What's wrong?" He knew her well enough to know that her smile was not genuine.

"What about us?" Her heart pounded in her chest, scared of what his answer would be.

He knew when Darshon told him Tressie was coming to visit she was going to ask about their future together. He loved this girl more than he loved himself. Despite the many times he'd hurt her in the past, her happiness was important to him.

He was up half the night trying to decide if they should continue their relationship with him being behind bars or go their separate ways. His heart told him to hold on tight and never let her go, but his conscience told him that it wouldn't be fair to her. She was far too beautiful to ask to wait for him.

He softly touched her face. "I want to tell you to wait for me, but I can't. I love you too much to ask you to put your life on hold. I wasn't lying when I told you that I want what's best for you. You are beautiful, smart, and deserve the best. I'm not going to hold you back. As much as it hurt me the last time we were together and I told you to move on, I'm going to tell you again. Go ahead and live your life. As you can see," he looked around. "I'm not going anywhere. Our paths will cross again."

Her heart ached; she didn't want to go on without him. She wished he wasn't locked up so they could be together. "Three years is a long time." Tressie sniffled.

"I know, but it isn't forever."

"I love you," she told him and hugged him tightly.

An hour later, Payce stood at the far end of the gymnasium where a group of inmates were in line waiting for a prison guard to escort them back to their cells. Payce turned around one last time and waved good-bye to Tressie.

An inmate standing behind Payce looked up and recognized Tressie. He couldn't believe his eyes. She was here. He had been thinking about her for years. He wondered what she was doing here. He saw her waving to Payce. He didn't know who Payce was, but he did know that Payce was the new kid on the block. He had to find out what his relationship was to Tressie.

The stranger walked up to Payce to introduce himself. "Hey man, what's up? I don't believe we've met. My name is Jabril."

Tressie, Val, Danyelle, Olivia, and the baby all sat in church and listened to the choir finish their first hymn.

Mrs. Simms stood up before the congregation. "The time has come for us to bring our burdens to the Lord. If there is anyone here who has committed a sin that has put a burden on his or her heart, I encourage you to come forward. Maybe you said something nasty or mean to a coworker or even someone in your household. Perhaps you did something that you now regret. It could have been something you did last year and the Holy Spirit has laid it on your heart to ask for forgiveness. Now is the time to repent."

Everyone remained seated. "Come on, church. It's hard for me to believe that no one has sinned, for the Bible says, 'For all have sinned and come short of the glory of God.'"

Everyone in the congregation still remained seated until Elise walked in through the church doors and up to the front of the church.

Danyelle leaned over to Olivia and whispered. "I have a feeling there's going to be some drama in the church this morning."

"Bless you, Sister Elise. Tell us what is plaguing your heart," Mrs. Simms encouraged her.

"I came up here not to confess my sins to the church and not to ask the church for their forgiveness. I'm here because I love the Lord."

"Amen," the congregation replied.

"I am a sinner, but Jesus saved me from sin. That's why he died on the cross. So the things that I did wrong in the past, present, or future will be forgiven and not held against me." She took a deep breath. "I made excuses for the church when it wanted to exploit other people's sins and not confess its own. The church is composed of sinners. There is not one without sin!" she yelled into the congregation. "We have no right to label others as sinners and not look at our own flaws." She looked over toward Olivia. "Livie, I'm sorry. I'm sorry if we hurt you in any way." Olivia nodded her head.

Mrs. Simms walked up to Elise and whispered in her ear, "Elise, maybe you should sit down now."

"No, I'm not finished," Elise replied. "I need to repent. I'm not going to disclose the details of what has been going on in my life, but I will tell you that the consequences from my sins will last a lifetime."

The church fell silent.

"I'm leaving the church. From now on anything I do will not be judged by you, but by God." Elise walked out the church doors and didn't turn back.

A buzz filled the church. Whispers ran rampant throughout the sanctuary. Reverend Kane called for the church's attention.

"Can I have everyone's attention? I also have an announcement to make. Elise was right; we should acknowledge our own sins before we ask anyone else to acknowledge theirs. I have a sin of my own that I'd like to confess. I don't think I would have ever been able to face who I really am without the help of a good friend who isn't here right now, but he's here in spirit."

"I told you there was going to be drama up in here today," Danyelle whispered to Olivia again.

Reverend Kane continued, "I'd like to confess before God and the church that I am a lesbian."

There were no amens shouted through the church. No one caught the Holy Spirit. The only sound came from baby Bryce, trying to make his presence known. A few of the older members looked at the reverend strangely.

"I am sexually attracted to women," she clarified so everyone understood. "I realize that the church sees this as a sin, but that hasn't stopped the Lord from loving me."

She held out her left hand. Mrs. Simms walked over and gripped her hand tightly. "And this is my lover. Mrs. Simms and I have been in a relationship for months."

Reverend Simms ran over to them. "Is this true?" he asked his wife.

Mrs. Simms held her head high. "Yes, it is."

"Shall we?" Reverend Kane asked Mrs. Simms and the two quietly walked around Reverend Simms and out the church doors.

More Drama in the Church

Dedication

Dedicated in loving memory of Alberta Stewart
May you dance among the stars forever.

Acknowledgments

This time around I don't have too many people to acknowledge. But I would like to express my gratitude to a few special people.

My stylist, Rau'berd at Studio Whisper. You are such a good friend; not just to me, but I've witnessed first hand your generosity to others. You are such a giving and caring person. Every customer who has the pleasure of sitting in your chair will leave with not only a fly do but also intoxicated with positive enthusiasm. Every life you come in contact with is encouraged. It's an honor to call you a friend . . . and FABULOUS HAIR STYLIST . . . Love ya

To my new family the EXTENDED FRIENDS BOOK CLUB. I look forward to spending time with you every time we meet. You ladies are not only fun, but also an answer to a lonely writer's prayer. I prayed for a book club, and as we know . . . God answers prayers. He not only sent me the best group of women to meet with, but also a hoard of new friends.

Acknowledgments

In Baltimore I made two new friends, Mondel and Tracy at Urban Knowledge Bookstore at Eastpoint Mall. I thoroughly enjoyed the time we spent together. Mondel, you are now a part of my inner circle. It's a pleasure conversing with you about different books. Please keep the suggestions coming. Thank you for being so real with me.

I'd like to shout out two special fans. First is Malika D. from Dayton, Ohio. Receiving your e-mails on the regular always makes me laugh. Secondly, I owe plenty of thanks to my MySpace friend Sharlean Frazier, you were always looking out for my best interest. Thanks for the support and encouragement.

Love,
Dynah
Dynah.Zale@comcast.net

Prologue

1961

"Albert, make sure you get back here before the sun goes down." Those were the last words Albert heard his momma say before he raced out of his aunt's house and down the dirt road toward the church. It was his turn to pick up his family's monthly stipend of government milk, butter and cheese the church distributed every month.

Albert ran a few feet before losing momentum. He slowed down to a turtle's pace and dragged his feet along the dusty road while kicking up rocks along his path. It was hard being the oldest of three. At twelve years old, he was the man of the house. He chopped wood, washed clothes, cooked and even worked a part-time job with his uncle. Albert would do anything to help out his momma.

From across the field Albert could see the sky turn different shades of pink, a sure sign that the sun was beginning its descent to retire for the night.

Albert jogged the remaining distance to the church. The last to arrive, he pushed through the church doors and gathered in his arms the last package sitting on the table.

"I didn't think you were gonna make it here in time." The reverend's smile condemned him for being so tardy. "Your momma called and said you were on the way."

"Yes, sir. They need this stuff to prepare our Easter Sunday dinner tomorrow," Albert replied.

"Are you ready to star as Jesus in the Easter play?"

The reverend and Albert walked to the church doors together.

"Yes, sir." Albert regarded it an honor to portray Jesus and took his part seriously. He rehearsed his lines at least twice a day and prayed for a flawless performance.

"Good." The reverend patted Albert on the back and guided him out the door. "It's getting dark out, would you like for me to give you a ride home?"

Albert opened his mouth to accept the offer, but quickly changed his mind. The Reverend liked to talk, and he had bad breath. Albert couldn't fathom being locked in a car with him for any period of time.

"That's okay, Reverend. It won't take me long to walk home."

"Okay, son, but make sure you go straight home. It's unsafe for a young man to be out alone after dark."

Albert waved good-bye and pressed on toward his final destination. Suddenly, he stopped. Only a few hundred feet away from the church steps Albert heard the familiar call of crickets. Certain he could catch at least a dozen crickets for his fishing trip before nightfall, he disregarded the strict instructions from his elders to go directly home and stopped by the banks of the swamp that stretched out behind the church.

Albert pushed his way through the thick brush and knelt down close to the ground. He set the package by his feet and listened closely for the crickets' mating call.

He was on the verge of capturing his first prey, when out of nowhere, the roar of the reverend's car engine frightened the crickets into silence. In a swift motion, the car's headlights swept over Albert. When he looked back, Albert saw the Reverend's car driving off into the distance.

Caught unexpectedly, Albert looked around at the darkness that surrounded him. Without him realizing it, the moon had crept into the sky and its light cast an uneasy feeling deep down in Albert's bones. Regret filled his mind. He should have obeyed his momma. As he prepared to gather his things and leave, Albert stood up straight to stretch his legs. Then, he heard a menacing voice holler, "Get 'em, boys."

Without warning, Albert's frail, thin eighty-pound body was lifted up off the ground. He kicked and screamed for his captors to let him go, but it was to no avail.

"Shut him up," another man commanded before Albert's mouth was gagged with a handkerchief.

His eyes frantically perused the white faces that surrounded him, searching for a look of empathy. Instead he found a slew of pale faces, all with beady black eyes that expelled hatred from within their soul.

While a pair of strong arms wrapped themselves around Albert's neck and held him in an unbearable chokehold, sharp fingernails pressed hard into his arms.

From behind the gag, Albert released muffled and distorted cries for help. The men shoved him against a nearby oak tree that sat in close proximity to the church's front door. Next, they pulled his hands around the tree and tied him to it.

Albert was terrified. At school, stories circulated the schoolyard about missing children who were rumored to have been torched alive. Their bodies were burned until there was nothing left but ashes.

"Is he tied to that pole tight?" Wet, sweaty, loose strands of hair hung in the man's eyes as he chewed on a piece of hay. "Fellas, look at what we've caught. Didn't your momma tell you not to go anywhere by yourself?" The man's tart breath ripped through Albert's nostrils.

Tears gathered in the corners of Albert's eyes, but he wouldn't allow them to see him cry.

"What do you think we should do with him?" The man swallowed the remainder of his beer from the can, dropped it to the ground and crushed it with his boot.

"I think we should stone him."

While everyone laughed at the man's suggestion, the guy who asked the question held up his hand to quiet everybody. "A modern-day stoning is not a bad idea."

"I was just joking."

The two men talked as the others tortured Albert by pulling his hair and spitting in his face.

"I wasn't. Stone him like they did in biblical times." The burly white guy snatched up a huge rock from the ground and tossed it from one hand to the other.

Albert's vulnerability gave his oppressors power. Their ringleader felt like Goliath, and Albert was David. Through his eyes, Albert was a worthless nigger. His chapped lips, knotty hair and charred skin were enough reasons for him to rid the earth of his kind.

The white man stepped a few feet away from Albert, and with all the strength of a baseball player trying to strike out a batter, he threw the rock at Albert's face. It hit him an inch above his right eye. His skin split open, exposing a bloody wound. Again, the man picked up a few more rocks, and with even more force, he aimed each one at

Albert's face. The other men mimicked their leader's actions, and within minutes they were simultaneously stoning Albert with rocks. Every rock was treated like a missile that was aimed at Albert's face and body. He was defenseless against their torture, and while they attacked him they jeered and taunted him by calling him names.

"Hold up!" Another man pushed his way to the front of the crowd. "We can't do this . . ." he said to the crowd.

Albert's swollen left eye prevented him from clearly seeing the man who was shielding him from their torture.

". . . Without a crown for his honor." He strutted up to Albert and placed a crown made of barbwire down on top of his head.

Everyone watching laughed heartily.

"Where'd you get that from?" someone asked.

"I used this to keep the sheep at Old Man Crother's place safe from those sly foxes that come around at night." He pressed the crown down hard on top of Albert's head so it fit securely.

The pressure of the crown felt like thorns being crushed into Albert's skull, and he cringed at the pain. A small stream of blood slid down the side of his face and onto his shirt.

"This is your lucky day, kid," the man teased. "You can pretend to be Jesus and ask God to forgive us for our sins."

The entire group of men screamed out in laughter.

The minute the man removed himself from the line of fire, the constant hammering of rocks being thrown against Albert's slim body continued. Ultimately, he endured the suffering until he finally passed out.

Albert's head dropped down in front of him, and his body slumped forward. The men noticed his body become limp and stopped their persecution against him. The man in charge tried to push the kid's head straight up, but it instantly dropped back down. The power he'd had ten minutes prior was gone. The kid was dead. The rocks in his hand fell to the ground, and he ordered everyone back in their pick up trucks. They left the scene as dark rain clouds moved in and rain poured down on the kid's head.

The rain revived Albert long enough for him to part his lips to speak with God, "Father, forgive them, for they know not what they do."

It rained all night, and the following day was Easter Sunday. The boy's body was discovered at sunrise service.

Chapter 1

December 2007

The serious look on Reverend Simms's face spoke volumes throughout the church.

" 'Why are you persecuting me?' That's what Jesus said to Saul," he screamed from the pulpit. "I want everyone here to recognize how some of our ways are displeasing to God." He slammed his fist down on the podium. "We gossip. Oh! Do we gossip?" The reverend exaggerated his words. "We gossip so much that we'll talk about anybody. We talk about our friends, our family, our co-workers, and we even talk about complete strangers. 'Look at him with that shirt on that's two sizes too small.' "

The congregation giggled.

"The things we say about others, whether it's said out loud or private thoughts we keep to ourselves, hurt God. Let me give you an example. Yesterday, the daily newspaper reported a story of a junior high student who died as a result of an eating disorder. When they laid her to rest she weighed a mere forty-six pounds. The reporter talked with family and friends, but the most frightening revelation came from the girl's best friend." Reverend Simms read directly from the news clipping. "The thirteen-year-old was apparently the victim of vicious name-calling by classmates. *Fatso, hippo,* and *wide load* are just a few of the insults that were hurled at her within the hallways at school. To lose weight she starved herself, purged her meals and allowed herself to only eat two meals a week."

Reverend Simms rubbed his chin, heavy in thought. "Those children who did the teasing did not set out to intentionally kill their classmate. They thought they were being funny. But the consequences of their words were slowly killing not only her spirit, but also the healing process of her loving herself. They were persecuting her through their speech. My final words—Beware of what you say to others."

The moment Reverend Simms sat, the women's choir rose to their feet. Clothed in matching button-down blouses and blue denim skirts, they waited for their cue. Danyelle, the soloist, climbed her way out of the cramped and crowded choir box over to the microphone. The piano keys spun a familiar melody that embraced her soul.

Danyelle closed her eyes and swayed her forty-four-inch hips from side to side. Without thinking, she pushed a single braid away from her eye before performing her rendition of "Oh Mary, Don't You Weep."

The passion Danyelle poured into the song was reflected in the tears she cried. Her strong soprano voice touched everyone. A few members dropped to their knees, while others waved their hands back and forth, thanking God for his goodness. Sister Gardner did her usual insanity act by grabbing the Christian flag, lifting it high in the air and sprinting through the church as if she had just lit the Olympic torch. Afterward, she always claimed Jesus had embodied her spirit.

Once the song concluded and Sister Gardner finished her marathon, Reverend Simms again approached the podium.

"I'm not going to hold you this morning, but I must mention two things. First, I would like to thank Reverend Baxter for joining us again for the second Sunday in a row." He turned around to give his colleague a firm handshake. Then the congregation rose to their feet and gave him a round of applause. Reverend Simms stepped to the side and encouraged him to speak to the crowd.

The strikingly handsome thirty-something man possessed a close resemblance to Matthew McConaughey. His blue eyes sparkled. Golden locks of hair swept away from his face. His smile was charming. Dressed in black from head to toe, he stepped up to the podium. A tarnished cross dangled from around his neck. "Thank you, First Nazareth and Reverend Simms. It's such a blessing to be in the house of the Lord. Now, I know when Reverend Simms told me to come back soon, he didn't think I'd be back the very next week." He laughed. "But my family and I"—he pointed to his wife and three young children who sat on the first pew— "enjoyed ourselves so much, we had to come back again."

Everyone applauded.

"Now I understand why Reverend Montgomery comes into work dancing on Monday mornings. He's filled with the Holy Ghost."

Reverend Colin Montgomery was First Nazareth's new associate pastor. One year ago the church began its hunt for Reverend Simms's successor. They prayed for a man of God who was not only a counselor, but also a teacher of the Word. Then they stumbled upon Colin at the Philadelphia Bible College. He was a professor there and happened to be looking for a church to call home. Colin was immediately interviewed and hired. His youthful spirit was refreshing, and that helped win the teenagers over to Christ.

"Church, Reverend Montgomery and Reverend Simms are both anointed. It's obvious how much they care about this church and their community."

The church gave Reverend Baxter a round of applause, and Colin stood to give him a manly hug.

The bond shared between Colin and Reverend Baxter went beyond the usual boss-employee relationship. Colin felt like he could talk to him about anything. Reverend Baxter was a shining example of the kind of preacher he strived to become.

Reverend Simms stepped back up to the podium. "Lastly, the time has come for anyone interested to register for our annual Singles Retreat. This year it will be held at Split Rock Resort in the mountains of Northern Pennsylvania, and before anyone asks, yes, Reverend Montgomery will be attending the retreat."

The single ladies blushed, the married women laughed, and the men in the church seemed upset over the amount of attention the new associate pastor received from the ladies. Reverend Montgomery's face turned red from embarrassment. He ran his fingers over his soft, curly hair. His thick eyebrows and heart-shaped lips made him the most sought-after man in the church. Women, young and old, flirted endlessly when in his presence.

"How old is Colin?"

Dean, Olivia's boyfriend, gave her a questioning look.

"I'm asking for my sister," she quickly cleared up.

"Twenty-seven," he whispered.

Satisfied with her man's answer, Olivia sat back in her seat with her four-year-old son Bryce sitting quietly on her lap. She nudged her cousin Val with her elbow to get her attention. "Cuz, are you going to sign up to go on the resort with me?"

Without hesitation, her fiancé, Julian answered for her, "Valencia will be a married woman soon, and she won't have any reason to attend a singles retreat." He wrapped one of his long, thin arms around her shoulders and hugged her closer to him.

Olivia giggled inside. It was amusing to watch how overprotective Julian was of Val. Their love for one another seemed stronger than ever. Three years ago, Olivia thought she would never see them this happy again. The rough time they endured when Julian was drafted into the NBA put a rift between them that seemed beyond repair. The lure of money, women and cars was too much for Julian to bear. He gave in to his lustful desires, and a disastrous affair destroyed all Val's trust in him. Eventually he came to his senses and realized his mistake. Humiliated, he begged Val for a second chance. It took her a while to forgive him, but once she did, Julian wasted no time. He proposed, again. Their wedding was less than a week away.

Julian reached over Olivia and tapped Dean on his knee. "Yo, man, keep your woman in check."

Dean turned his lips into a loving smile before planting a soft, gentle kiss on Olivia's cheek. She giggled like a teenager in love.

They'd been dating for close to two years, and it was apparent to any bystander that they were madly in love. A day wouldn't go by without someone asking, "When's the wedding?"

Dean West, a devoted Christian, also was raised at First Nazareth and lived on the same block as Olivia when they were kids. Growing up, Dean was quiet, kept to himself and didn't have many friends. Throughout high school he was often found in the library with his head buried in a book. Right after graduation he left Philadelphia to attend Tuskegee University on a full four-year academic scholarship.

Like Olivia's parents, Dean's parents died when he was young. When he was eight months old, Dean's mom and dad were killed in a car accident, leaving him in the custody of his paternal grandparents.

It wasn't until he'd finished school and returned home from Alabama that Olivia appreciated his less-than-average looks. The product of a white father and black mother, his blonde, curly hair and blue eyes were in stark contrast to his full lips, wide nose and chestnut brown complexion. He was nicknamed "Soul Man" after the movie, because of his close resemblance to the main character.

At the onset of their relationship, their love for one another blossomed. Dean treated Olivia like a precious jewel and would do anything to make her and Bryce happy. He loved them both and couldn't wait until they were a family.

Olivia felt blessed to have Dean in her life. He was not only a good man, but also a positive role model for her son, unlike his father. Bryce's biological father, Bryant, was currently doing time in a federal prison for trying to sell their son through an illegal adoption. Olivia would never forget the way he manipulated and used her. By being so naïve she almost lost her son forever.

That experience marked the beginning of a life makeover for her. Determined to make a drastic change, she cut twelve inches of her hair, leaving a short, classy, chic haircut tapered above her ears. Then she upgraded her outdated wardrobe by dressing more like a mom instead of a grandma.

Her final act of independence was noted by moving out of the apartment she shared with her sister. She no longer lived with Danyelle. Her need to be a responsible parent meant putting distance between her son and her sister's weed smoking.

Bryce bounced up and down on Olivia's lap and pointed excitedly. Olivia figured by her son's reaction that he'd spotted Tressie sneaking into church. Late as usual.

Tressie slid into the pew behind her friends. After taking off her coat and hat, she quietly acknowledged everyone before reaching out for Bryce to sit with her.

Olivia did a double take when she glanced back at Tressie. "You colored your hair?"

The entire pew turned around to get a good look at Tressie's honey blonde hair.

"Do you like it?" Her medium-length hair was full of bouncy, vibrant spiral curls.

"I love it," Val responded. She ran her fingers through her shoulder-length hair. "Maybe I should get something done to my hair."

"No." Julian loved everything about Val. Her smooth ebony skin, thick shoulder-length hair and wide hips were what he dreamed about every night.

Bryce flashed the picture he drew in Sunday School class in Tressie's face.

"This is beautiful," Tressie complimented him.

"It's for you." His cheeks turned beet red when Tressie expressed her gratitude by kissing him on the cheek.

Olivia was mindful of the fact that her son was a flirt. That was why she prayed daily that he wouldn't grow up to be like his father.

Olivia beckoned Tressie closer with her index finger. "It's nice of you to join us this morning."

"You know I was out of town on business. My plane arrived late, but I came straight here from the airport," Tressie replied.

"Every week she has a different excuse." Val eyed Tressie suspiciously. "Are you sure you're not meeting a man?"

Tressie gave her a ridiculous look. "It's not my fault my job requires extensive traveling."

"Aunt Tressie." Bryce tapped her shoulder. "Did you bring me anything?"

"I sure did."

"Whatever it is, I hope it doesn't make any noise."

Last Christmas Olivia had made all the girls promise to not buy Bryce any more toys that made any sound.

"I brought you back a drum set."

The entire pew turned around to see if she was telling the truth. Tressie excitedly nodded her head.

"She's not bringing those drums to my house," Olivia whispered to Dean before turning around. Then she summoned Tressie to her. "Tressie, will you go with me to the singles retreat? I don't want to go by myself."

"Julian must have told you that Val couldn't go, because that's the only reason you would invite me," Tressie sarcastically replied.

When Julian snickered, Tressie knew she was right.

Olivia pleaded her case. "That's not true. I always ask you to go."

"Only after you ask Val." Tressie shook her head. "It doesn't matter, because I'm not going. I don't like those singles retreats. The only thing there is saved men." Tressie held up her hand to stop Olivia before she said something smart. "I already know that we're supposed to associate with saved men, but you know what kind of man I'm looking for. I want a—"

"A thug that knows Jesus," Val, Julian and Olivia said in unison. The kind of man Tressie desired had been branded in their minds through the years, and everyone knew she would settle for nothing less.

Her infatuation with roughnecks who usually led a life of crime that eventually landed them behind bars was a mystery. Payce, Tressie's last boyfriend, cheated on her, conceived two children and jeopardized her freedom, but that wasn't a deterrent for her. Instead, she remained persistent, faithful and prayerful that God would send her the type of man she longed for.

Reverend Simms rambled on for another five minutes before praying over his congregation and bringing services to an end.

As Dean and Olivia gathered their things, Dean's grandpa approached them. "Don't you two forget, I'm expecting the both of you over for dinner tonight."

Judge Ernie West, the only white member of First Nazareth's congregation and Dean's paternal grandfather, was a faithful member who demonstrated his love for Christ by helping his community. He took advantage of his power and position to put a stop to the injustices targeted toward minorities. Plus, he promoted programs that encouraged self-empowerment for the youth.

"Not to worry. We'll be there." Olivia reached out to give him a hug and quick peck on the cheek. "Bryce is looking forward to spending time with you."

"Bryce reminds me of Dean when he was his age. I enjoy the time we spend together, but if you two will excuse me, I see Reverend Simms calling me over." He quickly wobbled away on his cane.

"All right, Grandpa, we'll see you later." Dean turned toward Olivia. "What would you like to do before dinner?"

"I thought maybe we could surprise your grandpa and cook dinner for him this time. He always cooks us a delicious supper. I need to stop by the market and pick up a few things before we head to his house. By the time he gets home we'll have everything waiting for him."

Dean loved Olivia's thoughtfulness. "That sounds wonderful." He lifted her lips to meet his.

An hour later Judge West, followed by Reverend Montgomery, Reverend Baxter and his entire family entered his home, greeted by the tantalizing aroma of sweet cornbread.

"Thanks for inviting us over, Judge West," Colin said. "I was going to take Reverend Baxter and his family over to Mrs. Tootsies for some soul food."

"Boy, don't you know I can cook soul food? Just because I wasn't born with soul don't mean I can't get down in the kitchen."

"Judge West, don't look now, but I think somebody is already cooking in your kitchen," Colin kidded his elder.

"It smells as good as my cooking." He sniffed the air.

Dean came out of the den and met them in the dining room.

"Boy, what are you doing here? I thought you and Olivia were coming over later."

"She wanted to surprise you by having dinner ready for you by the time you came home from church."

"She is so sweet." He pushed by Dean. "Let me go give my future granddaughter-in-law a hug for always thinking of others."

Colin took off his suit jacket and draped it across the dining room chair.

"What are you doing here?" Dean held up his hands in a boxer stance and playfully swung a punch at Colin.

"Your grandpa invited me not only for dinner, but to also continue our discussion on the deteriorating school systems in the neighborhood." He pointed toward Reverend Baxter. "Reverend Baxter thought he might be able to assist us in some way, so were all here to put our heads together."

"Good. The more the merrier." Dean invited the adults to sit while Bryce and Reverend Baxter's children took off toward another part of the house to watch television. "Olivia made plenty of dinner for everybody."

Twenty minutes later the men talked amongst themselves and Mrs. Baxter helped Olivia in the kitchen.

"Fellas, I don't have to tell you the number of school officials who have been indicted on charges of embezzlement," Judge West said.

"It makes me sick to think how these men are stealing from the poorest schools in the city. Their gain is these children's loss." Colin popped a peppermint in his mouth from the candy dish that sat on the end table.

"I went to visit one of the elementary schools so I could see for myself the damage lack of funding has done in the schools. It was horrible. I've never seen such conditions in a school. The first grade classes have huge rocks placed along the walls to block the rat holes. There are approximately thirty-seven to forty-seven students per class. I spoke to one of the teachers, and she complained that because there weren't enough desks or books to go around she moved all the desks out of the classroom and everyone sits on the floor."

"This is so unfair. They don't have these kinds of problems in the suburbs." Reverend Baxter shook his head in disgust.

"That's why I want the church to build its own school for the community," Judge West said.

"That's a great idea, Grandpa, but that is going to cost a lot of money," Dean said.

"Boy, I've already done my research. I do have a law degree," he reminded his grandson. "We can start off by getting grants from the government, and the rest of the money we need will have to be provided by the Lord. This school will have a huge impact on the community. I've already outlined a curriculum, and since I have two professors in the room I was hoping one of you could review the initial business plan I put together." Judge West pulled the papers out and handed them to Reverend Baxter.

"This sounds like you put a lot of thought into this." Reverend Baxter studied the plans a moment. "You want to extend the school day and place students in an environment that speaks primarily in a foreign language. Plus, it looks like you have an intense math and science program here."

"Yes, we are one of the richest countries in the world with the poorest educational systems."

"What about this negative two hundred and nineteen thousand in the budget section?" Reverend Baxter pointed out.

"That's the part I was talking about when I said we will need to rely on the Good Lord's help."

The men all laughed together.

"With God, anything's possible."

"Why don't we hold a fundraiser?" Dean suggested.

"I don't think a fundraiser will solve this problem." In Judge West's mind, he knew he had to think bigger than a fundraiser.

Olivia stuck her head into the den. "Dinner's ready," she hollered.

"Great! I'm hungry." Dean was the first one to run to his place at the dining room table. The other men rose from their seats and followed.

"Judge West"—Reverend Baxter patted the old man on his back—"I don't know why, but since the first time I met you at church last weekend I can't get rid of this feeling that I've met you somewhere before."

"It's possible we could have been on a committee at one point together. Your face isn't familiar to me, but I'm getting old. I can't remember every face I met. I hope you don't remember me from being in my courtroom."

"No. I know for sure I've never been in any trouble with the law," Reverend Baxter replied.

On their way to the dining room, the judge was stopped by a knock at the door. He told his guests to go ahead and he would join them once he answered the front door. It would only take him a moment, and then they could bless the food.

When the judge swung open his front door, uneasiness filled his soul. Standing before him was a deliveryman holding a huge dark-brown box in his arms.

"I have a package for Judge Ernie West."

Hesitant to answer, the judge gave the young delivery guy the once-over look. "It's Sunday. I thought you guys didn't make deliveries on Sundays."

"No, that's not true. We deliver packages seven days a week. Anything to satisfy the customer."

West doubted the man's story. He was ready to shut the door closed in his face when he pushed the clipboard out toward him.

"I need you to sign here." The deliveryman pointed to the dotted line.

Judge West could usually discern if strangers he met were friend or foe. For some reason, he felt this man was foe. Before taking the clipboard, he noticed the man's nicely manicured hands. He didn't look like a blue-collar worker. In fact, he looked like someone who rarely got his hands dirty.

The judge didn't want to cause a ruckus, with his family in the next room, so he decided to take the package and immediately discard it outside his home. He signed the form and took ownership of the box. "Have a blessed day, young man."

The judge's well-wishes were insincere. "I wonder what this is," he mumbled to himself. He turned around to walk back inside. As he attempted to close the door, it was suddenly thrust open and Ernie was forced against the wall.

"FBI," an agent screamed in his face and flashed a badge. The agent pulled out his handcuffs and slapped them around the judge's wrists. "You are under arrest for murder."

The commotion made everyone in the house run to the door.

"What's going on?" Reverend Baxter stepped toward them.

Another agent stepped in front of him and held out his arm. "I'm sorry, sir. Don't come any farther, or I'll be forced to arrest you."

The entire house watched as the police treated Judge West like a criminal. The last thing the judge remembered seeing before they hauled him away was the sad look in Bryce's eyes.

Chapter 2

"I don't understand." Olivia slammed a folded wedding program down on the table so hard, it disturbed her two sleeping shih tzus. "I'm sorry," she spoke to her puppies. "Mommy didn't mean to wake you."

"You act like you actually gave birth to those two mutts," Val said.

Olivia lightly punched her in the arm. "Don't call my babies mutts. They're sensitive. Anyway, back to what I was saying. Dean has been down to the justice building three times. Everyone he speaks to acts clueless. He can't get any information on his grandpa. The only thing we know for sure is that his grandpa is in their custody for the murder of a little black boy."

"That's hard to believe." Val listened closely to Olivia's every word.

"I said the same thing. Dean thinks he's being set up because Judge West is such a huge advocate for equality for minorities, but we can't say for sure because he hasn't talked to his grandpa."

Val threw her a look of shock.

"Every time he requests a visit they tell him that Judge West refuses to see him. Dean is so upset, he doesn't know what to do."

"Reverend Simms was furious when he got the call on Sunday. Julian and I were in his office for our very last counseling session when he politely kicked us out. I had never heard him in such an uproar."

Olivia took a deep breath to calm her nerves. When she looked across the table, Val's three-carat canary yellow diamond caught her eye. The brilliance of the diamonds dazzled under the light. "I remember the day Julian proposed and placed that on your finger." She pointed to the ring. "Time sure does fly." Olivia folded another wedding program in half before handing it to Val to place in the huge stack of programs already assembled. "I can't believe you're getting married in only a few more days."

Val's face glowed from happiness. Thoughts of her big day made her cheeks rosy and her heart skip a beat. She couldn't believe the day she had dreamt about her entire life was finally here. "I can't wait to walk down that aisle." She paused a moment to try and picture what the church was going to look like. "Livie," Val addressed Olivia by her childhood nickname, "did I tell you I ordered twelve thousand dollars worth of calla lilies for the church?"

Olivia sighed, smiled and nodded her head yes. Val had repeated every detail of the wedding to her several times already. There wasn't anything she didn't know.

"Last night my wedding planner told me that the church had approved the candles I wanted set throughout the church." She tapped Olivia's shoulder to make sure she was listening. "Picture this, the entire sanctuary lit with long white candles, the intoxicating fragrance from the flowers surrounding our friends and family. Then, at the stroke of midnight on the New Year, Julian and I will be joined together as husband and wife." A serene look spread over her face.

"You don't appear to be nervous at all," Olivia said.

"I've been ready to become Mrs. Julian Pennington." Val grabbed a handful of grapes from the bowl of fruit set in front of her. "The part I'm nervous about is the wedding night."

Bryce ran over to Val full speed and crashed into her lap. "Aunt Val, can I spend the night with you and Uncle Julian tonight?" he begged.

"Baby, I'm not going anywhere. I'm staying the night here with you and your mother. Besides, don't you want to wake up here? Tomorrow is Christmas." She kissed him on the cheek.

"I forgot tomorrow is Christmas," he replied. "Is Uncle Julian staying the night here, too?"

"Your uncle is out of town. He has a game tonight. So we're going to watch him on television later tonight."

Bryce cheered before running back toward his bedroom.

"I don't know how he forgot tomorrow is Christmas. He asks me every morning how many days until Santa comes back to our house. Now, back to you. You never let on that you were scared to share your bed with Julian." Olivia felt insulted that Val hadn't voiced her concerns sooner.

Val carelessly shrugged her shoulders. "It's funny, because I have every detail of my wedding planned out. In my mind I can picture how the church will look, the smell of the flowers and the taste of each entrée served at the reception, but I have no expectations for my honeymoon. Do you think that's weird?"

"I think you need to stop worrying and allow your love for Julian to lead you through the night."

Val got up from her chair and grabbed a shopping bag. "Let me show you what I bought." She pulled out a black-and-red teddy and dangled it in front of her bosom.

"Is your chest going to fit in those cups?"

Val's full-size breasts developed at the age of ten, and the rest of her body was still trying to catch up.

She playfully punched Olivia in the arm. "Yes, it's going to fit. I tried it on and I must say that it looks good on me."

"I'll take your word on that."

A hard and rapid knock at the front door interrupted their conversation.

"I bet that's Danyelle and Tressie."

When Olivia opened the door Danyelle rushed past her and down the hall to the bathroom. When the dogs saw her running they jumped up and started chasing her, biting at her pants legs.

"Clinton! Kennedy! Get off!" Danyelle yelled. "Livie, call your imitation guard dogs off me."

Olivia whistled and the dogs came running to her side.

Tressie knelt down and played with them a moment before giving Olivia a quick hug. "I didn't think we were going to make it here in time. Danyelle has been drinking herbal tea all day, trying to clean out her system for this drug test she has to take tomorrow."

Olivia closed the door behind Tressie. "When will my sister learn that all she has to do is quit smoking and she wouldn't have to do these things?"

When Tressie stepped into the dining room she sucked her teeth at the sight of numerous wedding materials scattered around. "Please don't tell me this is going to be another night of wedding planning," she wailed while pulling out a chair. "Why did you hire a wedding planner when we're doing all the work?"

"Stop complaining." Val placed a pile of unfolded programs down in front of her.

Olivia chuckled at their innocent bickering.

Danyelle finally joined them at the table. "If you can't keep those dogs under control I'm going to have them picked up by the animal shelter." Danyelle sneered at them from across the room. "Anyway, guess what I did today?" Danyelle expected the girls to fall out in surprise when she shared with them her news.

"You guys will never believe this. I still don't believe it." Tressie sat up straight in her chair so she wouldn't miss their reaction.

Danyelle cut her eyes at Tressie. "I applied to Bible College."

A hush fell over the table. Val and Olivia eyed one another before breaking out into a hearty laugh.

"Right, stop playing with us. What did you really do today?" Olivia couldn't stop laughing.

"I told you they weren't going to believe you." Tressie placed her first finished program in the pile.

Shock filled Olivia's face when she realized Danyelle was serious. At a loss for words, she looked to Val to rescue her.

"I've been thinking about it for a while," Danyelle said.

Olivia wasn't sure what to say and was glad when Val finally spoke up, "What brought on this decision?"

Danyelle's decision to enroll in college was so sudden she couldn't explain it herself. Recently, episodes of uneasiness nagged at her soul. She prayed, fasted and studied the scripture, looking for peace.

Suddenly, His plans for her life poured into her heart like the feel of a refreshing ice-cold glass of spring water on a hot, sweaty summer day.

Danyelle was considered an expert when it came to exploring facts, memorizing scripture and interpreting meanings within the Bible. She believed her intellect came from smoking at least one blunt a day, until it dawned on her that her wisdom was one of her God-given talents that was supposed to be used to glorify Him.

"Did you think I was going to work at the drugstore forever?"

The three of them slightly nodded their heads in agreement.

"Okay, I must admit, college has never been a part of my game plan, but I feel like I'm standing on the sidelines watching the three of you advance in your field while I'm stuck in a bottomless pit. Val's in law school. Tressie is a child counselor working toward her masters in psychology. When Reverend Baxter spoke at our church it was plain to see how close his relationship with God is. A part of that is because he understands the Bible. I want that relationship. I want that insight."

Olivia got up from her seat, walked around the table and wrapped her arms around her sister.

"I'm so proud of you. I believe you can do anything you set your mind to, and that includes school."

Academically, Danyelle had been labeled the underachiever in the family. Mediocrity was acceptable for her, and she never strived for anything greater. Olivia saw her potential and realized the initiative it took for her to enroll in Bible College. This was not only a blessing, but a miracle only God could do.

"Did you choose a major?" Val asked.

"I've decided to take on a double major in biblical studies and children's ministries, and I've chosen to minor in church music."

"Big sister, don't take on too much," Olivia advised before taking her seat again.

"I won't. I'm fully prepared to battle this small hurdle." Danyelle was proud of herself, and she wasn't going to allow anything to hinder her calling from God.

Tressie's head was bowed down working on wedding favors, but she shifted her eyes up. "You know they don't allow drugs on college campuses."

"That's okay. Because I plan to smoke before I get there." Danyelle had decided that the day she received her acceptance letter. "Tressie, will you go to the school with me during registration? It's the second week of January. You know how hard it is for me to make a decision."

"Sorry. I'll be out of town. Right after the New Year my boss has me scheduled to fly to Milwaukee. An eleven-year-old cut his classmate's throat and killed her," Tressie said as if she were giving a weather report.

"Doesn't it bother you that your job is to get inside the minds of kids who have committed such violent crimes?" Val asked.

"Of course not. Tressie's used to it. She used to date them."

Everyone looked at Danyelle because her joke wasn't funny.

"It gets a little disturbing sometimes," Tressie admitted. "Sometimes when I speak with these children, some have no remorse. It's like they have no value for life and I'm looking straight into the eyes of an empty soul. The others act like they have no idea of the seriousness of what they've done. They play head games, and sometimes they are so smart that I get confused. It's a hard job."

"We live in a horrible world," Olivia said out loud. Everyone gathered around reflected on her words.

The girls talked and worked well into the early morning hours. They managed to finish folding the programs, assembling the wedding favors and even helped Val memorize her wedding vows. In the end everyone was tired and ready for bed.

In the process of everyone cleaning up their mess, Val's cell phone rang.

"Hey, baby!" The fatigue Val felt a moment ago disappeared at the sound of her fiancé's voice.

"Hey, baby!" The girls mocked her in unison and laughed at her. They knew it was Julian on the other end. It was customary for him to call her after every game.

Val rolled her eyes and fled to Olivia's room for privacy.

"Did you watch the game?" Julian screamed over his celebrating teammates in the locker room.

"Yes, I did. I wish I could have come with you." Val missed him so much. She hated being away from him. "But there is no way I could leave with all the things that still need to be done before the wedding. I called the caterer and told him you wanted to have one last meeting with him to discuss a few minor details. At first he told me he wouldn't have any free time until the day before the wedding. You know the holidays are the busiest season for him, but I told him you had to get in there sooner than that. It took for me to be a little persistent, but he's going to go into work an hour early the day after Christmas. So we have to make sure we meet him at the restaurant no later than nine. So when does your flight leave?"

Julian kept trying to interrupt her, but she talked so fast.

"Valencia." Julian knew his future bride was not going to be happy with what he had to tell her. "Baby, the weather is so bad here that I don't think I'm going to make it."

"I heard it was snowing there, but I didn't think it was that bad. Did they close the airports?" Val's temperature rose. She hated it when things didn't go as planned.

"No, but my coach suggested I leave out tomorrow morning with the rest of the team." He loved Val, but there were times she could be spoiled and intolerant.

"Julian, I don't want to spend Christmas without you. You promised you would be here," she reminded him.

"I know, but I'll still get there in time for Christmas. I just won't get there until late in the afternoon."

"Late afternoon," she repeated.

"Yes. You have to account for travel time and we're in a different time zone." He tried to explain, but his argument wasn't very convincing. Julian was the kind of man who didn't like to go back on his word, especially to his woman. He broke the uncomfortable silence over the phone. "All right! I'll catch the next commercial flight out of here. Once we get married you're going to stop getting your way all the time."

Val giggled. "Do you need me to pick you up from the airport?"

The sound of happiness in Val's voice assured Julian that he had made the right decision. He couldn't wait to pledge his love and life to her in front of God, family and friends. Val was a priceless jewel, and nothing in this world was more valuable to him than her. He vowed to spend his life making her happy.

"You don't have to do that. I'll catch a cab to my mom's house and I'll pick you up from Olivia's. See you in the morning. I love you, Valencia."

"I love you, too." She disconnected the call and savored the moment. She couldn't believe how the sound of Julian pronouncing her full name still sent chills down her spine. He refused to call her by anything other than Valencia.

Val reentered the living room just in time to see Tressie and Danyelle gathering their things to leave.

"I thought you two were going to stay with us tonight?" Val settled into the fluffy couch pillows.

"I can't. My parents pressured me into staying the night at their house tonight. They miss having their only child." Tressie reached out to give the girls a goodnight hug. "I think my mother is experiencing the empty nest syndrome." She rubbed her temples and strolled out the door with Danyelle following close behind her.

Olivia put Bryce in the bed with her and told Val she could sleep in his room. Afterwards, Olivia checked to make sure all doors and windows were locked before heading to bed. As she passed by Bryce's bedroom, she saw Val pulling the blankets over herself.

"Hey." She walked into the room. "If I haven't already said this"—She paused a moment—"I am so proud of you."

Dimples formed in Val's cheeks. "Why?"

Olivia walked over and sat on the side of the bed. "When Julian came home from Seattle I was sure you were never going to be able to forgive him. You treated him like dirt."

They laughed together.

"But I'm glad to see that you finally found it in your heart to forget the past."

"Livie, his lies and infidelity blinded me from seeing that just because he made a mistake he didn't stop loving me. But it's him who deserves all the credit for us being together. He was the one who made the sacrifice. He loved me enough to forgo his multi-million-dollar contract in Seattle to play in New York for only a third of what he's worth."

"The trials we endure in life can do nothing but make us stronger," Olivia reminded her.

"I've learned that, although my last name will change, who I am on the inside will still remain the same. I'm going to be a wife and hopefully one day a mother, but I still want a life of my own. I will never put my life on hold like I did before. Don't get me wrong, you know I will support Julian, but not at the expense of me falling back ten steps to push him forward two. Am I making any sense?"

"I understand and I'm jealous of you."

Val gave her a puzzled look.

"God has blessed you because it's not too many women who can say they have it all. You have the degree, the man and pretty soon you'll be adding babies and a career to your resume. God has blessed you." She wrapped her arms around Val. "I love you."

"I love you, too." She pushed Olivia back away from her. "But I need to get some rest for tomorrow and so do you, miss maid of honor."

Olivia's insides tingled at her honorary roll in the wedding.

In the early morning hours, while the outside temperatures were still way below zero and the wind made the chill factor in Philadelphia feel like it was in the negative twenties, Olivia was awakened by the sound of someone pounding on her front door. She turned over to check on Bryce. He was sound asleep.

"My son could sleep through the second coming."

She crawled out of bed and threw her robe on. Olivia was going to kill Julian for waking her up so early in the morning. She knew it had to be no one but him. He was the only person who would be up at this time in the morning. Julian lacked patience, which would explain why he couldn't wait until later that morning to see Val. When she flipped on the living room lights the knocking became louder. She looked for Kennedy and Clinton, who were sleeping soundly under the dining room table. Then Olivia fixed her mouth to tell Julian to quiet down, but when she flung the door wide open it wasn't Julian on the other side. It was Julian's stepfather, Mr. McCormick.

The distraught look in his eyes made Olivia's body tense up. She sensed that he was there to deliver bad news. This man who usually stood tall and strong like a tower was now bent over. He leaned his muscular body against the doorjamb for support. The whites of his eyes were bloodshot, and Olivia could see his eyes full of tears. She was scared to ask what was wrong, because she knew it couldn't be good.

He finally parted his lips to say something, but choked on his words. He held out his arms for Olivia, and she helped him into her apartment.

When they sat down together on the sofa, Mr. McCormick's head fell down in front of him. He had cried the distance to Olivia's house, and it took him another twenty minutes before he found the strength to get out of the car and to her door. Eventually he would have to tell her why he was there, and once he did, this nightmare would become a reality.

"Mr. McCormick, is Mrs. McCormick okay? She's not sick, is she?"

He lifted his head so fast that the look in his eyes startled her. "It's Julian," he sobbed. "His mother sent me over here to tell her in person before she heard it on the news."

"Heard what?" Olivia braced herself for the worst. Goose bumps broke out along her arms, and she prayed that Julian was all right.

"Julian's plane crashed last night right after takeoff. We received a call about an hour ago. There were no survivors."

Shaken to the core, Olivia fell back in her seat. Mr. McCormick hugged her numb body tight. She immediately assumed he must have been mistaken. Julian wasn't dead. Just a few hours ago they were watching him on television. He was alive and well, jumping, running and slamming the ball into the basket.

Across the room sat over two hundred wedding favors and programs for a wedding that was not going to take place. "No," she cried. The pain was too deep for her to contain, and she cried hysterically.

"How am I going to tell Val?" Olivia said more to herself than to Mr. McCormick.

"You don't have to."

They turned around and found Val watching them.

"I've known for hours."

Olivia rushed to comfort her. She expected Val to cry, kick, scream or get mad. Instead she stood frozen, emotionless like a statue. Olivia helped her to sit down, but Val remained unmoved. Olivia figured she was upset and in shock. She and Mr. McCormick sat with Val until her parents arrived later that morning.

Chapter 3

Dark gray rain clouds hung suspended over First Nazareth A.M.E. church. A long black hearse sat parked in front of the church, several black limousines lined up behind it. The police blocked off the street, and barricades held back fans holding up signs expressing their condolences. News vans filled every corner with correspondents trying to get a glimpse of the coffin that held Julian's last remains.

Inside, the church pews were full of Julian's friends, family, colleagues and teammates all gathered together to say good-bye. The entire New York Knicks team stood in attendance along the back wall along with people from the NBA organization, including Commissioner David Stern. Even Owen Torres and a few of Julian's old teammates from Seattle showed up. Flower wreaths surrounded Julian's coffin and a soft melody drifted from the organ.

On the first row, Julian's stepfather cradled his wife in his arms as she wept loudly.

The days following Julian's death were hard on everyone. Mrs. McCormick wouldn't leave the kitchen. She mourned her only child by baking cakes, pies, and loaves of bread all from scratch.

Mr. McCormick pulled out videotapes of Julian's high school basketball games. For hours he locked himself inside his bedroom and watched Julian turn his basketball skills from average to phenomenal.

Val fell into a deep depression. She wouldn't eat, sleep or talk to anyone. Her parents tried to convince her to get her mind off of things by getting her out of the house, but she refused to go anywhere. Even when Mrs. McCormick went to visit her she wouldn't leave the confines of her bedroom.

When it came time for Val to attend the funeral her mental state hadn't changed, so her parents chose to stay at home with her.

From the choir box Danyelle stared down at the closed coffin that held her good friend. She wondered why bad things happened to good people. Val and Julian were on the verge of making a commitment to spend the rest of their lives together, and on the day they were supposed to be standing in this church saying their I do's, the groom was being buried.

"God's ways are not our ways," Danyelle softly recited to herself.

"You may not know how much it hurts my heart to stand before you this morning," Reverend Simms stuttered from behind the podium. "I've watched Julian grow from a little boy into a man and to have him taken away . . ." Reverend Simms paused. "I'm sorry." He wiped a single tear away from his eye.

Colin patted him on the back and told him to have a seat.

"I may not have known Julian as well as most here, but the few times that he and I did speak, I felt in my heart he was a man of God. He was a consistent figure in church, and it's rare to find young men his age so committed to the Lord. The last time Julian and I talked he asked me to pray for him. He told me that he would be on the road for a few weeks playing away, and it was important for him to stay close to God while he was on the road. It's a hard thing for a man not to be taken in by money, fame and power, and I commend him for that. I'm proud to say that now that he's been called home he doesn't ever have to worry about being separated from the Lord ever again."

Olivia tapped her foot on the floor, trying to hold back her tears. It was important for her to remain strong for her son. When the time came for Olivia to explain to Bryce that Uncle Julian had died, she was unsure of how he would react. Since Bryce's father wasn't in his life, Julian stepped up as a surrogate dad and he often did a lot of father-son things with Bryce. They were close, and she feared her son would act out in a negative way.

Christmas morning was when Olivia told him the news. She didn't plan to, but when he kept asking for Val and Julian she felt as though she had no choice. His reaction to the news was not what she expected.

"Honey, did you hear what Mommy just said?" Olivia sat in one of her son's miniature beanbags in his room.

Bryce walked around his room, picking up toys from off the carpet. Olivia had been trying to get him to clean his room for weeks, and she wondered why he had chosen that moment to start listening to her.

"Yes, Mommy. Uncle Julian is in heaven and I won't see him anymore because he's with God."

She watched him put his books back on the shelves and store board games away under his bed before suggesting they go out to dinner to talk some more.

Olivia felt Bryce had taken the news too well, and she kept a close eye on him for any unusual behavior.

It wasn't until they were getting ready for the funeral that Bryce started asking questions.

"If Uncle Julian is in heaven, how can he be at the church?" His innocent eyes waited for an answer from his mother.

Olivia knelt down in front of him and searched for the right words to say. She knew it was too confusing for a four-year-old child to understand.

Dean could see Olivia was nearing her breaking point. He intervened and brilliantly explained how important it was for them to say their final good-byes to Julian's memory. Olivia was thankful.

Now they sat in the church, surrounded by hundreds of flower wreaths, songs that serenaded the dead and enduring heartfelt words that made the funeral that much sadder. Several people spoke beautifully about Julian's short life, and afterward the choir sang one final song before the last viewing.

The choir stood, and just as Danyelle opened her mouth to lead the choir, the church doors abruptly swung open and Val entered the sanctuary. The entire church gasped loudly at the horror they witnessed.

Val marched slowly down the aisle in her white Jessica Zamir backless wedding gown. The form-fitting twenty-seven-thousand-dollar gown was badly wrinkled and looked slept in. A tattered train with small holes and dirt stains trailed behind her. Over one hundred man hours was needed to custom make the veil that hung haphazardly over her head. She held a bouquet of red roses directly in front of her belly.

She paraded down the aisle and stopped directly in front of Julian's casket.

Scared of what Val might do next, Olivia lifted Bryce up from off her lap and handed him to

Tressie. She raced out into the middle aisle. "Val."
Olivia walked up behind her and placed one hand
on her shoulder. "Sweetie, let's go."

Olivia tried to steer her away from the casket,
but Val refused to move.

From the back of the church Val's father raced
in after her. He charged toward them, but Olivia
put up her hand to stop him.

"I can't . . . I can't leave without . . ." Val whispered before pressing her hand against the top of
the casket, searching for a piece of herself that was
lost. She dropped her bridal bouquet to the floor
and cried for the first time.

Olivia hugged her in front of the church for several minutes before again trying to get Val to leave
with her.

"Are you ready?"

Val looked down at her engagement ring one
last time. She pulled it off her finger and placed it
on top of the casket. "I will always love you," she
whispered before she allowed Olivia to lead her out
of the church.

When they walked outside, the photographers
snapped pictures, and reporters asked for comments, but Val remained silent as Olivia led her to
Val's Mercedes Benz, left running in front of the
church.

Olivia took Val back to her parents' house and,
once they were safely inside, Olivia helped Val out
of her wedding gown and back into bed.

Val balled herself into a fetal position and cried into her pillow. Olivia lay next to her and rubbed her back for over an hour. She knew the girl was releasing grief she had been carrying around for over a week.

After Val's cries subsided, Olivia went into the bathroom to run her a bath. She lit a few of her aunt's aromatherapy candles and hoped it would help Val relax.

She was gone for less than ten minutes before she went back into Val's bedroom to find her missing. Olivia panicked. She searched Val's parents' room and then the guest bedroom before she smelled something burning.

Olivia rushed down the stairs and toward the living room. When she walked in she saw Val standing in front of the fireplace with nothing on but her underwear.

"Val, what are you doing?" Olivia didn't realize until she stepped closer that Val had stuffed her wedding gown into the fireplace and set it ablaze. She rushed over and tried to pull the remains out of the fire, but it was too late.

"Olivia!" Val cried. "Why? Why did Julian leave me? Again?"

Olivia pulled Val into her arms.

"It's not fair!" She fell into Olivia's arms. "It's just not fair.

Chapter 4

January 2008

From his cot, Judge West could see the sun sprouting rays of light across the sky. "Lord, thank You for allowing me to see another day." The judge never missed an opportunity to give God praise for the things he took for granted.

He stood to his feet and stretched his limbs. Against the far wall, right beneath the window West had started keeping track of how many days he had been locked away. He picked up a piece of drywall that he used as a pencil and drew another mark down on the wall. Today was the twenty-first day of his incarceration. Twenty-one days, and he hadn't seen anyone. No visits. No letters. No lawyers.

After his arrest he was shoved into an unmarked car and brought here. No newspaper. No books. No radio. He did nothing but stare at the four walls. He had no idea what was going on, but he had a funny feeling that his past had come back to haunt him.

The first few nights he spent in that cell he racked his brain, trying to figure out what was going on. He wondered if he had done something wrong. Then he thought back to when he was a confidential informant for the agency. They had worked on numerous cases together, and he had helped them convict a lot of heartless murderers, but it had been over twenty years since he'd last heard from the bureau.

West sighed heavily and sat back down on his cot. For the time being, he would have to wait for them to come to him. The government was known for taking its time in everything they did, so he expected this to be a long wait.

"Are you hungry, West?" a familiar voice shouted out to him from outside his cell.

West jumped up. "Stevens, is that you?"

Stevens, a white man in his late thirties, stepped in front of West's cell, holding a tray of breakfast food. He stuck his hand through the bars for a handshake. "Sir, how are you doing?"

West was happy to see an old face. "It's been years, but I would recognize that voice anywhere." West looked him over. "It looks like you finally grew up. When we first met you were a fresh face in the bureau."

"Yes, it's been some years." He handed West the tray of food.

"Listen, if you wanted me to come in to talk with you, guy, you didn't have to set me up and take me out in front of my family like that."

"I know it was kind of harsh, but we were in a hurry. Ernie . . . they found you."

Judge West knew the day would come when he would have to face the group of people he went against and helped put away. "I knew it would only be a matter of time."

"Yeah. They put a huge contract out on your head. Remember what I said the last time we were together?"

"You said that if they ever found me, I would die," West repeated slowly.

"Yes, and because of what happened to your son and his wife, I made a promise on behalf of the bureau that no harm would come to you or your grandson as long as I was alive." Stevens stepped back away from the cell and folded his hands. "We always knew that there was a great possibility that because of your position as a judge we wouldn't be able to keep your identity a secret forever."

"That was a chance that I was willing to take. The number of lives I have helped save far exceeds me living another day."

"You've always been such a noble man. The day of your arrest we intentionally leaked the story to the newspapers and television stations so that they would be there waiting for you by the time you were brought in for processing."

"But I—"

Stevens held up his hand to stop him.

"We brought you in the back entrance. We set up a decoy that looked just like you to act like you." Stevens held up the newspaper for him to see.

West stared at a snapshot of a man who looked just like him hiding from the press as he is ushered into the county jail. The headline read THE MAN WHO CONVICTED MURDERERS IS ACCUSED OF MURDER.

Stevens folded the paper back and stuck it under his arm. "Remember that murder you told us about the black kid that was found stoned to death next to the church?"

West nodded his head yes.

"They are pointing the finger at you as being responsible for that."

"But I told you exactly what happened that night," West protested.

"Yes, we had that story and we were following up on some leads against that story when your name came up."

"What now?" West asked.

"I'm not sure. My superiors have taken me off the case, because they feel as though I'm too close."

"You don't have any additional information you can tell me?" West was anxious for any news he could get. "Stevens, you're just about the only person I trust in the bureau."

"Well, one thing I know for sure is that they hate you. They want you dead. The bounty on your head is for one hundred and twenty-five thousand dollars."

"What about my family? Will they be safe?"

"They haven't made any threats against your grandson, but I'll make sure they keep an ear out for anything suspicious."

"So what's going to happen to me?"

"For now you sit and wait."

At his reply Judge West dropped his head. There was nothing more he could do.

"Excuse me." Danyelle pushed her way through a crowd of college kids loitering in the middle of the registration office. She navigated down several wrong corridors until she found her final destination, the student lounge area.

Anxious to enroll for the spring semester, Danyelle arrived at the Bible College before its doors opened. At seven-thirty in the morning she raced inside to secure her name on the roster for each one of the classes she desired.

Four and a half hours later she was still registering for school. The process wasn't going as smoothly as she had hoped it would. At the start of her day she learned that students who attended last semester had pre-registered, leaving most of the classes she wanted already closed.

Danyelle spotted an empty seat and raced to it before another lazy teenager got to it first. She placed her backpack down by her side and pulled out the school's catalog. She was determined to carry a full load this semester, and she wasn't leaving until she picked out three more elective classes. She focused hard to find classes that revolved around her work schedule, but the girls sitting close to her kept breaking her concentration each time they bobbed their head or snapped their fingers to the music blasting through their earphones. Danyelle sent annoyed looks their way as a hint that they were disturbing her, but they appeared to be in a music-induced coma and never acknowledged her presence.

She scanned her most updated list of available courses. It was a long list, which made it more difficult for her to narrow down which ones were the best.

The aggravation of such a long day gave Danyelle a throbbing headache. She massaged her temples to relieve the pulsating pound against her head, but the suffering continued.

Tired, Danyelle peeked inside her book bag, searching for her medication that could cure all ailments. She breathed a sigh of relief when she spotted the stash she stuck in her bag before leaving home that morning. In a hurry to relax her mind, she raced out of the student lounge and into the brisk, cold air.

The temperature outside hovered around the freezing mark, and the weatherman predicted snow for the remainder of the week. Upset because she forgot her gloves, Danyelle wrapped her scarf tight around her neck and pushed her naked, cold hands deep into her coat pockets. The powerful winds pushed her across the courtyard. To shield herself from the cold she ducked behind the library.

A few feet away she saw a cluster of trash dumpsters. *That would be the perfect place for me to get in a few puffs.* Once she was safely behind one huge dumpster, she dropped her bag on the ground and dug for the blunt she rolled that morning. She found it and stuck it in her mouth. It was going to be hard to get a light, so she turned away from the wind. After several tries she finally lit the blunt and inhaled.

After only a few puffs she heard footsteps walking in her direction. She stood still, praying that whoever was coming her way wouldn't notice her. She held the blunt down by her side and listened intently. The footsteps stopped, then the sound of gravel underneath feet alerted her that she was caught.

In a hurry, she extinguished the blunt against the trash dumpster and tried to wave the smoke away. Her heart was beating fast. She was scared she would get caught using drugs on school property. It would be embarrassing to tell her sister that she was kicked out of school before she even attended her first class.

When her unwanted visitor rounded the corner, she was surprised to see a familiar face staring back at her. "Danyelle, I thought that was you." Reverend Montgomery greeted her with a huge smile.

Her eyes were filled with surprise. "Reverend Montgomery, what are you doing here?" Danyelle wrung her jittery hands in front of her pastor.

"I teach here."

It wasn't until he said those words that she remembered that he was a professor at the college.

"I was in the student lounge when I thought I saw you head out the door." He looked around at her surroundings. "What are you doing out here?"

"I um . . ." Danyelle tried to think of an excuse, but her mind went blank.

He was amused and tried to help her out. "Are you registering for classes?"

"Yes. I was registering for classes and it was so stuffy in that building that I had to come outside for some fresh air. I thought maybe if I cleared my head it would help me decide what electives to take."

"Oh! If you need some help, I'll be glad to help you. I have an office on campus. We can go there now and I'll answer any questions you may have."

Reverend Montgomery's generosity made him sexier than usual. Typically, Danyelle wasn't impressed with the reverend, but looking at him now she understood why more than half the single ladies at First Nazareth were chasing him down. He had a physique molded after one of football's greatest running backs, Terrell Owens, and a face that closely resembled basketball sensation Dwayne Wade.

"Are you coming?" he asked when he realized Danyelle hadn't gathered her things to follow him.

"Yes." She quickly grabbed her book bag and followed him to his office.

Unfortunately, Colin's office wasn't in close proximity, and they had to walk to the far end of the campus. As they settled in, Danyelle's teeth chattered from the cold.

"I'm sorry. It's not as warm in here as it is in the registrar's office. Let me get you a cup of hot chocolate."

He disappeared out of the office and minutes later returned with two steaming cups of hot chocolate from the vending machine. He placed her cup down in front of her, while she peeled out of her hat and scarf.

Danyelle wrapped her numb fingers around the hot Styrofoam cup. Eager to thaw herself out, she drank. When the hot chocolate reached the back of her throat, she gagged and pushed her lips out. "This stuff is horrible."

Colin rushed to her side and patted her back. "I'm sorry. I know how you feel, but this is the best we have."

Danyelle rolled her eyes and sucked her teeth.

He wasn't offended by her response. In fact, it made him sit up and take notice of how Danyelle's beauty was blossoming right before his eyes. Her curvy body, rosy cheeks, and sexy eyes drew Colin into a trance.

"Rev. Rev." She lightly nudged him with her arm. "Are you ready?"

Lost in his own thoughts he looked around.

"Reverend Montgomery, are you all right? Maybe I should come back another time. I think maybe you were standing out in the cold for too long." She got up to gather her things, but he stopped her.

"No, I'm fine." He reached behind his desk to boot up his computer. "Why don't you show me what you have so far?"

Then they were interrupted when Reverend Baxter barged into his office. "Colin, I have this great opportunity for you and I hope"—He stopped when he saw Danyelle— "I'm sorry. I didn't mean to intrude. Hi." He studied her face for a moment. "I remember you. You're the one with the angelic voice. Don't you attend Reverend Montgomery's church?" He saw her book bag on the floor by her feet. "Are you going to school here this semester?"

She said yes.

"That's great. Isn't that great, Reverend?" He turned to Colin and, for the first time, noticed the look of infatuation in his eyes. It was the same lovesick expression he wore on his face the entire time he courted his wife.

Instantly, he felt like he was intruding on something special. "I'm going to excuse myself and allow the two of you to get back to business. I'm sure the registrar's office could use my help." He quickly let himself out.

Danyelle disregarded Reverend Baxter's odd behavior and pulled out a pile of papers from her bag.

Colin chewed on the end of his pencil while looking over her class schedule.

"You're going to get lead poisoning if you keep doing that." She reached across his desk, pulled the pencil from his mouth, then threw it in the trashcan.

Colin appreciated her gentle chastising. She reminded him of his foster mother. Brassy and bossy. Then he focused his attention back to her schedule. "Why did you pick these three classes?" He pointed with his finger.

"I really didn't have a choice. Most of the classes I wanted were already full. If you could help me find two more classes, then I'll have a full schedule for the spring semester."

He nodded his head while searching through different screens on his computer.

"But it would be great if you could get me morning classes."

He questioned her preference with his eyes.

"I usually work in the afternoons and evenings."

"Would you be interested in this?" He pointed to his screen. "It's a class called 'The facts behind the book of Isaiah.'"

Danyelle jumped up from her seat and looked over the reverend's shoulder. "I tried to sign up for that class, but the counselor at the registrar's office told me it was closed."

"It is closed, but if you get the instructor's permission you can still sit in on his class," Colin educated her.

"Really?" Danyelle knew it would be worth it to hold on and God would open a few doors for her. "Do you know the instructor?"

"You're talking to him. I can lift the closed status long enough to add your name to the roster." He punched a few keys. "And, *ta-da,* you're in."

Danyelle felt God's favor shine down on her. "Thank you, Reverend Montgomery." Without thinking, she wrapped her arms around his neck and kissed him on the cheek. "I really appreciate this." When she noticed how warm his body felt next to her, she quickly stepped back away from him.

"Please." He enjoyed feeling her body so close to his. He placed her hand in his. "You can call me Colin."

His touch placed a fire down in her pants that she had never felt before. Her heart dropped to the bottom of her stomach. Whatever she was feeling scared her enough to run from him. "Reverend—I mean Colin—I have to go." She hurriedly grabbed her book bag to leave.

"What about your other classes?" he asked.

"That's all right. I'm fine with just three," she hollered out before closing the door behind her.

Colin smiled. He knew there was something special about her.

Chapter 5

Val banged her head against the car's steering wheel three times before her vision became blurred and she had to stop. "What am I doing here?" The rows of headstones surrounding her car pulled her back to reality. This was Julian's final resting place, and she was there to say good-bye.

It was her fifth attempt that week at trying to visit his grave. Each time before, she could never find the strength to get out of the car, but this time she prayed for God to hold her hand along the way.

It was hard for her to accept that Julian was gone. In her mind she understood that he was gone, but the gaping hole left in her heart kept growing every day. That's why she was there. She wanted closure. She thought that if she could feel his name etched in his headstone then she would be able to move on.

Not a day passed when she didn't ask God to turn back the hands of time. Just this once, she wanted to play God and change life events.

It was time for her to face her fears. Val swung her car door open. When she stepped out into the brisk air, that's when she noticed her labored breathing. Anxiety swelled in her belly, and doubts filled her head. She wasn't sure if she could do this.

She pulled out from her pocket a map the groundskeeper had given her. He said it would take her straight to Julian's grave. Her hands shook from nervousness. She set out on her journey and followed the directions through the maze of gravesites until she came upon another visitor who was crying hysterically at their loved one's final resting place.

"I'm so sorry," the girl repeated while lying face down on top of the grave. Her clothes were full of dirt stains, and a small shovel lay by her side. She had just finished planting flowers, and her cries were so loud that she didn't notice she had company.

Val didn't want to intrude. She sympathized with this girl. She understood the kind of grief she was experiencing.

The temperatures were predicted to reach no higher than fifteen degrees. It was far too cold for anyone to be lying out on the ground, and Val began to wonder if this wasn't the Lord's work at hand. She thought perhaps she could have someone to talk to about the way she was feeling.

"Excuse me." Val softly tapped her shoulder. "You look like you could use a friend to talk to."

The girl swept the hair away from her face and sat up. When she turned around, all of Val's sympathy instantly vanished and was replaced with disbelief. Val was stunned to see her face. It was

Caitlyn from Seattle. Val's eyes darted to the tomb-stone of the grave she cried over. It was Julian's.

"How dare you show up here?" Val viciously hollered.

"I-I-I," Caitlyn stuttered.

Then Val hit her with a right hook straight in the jaw. "Why can't you just leave us alone?" Val jumped on top of her and flung her arms wildly at Caitlyn's face.

Caitlyn was powerless against the blows Val threw. She was so full of remorse that all she could do was cry out, "I'm sorry!"

Val beat Caitlyn's face until her fists began to hurt. By the time she stopped, Caitlyn's face was so bloody, she hardly recognized her. She got up off Caitlyn and pointed in her face. "You're not welcome here." Val walked over and pulled out the flowers Caitlyn had planted and flung them as far away from Julian as she could. Then she staggered back to her car and pulled off.

The moment Dean stepped foot in his grandpa's attic he felt like a little boy again. He stared at the low beams he used to swing from and the dusty boxes he would duck behind when playing hide-and-seek with his grandfather. He wiped a few cobwebs out of his way so he could get a better look at the place. "Nothing's changed."

"Remind me why we're here again." Olivia stepped up behind him and wrapped her arms around his waist.

"I have to find the deed to the house." Dean broke away from her embrace. "That's the only collateral I have to get my grandpa a lawyer."

"How can you retain a lawyer when your grandpa is still refusing your visits?" Olivia shadowed Dean's every move as he pushed boxes around. "Doesn't it bother you that your grandpa won't talk to anyone? He's turned you and Reverend Simms away. He won't even talk with his public defender."

Dean's eyesight turned blurry and he suddenly felt faint. Scared he was going to fall, he held his hand out to steady himself.

"Are you okay?" Olivia saw that he didn't look too well.

He held on to her hand tight as Olivia led him to sit on a nearby box. "I'm fine. It's so cold up here. I think that blast of cool air caught me off guard." He closed his eyes for a second and squeezed her hand tighter.

"Are you sure there's nothing wrong?" Her voice was full of concern.

He didn't want her to worry about him, so he swiftly pointed the conversation in a different direction. "Do you think he's capable of murder?"

Caught off guard by his question, Olivia answered the best she could. "The first time I heard that news report accusing Judge West of killing a twelve-year-old black boy back in the sixties, I was sure this was some kind of political conspiracy to hurt the black community by filing bogus charges against someone we all love and trust. That man has become our foundation, and if we lose that, our foundation crumbles. Last night I thought he could be protecting somebody. That would help explain why he won't see you. He's probably scared."

"I'm sure he is scared. He's a white man being accused of killing a black kid in the South. I also think he's embarrassed to look anyone in the face." He patted Olivia on her back and stood to his feet. "We need to get started looking for those documents. I promised Bryce we could go to the movies later this afternoon."

"I'll start with those boxes over there." She pointed to a box sitting in the far corner, while Dean began laboring through another box in the opposite corner of the room.

Dean pulled open the flaps and dug his hand deep inside pulling out a mound of Polaroids. He browsed through them, finding snapshots of him he never remembered posing for. Then a picture of his parents brought his journey down memory lane to an abrupt halt. He analyzed the loving picture of his mom and dad together.

This was the closest he had ever been to a picture of his parents. His grandpa refused to hang any pictures of them in the house. All pictures of his mom and dad were kept locked away. He remembered his grandma telling him that having pictures of his parents around was too painful for his grandpa to handle.

Every so often his grandma would surprise him by pulling out a picture of them. But he was never allowed to keep it for long, and she always made him promise to never tell Grandpa.

His grandma always said he was a carbon copy of his father. This was the first time he got to see for himself the close resemblance. Dean thought they shared the same square jaw line, build and smile. It was obvious where his perfect bronze tan came from. The woman with beautiful dark brown skin and curly hair was no doubt his mother. A shockwave of hurt penetrated his heart. He wished they had lived.

"Olivia, have you found anything yet?" Dean put the pictures away and turned toward his girlfriend.

"No, not too much of anything. Just a lot of photos of white people," she replied.

Dean laughed to himself and started working on another box. Inside he discovered an abundance of official documents and files. Dean's birth certificate, his grandparents' wedding license and a copy of his parents' death decree were the only contents found within the box. As he skimmed through, he realized his grandpa kept his paperwork in order. Every piece of paper was neatly filed and labeled.

"Dean, it's cold up here." Olivia wrapped her arms around herself and rubbed to get warm. "Would you like a cup of hot tea? Oh, Dean! I forgot to tell you. I found a bunch of linens stored away in a box over here. I'm going to leave it by the stairs, and before we leave I need for you to take them downstairs. I figure your grandpa could use them, and if not, I may be able to use them for myself."

Preoccupied with his hunt, Dean said okay. Once Olivia left, Dean threw the documents he held in his hand back in the box. Then he counted the number of boxes they still needed to comb through. There were at least thirty. "God, give me strength!"

Ready to give up, he shoved the box in front of him away. He decided to save this project for another day. He figured they could pick Bryce up early and catch a bite to eat before the matinee. He stood up and maneuvered his way toward the exit. A short lapse in memory almost made him forget about the box Olivia wanted. He did a quick check to make sure the box he was looking in was what she wanted. When he did, he noticed something out of the ordinary about the way the sheets looked. "She did say there were bed linens in this box. Didn't she?"

Dean examined the sheets a little closer before finally holding one up before him. It looked like a Halloween costume. "What is he doing with this?" Dean looked at the backside before turning it around. Stitched over the left hand side of the breast pocket was an emblem. Dean closely studied the white cross set inside a bright red circle. The most interesting detail of the emblem was the red teardrop set in the center of the cross. For some reason his heart rate accelerated and his hands shook uncontrollably. He had never seen this symbol before, but for some reason it scared him.

When Dean blinked his eyes three times what he was looking at became clear to him. In his hands he held a Ku Klux Klan robe. He threw it across the room and dug further down in the box. He found the matching hood. Dean rubbed his forehead. He was confused. *Why is this stuff in my grandpa's attic?*

He tore through the box, searching for an explanation. On the bottom of the box was a manila envelope. Hastily, he ripped it open. Horror surfaced on his face. He stared at a picture of his grandpa posing for the camera along with a bunch of Klansmen. As cool as the room was, Dean couldn't help but sweat with perspiration. Ten men all dressed in white robes with white hoods covering their faces. Judge West and another man were the only two in the picture not in disguise.

His grandfather stood right next to the grand wizard and held up a flag bearing the same symbol he found on the robe. "I don't believe this."

"Sorry, it took me so long." Olivia was on her way back up the stairs with their tea. "I added honey to yours, just the way you like it."

Dean hid the robes by throwing them back in the box and stuck the photo in his back pocket. He wasn't ready to tell her what he found.

"Livie, I don't want to spend any more time here. Let's go pick Bryce up from your sister and take him out to eat."

She looked at him strangely. "Okay, but I thought it was so important for you to find that deed."

"It was, but I can get it later." He gestured for her to turn back down the steps.

"What about the box with the linens in it?" she asked.

"I'll pick that stuff up later," he replied.

Chapter 6

Three weeks later

Val reminisced back to her first year in law school. She had one class where the professor would make the entire class act out a mock trial. Each time she played a lawyer she dreamed of the day she'd stand before a real judge in an actual courtroom. Unfortunately, today she was in a courtroom, but not as a lawyer.

The bailiff screamed out Val's name, shaking her from her thoughts. She half-heartedly got up from her seat and stood before the judge.

Olivia sat in the courtroom worried about her cousin's mental state. Val used to be vibrant and so full of life, but after Julian died, she seemed to have lost the will to live. The blue pinstriped blazer with matching skirt looked good on Val, but it wasn't enough to make her look presentable. Her face looked naked and drab without any makeup. The dark circles under her eyes revealed her lack of sleep, and hair that never had a strand out of place was haphazardly piled atop her head.

Olivia prayed that Val would bounce back to her old self, but after she heard about the fight with

Caitlyn, it looked like things were getting worse. Then Caitlyn pressed battery charges against Val. Olivia felt helpless and wondered how much more Val could bear before losing all self-control.

The judge pulled her eyeglasses away from her face and lay them down beside her. She recognized Val the moment she walked into the courtroom. Val was one of the law students she'd met with last year. Every year the university asked the judge to speak with a group of law students who were still undecided about what kind of law they wanted to specialize in. The judge remembered Val from that meeting, not because she was the only black woman, but because she was the most focused, detailed, and showed so much empathy for others. Val's passion for law was rare, but refreshing. The judge was very interested in seeing how far Val's ambition would take her.

This morning the judge was disappointed to see that Val had gotten off track and lost sight of her goal. "Ms. Benson, you admit to the court that you are responsible for the bruises on Ms. Haas's face."

"Yes, Your Honor." Val's response was uncaring, cold and lacked remorse.

"Are you sorry for what you did?" The judge wondered what would drive this girl with such a bright future to jeopardize it all.

"No, Your Honor."

Olivia wished she had insisted that Val retain a lawyer. Only a fool would represent herself, and that was exactly what Val looked like.

Across the courtroom sat a slew of lawyers all hired to represent Caitlyn. "Your Honor," one of Caitlyn's lawyers spoke up, "this is not the first time Ms. Benson has attacked my client. They did have an altercation when she"—The uptight Jewish man cut his eyes in Val's direction and turned his nose down—"lived in Seattle. We are asking that the court grant us a restraining order against Ms. Benson."

Olivia stood and yelled from her seat. "This is ridiculous."

The judge's face turned to annoyance when she heard Olivia's outburst. She picked up her gavel to slam it down, but before she could say anything, Olivia pressed on with her protest. "Your Honor, that girl"—She pointed toward Caitlyn—"did nothing but torment my cousin the entire time she lived in Seattle."

The judge questioned Caitlyn's counsel with her eyes. "Is there any truth to this?"

"Your Honor, we are not aware of our client ever being responsible for baiting Ms. Benson in any kind of way."

"Of course you wouldn't." The judge was stern and was losing all patience with both sides. She glared at Caitlyn then noted a few things on the file in front of her before turning to Caitlyn's lawyer. "Is it safe to assume that your client will be returning back to Seattle shortly, since that is her current address?"

"Yes, Your Honor. Ms. Haas has concluded her business here and will be returning to Seattle later this evening," Caitlyn's lawyer replied.

"I'm not sure what the entire story is between the two of you, but I'm going to fine both of you court costs for wasting my time with something that could have been resolved outside of court. Ms. Haas, I feel like you're not entirely innocent in this matter."

Caitlyn shifted uncomfortably under the judge's watchful eye.

"But, Ms. Benson, that doesn't mean you can assault people any time you lose control of your temper. You could have done some permanent damage to her face. Your punishment will be two hundred hours of community service."

The judge dismissed the hearing, and Val strolled out of the courtroom with Olivia on her heels.

"I should have hired you as my lawyer," Val cracked a joke.

"I'm sorry, Val. I didn't mean to embarrass you, but I couldn't sit still and allow Caitlyn to make you look like the culprit when she had no right being at the cemetery."

"It's not her fault I lost control."

They stopped at a bench and sat.

"I'm glad you came with me today. I don't think I could handle seeing Caitlyn today without finishing what I started. I think what made me so mad about seeing her again was how guilty I feel about Julian."

"Why would you feel guilty?" Olivia asked.

"I'm the reason Julian died in that crash. I begged him to take that flight. He knew it was too dangerous to fly, but he boarded that plane to please me. If he would have waited for the morning flight, we would be married right now."

"Val, you can't blame yourself for something that was set in motion before we were even born. God called Julian home. It was his time, and you have to let this go. What I'm saying may seem impossible, but if you don't let go of that anger, you will never be able to feel God's love surrounding you." Olivia grabbed hold of her cousin's hands. "Close your eyes. Can you see God's hand reaching out toward you? He wants to stop the hurt, but you won't allow Him to heal you because you're punishing yourself for something that wasn't your fault. Are you going to take God's hand and love, or are you going to leave God hanging?"

Val wiped away the tears that fell from her eyes.

"If you don't move on with your life, then you will never experience the abundance of blessings He has waiting for you."

***

Danyelle grabbed her duffle bag from the front seat of her car and ran up the church steps. She was running late, and if she didn't hurry, the kids in the children's choir would leave and say it was her fault for being late.

She swung open the church doors out of breath. The church was full of children. There were thirty-two kids in the choir, and today every one of them had shown up for rehearsal. Instead of publicizing her arrival, she took a moment to observe how the children acted without parental supervision. She wasn't pleased.

More than half the children jumped over church pews, ran across the altar and played in the pulpit. The few remaining kids who were serious about rehearsal surrounded the piano exercising their voices.

"That's enough." She stormed inside and dropped her bag on the first pew. "You know better than to play in the house of the Lord."

The children dropped their heads in shame.

"Let's get started."

Everyone quickly shifted into formation like soldiers in the Army. Danyelle handed out copies of a song she had written herself. It was an upbeat a cappella song that she was sure would bring the congregation to their feet.

She softly clapped her hands to establish a beat. At her direction, the choir sang softly and tapped their feet. Danyelle picked the two strongest voices in the choir to sing the lead. When she pointed to them, they performed a duet like Roberta Flack and Peabo Bryson. She was so excited, she couldn't wait for the congregation to hear them Sunday morning. They practiced the song several times before she could finally call it perfect and dismissed rehearsal.

"Well done," a deep voice drifted to her ears from the back of the church.

Danyelle was surprised to see Colin standing behind her. She turned back around embarrassed that he was watching them.

"That was beautiful."

This man is always sneaking up on me when I least expect it.

"Colin, I had no idea you were here."

"I was in my office working, but when I heard the children singing, I had to come witness their divine voices for myself."

"I hope we weren't too loud."

The children raced out of the church, and Danyelle cleaned up any papers left behind.

"No. I'm glad for the interruption." Colin shoved his hands in his pocket. "How are you making out at the college? I already know you're the star pupil in my class, but what about your other classes?"

"They're going well." This time Danyelle was ready for him. The last time they were alone together Colin caught her off guard with the way his eyes seduced her, but not this time. If it happened again, she was prepared to give him a dirty look. "Thanks for asking."

His eyes followed her every move.

She abruptly spun around and caught him looking. She marched up to him. "Is there something you wanted?" Danyelle stood eye to eye with Colin.

"Well"—He paused a moment and swallowed hard—"if you're not in a hurry, I was thinking maybe we could get a bite to eat."

"Dinner?" She didn't expect him to ask her out. She was sure he would have backed off from her once he realized she wasn't intimidated by him. "You want to take me out?"

"That is what I said."

In his suit underneath the church's lighting, Colin looked even better than he did on Sunday's or even in class. His sleepy, dark eyes were alluring. She felt like she was under a spell.

Danyelle lightly shook her head to regain consciousness. She playfully wagged her finger at the reverend. "Colin, why are you playing games with me?"

"What? I didn't do anything wrong. All I did was ask a beautiful woman out to dinner."

"Did you forget that you're not only my pastor, but also my teacher?"

He snickered a bit.

"Isn't it against the rules for a professor to date his students?"

"Actually, that is true, and I apologize if I overstepped my boundaries, but you and I are both adults, and like you said, we do attend the same church. Now, if someone saw us out together, they could get the wrong impression and assume you were a straight-A student because we were dating."

"That's why I don't think it's a good idea for us to go out together."

"But, again, we are both adults, and it's only dinner. I just want to get to know Danyelle Benson a little bit better."

Colin's brown eyes made her vulnerable. "I guess dinner would be fine." Danyelle was not sure why she agreed to eat with him, but there was no turning back.

"Great!" He was so excited, he jumped in the air and clicked his heels together.

Danyelle laughed at his animated performance.

"I know a small restaurant that has great food. It's not that fancy, but I like to support the small businesses."

In the car, Colin wouldn't stop talking. When he was nervous he had a tendency to talk for long periods of time. This was an example of one of those times. With Danyelle sitting so close to him he couldn't keep his mouth closed. He talked so fast, he held up both ends of the conversation by himself.

A short ride later, Colin pulled his car over in the heart of North Philly. Danyelle looked around. She was quite familiar with the area. She used to frequent this part of the city often to buy her weed. But, with the rise in violent crime and the drug task force storming the weed corners, it was too much of a risk. She couldn't endanger her life or her freedom over a dime bag of weed. Now, she traveled the short distance to New Jersey to get her stash.

The Cabana Club's sign hung above the front door of the building.

"A club?" Danyelle gave him a critical look.

"It's not just a club. It's also a restaurant."

They got out of the car, and before they could enter the establishment, Danyelle heard a familiar voice call her name.

"What's up, girl? I ain't seen you in a while." Javier was walking by and noticed her. He reached out to give her a hug.

Danyelle gave a quick wave of her hand and tried turning away. She prayed he would leave her alone. Danyelle used to be one of his best customers. He would look out for her and often sold her herb at the lowest price.

"Listen, if you need anything, look me up. I just got in a supply and I'm telling you this stuff will set you off." Javier bounced up and down as he talked.

Danyelle could see he was high by his sleepy eyes. Then Javier chuckled to himself and swayed to one side. "I got a few bags on me now if you need something." He dug into his pocket, and Danyelle stopped him before he pulled anything out.

With her eyes she tried to hint to him that this was a bad time, but he was so high he was unaware of what was going on. She knew that standing in front of her pastor with a drug dealer trying to sell her a bag was just as bad as a crack addict trying to buy a bag in front of the cops. She desperately wanted to shake him and scream for him to wake up.

"Excuse me." Colin inched himself between the two of them. "I don't think Danyelle will be buying anything from you tonight. We came here to eat. Nothing more."

Javier looked at him strangely, as if the reverend had just appeared out of thin air.

"Oh, okay." He turned away, but turned back as if he forgot something. "Girl, you know where to find me."

Danyelle slightly nodded her head and rushed into the restaurant. When Colin caught up with her, he acted like nothing happened. He told the hostess they needed a table for two.

"My name is Rosa. I'll be your server for the evening." She led them to a table and placed their menus down.

"If you don't mind I'll order for the both of us," Colin politely requested permission from Danyelle before proceeding. She agreed, and without hesitation Colin ordered them Spanish entrées.

This was Danyelle's first time at a Latino restaurant. Vibrant colors brightened the dining area. Miniature Puerto Rican flags sat on every table, and Latin music playing from the radio filled the air.

"The way you accurately pronounced those Spanish meals, I assume you speak Spanish fluently?" Danyelle snapped her fingers to the beat.

"Yes, I used to live in Spain for two years."

"Rev, it seems like you've done so much to be so young. You haven't lived in Philly long. What brings you to the city of brotherly love?"

"I'm searching for my mother. My parents divorced when I was still an infant, and when my father walked out on my mom she also walked out on me. My grandma raised me, but after she passed away two years ago, I figured it was time I try and find my mom."

"Does she live in Philly?"

"I'm pretty sure she does, but the trail has gone cold."

"Don't give up. God will place her in your path when you least expect it," Danyelle replied.

"That's what I like about you. You have unshakable faith." Colin found something special in Danyelle that most men couldn't appreciate. The day Reverend Simms introduced them he was immediately taken by her enthusiasm for Christ. The way she worked with the youth was endearing, and the passion in her voice put him under a spell.

He wasn't sure what had gotten into him, but a few times he had to scold himself for watching her hips shake from side to side as she walked down the center aisle during Sunday service.

Rosa returned with their meals. Danyelle looked from his plate to hers. Their meals were identical.

"I thought I would order you something simple for your first time." Colin blessed the food, and they dug in.

Right away, Danyelle tasted how spicy and full of flavor her meal was. The rice, beans and meat were filling.

"Are you enjoying the meal?" Colin asked after he saw her plate was half empty.

"It's delicious." Danyelle pushed another mouthful of beans in her mouth.

The table was silent as they ate, and afterwards Rosa came around to clear the table. "Would you like dessert?" she offered.

Danyelle declined, while Colin ordered a cup of coffee.

After Rosa left their table, the proprietor of the place began moving chairs and tables out of the way to open up the small dance floor. On Friday and Saturday nights the restaurant turned into a small nightclub. They sat long enough to watch a band set up, and soon that conga sound entered Colin's body and stirred his soul.

He snapped his fingers and bounced his shoulders to the beat. "Can you salsa?"

"There's not much I can't do," she got up and shook her hips seductively.

Colin smiled broadly as he took her hand in his. "Would you care to dance?"

Danyelle was never one to turn down a challenge, but she had never done the salsa in her life. The two joined several other couples already on the dance floor.

Colin gripped Danyelle's hand tightly and spun her out until she was arm's length away from him. She felt a bit out of place in the midst of seasoned dancers, who obviously knew what they were doing. This music wasn't like the hip-hop music she kept in her car's sound system.

She stood for a moment and watched the reverend move like a well-trained dancer, until he noticed her watching him.

Placing his hands around her waist, he pulled her close to him and this was where their love affair started. He led her in a simple two-step, until the music spoke to her heart through the sounds of each instrument.

Each beat of the drum drew a pattern for their footsteps to follow. The beat was fast, and they worked up a sweat as the music hypnotized every movement of their body. With every backward step taken by Colin, Danyelle would step in.

For thirty minutes they danced like professionals. Then Danyelle's footsteps started to get sluggish. Colin could see she was tired. Salsa dancing could be exhausting. He spun her around once. Twice. Three times. Then he called it quits.

Colin dragged Danyelle off the dance floor and back to their table. He gathered their things, tipped the waitress and they departed the restaurant together.

"That was fun." Danyelle danced in her seat. "I enjoyed myself. Thanks for the treat. If I didn't go out with you, I would probably be at home studying."

"No problem. It's good to get out of your usual routine and do something a little different every once in a while." He glanced at her from the corner of his eye. "I haven't done that in a long time." He laughed to himself. "You didn't do so bad yourself.

I was kind of worried when I saw you standing their watching everyone else, but you did better than I did my first time." She smiled.

"Would you like to do it again sometime?"

This time Danyelle's heart dropped. She couldn't believe the reverend was asking her out on another date. "Okay, Colin, what's up with you? In your office you kept looking at me with those sexy bedroom eyes and then you ask me out to dinner. Now you want to see me again? What is going on? You don't have enough women chasing you around church?"

He was shocked at how confrontational she was. "I like you and I want to get to know you better."

Colin pulled his car next to Danyelle's in the church parking lot.

"Okay, I'll go out with you again, but don't think I'm easy."

He laughed. "I never thought that."

"Because, I'll probably be the hardest woman you ever worked for." Those were her final words before she got out of the car.

"I never doubted it for a second." Colin watched her get in her car and pull off.

Chapter 7

The steel door slammed shut. "West, get up." Still in a comatose state, Judge West lifted his head up off the table before closing his eyes and falling back off to sleep.

"Old man, you have to get up." Instead of sitting in one of the other chairs in the room, the federal agent sat on the edge of the table. "Sorry, I'm late. I was in a meeting."

"They brought me down here three hours ago," the judge mumbled.

"West, it's not like you have anywhere to be. I thought you would be happy to get out of that cell for a while."

The judge replied with a sarcastic smirk. "How long am I going to have to stay cooped up in this miserable jail? I thought being in federal custody meant I would be living the good life. For weeks, I've been in solitary confinement. If you didn't know it or not, total isolation is enough to make a man go insane."

"I'm fully aware of that. That's why we have it." The cocky agent winked his eye. "But that's not why we have you in exile from the other inmates."

"Can I make at least one phone call? I've had not one visit."

"That's what protective custody means—No contact with the outside world. We're trying to protect you." He slammed a file folder down on the table. "Listen, if you want to leave, I can call a guard and you'll be released within the hour, but if you leave, I can no longer guarantee the safety of you or your family."

Judge West knew the man was serious. He released an aggravating moan and grabbed at his hair. "How did they find me?"

"I'm not sure, but the important thing is that we got to you before they did. Somebody must have tipped them off that we were bugging their offices, because they started feeding us false information to take us off their trail. They pointed the finger at you for most of the crimes we're trying to tie them to, in particular, the murder of that little boy."

"You must have a mole inside your organization."

"Yes, but that's why we have to be careful of who we talk to. Only the highest-ranking officials in the FBI have access to your case. We have hundreds of agents who don't know the real truth." The agent saw the leery look in West's eyes. "You don't have to worry. The FBI has conducted a comprehensive look into my background. I'm clean."

"Since I've worked with the FBI before, I'm fully aware of the fact that they will only tell me information on an as-needed basis."

"You're right about that." The agent laughed.

"Well, what can you tell me?"

"The brotherhood is fully convinced that you're going to be prosecuted. We leaked incriminating evidence to the press, and if you were to go before a jury they would definitely send you to the chair."

West did a gesture with his hands for him to continue.

"We plan to release you as soon as we get enough evidence to prove that they were the ones responsible for that kid's murder in nineteen sixty-one."

West sighed. "After all this is over, am I going to be able to return to the life I had before?"

The agent looked at him and solemnly replied, "Let's hope so." He pulled a letter from the folder and handed it to West. "This came for you sometime last week."

Judge West stared at it a moment before snatching it out of the agent's hand. He glanced at the return address. The envelope looked like it had gone through Baghdad before coming to him. It was torn, taped, and the corners were worn. He knew the letter had probably been examined by practically every government agency. "You know once you find out my mail isn't a bomb or death threat from the brotherhood you should give me a chance to read it first."

"West, you know we have to take the necessary precautions to keep you safe."

Judge West skimmed through the letter and threw it back on the table.

"Your grandson said he found out something about your past."

"He couldn't have found out anything to be overly concerned about." Judge West was sure Dean was overreacting.

"I'm not so sure about that. The guy has been up here every day for the past week trying to see you. He knows something." The agent pushed the file folder toward him. "That's what this meeting is about. In this folder we typed up explanation scenarios for you to read through. Once you talk to your grandson, you feed him one of the stories we provided. You may have to add your own spin to make it sound believable, but it's the best we could do."

"So, you want me to tell him a bunch of lies?"

"It's not lies. We just altered the truth."

West rolled his eyes.

"Like I told you before, this is for his safety as well as yours."

"We've set up a special room just for your visit with your grandson. The room is tapped. Everything you say will be monitored." The agent got up and walked toward the door. "Read through the material. I'll tell the guard to give you some time alone in here before taking you back to your cell. It's going to take you a while to read through that."

The door slammed shut again, and Ernest pulled the contents out of the folder and began reading.

***

Dean sat in the county jail visiting room in a dazed state of mind. It was hard for him to clear his mind of the picture he'd found in his grandpa's attic. He studied it from every angle, praying that his eyes were somehow deceiving him.

Before leaving the house, Dean dropped to his knees in prayer. He had to see his grandpa, and only a miracle worker could make that happen. Each time he tried on his own he was turned away, but today he received a pleasant surprise. When he requested to visit with Ernie West, the gates were opened and he was allowed entry.

Dean checked his watch three times. He wondered how much longer it would be before his grandpa arrived. Suddenly, the lock outside the room turned and the door swung open. Judge West entered the room wearing a bright orange jumpsuit and shackles that bound his hands and feet. His prison escort pushed him over to the table across from Dean. Then the guard securely handcuffed his feet to the floor and hands to the table.

Dean stared in astonishment. He could not believe how prison life had changed his grandpa for the worse. The man who stood before him was a stranger. He had dropped ten pounds, his skin was a ghastly white, and his hair had grown so long that strands reached his shoulder.

This wasn't the same man Dean idolized as a child. The Judge West he knew stood up to injustice, but the man who sat before him had accepted defeat and was now a coward.

"How are you doing?"

The judge grunted in response, and silence planted itself at their table.

Dean kept trying to make eye contact with his grandpa, but he refused to look in Dean's direction. "If a man avoids looking you in the eye, that means he can't be trusted."

Judge West glared at his grandson.

"That was one of those precious jewels you preached to me as a kid. You promised it would be beneficial to me when I became an adult." Dean cleared his throat. "We'll, I'm an adult now."

Although Dean was talking to his grandfather in a stern, cold manner he could see how humiliating this was for his grandpa. Dean didn't want to waste any more time. He pulled the picture out his coat pocket, laid it on the table and pushed it in front of his grandpa. "When you were arrested I told myself that it had to be a mistake, that you would never do any of the things that they were accusing you of, but this picture proves otherwise."

The judge lowered his eyes. He wasn't ready to face the truth. It was hard to see his past stare back at him. Judge West picked up the photo and moved it closer to his face. He was immediately taken back in time to the day the picture was taken.

"I thought I knew who you really were, but this photo paints a different picture. Do you know what I see when I look at this sickening picture?" Dean was angry.

"I . . . I . . ." Judge West's voice cracked, and he put his head down momentarily to regain his composure. "I never wanted you to find out this way. I'd give my life to protect you from the truth."

"What is the truth?" Dean pounded his fist against the table.

The urge to confess everything was strong, but if he deviated from the script a horde of federal agents would burst in and cut his visit short. Then they probably wouldn't allow him to have any more while he was in lock up.

"The truth is, at one point in my life I was an active member of the Ku Klux Klan."

Dean shut his eyes to block out his grandpa's upsetting words. "Why?" Dean shook his head, as if to dispel the thoughts from his head.

"I know it's hard to understand, but I was raised in a house that lived and breathed hatred. Both my parents were card-carrying members of the brotherhood. My grandfather was a high-ranking official in the Klan, and my great-great-granddaddy owned at least forty slaves on his plantation. That's the kind of ancestry I inherited from my family."

For the first time in his life Judge West saw disappointment in Dean's eyes.

"From the moment I learned to read, I was forced to study books that depicted whites as the superior race. It consumed my life. Wherever I went, white purity and segregation was preached. 'Don't allow the coloreds to move next door to you, or your property value will fall. Don't allow those Negro children in our schools or your children will turn out dumb just like them.' It went on and on."

"What about the kid you're accused of murdering?"

Repulsed by the sight of that picture, the judge flipped it over face down on the table. "I told you I was brainwashed. I believed I was doing the Lord's work."

"That included killing an innocent kid?" Dean jumped up and kicked his chair across the room. It crashed loudly against the wall. He paced the room hysterically, repeatedly slamming his fist into his bare hands. "I don't know you at all," he shouted. "I've been living with a liar my entire life."

"Dean, I understand you're upset, but I won't allow you to continue disrespecting me. I'm still your grandfather."

"Please! Don't talk to me about respect when you're chained to the table," Dean yelled from across the room.

"Please," his grandpa begged him. "Hear me out?"

Dean wasn't sure if was ready to hear any more. It took him a moment to get control of his feelings. Eventually he picked his chair up from off the floor and sat back at the table.

"Every member initiated that enters the brotherhood must take an oath of secrecy. I vowed to never divulge any information that could harm myself, the order or any members in the brotherhood. That night I accepted a lifetime membership into one of America's most powerful circles. The Grand Wizard made it clear. The only way out was by death.

"When hate simmers it fuels anger, and when you least expect it, that anger will boil over and lash out at the first person you see. That's what happened the night that kid died. They pumped so much hate into me that for me to take that young boy's life meant nothing."

The judge could tell Dean believed every word of his story. He wished he could tell him the real story. "A few days after the"—West chose his words carefully—"incident, pandemonium broke out throughout town. Racial tension was high. Everyone wanted to know who killed that kid. The mayor and governor were under a lot of pressure from the White House to place someone under arrest.

"I steered clear from a lot of my friends for the next few days, then before I knew it, a man I had never met before confessed to the killing and his trial started shortly thereafter. I could not figure out why that guy would admit to a murder that could send him to jail for life. During the trial, I sat in the back of the courtroom thinking it could've been me sitting before a judge and jury.

"I will never forget the prosecution's closing remarks. He called that man names like Satan and the Prince of Darkness. He described the killing as cruel and vile and said that no respectable human being could commit such an act. The prosecutor's words convicted me. The more he talked, the more I felt like he was peeling away layers of who I really was. For the first time in my life I felt unworthy. I didn't even think I deserved to live among society any longer. I thought the brotherhood would revoke my membership and make me an outcast.

"An all-white jury found him guilty, but he was only sentenced to ten years probation. The coloreds were outraged he received such a light punishment, but there was nothing they could do about it."

"Did you ever find out why that guy took the blame for you?" Dean eyes were full of curiosity.

Judge West nodded. "When I exited the courthouse I was surprised at the number of people who had descended upon the courthouse steps. Never in my life had I seen so many people assembled in one place before. It was amazing the crowds this case had attracted. I looked to the left and there were thousands of colored people holding up signs demanding justice, and to the right were the whites who wanted the murderer to go free. Straight down the middle, keeping the two groups separated, stood the National Guard in army fatigues, holding rifles in their hands. Ready to point and shoot.

"From the corner of my eye I spotted the Grand Wizard standing behind a pillar, quietly observing the crowd. This was the first time I had ever seen him not adorning that bright red satin robe. When I approached him I started to talk, but he stopped me with his hand. Then he pointed for me to listen. We watched the stylish, educated, and articulate prosecutor step up to the podium.

"I watched him carefully explain to the crowd that justice had been served that afternoon. He said, 'The accused has been found guilty, and although his punishment may seem minimal, it isn't. The state of North Carolina is committed to protecting its people.'

"Hypnotized by his words, the crowd digested his sincerity and walked away believing every word he said. No one questioned or doubted his position. They assumed because he took an oath to uphold equality for all that he had done his job. The Grand Wizard turned to me and said, 'See what he did?

He's a lawyer who has mastered the art of persuasion. His body language and voice tone represents a trustworthy man. He is one of our most valuable assets. That's why I couldn't allow you to get charged with killing that boy. One day you're going to be standing at that podium speaking the same words he did today.'

"That next semester I enrolled in law school. The brotherhood paid for every bit of my education. Through huge charitable donations, my entire college education was paid for.

"While I was away at school the one phrase I couldn't get out of my head was when that prosecutor called that man the Prince of Darkness. I wondered if that was how people viewed me. I thought I was doing the Lord's work by upholding racial justice. That is when I did something that I rarely did. I prayed on it. I mean I prayed morning noon and night. I asked God to ease the tension that was bothering me every day.

"After graduation, I was still confused about the purpose for my life. I wasn't sure if I wanted to go back to the brotherhood and do the things they expected me to do. I ran away and that is how I landed in Washington, DC.

"That's where I met your grandmother. She came from a very rich liberal family, and her passion in life was to help the less fortunate. She organized various charity events throughout the city, and it was only because of her that I began to understand that things aren't always what they seem. Your grandmother wasn't a lawyer, but she sure debated like one." He laughed. "She could quote me facts and figures on everything from inequality in education to unfair hiring practices. I loved her passion. That's one of the reasons why I married her." The judge lingered in the moment. "Life was good for us. We were married, bought a house, then along came your father. I couldn't have been happier."

Chapter 8

Spring 2008

"I'm curious. What made you two sign up for a singles retreat?" Danyelle lodged her head between Dean and Olivia. "After close to two years of dating, I consider neither of you single."

Dean glared at Danyelle from behind the wheel of his Lincoln Navigator. Her witty sarcasm was annoying, especially when he knew they had a three-hour road trip ahead of them. He should have listened to Olivia when she suggested Danyelle ride to the resort on the church bus. *It isn't too late,* he thought. Members were still loading the bus, and if Danyelle kept running her mouth, Dean was very close to putting her bags on the curb.

"Dean and I look forward to strengthening our relationship with Christ this weekend. Reverend Simms reminded us how important it is for Christian couples to have Jesus as their foundation." Olivia adjusted her seat belt in the front passenger seat.

"The life we build together will endure a few tremors and probably a few earthquakes that will make us feel like the world is going to swallow us whole. But, if the structure we build is set on solid ground and not sinking sand, we will get through the hard times." Dean caressed Olivia's hand.

"That was corny." Danyelle rolled her eyes. Her suspicions were finally confirmed. Dean was a fool ridiculously in love. Olivia was just as hopeless as her boyfriend. Danyelle watched them smile lovingly at one another. She sucked her teeth.

Danyelle was a pessimist when it came to matters of the heart, and she preferred to live her life according to the teachings of Paul the Apostle. He wrote in the book of Corinthians that it's best to stay unmarried and focus on the work of the Lord. Paul never condemned those who did get married, but Danyelle knew marriage was not for her. She always thought that being married was a full-time job. That was too much work.

Danyelle sat back in her seat and accidentally bumped into Val. "Sorry."

Val never acknowledged Danyelle's apology. Instead, she continued to stare out the window.

Danyelle was fully aware that Val was probably still mourning the death of her boyfriend, but she felt like her own safety was in danger. She feared that Val would unravel at any moment and take her anger out on the wrong person.

Careful not to make any sudden movements, Danyelle cautiously whispered in her sister's ear, "I don't think it's wise for her to be around people."

Danyelle nodded her head in Val's direction. "She looks unstable. Look at her."

"She's fine," Olivia insisted. "Aunt Stephie and I agreed it would do her some good to get out the house and immerse herself in some fresh mountain air."

"I haven't heard her speak in weeks," Danyelle replied.

Olivia noticed that since Julian's death Val had turned into a recluse. Everything about her had changed. Buried along with Julian was that friendly, outgoing and confident black woman Olivia admired her whole life, leaving behind someone she didn't recognize. Val had crawled into her own private cocoon and watched the world as it passed her by.

"Danyelle, please sit back and be quiet." Olivia pulled out a book from her bag and shoved it toward her sister. "Here, read this."

"This is Bryce's Winnie the Pooh book," Danyelle complained.

A headache quickly formed at the corners of Olivia's temples from Danyelle's constant chatter. She lay back on the headrest.

Suddenly, she shot straight up from the abrupt knocking on her window. Tressie stood outside waving her hand and motioned for Olivia to roll her window down.

She pushed the power window down. "What are you doing here?" Her eyes settled on the small carry-on luggage bags sitting next to Tressie's feet. Olivia jumped out of the truck. "Oh! No! You're not going with us. You told me you didn't want to go on the retreat."

"Dean, could you put my bags in the back please?" Tressie looked over Olivia's shoulder and directed her request toward Dean.

He obediently got out and made room in the trunk for Tressie's things.

"You can't go! There are no more tickets left," Olivia objected. "The church sold out weeks ago."

Tressie dug in her purse and pulled out her ticket, then slowly waved it in Olivia's face.

"Where did you get that from?" Olivia asked.

"Ms. Young." Tressie smacked on a piece of Bubblicious gum. "She said her bunions were giving her trouble and she wasn't up for making the long trip. So I offered to buy her ticket." Tressie cocked her head to the side and gave Olivia an overconfident smile, while ordering Danyelle to scoot over.

Olivia pulled her sunglasses down from the top of her head and over her eyes. Any ideas she had about this being a nice relaxing oasis for her and Dean to escape to were now wiped away. With Danyelle, Val, and now Tressie tagging along, she was bound to get no rest at all.

Their journey up to the mountains was a quiet one. Everyone slept most of the way, and just before they arrived at the resort campgrounds Olivia mentioned to Dean how tired he looked.

"I am tired," he replied. "I need to take a nap before dinner, if that's okay with you."

"Sure. I know how exhausting it was for you to do all the driving. Plus, having to deal with my sister didn't help any." Olivia cracked a smile, but Dean didn't seem amused. He looked like he was worried about something.

"Is everything okay?" she asked.

"I'm fine." He pulled his truck into a parking space right beside the church bus. "We're here," he announced loudly enough to wake up each one of his passengers.

The girls looked around and stretched their arms and legs as much as they could before getting out. Dean unloaded the bags and offered to carry them for the ladies, but Olivia insisted they could carry their own bags.

Dean's lack of energy left Olivia concerned. It may have been his job that was wearing him out, but to be on the safe side she was going to make a doctor's appointment for him when they returned home.

Olivia puckered her lips for the quick peck Dean placed square on her lips then watched as he walked toward the men's cabins, located on the left side of the lake.

Dean walked as if he were carrying a barrel full of adversity on his back. His head hung down low, his shoulders slumped over and his legs wobbled unsteadily. The invisible burden slowed down his journey. With each step he was losing momentum.

She wondered what the burden was that was weighing him down. It had to be something important because he rarely kept anything from her. They shared everything.

"What did you do that for?" Tressie complained, referring to Dean's offer to carry their bags. "I can't carry all these bags by myself."

"No one told you to bring five pieces of luggage for a three-day trip." Olivia lifted her bags over her shoulder and set out to find their cabin.

After being pointed in the wrong direction several different times, the girls finally found their cabin.

"This is not what I expected when the brochure I read said luxury log cabins," Tressie moaned. "Where is the plush king-size beds, huge garden-style bathtubs, wood-burning fireplace, television and microwave?"

"Do I have to remind you that this is a singles Christian retreat? Your focus is supposed to be on God's will for your life, not the amenities included with this cabin." Olivia pulled out her hiking boots and slipped them on her feet. "Are you ready for our hike?"

"Yes!" Danyelle exclaimed. "This is the best part of the trip."

Hiking to the mountaintop became an annual ritual for the girls since their first visit to the camp three years prior. Olivia called it "A Spiritual Cleansing." Each one of them struggled with uphill battles every day in their personal lives. Every once in a while someone might stumble along the way or stray from their given paths, but fortunately they had God to put them back on track.

The girls started up the steep trail that seemed so much harder to climb than the previous year. They hiked less than a mile before Danyelle rested against a nearby tree. "I'm sorry, but I'm tired. Can't we rest a moment before going any farther?"

"No." Olivia pulled her sister along. "We're not going to stop until we reach the top."

Another half hour passed before Tressie noticed that Olivia was losing her momentum. It was too soon for Olivia to get tired, so Tressie struck up conversation. "Livie, do you think you and Dean will get married soon? You two have been dating for a while and the next step is marriage." Tressie hung onto Danyelle's arm to keep her balance, while Olivia and Val helped one another a few feet behind them.

"I'm not sure. We've talked about marriage, but I think Dean has so much going on, with his grandpa being arrested."

"Has Dean learned anything new?" Danyelle asked between breaths.

"No. Every time I ask him about it he says he doesn't want to talk. A few weeks ago he was determined to find his grandpa the best defense lawyer in the state, and now he acts like he doesn't care."

"Well, until you find out what's up with his family, I think you need to hold off on any marriage plans. I don't need my sister marrying into bigotry," Danyelle screamed. "Plus, I think you need to take my advice."

Olivia gave her a puzzled look.

"Sex. You can't buy a car without giving it a test drive. How can you marry a man without knowing how he is in bed?"

Olivia's face turned red. She gripped Val's hand so tight that Val winced in pain. "Look who's talking. That chastity belt you wear around your waist has never been taken off and, until it is, don't talk to me about sex."

"I'm not ashamed of my virginity," Danyelle proudly announced. "But I'm not walking down that aisle without first getting in that man's pants."

"What would Mommy say if she heard you talking like that?" Olivia shouted.

"I realize we were raised on the 'no sex until after marriage' principle, but times have changed. How many people actually wait?"

"Unfortunately not many, but we should learn from other people's mistakes. We are taught to be wise through Biblical principles," Olivia explained.

"Imagine your wedding day." Danyelle turned to look her sister in the eye. "You, dressed in a flawless white wedding gown that symbolizes your purity. You've saved yourself for this man and are giving him a gift that is priceless. Then comes the honeymoon. You two are in bed, getting ready to get busy, then come to find out he's this big." Danyelle used her thumb and pointer finger to measure an inch. "You ain't feel anything. What are you going to do?"

Everyone was surprised when Val was the first one to laugh out loud. "You know we joke a lot about Danyelle smoking too much weed, but she does come up with some convincing arguments." She turned to Olivia. "Your sister has a point."

"Not you too!" Olivia complained.

"You can't divorce him or send him back to his momma," Danyelle ranted on. "Or would you file for annulment?" Danyelle asked. "What would you do?"

"Marriage is about so much more than sex. When I was with Bryant, we moved so fast that we never got a chance to know one another. I want it to be different with Dean," Olivia defended herself.

Danyelle pressed the issue. "Having sex can only bring the two of you closer. Dean is a cool guy, but he's still a man." Danyelle tilted her head to the side and considered her next words carefully. "Unless Dean's a virgin?" she spat.

Olivia's body instantly turned tense and she stopped climbing. "Not that it's any of your business, but my man is far from a virgin."

"Livie, don't misunderstand my point. I know you're worth the wait and Dean is a great guy, but don't ignore the obvious. For one, he loves you and adores your son. Second, he does everything he can for you. Lastly, he works to give you money, keep gas in your car and help out with your monthly utility bills. How much longer do you think it's going to be before he gets sick of putting all his eggs in your basket without getting anything in return?"

Olivia reflected on Danyelle's mini-sermon. *Am I being selfish?* She never considered the possibility that Dean may want to have sex. Olivia loved Dean and didn't want to lose him. In her heart she knew that sex would never keep a man, but Danyelle's argument sounded so convincing.

"Look!" Tressie pointed to a narrow trail that looked like a shortcut to the top. "We can go through here."

"I don't know, Tressie." Olivia looked skeptical of the path Tressie had found. "I think we should stay on the designated path."

But it was too late. Danyelle was already following Tressie through the thick brush of bushes.

Olivia followed, and it wasn't long before the girls made it to the top.

"See, I told you this was a quicker route," Tressie shouted.

"Yeah, but was it worth it? My arms have scratches from the thorns and pointy sticks," Danyelle complained.

At the mountaintop, each girl found a huge rock to relax on and basked in God's glory. Sunrays trickled down from heaven, painting a beautiful array of pink and yellow light across the sky. Total silence surrounded them.

"If I was you, I would go ahead and enjoy Dean in as many ways as I could," Val said. "If you don't take advantage of the opportunity, it could be snatched away from you and you'll never get to feel the touch of his hands over your body."

Tressie, Danyelle and Olivia looked at one another. They knew Val was regretting her decision to wait until after she was married to consummate her relationship with Julian.

Chapter 9

Anxious to get back to their cabin and get ready for dinner, the girls retreated back down the mountain trail. "Thank God the climb is always easier going down than the climb up," Danyelle hollered, out of breath.

In their absence, the campgrounds grew into a stampede of activity. Buses carrying passengers from different churches passed them by. Men and women, young and old, hauled luggage, duffle bags and coolers in search of their cabins.

"Look at the shortage of men around here," Tressie griped. "I knew I should've stayed home."

The moment the girls stepped foot in their cabin, the bickering between Danyelle and Tressie began. They fussed over who would be the first to take a shower. Then they argued over who would sleep closest to the window. The final straw came when Danyelle threatened to put Tressie's things out.

"Would you two stop it?"

Olivia was tired of hearing them act like children. She snatched her cell phone off her bed and stormed outside to call her son. Pressing the number three speed-dial number on her phone, she called her aunt. "Hey, Auntie, how's everything?" Olivia shouted.

"Olivia!" Val's mom sounded relieved to hear from her. "Did everyone get there safely?" Her aunt wasn't as concerned about everyone as she was about Val. That's why she sounded the way she did.

"We had no problems, and everyone is fine," Olivia replied.

"Good!" She released a sigh of relief. "I know you're anxious to talk with Bryce, so here he is."

"Mommy, we've been waiting for you to call," Bryce sounded upset.

"Why honey? Is everything okay?" Worry filled Olivia's mind.

"Aunt Stephie was going to take me to Chuck E. Cheese, but she said we couldn't leave until after you called. Can we go now?" He spoke away from the phone and toward his aunt.

Olivia could hear her in the background telling Bryce they could leave once he hung up the phone.

"Bryce, I'm not going to hold you up. I just wanted to make sure you were all right and tell you that I miss you."

"I miss you too, Mommy."

She thought he was going to hand the phone back to Aunt Stephie, but he continued to talk.

"Mom, why couldn't Kennedy and Clinton come with me? Aunt Stephie said it was okay."

"Bryce, I explained this to you before we left home. It was time for Kennedy and Clinton to get their shots. The kennel is going to take care of that and give them each a bath. By the time we pick them up on Monday, they will be as good as new."

"Okay, Mommy."

Olivia wasn't sure if he was satisfied with that answer, but he handed the phone back to his aunt and went to the guest room to get his jacket.

"Olivia, don't worry about us," Aunt Stephie said. "We'll be fine. Enjoy your trip and make sure my daughter has some fun while she's there."

When Olivia hung up the phone, her heart stung a little from the way Bryce brushed her off for Chuck E. Cheese. The hardest part of being a mother was watching her child become so independent. He demonstrated new self-reliance in the mornings by dressing himself and rushing off to class without giving her a kiss good-bye. She could feel him pulling away from her, but there wasn't much she could do about it. Dean warned her that eventually she would have to allow her boy to grow into a man.

After dinner a small group of campers gathered around a bonfire to sing church hymns. The sky was clear, the fire blazed high, and the songs they sang sounded like a professional mass choir. Part of the reason was due to Danyelle. She had taken the initiative to divide everyone into groups and instructed everyone on different song arrangements. When it came to music, Danyelle was a professional.

Late into the night, Olivia announced she was tired. "Danyelle, I'm glad you're the musically inclined one in the family, because I can't sing one more song. My tonsils hurt. I'm going to bed." Olivia placed her hand on Danyelle's shoulder.

"You're leaving already?" Then Danyelle noticed that everyone was leaving. "It's still early."

"It's close to midnight. We're tired." Tressie lifted herself up from off the log she was sitting on.

Olivia ran to catch up with Dean. "Are we still going canoeing in the morning?"

His eyes flashed an affirmative response. "I'll meet you on the dock." They kissed good-night and retired for the night.

"Danyelle, are you going to walk back to the cabin with us?" Tressie asked.

Disheartened that her singers had bailed, Danyelle looked over her shoulder and responded with a no. "I think I'm going to sit out here a bit longer and review a couple pages of notes from class. I have an exam Monday morning, and I need to be prepared for it."

The girls left her alone, and Danyelle picked up a three-ring binder that sat at her feet. She flipped it open to the first page and began testing her memory. To help her relax, she grabbed her book bag and pulled out the only blunt she had brought with her. She used the bonfire to spark it up.

I can study better once I get a few puffs in.
Danyelle took a small hit and focused her attention back on her schoolwork.

"Can I join you?" Startled, Danyelle jumped up and dropped her notebook to the ground. It was Colin Montgomery. She quickly hid the blunt behind her back and smiled in his direction. *Why is it that this man always manages to find me when I'm trying to get high?*

"I'm sorry, did I scare you?" He walked around to one of the logs that was positioned around the campfire and picked up her notebook. "I'm glad to see my star pupil is studying. I wish all my students were like you."

Danyelle wanted to respond, but the smoke that filled her lungs prevented her from saying anything. She didn't want to blow smoke in the reverend's face, but she couldn't hold it in any longer. Her eyes began to water. The smoke started to choke her. She finally had to let it out. Loudly, she coughed, bending over to release the smell of marijuana into the air.

"Are you all right?" The reverend patted her on the back. "You know you really shouldn't be smoking out here."

Danyelle cleared her throat, her face red from embarrassment. This was the second time he had caught her. She pushed his hand away and told him she was okay.

An uncomfortable silence filled the air.

"Does it help you to study alone?" He walked around to the opposite side of the fire, where she could barely see his face.

"Yes, there are fewer disturbances. I can concentrate and retain more. I have this teacher who likes to kill us with scripture." She gave him a playful smile.

"Sounds like a man after my own heart." He walked around the fire closer to her, but she backed away.

She still held the blunt behind her back as it slowly burned.

When he realized she was intentionally avoiding him, he stopped coming toward her. He tried a different approach. "What did Jesus say is the first great commandment?"

"We are commanded to love the Lord with all our heart, mind and soul," she replied with ease.

"And the second?"

"Love our neighbors as ourselves."

Their eyes locked. The bonfire danced around them, and their body temperature rose ten degrees.

Danyelle felt an unfamiliar feeling in the pit of her stomach. She shifted her eyes away from him. It was the first time she felt nervous being the center of attraction.

"Danyelle, you are a mysterious young lady. What made you enroll in Bible College?"

"Although my parents are gone, they left my sister and I with a gift that I consider priceless: a Bible full of God's infinite wisdom." She pointed toward her Bible. "Daddy would often tell us that securing the Lord's Word in our hearts would benefit us later on in life."

"It's obvious that your parents were a big part of your life."

She smiled to herself. "I really wish my dad were around to see my nephew. Bryce walks just like him." She laughed out loud.

"I'm sure they would be so proud of you."

He reached out to hand Danyelle back the notebook she'd dropped earlier. When she grabbed a hold of it, he used it to pull her closer to him. Then he kissed her.

The feel of lips locked around hers was something she had never experienced before. She closed her eyes and enjoyed the feel of his tongue wrestling with hers.

They kissed for thirty seconds before she abruptly pulled away. She couldn't believe she had just experienced her first kiss and it was with the pastor of her church.

"Reverend, I'm sorry. I don't—" Danyelle stuttered.

"Don't be sorry." He gently kissed her again. "It was my pleasure." He checked the time on his wristwatch. "I have to get back to the cabin. The men are waiting on me to lead them in prayer.

Would you like for me to walk you back to your cabin?"

She looked at him with a dumbfounded expression on her face, but he laughed at her response and asked the question again.

This time she replied, "No, Reverend. I'm okay."

Then, as he disappeared into the night she couldn't help but wish he had kissed her again.

Chapter 10

At the midnight hour West tossed from side to side. His sleeping mind replayed the last time he saw his son alive.

"Pop, are you sure you don't want to go?"

"Son, I've been to plenty of these charity events. I've got so many invitations this month that it won't hurt if I miss this one. The same people you see tonight will be the same people I see next month at the next gala event."

"Belinda and I really appreciate this."

"I'm glad to do it. I know how excited she is to finally get out of the house. Since she had the baby, you two don't go out anymore. It's okay to get a break and go out to dinner every once in the while." Judge West took his eight-month-old grandson into his arms. "Plus, I think this would be a great place for you to network with other young lawyers."

At that moment Belinda descended the stairs. She looked radiant in a black and silver form-fitting gown that shimmered every time she moved.

"Bye, Dean." She walked over and kissed the baby's fingers. "Don't you cause your grandparents any problems tonight."

"You two get out of here." Judge West shooed them out the door. "Enjoy yourself and don't you two worry about the boy."

His son opened the door and led the way to the limousine waiting by the curb.

After the limousine safely pulled away from the curb West held his grandson up to face him. "Dean, you're going to be a lawyer just like your father and I, but you're going to be better."

Judge West's wife, Martha, interrupted their private conversation, "Ernie, don't put expectations on my grandson. He could be an athlete, an engineer or better yet a billionaire."

"You're right about that. He's a West; he could be whatever he put his mind to," Judge West replied.

"Honey, why don't you take the baby out on the back patio while I make a few glasses of fresh lemonade?"

"Okay." He walked out on the patio and relaxed in his usual lounge chair. Then he heard the phone ring.

"Ernie!" Martha released a loud high-pitched cry. "Ernie!"

He could hear trouble in the way she shouted. He jumped up and raced in the house.

A look of horror covered Martha's face. Her right hand covered her mouth and she used her left hand to hold the phone out to him. When he took the phone she took Dean in her arms.

He listened a moment before he said, "I'll be right there." He hung up the phone and rushed out the door. As he pulled out of their driveway, he could hear Martha yell.

"Ernie, I love you."

When Judge West arrived on the scene, police cars, ambulances, detectives and the media surrounded the limousine that his son and daughter-in-law left in. He stopped his car and ran to the scene.

"Judge West." A detective stopped him. "We need to prepare you—"

Judge West slapped the young detective's arm away from him. When he ran over to the limo the first thing he saw was the limo driver with a gunshot straight to the temple.

West's eyes doubled in size. "What happened here?" West screamed. "Somebody needs to tell me exactly what is going on."

Another police officer, this time a sergeant, came over and pulled West over to the side.

"Apparently, this limo that carried your son and daughter-in-law was ambushed by unknown assailants, who apparently fled the scene, and we have no witnesses. Whoever shot the driver is responsible for the kidnapping of your son and his wife."

"Kidnapped?" Judge West was in shock.

"Yes, they were not killed. We know they were in the car because their identification was left behind. Do you know who would do this?"

Tears welled up in the corner of West's eyes.

"Sir, I don't think that your son and his wife were the intended target."

The judge spun his head in the sergeant's direction.

"We called the charity event, and this limousine was reserved for you and your wife. I think that whoever raided this car was expecting to find you, and when they found your son and his wife, they took them as hostages. Right now our number one priority is to find your son and his wife."

Days passed. The police placed a wire tap on Judge West's phone, and their house was under twenty-four-hour watch by the police, but they heard nothing from the kidnappers. No ransom. No bodies. Nothing. Judge West went into work every day with nothing on his mind except finding who was responsible for the abduction of his grandson's parents.

Two weeks after their disappearance, the identity of the kidnappers were revealed. Judge West sat in his chambers reviewing cases when he came across a plain manila envelope that he hadn't seen before. He opened it up, and inside were pictures of his son and daughter-in-law blindfolded, their hands tied behind their back. They looked scared, and he could plainly see they were badly beaten. Scrawled on top of the photo were the words: HELP HAINSWORTH OR THEY DIE.

Judge West shifted through the file folders until he came across Darden's file. He was already familiar with the contents of his file. Creighton Hainsworth, a doctor who volunteered his time at the free clinic in one of the poorest sections of the city, had injected over two hundred and thirty babies with HIV. During the trial, Hainsworth showed no remorse for his actions, and when he got on the stand, he blatantly admitted he would do it all over again if he had the chance.

This was a high-profile case that had received national media coverage. The city was in an uproar over it. West was expected to give the doctor the maximum sentence allowed by law, but was confronted with giving him the minimum sentence of eighteen months in jail. If he did anything different than the maximum, every African American and Latino civil rights advocate in the city was ready to storm his office.

West stared at the picture of his son for over an hour. In his heart he knew who was responsible for their disappearance. This was a group of people he was very familiar with. He knew because he used to be one of them. The brotherhood was a powerful organization, and he knew what they could and could not do. He wasn't sure before, but he now knew they were trying to blackmail him into releasing one of their own.

Finally, it was time for him to announce Hainsworth's fate. For the first time in his career, West was still unsure of what would happen to the guilty. He sat down and looked out at the crowd of people. The courtroom was full. West rubbed his temples then began to speak.

"Mr. Hainsworth, would you please stand?"

Hainsworth stood to his feet.

"You have been found guilty of a hcinous crime that has crippled an entire generation of children." Judge West paused and took a small sip from his glass. He stared out at the families of each victim then looked at the doctor. Just the mere sight of him made the judge sick. "On behalf of the state of Pennsylvania I am sentencing you to"—He looked out at the families of the victims—"two years in a state correctional facility."

The families gasped and cried out in anger.

West abruptly left the courtroom and rushed back to his chambers. He grabbed his things and told his secretary he had an emergency at home.

When he barged through his front door, he found his wife and grandson sitting in the living room watching television.

"Martha, I know who's responsible for the kidnapping."

"Who?"

At that moment, the nightly news interrupted the program they were watching. The news correspondent reported, "This just in, a few hours ago a fisherman discovered two torched bodies floating in the Chesapeake Bay. Speculation suggests that these could be the bodies of Judge West's missing son and daughter-in-law."

Martha screamed out. "No!"

The judge hugged his wife as she grieved her only child's death.

"I had a feeling they were already dead."

He pushed her away from him and looked her in the eye. "It's the brotherhood."

"Nooooo!" Martha cried. "Not my babies."

"Martha, we have to go. We have to pack our things and leave town."

Martha rushed over to the phone. "Call the police, Ernie. You have to tell the police what you know. They have to pay for what they did to our children."

Ernie walked over and took the receiver out of her hand and placed it back in the phone cradle. "I can't do that."

With her eyes she asked why.

"Our first priority is to take care of the baby. If we point the fingers at anyone in that organization, they will kill us and Dean."

Martha wept in Ernie's arms because she knew he was right.

Suddenly West woke up from out of his sleep. He looked around at his surroundings. It was still dark outside. "Martha," he said out loud, "you were right. I should have turned them in when I had the chance."

Chapter 11

The following morning Olivia rose to her feet at six a.m. to meet Dean at the dock. Darkness filled the cabin, making it nearly impossible for her to see. She blindly moved around the room, allowing the furniture to guide her to the bathroom. She closed the bathroom door before turning on any lights. She didn't want to wake anyone.

Olivia quickly undressed and slipped underneath the showerhead. This morning was her time to spend alone with Dean, and if one of the girls woke up she was scared they would insist on tagging along.

"Mission accomplished," Olivia sang after she gently pulled the cabin door closed. She was finally free.

When she reached the dock she was surprised to see such a huge crowd of people gathered that early in the morning to go canoeing. Every face she saw was foreign to her, until she spotted Dean talking with a girl.

Olivia quickly sized up the girl and considered her foe, not friend. Her perfect size six fit snug in those pink Daisy Duke shorts, showing off her long, shapely legs, and she batted her fake eyelashes in Dean's face.

Jealousy pumped through Olivia's veins. Her first thought was to step directly between the two, but the Holy Spirit kept her in control. If she over-reacted, it would only make her look like a fool. So she stood back and watched Dean.

Olivia watched as the girl playfully hit Dean on his shoulder then whispered something in his ear. Whatever she said must have been funny because Dean's smile was so wide, she could count every tooth in his mouth.

The girl then took off her T-shirt to reveal double-D cups stuffed into a bikini top that was no bigger than her hand.

Olivia wished she could crawl into Dean's mind and read his thoughts. Was he turned on by her sex appeal? Did he want to sleep with her? Olivia couldn't tolerate watching them any longer. She rushed over, snuck up behind Dean and tapped him on the shoulder.

When he turned around it was apparent by the joyous expression on his face how happy he was to see her. He wrapped his arms around her and held her like his life depended on it.

The girl had to clear her throat a few times to bring Dean's attention back to her. He introduced Olivia to his new friend, and when they shook hands Olivia could hear Danyelle's words ring in her ears.

"If you don't satisfy him, somebody else will."

The girl politely made small talk with Olivia until she could no longer tolerate the public displays of affection between the couple. She excused herself from their company.

"How long were you going to stand over there watching us before you came over?" Dean busted her.

"You saw me?" She was surprised. "I didn't want to intrude. It looked like you were enjoying her company."

"You know I wasn't interested in her." He laughed at her jealousy. "Come on, let's get going before the line gets too long."

They stood in line for over twenty minutes before it was their turn to climb into the tiny boat for two. Olivia got in first and scooted to the front of the canoe, while Dean sat behind her. Together they stroked the water with paddles.

By the time they reached the middle of the lake, Dean filled Olivia in on the guys he shared a cabin with. "Livie, one guy snored so loud, I didn't get a wink of sleep."

"I'm sorry you didn't get any rest. I know how tired you were."

"It's all right." He grabbed Olivia around her waist and pulled her closer to him.

She sat between his legs and laid her head on his chest.

"But as long as you're in my arms, I'm fully energized."

"Good, because you seemed so distant yesterday. I was worried."

"Baby, I'm sorry. I've just a lot on my mind lately," he said.

"Do you want to talk about it?"

"It's not that important to intrude on our time together." He hugged her tighter.

The two sank deep into their own thoughts. Dean's mind was on his grandfather, and Olivia agonized over her relationship with Dean.

The conversation she'd had with the girls on the hike haunted her. To remain celibate until her wedding night was important to her. It scared her to think she could lose Dean to another woman over something as simple as sex.

Olivia prayed most of the night. In her heart she could hear God's voice telling her to sit still and do nothing, but it made her nervous when she saw girls, like the one Dean was talking to earlier, flirting with him. If she waited any longer, she could end up losing Dean and be left with the similar regrets Val now carried around with her. She couldn't allow the same fate to befall her. So she chose to take Val's advice, even if it was against God's will.

Dean's stomach growled. "Baby, I told you we should have stopped at the cafeteria before coming out here. My stomach is screaming, 'Feed me.'"

"Dean"—Olivia took a deep breath—"Do you miss having sex?"

Dean's mouth dropped wide open. He was speechless. It took him a moment to respond to her question. "I wouldn't say I miss it. I haven't thought about it much."

"Why haven't you asked me to go to bed with you?"

Dean's face turned red from embarrassment. "Why are you asking me these questions? We've talked about this already. Bryce's father hurt you, and I would never push you into doing something you don't want to do. I can wait until after we're married."

"I know what I said, but if you want to do it, I will. For you, I will."

"Don't say that. Don't do anything just for me. If we . . . were to do anything, then that would be a decision we would make together."

"Okay." Olivia sighed and relaxed.

A few minutes passed before Dean suggested, "Why don't we get married?"

"What did you say?" Olivia spun around to face him and was blinded by the diamond ring he held in his hand.

"Olivia, will you marry me?"

The huge marquise diamond sparkled under the morning light. Olivia opened her mouth, but the words slid back down her throat. She tried, but her tonsils still failed her.

He gave her a peculiar look as he waited for a response.

"Dean, this comes as a total surprise." With unsteady hands she gently took the ring from his fingers.

"This is what you want? Isn't it?" Dean asked. "Olivia, we planned this. The time has come for us to get married."

Olivia admired the ring for a moment.

"Please say yes." He placed the ring on her finger. "Look at how beautiful it fits on your finger. This ring was made to be worn by you." He kissed the back of her hands. "If you say yes, I want us to get married as soon as possible. Let's say, next week."

"Next week?" she sounded alarmed. "Why so soon?"

He took her hand in his and sat up on the bed next to her. "I love you, and I don't want to wait any longer to spend the rest of my life with you."

Olivia could feel God's favor pouring down on them. She looked up to the sky. "Yes! Yes! Yes!" she screamed. Then she stood up in the canoe to give him a hug.

"No, Olivia," Dean warned, but it was too late.

The canoe tipped over, and they fell over into the water. The lifeguard's whistle blew, and everyone watched as the two kissed in the middle of the lake.

After Dean and Olivia were rescued, they returned to their cabins to change clothes before catching up with their friends in the cafeteria.

Olivia was so excited. She couldn't wait to show off her engagement ring and start on the wedding plans, but despite her happiness, she asked Dean to keep their engagement a secret from the others.

Val was still upset and very sensitive over Julian. Olivia wanted to break the news to her in private, so it wouldn't be so upsetting.

"How was the canoe ride?" Danyelle questioned the couple as they approached the table with their trays full of food.

"Fine." Olivia's tone was full of cheer, and it didn't go unnoticed by the girls. "Can you pass me the salt, please?"

Val reached across the table and handed her the salt shaker. Val, Tressie and Danyelle simultaneously turned their head to look at Dean.

He could feel their questioning eyes bearing down on him, but he refused to look up. He was scared to say anything. He couldn't risk Olivia getting mad at him and calling off the engagement.

"Good morning, members of First Nazareth." Colin took a seat next to Dean. "I signed us up for the men's fishing exhibition this afternoon," he told his friend then smiled brightly, wondering why everyone at the table was so quiet. He pounded out a happy beat on the tabletop. When he looked up and caught Danyelle staring at him, he winked his eye at her, and she quickly turned away.

Danyelle looked down and refused to lift her head.

Olivia asked her a question and she answered by talking to the tabletop.

Tressie was used to Danyelle acting odd, but just a few minutes ago she was the loudest one at the table. Suddenly she was reserved. "Are you all right? You're awfully quiet."

Danyelle shrugged her shoulders and played with her food. "I'm fine." Tired of picking over watery eggs, she got up and took her tray to the trashcan.

Colin's eyes followed her. "Man, are you ready to catch some fish? I brought my golden rod. I love fishing. As a kid the boys and girls club used to take us all the time and—"

Dean stopped him with his hand. "Colin, what's up with you this morning? I've adjusted to your upbeat personality, but this morning you act like you've drank twelve cups of coffee."

Colin ignored Dean's questions. The reason he was so happy was because he was in love. "Are you ready? Throw that stuff away." Colin referred to Dean's plate full of food. "Save that appetite for all the fish we're going to catch out on the water."

Dean stood to his feet. "Ladies, we'll see you later." He and Colin left together.

"He is such a nice guy," Olivia said out loud, referring to Colin. "It won't be long before one of the single ladies at our church gets their hooks into him. I wonder who it will be." Olivia finished up her thought just as Danyelle returned to the table.

"Come on. We're going to be late for the afternoon seminar."

"Ladies, I'm glad to see each and every one of your faces here today," an evangelist spoke loudly into the microphone. "Today you are going to be blessed. The spirit is going to pour wisdom into your hearts that is going to enable each of you to correctly choose a good mate. You are going to be able to hear his call when he whispers your name, and most importantly you will learn how to place God first in your lives without neglecting those boyfriends or husbands."

Hundreds of women seated underneath the picnic pavilion hollered out in praise. Enthusiasm pulsated throughout the area.

Every woman there was looking forward to a positive experience, except for one. Val was inconsolable. A faded Phillies baseball cap was pulled so far down on her head that it practically hid the bags underneath her eyes. She'd lost a lot of her inherited Benson curves because her behind was now flat after losing over fifteen pounds. Her grief was stealing her natural beauty.

Val wasn't in the mood to listen to a bunch of women lecture her about what she needed to do to get a man, when God had taken hers away. Unable to withstand the raising cheers, she got up and walked toward the riverbank. She sat on a nearby log and watched the guys across the river fishing for the night's meal.

"Val"—Olivia came up behind her and sat beside her— "I'm sorry, I shouldn't have talked you into coming. I thought you were ready to attend this kind of retreat, but I can see I was wrong. I can be kind of pushy sometimes."

"Sometimes?"

Val chuckled, and Olivia playfully hit her on the shoulder.

"Olivia, I've been through so much, and I know everyone is worried about me, but I'm beginning to worry about myself. Sometimes I don't even know who I am. Each day I get up out of bed, I don't know what to expect. Sometimes I'm sad and I cry all day, but then the very next day I can be so angry that I buy thousands of dollars worth of stuff from the Home Shopping Network. Things I don't even need."

Olivia nodded her head in understanding.

"Other days I'm fine, but I can't get Julian off my mind. I can hear him in my dreams calling my name. Valencia." She mimicked his voice. "I often dream about us making love. Livie, that's why I told you to go ahead and do it. You have no idea how big a hole Julian left in my heart."

Olivia hugged her tightly.

"Livie, I'm ready to go home. If it's all right with you, I'm going to ask Dean to drive me to the train station. I can't take this anymore." She threw a stick she was playing with down on the ground. "Besides, I have to get ready for my big day at the homeless shelter on Monday."

"Honey, I understand."

Val stood up.

"We'll go back to the cabin together and pack your things. Then I'll call Dean on his cell phone."

"Man, I don't believe we've been out here for over an hour and not one fish has nibbled on my line." Dean sat staring at his fishing rod extended into the lake.

Colin laughed. "You're the one who suggested we go fishing. There were other things we could have done, but I thought you were tired of me beating you on the basketball court so that's why you suggested fishing."

"I chose fishing because I thought that didn't require much skill. I guess I was wrong."

Disappointment settled in Dean's eyes, and Colin lightly punched him in the arm to alleviate any pressure Dean put on himself.

"Don't take it so seriously. We're not here to compete against one another. This is about our individual relationship with God," Colin said.

"You're right." Dean turned to Colin. "I'm surprised you decided to participate in this retreat. I thought you hated coming to these kinds of things."

Colin laughed at him.

"Correct me if I'm wrong, but I believe it was you who said that women who attended these types of functions treated it like a hunting expedition for men."

"I said that?" Colin acted confused.

"Yes, man! It was you," Dean reminded him.

Colin looked around to make sure no one else was listening. "I think I found somebody I'm interested in," he whispered.

"Get out of here." Dean had never heard Colin say he was interested in anyone. Colin believed that a man should not pursue any woman unless first led by the spirit. "She must be awfully special if you're interested in her."

"She is," Colin replied.

"Is she here?"

"Why are you asking so many questions about me? What's up with you and Olivia?"

"I love her," Dean admitted. "I've never found anyone more beautiful or perfect. I'm going to marry her."

Colin gave him a startled look. "I didn't know it was that serious."

"I have no doubt in my mind that Olivia was made for me. My soul soars every time she smiles," Dean explained. "If the way you feel about this girl compares in any way to how I feel about Olivia, then I say go for it. Make her yours before somebody else snatches her away."

"I'm working on it," Colin replied.

"I don't know who she is, but I hope she's like Olivia and nothing like her sister," Dean replied.

"Why would you say that? I think Danyelle's cool," Colin subtly replied. He wasn't ready to tell Dean that Danyelle was the woman of his dreams.

"She is cool, when she's drug free," Dean replied. "But when she's high she can get on your nerves. Ask Olivia." Dean heard his cell phone ringing and quickly answered. He listened for a moment. "No, it's fine. I was tired of fishing anyway."

Colin laughed at his friend.

"I'll be right there." He snapped his phone shut. "Man, I have to make a quick run," Dean shouted as he walked away from where they were fishing.

At that moment Colin saw his line move. "It's a good thing you're leaving, because it looks like I've got something." Colin pulled up on his rod and struggled with the fish he caught. "And it looks like this is a big one."

Chapter 12

Later that evening as the sun set behind the mountains, the men returned from their fishing trip with Igloo coolers full of fish. In the cafeteria, an award was presented to the camper who caught the largest fish.

"Can I get everyone's attention?" A deacon from one of the other churches paced the cafeteria floor with the mic in his hand. "We have a gentleman who has broken the record for the largest fish caught."

A thunderous applause filled the room.

The deacon quickly glanced at the index card in his hand. "Reverend Colin Montgomery caught a trout that weighed seventy-five pounds." He motioned for Colin to join him.

Colin stood and posed for pictures with his fish, just like it was a supermodel. Afterward, he took the mic to leave the crowd with one final thought. "This is a pretty big fish, but I know I'll never catch as many fish as Jesus can."

The crowd laughed and agreed with him. As he walked back to his table various people congratulated him.

When Colin sat down, he overheard Olivia talking to Dean. "Honey, how did you do?"

Colin laughed. "Our friend didn't do as well as others. He didn't catch anything. I don't think fishing is his sport."

"That's all right, baby. I didn't fall in love with you for your fishing ability." Olivia kissed Dean on the cheek while those sitting around jokingly laughed at him.

The men's fishing trip was a success, despite Dean's lack of contributions. They'd caught enough fish to feed everyone that evening, and there were even leftovers. For those who didn't eat fish, the cafeteria staff also served chicken, meatloaf and an assortment of desserts.

Olivia picked up a copy of the retreat itinerary that lay on the table. "Oh, look, they're holding potato sack races across the river. Do you guys want to go?" she asked.

"I'll pass," Tressie replied. "I have a date."

"A date?" Danyelle and Olivia asked in unison. "With whom?"

Tressie's pointer finger led them across the room to a young distinguished gentleman. A pair of black square-rim glasses surrounding his eyes made him look like a scholar. A button-up plaid shirt that perfectly matched his blue Dockers and tan loafers was a change from Tressie's usual dates. "He asked me to take a stroll around the campgrounds with him."

Danyelle placed the back of her hand against Tressie's forehead. "Are you feeling all right? Because that guy standing over there looks a little stuffy and uptight. Definitely not your type," Danyelle assessed. "Besides, I thought no one here would interest you."

"Miracles do happen. He could be 'the one.'"

Tressie then ran off to catch up with her date.

"Come on, baby. Let's go beat everyone at the sack races." Dean stood and held out his hand for Olivia to join him. "Although I already have the trophy."

Olivia beamed. "Danyelle, are you coming?"

Danyelle looked around and noticed she was left all alone. A phone call had pulled Colin away from the table minutes earlier.

"No. I'm going to go for a walk down by the lake," Danyelle replied.

"She's probably going down there to smoke a joint," Dean whispered.

Danyelle overheard what Dean said about her, but this time he was wrong. Tonight her only desire was to spend time alone with her thoughts and God.

When she reached the lake, the sight of two fawns drinking water from the lake made her stop momentarily and enjoy nature.

"It's beautiful out here. Isn't it?"

Danyelle was startled by the sound of Colin's voice. She quickly swung around to face him. "You scared me. I was about to take off running."

"I'm sorry. I hope you don't mind me following you." He stepped in closer to her. "But I was hoping I could spend some time alone with you."

"That's funny"—she laughed—"because I was hoping to spend some time alone with God." She threw him a look full of attitude before switching away.

"Is that your way of telling me to get lost?" He ran to keep up with her.

She stopped and smiled. "No. I was just teasing you. I wanted to see how persistent you would be to follow me."

"I'd chase you all the way to heaven, if that's what it takes for me to get close to you."

She laughed loudly. "That was corny, but you earned points for trying." She stretched her hands up toward the sky and hollered, "Lord, can You please reveal to me this man's true intentions?"

He laughed at her crazy and outrageous behavior. "Why don't you ask me yourself?"

"How can I be sure you're going to be honest with me?"

He gave her a ridiculous look.

"I mean, there are plenty of women at this retreat who would love to have been kissed by you last night, but you chose me. Why?"

"Did my actions scare you?"

"No."

"Good, because I wouldn't want to frighten you off. I apologize for being so forward, but sharing a kiss with you is something I've wanted to do for some time."

She was still very suspicious of his motives.

"When I saw you at the school I was sure it was a sign from God telling me it's time. Time for me to court the woman who will be my wife."

"Wife?" Danyelle laughed. She was now convinced Colin was playing games. "Sorry, Rev, I'm not wifey material."

"If Jesus turned water into wine, I'm sure it would be no problem for him to turn you into my lifelong mate."

"You're funny, Colin." Danyelle laughed and walked away from him. "You almost had me thinking you were serious."

Colin watched her walk back to the campgrounds. "Watch the Lord work wonders in our relationship," he said as she walked away.

Later that night, before the girls laid down for bed, Olivia decided it was a good time to share her engagement. With her legs crossed Indian-style she patiently waited for Tressie to return from the bathroom.

When Tressie slipped underneath her bed sheets, Olivia couldn't hold back any longer. "I have some headline news to share with you ladies.

I couldn't tell you earlier because Val was still here and I didn't want to upset her, but Dean asked me to marry him this morning."

The news was so exciting that Tressie screamed out and ran to Olivia's bed. She wrapped her arms around Olivia's neck so tight, she practically smothered her.

"What?" Danyelle lifted her head from underneath her bed covers. "It sounded like you said you and Dean were getting married."

Olivia nodded her head yes. "That's what I said." Her cheeks were rosy red from smiling so much. "We set a date for two weeks from today. Dean wanted to get married next week, but I convinced him to give me an extra week."

"Livie, don't you think this is kind of sudden?" Danyelle asked.

"No." Olivia's temperamental attitude turned defensive. "On the hike yesterday we talked about how it wouldn't be long before Dean and I got engaged, so why do you sound surprised?"

Danyelle hadn't noticed it at first, but she could clearly see how her response had spoiled her sister's moment. Her sister's happiness was important, but this move was irresponsible. "I'm sorry." She walked over and kissed her sister on the cheek. "I'm just worried about my little sister. You know with everything that happened between you and Bryant I just want for you and my nephew to be safe."

Olivia and Tressie made room for Danyelle on the bed.

"Doesn't it seem odd to you that Dean wants to get married in the midst of all this controversy surrounding his grandpa? The man who has raised him and is like a father to him is behind bars for a crime he supposedly didn't commit, and Dean pushes all that to the side to marry you."

It suddenly dawned on her that Danyelle had valid reasons for being concerned. Instead of agreeing with her sister, Olivia quickly thought of a logical excuse. "As a matter of fact, we did talk about his grandpa, and Dean just wants us to have a reason to celebrate, instead of all the bad news he's been receiving."

Danyelle was skeptical of Olivia's explanation.

Tressie knew the sisters could debate all night long about the pros and cons of getting married, so she tried to move the conversation in a different direction. "Well, since we don't have much time, the moment we get back we have to make an appointment at the bridal boutique to look for dresses."

Danyelle sat across the room and listened as the girls discussed what colors would look best for the season. She was convinced her sister was making a huge mistake. It bothered her that Olivia was being so irresponsible, but there wasn't too much she could do about it then. So she went to bed.

***

He aggressively yanked her head back by the roots of her hair and forced her mouth open with his tongue. The warmth from his mouth warmed her entire body. She was a prisoner of his passion. He spun her around and planted tender kisses along the back of her neck. He caressed her thighs and massaged her voluptuous breasts.

She released a soft, subtle moan. Individual braids slid down her back like a waterfall. She grinded her backside into his pelvis. She was ready for him to take her. Thoughts of him satisfying her desire drove her crazy. Energy and passion grew until it came to a boiling point. Their breathing was labored.

She gripped the blankets around her, and just as she felt juices flowing from between her legs, Danyelle jumped up and sat straight up in her bed. She looked around and wiped the sweat from her forehead.

It was just a dream.

Danyelle leaned back against her headboard and sighed heavily. She rubbed her thighs together and felt how sticky she was. She never had a wet dream before, and it was embarrassing to think her first wet dream was of her pastor. She lay back in bed. "God, why me?" She rushed into the bathroom to wash all thoughts of Colin away.

***

Right before the retreat's final morning church services were about to begin, Colin felt his phone vibrate. He pulled it out and saw that the call was coming from the college. He wondered who would be calling him from the school on a Sunday. Then he thought that something might have been wrong, so he answered.

"Colin." It was Reverend Baxter. "I apologize for calling you on a Sunday morning and I know you're probably still up in the mountains on the retreat, but there is something I need to discuss with you."

Colin looked toward the hundreds of people being seated for Sunday service. He hoped Dean would remember to save him a seat.

"It's alright, Rev. What's up?" Colin figured that whatever he wanted to talk to him about must have been important for him to call him on a Sunday.

"As you know, the Assistant Dean position in our department has been open for a while. I've been trying to get the college to fill that position for months. Finally, after cutting the bureaucratic red tape, the administration finally approved it. I was hoping you would be interested in the position."

"Me?" Colin was surprised.

"Yes. Colin, you haven't been at the college very long, but you have a lot of potential. You're friendly, young, and it's obvious you have a promising future ahead of you."

"I'm shocked. I never thought this kind of opportunity would come my way so soon. I've only been teaching at the school for about a year."

"I realize that, and it's unfair of me to call you without calling anyone else at the school who might be interested, but I really do think you would be a perfect fit for this position."

"Thanks, Reverend Baxter, I appreciate it. I will definitely give it some thought." Colin was flattered.

"It's not too often that you people are offered an opportunity like this."

Colin pulled the phone away from his ear and looked at it. He must have heard his good friend wrong, so he continued to listen.

"I think it's about time we put some brown faces in authoritative positions."

Colin felt a little uneasy with his comment, but he didn't say anything.

"It wasn't until I listened to Judge West talk did I realize how disadvantaged black people are, and I want to do my part to help lift your people up. It's important for me to give to someone who is less fortunate."

Colin was speechless. He had never heard Baxter speak like this before.

"Colin, I'm not going to lie, I don't have a lot of black friends, but me and my wife were talking the other night and I had to tell her that you were okay.

You're not like the rest of them. You are definitely a credit to your race. You speak so articulate, and when I look at you I don't see color. It just goes to show you that anyone can succeed if they work hard enough. Plus, think about how comfortable the minority students would feel to have someone like you to speak with. Someone who understands what it's like to be black."

Colin couldn't believe what he was hearing. He started to say something, but when he looked up, he saw Dean waving him over. "Listen, Rev, I appreciate you calling, but I have to go. Church is about to begin. I'll talk with you when I return to work tomorrow morning."

"Oh, okay! Just think about what I said. Maybe we can get the cafeteria to start serving some soul food. It would be nice to have some cornbread and catfish."

Annoyed, Colin disconnected the call and joined his friends.

Chapter 13

"Are you surprised to see me?"

"I am." Embarrassed to look a man he highly respected in the eye, Judge West turned away. "I didn't think they were allowing me any visits.

"They weren't, but you know me. After I threw my weight around they saw the light and allowed me to enter like the parting of the Red Sea," Reverend Simms jokingly boasted.

Judge West chuckled at the reverend's sarcasm.

"So, how have they treating you in here?" the reverend asked.

"You're the second visit I've had in four months."

"I'm surprised Dean hasn't been up here to visit with you."

"Rev, he's upset with me right now, and he has every reason to be. If I told you the truth about my past, you would probably stop speaking to me too."

Reverend Simms got the feeling that Judge West wanted to get something off his chest. "Judge, you know that whatever you tell me is confidential. Being your pastor, I'm bound by an oath."

"I want to tell you, but I'm so ashamed," Judge West confessed.

"West, do you know what I do for a living?" Reverend Simms asked.

"Sure, everyone knows you're a doctor."

"Have you ever wondered why I refuse to treat or give medical advice to anyone at First Nazareth?"

"I always assumed it was because of ethical reasons. You didn't want the burden of being a patient's doctor and pastor."

"No, the reason why I won't treat anyone at the church is because I'm an abortion doctor."

Judge West gave him a startled look.

"That look you're giving me is the exact reason why I haven't told the church my medical specialty."

"Boy, Reverend, I thought I was going to be the one to surprise you today."

"That's my secret. Don't think I don't feel ashamed and that I should confess, but I'm scared that they'll look at me differently or, worse, force me out the church."

"Rev, I don't think the church would do that. They love you."

"People change when they realize you're doing something that they feel isn't aligned with God's will. Once I tell them, they won't want to hear any reasons I have for picking the profession."

"Why did you choose to be an abortion doctor?"

"When I went to medical school I could have been any kind of doctor I wanted to be, but when it was time for me to pick my specialty, I chose to be an OB/GYN and I asked for special training in abortions."

"I don't mean to sound disrespectful, but what would make you pick this expertise?"

"It may be difficult for you to understand, but the number of lost souls I've introduced to Jesus through the clinic far exceeds the number of people who stumble through our church doors. I've counseled teenaged girls who have been raped and molested, married women who are pregnant by their lovers and countless number of other women who are just plain scared. Trust me, at first I thought I was making a mistake by doing this. The number of killings and bomb scares being called into different abortion clinics around the country is frightening, but I couldn't allow death to stop me from what I feel I've been called to do."

It felt good to the Reverend to relieve himself of that burden he'd been carrying around on his back.

"West, I feel so guilty after every procedure. Immediately after, I have to repent, because I know I'm directly responsible for killing one of God's children. I always have to ask myself if what I'm doing is murder."

"Do you counsel any of the girls?"

"Yes, and a lot of them I've convinced to either have their babies or give them up for adoption. The others I can't get through to be so scared and lost that they go ahead with the procedure. A few of the young ladies from the clinic are now members of our church."

"I'm sorry. I didn't know."

"Now it's your turn. Tell me what burden is on your heart."

Judge West nodded his head and told the reverend every detail about his horrid past.

"Since you're a lawyer and I'm a pastor, we can leave here assured that what we said between us stays between us."

The judge agreed and shook the reverend's hand before their visit was over.

Chapter 14

Val parallel parked her black Mercedes 500 SL across the street from the Sixth Street Mission in North Philly. She thought her days of coming to the north side of the city ended when she graduated from Temple University last June, but because of her anger issues, here she was again. She skittishly glanced around at her surroundings.

Being in North Philly always made her nervous. It didn't matter that the sun was shining brightly, dozens of people were standing around, and it was the middle of the day. Being mugged, robbed or shot was an everyday occurrence in North Philly. She got out of the car and pressed the button to activate her car alarm before darting across the street to the long line of people waiting for a good hot meal.

Unsure of what to expect on her first day as a volunteer, Val nervously chipped the paint off her manicured nails. She remembered the day she received that letter from court. She thought she was hallucinating when it said that the judge had ordered her to serve out her community service by feeding the homeless. It wasn't that she had a problem with helping out those less fortunate than her, but she could barely peel a potato without cutting herself. How in the world was she going to pull off cooking for a multitude of people?

Val stepped inside the mission and noticed that the place looked as dreary on the inside as it did on the outside. The shabby walls, painted a depressing gray, made her want to brighten the place up with different shades of yellow and orange. Her gaze drifted to the ceiling lights. Half of the bulbs were blown out, and the ones that weren't barely provided any light to the facility.

"Can I help you?"

Frightened, Val swung around to face the soldier-like voice that spoke directly in her ear.

A tall, slim man with big bulky cornrows, broad shoulders and crossed muscular arms intimidated Val.

"Hi, I'm here to—" she stuttered.

"I know why you're here."

Val did a double take. He was a woman.

"Follow me," she ordered.

Val followed the woman to a door labeled STAFF ONLY. She unlocked the door and allowed Val to look inside. "You can leave your coat and purse in here."

Val carefully hung up her things.

"While you're in there, you might as well grab a new pair of rubber gloves, the ammonia, scrub brush and bucket."

Val did as told then trailed the woman until they stopped in front of the restrooms.

"Your first assignment is to clean the restrooms. The good news is that there's only one to clean because it's a unisex bathroom. The bad news is that it hasn't been cleaned in months, not since the last community service person was relieved of her duties. Kyle is the director of the center and the person you would usually report to, but he's running a little late this afternoon. He left me in charge until he returns. If you need anything, I'm Ms. Ward, and when you're finished here, find me and I'll show you what else needs to be done."

Ms. Ward strutted away like a pimp from the year 1970. Val rolled her eyes and sucked her teeth. She was so angry with herself for kicking Caitlyn's butt that she had to flex her fingers into a clenched fist several times before regaining her self-control and entering the bathroom.

The first scent that greeted her was urine. The smell burned her nostrils and filled her lungs. She quickly grabbed her shirt to cover her nose from the harsh odor. First she inspected the place to see where she should begin. She walked through a sea of used paper towels that covered the sticky floor. The one mirror was filthy, and the soap dispenser was empty. She pushed open the one bathroom stall. Inside she could barely bring herself to look inside at the stained commode. She knew that would be the hardest job for her to do.

She stepped into the bathroom stall with her bucket, gloves and brush. She bent down to begin her duties, but before she could start, she spotted a used tampon lying on the floor. Val's stomach turned. She dropped the brush in the bucket and turned to leave, but the judge's final words drifted through her mind. If she didn't complete the full two hundred hours she would have to serve jail time. She looked around at her surroundings.

"Maybe jail time wouldn't be so bad."

Two hours later Val emerged and stood outside the bathroom gasping for air.

"Valencia." A young man wearing baggy jeans, Timberland boots and dreadlocks in his hair approached Val with an outstretched hand. "I'm Kyle. I'm so glad you could join us." Kyle was a very handsome guy with straight, brilliant white teeth. He even had two dimples that appeared each time he smiled, which was often.

Kyle showed her around and later explained that his responsibility was to make sure that breakfast, lunch and dinner was served to the community on time.

After they had gotten acquainted, Kyle told her that she would probably be working closely with Ms. Ward for the remainder of the day.

Reluctantly, she reported back to Ms. Ward, who had a list of chores that had to be completed before the dinner crowd arrived.

Two hours later Val felt like a slave. She had never worked so hard in her life. The joints in her fingers hurt from scrubbing just about every pot in the place. She had been on her feet most of the day, and Ms. Ward wouldn't allow her a minute of rest.

Kyle snuck up behind Val and tapped her on the shoulder. "How's it going?" he asked.

Val was in the middle of rinsing out one of the pots used to make soup. "It's going good," she lied. Val prayed that the next five weeks would fly by.

"Val, can you take out the trash?" Ms. Ward, the kitchen sergeant, interrupted their conversation and pointed to the trashcan that was overflowing with debris.

Val looked to Kyle to save her from Ms. Ward's gruesome labor demands, but he simply shrugged his shoulders and walked away. That's when Val realized he was also scared of her.

She peeled off her rubber gloves and gathered the trash bag to take out to the dumpster.

"And when you're done with that, I have something else for you to do," she shouted.

Val grumbled underneath her breath. Ms. Ward treated her like Cinderella. Every time she needed something demeaning done, she called on Val.

Once she replaced the garbage can with a new bag she pushed open the back door and dragged the trash out behind her. Ms. Ward sternly warned Val to never leave the trash bag on the ground, because it would attract rats. But when she tried to lift the trash it was too heavy for her to pick up. "I'm not going to throw my back out for a job I'm not even getting paid for." Val slid the bag behind the dumpster. She was sure Ms. Ward wouldn't find it. It was hidden too well.

When she turned to go back inside, her attention was drawn to the sound of metal smashing against the ground. Val couldn't help looking to see what was going on. She stuck her head out in the back alley. There she saw three kids around thirteen years old beating up an old man. Two kids held the man by his arms, while the other took the lid from the metal trashcan and slammed it against his head. Even from where she stood at she could see blood spill from the gash in the man's head.

Without thinking Val screamed out, "Hey, stop it."

The kids got scared when they saw her and took off running. She watched the man fall, curl his body into a fetal position and moan loudly.

Val ran as fast as she could to help him. "Are you all right?"

He looked up at her.

That's when she realized this man wasn't as old as she thought he was. Underneath the smudges of dirt that filled his face and tattered hat that covered his head she found young eyes. She noticed the filthy trench coat on his back, worn sneakers on his feet and gaping holes in his pants. Val had never seen a person her age look so shabby.

"I'm going to go get you some help," she said.

"Daddy?"

From behind an abandoned car that sat nearby a little girl appeared. Her eyes were full of fear. Hesitant to come any closer to her father, she kept a careful eye on Val.

"Hope." He waved for her to come nearer.

She quickly ran to his side. The little girl was so small and beautiful. Val thought she couldn't be any older than three years old. She reminded Val of a chocolate brown morsel with dark brown hair. Hope wrapped her arms around her father and cried. Val watched them for a moment before noticing the light purple spring jacket Hope wore was not enough to keep her warm.

"Listen, you were beat up pretty badly. I can get somebody to help you," Val said.

"No," he screamed. "Just help me get back into that car and I'll be fine," he demanded.

"What will you do if those kids come back? You're too hurt to defend yourself." Val was sure this man wasn't thinking clearly. He was in no condition to take care of himself and a young child.

"Those kids won't be back. They were searching for money. When they didn't find any on me they"—He cut his eyes at Val. "Forget it! Either help me or leave."

Offended by how rude he was, she wanted to leave him lying helpless on the ground. Then she saw his daughter struggling to help her father to his feet. Val's conscience wouldn't allow her to leave without giving a helping hand.

She struggled to lift him to his feet. After a few attempts, they were finally able to stumble over to the passenger side of the car.

"Hope, you lie in the back seat while Daddy sits in the front."

She did as her father asked. Then the man leaned back in the passenger seat and breathed a sigh of relief.

Val was stunned to learn that they were living out of a car. Their home sat on four cinder blocks. The front windshield was cracked, and the hood of the car was missing.

"I appreciate your help," he mumbled, "but you can go now, and please don't mention to anyone that you saw us." He winced in pain.

It was obvious he wasn't from Philadelphia. His thick Southern accent was a dead giveaway.

She stood wishing there was more she could do for them, when she heard Ms. Ward screeching her name.

"Val!"

By the sound of her call, Val knew she needed something else done. Val and the stranger looked at one another one last time before she dashed back toward the mission.

"Girl, where were you? We have dishes piling up in here."

"Sorry," was all Val could muster. She looked behind her one last time and back at the abandoned car before reporting back to the kitchen.

The remainder of the day seemed to drag on for Val. The hands on the clock appeared to have stopped, and Val kept checking her watch to make sure it read the right time.

At last, when Val thought Ms. Ward would never let her go, Kyle told her she could go home.

Anxious to get out of there before Ms. Ward noticed she was gone, Val quickly gathered her things and exited the building through the front door.

During her tour of the facility with Kyle, he'd mentioned that the biggest incentive of working at a mission was the leftover food the workers were rewarded with. Her lips formed a small grin when she looked down at the packages of food she was given from the mission.

Val managed to pack a couple bowls of hot soup, two loaves of bread and a six-pack of bottled water. She was sure Hope and her father would appreciate the food. Once she was outside she snuck around to the back of the building and went straight to where she had left the man and his daughter. She prayed they were still there.

When she walked up to the car she found them both soundly sleeping. She figured they were probably hungry, but she didn't want to disturb them, so she gently placed the food down on the ground and tiptoed away.

"Thanks for not saying anything earlier," the man said, causing Val to jump.

She turned to face him with her hand still on her heart.

"I'm sorry. Did I frighten you?"

"No. It's okay." Her heart was nearly beating out of her chest. She pointed to the food she left on the ground. "I left you and Hope some food. It's not a lot, but I thought you might be hungry."

He looked back at his sleeping daughter. "Yeah, she usually gets hungry around this time." He picked up the soup container and took a spoonful. "It's still hot. Thank you."

"You know you are more than welcome to come into the mission to eat. It's all free and it's not half bad," Val joked.

"No, thank you. Hope and I are fine. Besides, Hope and I usually dig through the garbage and get the leftovers anyway."

The man missed the look of disgust that crossed Val's face.

"What's wrong with coming inside? At least you would have someplace dry and warm to eat your meal."

"Listen, I'm not taking my daughter into one of those places." He was hostile and talked to Val like she was the enemy.

"I didn't mean to upset you. I was trying to help," she whispered.

"Don't apologize. Past experiences have taught me that when you go into places like that they try to get all in your business, especially if you have children with you. I'm very private. I don't like people knowing much about me."

"Listen, they probably just want to help you. I'm sure they can probably get you off the street and possibly into your own home."

"We don't need their help." He tried to sit up in his seat, but when he did he cringed in pain.

"I can see that you're still in pain. Those kids put a hurting on you. You may need to see a doctor and have them check for any broken ribs."

"I'll be fine," he shouted.

When he said that, Hope woke up. She rubbed her eyes and glared strangely at Val.

"Hello," Val kindly spoke to the little girl, but Hope never answered back. She simply stared back at her with wide eyes. "She's so pretty. How old is she?" Val asked.

Her father looked at her suspiciously before answering. "She's three." Then he pointed to the driver's seat. "Honey, sit right here so I can feed you." He started talking to Val again. "You're lucky they didn't pull out a gun and kill you," the man said. "What were you thinking when you yelled out for them to stop?"

Val hadn't thought about how dangerous it was for her to interfere. "I wasn't thinking," she replied softly.

"What's your name?" he asked as he gave Hope her first spoonful of soup and a few slices of bread.

"Valencia, but they call me Val," she replied.

"Well, it's nice to meet you, Val. My name is Jonah, and as you already know, the sleeping beauty that has just woke from her slumber is my daughter Hope."

"You two live out here?" Val glanced around.

"Temporarily. We're out here until I come up with a new plan."

A light rain started to fall down around them. Val remembered the weatherman forecasted heavy torrential rains overnight. She couldn't dare go home to a warm bed and leave them to weather the storm all night in that old clunker. "Why don't you come home with me tonight?" Val realized she was being a bit impulsive by inviting a stranger into her home, but she couldn't leave him outside, injured and with a child to care for.

"Thanks for the offer, but we'll be fine. I've been taking care of us since she was eighteen months. We'll be fine."

"You've been on the streets that long?" Val screamed. "You don't have any family I can call to help you out?"

He gave a negative response.

She looked over at Hope. The bottom of her pig-tails swept the top of her shoulders. Hope scarfed down her meal as if she hadn't eaten a decent meal in days.

"Do you want to come home with me?" Val asked Hope.

His daughter adamantly shook her head no. Then she didn't think twice before jumping into the safety of her father's lap.

He winced in pain. Hope cried, and so did her dad.

"I don't think your ribs are broken, probably just bruised, but if you come home with me, then I can wrap them up for you," Val suggested again. "If you still want to leave once I'm finished I'll bring you right back," she promised.

He was hesitant to accept help from a stranger, but he agreed, and she helped him out to her car.

Chapter 15

Jonah securely buckled Hope into the back seat before fastening his own seat belt. "How long have you been working at the mission?"

"Today was my first day. I'll be working there as a volunteer for the next few weeks."

"Why would a pretty girl like yourself work at a mission in her spare time?" Jonah had a lot of questions for her.

"It's a long story. One I would prefer to forget."

"Are you a lawyer?" Jonah continued to dig for information.

"What would make you think I was a lawyer?"

"I don't know." He glanced out his window. "I guess I don't know too many jobs that pay enough to drive a car like this."

Val wasn't ready to share her past, so she cleverly danced around his question. "Let's just say that right now I'm trying to find myself."

"The only people I know who use those words are the unemployed kind."

They laughed.

"You drive this expensive car, and I noticed the shoes on your feet probably cost more than it did to feed everyone who came to the mission today.

Are you one of those spoiled kids whose parents buy them everything?"

"Are you trying to ask, am I privileged?" Val was more amused than insulted by Jonah's comments.

She made a turn toward Penn's Landing waterfront. This part of the city housed many wealthy celebrities, athletes, prominent city officials, doctors and lawyers. The neighborhood consisted of mostly townhouses and condominiums. It wasn't the ideal place to raise a family, but it was the perfect residence for a young couple just starting out like Val and Julian. That's why they purchased a lovely townhouse built on a small cobblestone lane protected by a huge wrought iron gate.

Val pulled her car up to a small stand that housed the keyboard she needed to unlock the gates. She wound down her window and tapped in the six-digit combination code. Then the mechanical gates opened wide. She drove around to the back of the house.

"It looks dark in there. You should always leave at least one light on in the house to ward off intruders," Jonah warned.

"Thanks for the tip." Val parked and turned off the engine. "I'll keep that in mind."

When they got out of the car, they realized Hope had fallen fast asleep in the backseat, her head dropped down in front of her. When she started snoring, Val and Jonah laughed at her.

"Let me get her," Val offered. "You won't be able to carry her." When she scooped Hope into her arms, her eyes opened momentarily. Val was sure Hope would cry. Instead, she laid her head on Val's shoulder and went back to sleep.

When they approached the back door, Val juggled her house keys in one hand and Hope in the other. She tried to insert a key into the lock then realized it wasn't the right one. It had been months since she'd been at the house, and it was hard for her to remember which was the right key.

Jonah watched Val try several different keys before one finally turned the lock.

She pushed the door wide open.

"It looks like you had a hard time finding the right key," Jonah commented.

Val ignored his observation. "It's cold in here. If you don't mind, I can go lay her down in one of the guest bedrooms upstairs and then I'll turn on the heat."

Jonah stared at her holding his baby in her arms. He really didn't want Hope out of his sight, but he allowed it. As Val disappeared up the back stairs Jonah switched on a few lights.

By the time she returned, she found him admiring the place.

"This house is an architect's dream. I was going to college for engineering before I had to drop out." He knocked on one of the wooden beams that supported the ceiling. "There's a lot you could do to this place. But by the look of things, you're just getting started." He pointed to the various boxes that were scattered around the room. "I guess you haven't had a chance to go furniture shopping yet."

Val looked around. The house was full of boxes, but there wasn't any furniture. She had forgotten about the boxes that were brought there weeks before her wedding. She and Julian decided not to unpack anything until after the honeymoon. Her mind was suddenly flooded with thoughts of the last time she was in the house.

"Valencia, right after we get married I want to start a family." Julian sat on the gray stone ledge right next to the fireplace with Val perched on his lap.

"I thought we decided to wait until after I finished law school," Val reminded him.

"Baby, I love you so much that I can't wait. I want us to create something that is a part of both you and me."

"You wouldn't happen to be feeling this way because the guy you play with just had a set of twins?"

His face turned guilty.

"Baby, I promise our time will come. Plus, I don't think either of our parents will rest until they hear they have a grandbaby on the way."

"Val. Val."

She looked up and realized she had been caught daydreaming.

"It looks like you left me for a second."

"No, I'm fine." She noticed Jonah sitting on the steps holding his side. "I'm sorry. I brought you here to get bandages and I'm in my own world. Let me go check the upstairs and see if there's anything here I can use. If not, I'll run to the corner store."

"You don't have to go out your way," Jonah yelled after her.

"It's no problem," Val screamed back. She searched the entire master bathroom but couldn't find one Band-Aid. When she returned to the first floor she began searching for her purse. "I'm gonna have to run out. I won't be long. It should take me no more than ten minutes." She spotted her purse lying on the kitchen counter, picked it up and raced toward the front door.

"I'll be right here." Jonah pointed to where he was sitting. "Val." He stopped her right before she closed the front door behind her. "Can you pick me up some over-the-counter pain killers? My side is throbbing."

Val hurried to the store and within minutes was back home again. "Jonah!" she cried. The last thing she expected to see was him laid out on the floor with his eyes closed. She panicked and dropped everything in her hand. "Oh God, please let him be all right. I knew we should have gone to the hospital." She checked his pulse.

"Hey, you back already?" Jonah opened one eye.

"You had me worried." She breathed a sigh of relief. "I thought you were unconscious."

He laughed. "No. Just tired. This floor is so comfortable. It beats sleeping in an old car any day." He wearily pushed himself up against the nearest wall.

"My offer still stands. You're more than welcome to stay the night. There are four bedrooms upstairs. I don't have much food, but what I have we can share."

"The Bible says, 'Share your food with the hungry and give shelter to the homeless,'" Jonah recited.

"Isaiah 58:7."

Val was shocked that he was familiar with scripture.

"My grandmother was a Sunday School teacher for forty-three years, and as her only grandson, she said it was important for me to memorize verses of wisdom. She said if we carried God's word in our hearts then we would never get lost."

"She sounds like a very wise woman." Val picked up everything she had dropped on the floor and placed them back in the bag.

"I can't get over how beautiful your home is," Jonah commented.

"Yes, it is a nice house."

Jonah heard the sadness in her voice when she referred to the structure as a house and not a home.

She carried all the first-aid items over to him. "Can you take your coat off?"

Jonah slowly slipped out of his coat and pulled his shirt up as far as it would go without causing too much pain.

Val knelt down beside him on her knees and wrapped around his ribs with medical tape.

"I would never mistake you as a nurse." He sighed.

"Did I do a bad job?" She tore off the tape and sat back on her knees to admire her work.

"No, but I can hardly breathe." Jonah gasped for air. "Did you tape me up this tight on purpose so that me and my daughter couldn't leave?"

"I'm sorry. Let me try again." She carefully tore the tape away from his body. The second time she was mindful to allow enough room for him to breathe comfortably.

"Hope must really be tired; she doesn't normally sleep this long," Jonah said.

"When's the last time she's slept in a bed?" Val dropped a couple pain pills in her hand and handed them to Jonah.

"It's been a while." He swallowed the pills simultaneously without any water.

"I would have gotten you a bottle of water," Val said.

"Sorry, I guess I'm used to living off the most basic needs. A house, food, water and heat; those are things that most people take for granted."

"Why don't you take my offer to stay the night? If not for yourself, then for your daughter. She looks so peaceful sleeping in that king-size bed."

"I guess it wouldn't hurt for Hope to sleep in a real bed instead of the back seat of that old sixty-nine Chevy."

"Great! I'll go make up the guest bedroom for you and you'll be right across the hall from Hope so if she wakes up you won't be far," Val rattled off.

"That's okay. You don't have to go to any trouble for me. I'll squeeze in the bed right next to Hope."

"Are you sure? Like I said, I have four bedrooms upstairs. I'm sure you would be more comfortable sleeping in your own bed."

Jonah shook his head. "Hope and I are used to roughing it out together; sleeping in a soft comfortable bed for one night will make me soft." Jonah followed her to the room where Hope was sleeping. He took off his shoes and made a comfortable spot for himself in the corner. When he pulled the cap off his head, his hair revealed itself. A mass of unkempt soft brown curls filled his head.

Val pretended not to notice how ruggedly sexy he looked. "If you need anything just yell." She closed the door behind her and retired to the master bedroom.

"Good-night," Jonah yelled before switching off the lights. In the dark he thought about Val. She was beautiful, intelligent and kind, but it was hard for him to trust anybody. He feared that any strangers trying to get close to him and his daughter would do them harm. He wanted to believe that wasn't the case with Val, but he wasn't sure. That's why he chose to sleep in the same room as Hope. He would have peace of mind that Hope was safe if he slept close to her.

Val locked her bedroom door and collapsed on her king-size bed. The ceiling lights blinded her. She never expected to be back in this house again. Not without Julian. The realtor called her several times to put the house back on the market per Val's request, but she never returned the call. The house and everything in it was the proof she needed to prove that Julian wasn't just a figment of her imagination. It verified that her dreams were at one time true. She was happy, in love and about to become somebody's wife. Until one day it all vanished. The box with Julian's name scribbled in marker taunted her. She ripped it open and the aroma from his cologne drifted past her nose. A box full of his toiletries. Tears gathered in her eyes, but she refused to cry any more. "No more tears." She quickly closed the box, grabbed a blanket and slept in one of the guest bedrooms.

The following morning Jonah lurched forward out of his sleep. He looked around confused at his surroundings. The luxurious silk sheets and brilliant white walls were foreign to him, until he saw Hope sitting in the middle of the floor playing with a stuffed talking dolphin.

"Hey, Daddy." She held up the doll. "See. His name is Ed."

He quickly recollected his thoughts and remembered where he was. "Where's Val at?"

Hope shrugged her shoulders.

As Jonah got up out of bed, he felt a little better. He slightly bent to the side. "My ribs must be healing." He held out his hand. "Come on, honey. Let's go see if we can find Val, so we can tell her goodbye." They wandered around upstairs still unable to find her.

Twenty minutes later Val rushed in the back door. She dropped several shopping bags down on the table and yelled, "Is anyone here?" She listened for sounds of movement in the house, but it was quiet.

"We're up here," she heard Jonah yell from upstairs.

Val followed the sound of his voice to the master bathroom. When she walked in she found Hope up to her neck in bubbles taking a bath.

"I hope you don't mind," Jonah explained. "When we saw how big your bathtub was we couldn't resist. This is like a swimming pool to Hope. She was so excited, I allowed her to take a bath."

Val giggled to herself. "No, that's fine. I'm glad to see you're still here." She turned toward Hope. "Did you get a good night's sleep?"

Hope looked at her with empty eyes and reached out for her father.

"She doesn't like me?" Val said.

"No, don't think that. It takes her a while to warm up to people. It even took her a while to trust me."

Val gave him a strange look. She wondered what he meant by that. *Why would it take his own daughter a while to trust him?* Val's interest in her houseguests just rose through the roof. Val assumed Jonah was just another overprotective father, but there could be other reasons why.

She tried to play it off as if she wasn't suspicious. "I picked us up some breakfast and bought Hope some new clothes. That's what took me so long. I'll go get her things." Val bolted down the stairs. Her cell phone lay on the kitchen table. She thought about calling the police, but she wasn't sure what to tell them. She tapped her foot against the floor. She was running out of time. "Jonah could be a kidnapper. There could be people out there searching for Hope." She stepped toward her phone, but stopped herself. "I need proof. The police won't do anything without evidence. I know what I'll do."

Before returning to the bathroom Val straightened out her composure. "I also picked up a few items for you. I'm not sure if they'll fit, but I figured you could use them."

Jonah helped Hope step out of the tub and dry off. "Thanks. If you don't mind, can you help Hope get dressed? I'm going to use the hallway bathroom to wash up and change. It won't take me long."

"Sure." While Val helped Hope get dressed, she figured this may be her only chance at finding out any details about Hope and her father. "Hope, do you know your last name?"

Hope was aloof toward her. She didn't speak and avoided looking in Val's direction.

"Where's your mommy?"

The little girl's eyes were emotionless.

"She's not going to answer you." Jonah snuck up from behind Val. "She still considers you a stranger, and so do I."

"I was just trying to—" Val was at a loss for words.

"You were just trying to find out about me and my daughter. If you wanted to know about her mother you could have asked me." Jonah grabbed Hope's coat and shoes and threw on his own hat, coat and shoes. "Come on, Hope. Let's go."

"Please don't go. I brought you something to eat. At least eat first."

"That's all right. You may try to lift my fingerprints from off the glasses." He grabbed Hope's hand, and they left out the door.

Val watched them walk down her sidewalk, away from the house. She prayed he took Hope somewhere nice with the twenty dollars she slipped inside his coat pocket.

Chapter 16

Colin dribbled the basketball in front of Dean, teasing him. "Come on, Dean. What's the problem?" He grinned. "You're wheezing like an old man."

"Old man." Dean stole the ball out of Colin's hands and stepped around him to make an easy basket.

Dean laughed, threw the ball to Colin and slowly made his way over to the benches. He grabbed his Temple sports bottle and collapsed onto the bench.

It wasn't unusual to find the two men at war on the basketball court any given Saturday. Colin was very athletic and loved all sports. Dean wasn't as competitive as Colin, but there were some sports he excelled at, and one of them was basketball.

"Man, what's up with you?" Colin watched him drink the entire container. "We usually play at least three of four games before you need a break. We haven't even finished the first game."

Dean grinned. "I'm getting old. Everybody can't be as young as you." Colin sat down next to him.

"So finish telling me what happened when you went into Baxter's office."

"Well, I didn't go in there going ballistic. I prayed that morning and asked the Holy Spirit, 'What would Jesus do?' I really didn't expect God to answer, but He did. When I walked into Baxter's office, I felt tranquility overcome me. It was like being in a room filled with the presence of the Lord. I calmly and professionally explained to Baxter how offended I was by what he said. In the end he apologized and said that he didn't mean anything by it."

"Do you believe him?" Dean wasn't convinced it was that easy. "I mean, there is such a thing as unintentional racism. Some people are bigots and they don't even know it."

"I thought about that when it first happened, but I'm not going to hold this one incident against him. It happened, he apologized, that's the end of it."

"Well, I have some great news to share," Dean stated loudly. "I asked Olivia to marry me."

"Congratulations!" Colin gave Dean a firm handshake. "I knew it would only be a matter of time."

"I couldn't allow her to get away from me. She completes me. Every time I look at her I see my blessing. I can't stop praising God for having favor on me. When she's in my presence, I feel like she has me under a spell, because no other woman can compare."

"Dean, a lot of people don't realize how blessed they are to have a woman like Olivia until it's too late." Colin stood up and dribbled the basketball.

"Man, I'd be honored if you stood up with me as my best man at my wedding."

Colin was caught off guard by Dean's request. He wasn't expecting Dean to ask him to be a part of the wedding. "I wouldn't miss it for the world." He held the basketball in his hand. "What's up with your grandpa? You haven't said anything about his case. You know the whole church stands behind him. Those allegations are preposterous."

"I can't worry about my grandpa. I'm going to go on with my life. I wish him the best."

Colin gave an awkward look. "Man, I know it may be hard to read the horrible things they print in the daily newspaper, but don't allow one reporter's opinion of the case put doubt in your mind about a man who has been like a martyr to the black community."

"What if you put all your trust in my grandpa and he's not what you thought he was?"

Colin guessed there was more to the story than what he knew. "He's only a man, and man shouldn't judge man. We can't expect him not to have made any mistakes. Your grandpa has genuine love in his heart for God and all God's children. Black or white. Latino or Asian. It doesn't matter to him. Maybe you need to do some soul-searching and ask God to reveal what's blinding your heart from seeing the truth. I'll pray for you, and when you're ready to share, I'll be here."

"Colin, there is something I haven't told you yet."

Colin saw fear in his friend's eyes.

Before Dean could say anything, his breathing became erratic. He clutched at his chest and fell to the ground.

"Dean!" Colin hollered out. He tilted Dean's head back and tried to breathe life back into him. He pumped down on his chest for three counts and tried again. Seconds later Dean was gasping for air. Colin pulled his cell phone out of his gym bag and dialed 9-1-1.

Colin told the operator where they were, and it seemed like a lifetime before he heard the ambulance sirens in the background. "Hold on, Dean! The paramedics are on the way." Colin could see Dean was still having a hard time breathing on his own.

Finally, the paramedics arrived. They lifted Dean onto a stretcher and placed an oxygen mask over his face. As they rolled him away, he reached out for Colin and moved the mask from his face.

Colin bent down close to his mouth. Dean whispered Olivia's name. Colin ran to his car, and the first thing he did was call Olivia.

Across town at the bridal boutique Olivia, Val and Danyelle searched for dresses. Olivia searched the racks for the perfect gown. Plus, she had to find dresses for her maid of honor, Danyelle, and bridesmaids, Tressie and Val.

"Val, are you sure you're all right?" Olivia asked from inside the changing room. She worried that Val would have a mental breakdown from being around so many wedding dresses.

"Would you stop asking me that? I'm fine." Val looked around for Danyelle. She spotted her lounging in one of the plush leather chairs. Her feet were propped up on the footstool while drinking sparkling apple cider and munching on sweet strawberries from a fruit tray.

Val walked over and poured herself a glass. "Look what the cat done drug in." Val sipped from her glass and watched Tressie sashay through the store like a runway model.

Danyelle turned around just in time to see Tressie pick up a burgundy bridesmaid dress from off the rack.

"I love this. They have this hanging in the window. This is the dress for me."

Danyelle studied the dress. "It's cute, but they don't have that dress in the color we need."

"We already checked." Val sat down in the lounge chair next to Danyelle.

"Damn." Tressie looked up towards the sky. "Lord, I didn't mean that. Maybe I can get Livie to change the color," Tressie reasoned out loud.

"I don't think so," Danyelle told her. "Anyway, it's too late for Olivia to change the color scheme of the reception."

"I wouldn't change the colors anyway," Olivia hollered from the dressing room, "because it's my wedding."

Tressie sucked her teeth and leaned against the wall. "Where you been at?" Val asked.

"You were supposed to meet us here forty-five minutes ago."

"They had me sitting in court all day long for jury selection. It was a complete waste of time," Tressie replied.

"I guess that means you weren't chosen," Danyelle said.

"I think I would have been chosen if it weren't for the fact that every black man that entered the courtroom in shackles and jailhouse clothes I knew."

Val and Danyelle laughed. "I couldn't believe it. I knew every single one of those guys. It was embarrassing. Once I found the courage to raise my hand, the judge would call me out, and then I had to ask to be excused because I was an acquaintance of the defendant. It got to the point where the judge would start the selection off by asking me, did I know the accused."

Danyelle laughed even harder. "I even saw Payce's best friend, Darshon, there."

"That goes to show you that you need to start having a better choice of friends," Val said.

"All those people are from my past. It's not my fault that fate brought a bunch of shady characters in my life."

"Don't blame fate for your mistakes," Danyelle replied. They waited outside the dressing room another ten minutes before Danyelle got tired of eating fruit. She stood up and marched toward the stall Olivia was in. She banged on the dressing room door. "Would you hurry up? Livie, it doesn't take that long to try on no dress."

Customers standing close by turned to look at the commotion Danyelle was causing. Olivia slightly opened the door and looked around for her sister. "How can you expect me to do this all by myself? Most of these dresses weigh more than I do. Could you help me out?" She turned around so Danyelle could button up the back of the dress she had on.

"Okay, you two are making a scene." Val stepped in between the two of them. She turned toward Danyelle. "Stop upsetting the bride-to-be."

The perky and vibrant Bridal Boutique sales clerk came over with more dresses for Olivia to try on. "Here you are." She handed Danyelle four more wedding dresses.

"More dresses?" Danyelle questioned.

"Yes, your sister said she would like to try these on, and since you're not only the bride's sister, but also the maid of honor I figured that you could hold the dresses while she tries each one on."

"I thought that was your job," Danyelle dryly replied, but the sales clerk giggled her way to the far end of the store.

Olivia spun around to face the girls. Like children with a staring problem each one of her friends looked at her, but didn't say a word. The smile quickly faded from Olivia's face. "What's wrong?" She stood in front of the mirror. "Does the dress look that bad?" She turned toward them.

Danyelle set the dresses she was holding down on a nearby chair and walked up to her sister with tears in her eyes. "Livie, you look just like Mommy. If I hadn't seen you go into that room, I would have thought you were her."

Olivia was relieved. "You really think so?"

Danyelle turned her sister around to face the mirror. "I think this is the dress for you."

Olivia didn't realize how much this dress resembled her mother's. The simple country linen dress with delicate pearl beading was practically an exact replica.

"Oh, my!" Madge, the sales clerk, walked up and placed her hand over her open mouth. "I have never seen a bride look lovelier. Isn't she breathtaking?" She nudged Danyelle.

"I think I'm going to take it," Olivia said.

"All right." She took one final glance at the dress. "I don't even think it needs any alterations. If you go into the dressing room I'll bag this up for you."

Tressie helped Olivia unsnap the back buttons, and Olivia went back into the dressing room to change.

Olivia admired herself in the mirror. It was still hard for her to believe she was getting married. "Olivia!" Her sister's big mouth frightened her. "What's taking you so long? The sales lady is out here waiting for you."

Olivia pulled the dress over the top of her head and put back on her own clothes. As she was tying up her sneakers, she noticed a missed call on her cell phone.

As she listened to her messages she got scared when she heard Colin's message. He didn't say what happened, but he did say he was on the way to the hospital and that she should get there as soon as possible.

Adrenaline pumped Olivia's heart so fast that she broke out in a sweat. The walls seemed to close in around her and she couldn't breathe. She grabbed hold of the wall and finished putting on her sneakers then dashed out of the store and toward her car.

"Olivia! Olivia!" Danyelle called after her sister, but Olivia never turned around.

***

In the hospital Colin sat next to a sleeping Dean. He hadn't left Dean's side since they arrived. Colin pushed back in his chair. Scenes of how Dean collapsed to the ground flashed before his eyes. That was a scary moment for Colin.

A doctor entered the emergency room cubicle and introduced himself. "Has he been sleeping long?" the doctor asked.

"Since, I've been here," Colin replied.

"I'm not 'sleep." Dean rubbed his eyes to adjust to the bright light. "Just resting my eyes."

"Good. Is it all right if I speak in front of your friend?" After Dean nodded, the doctor sat on the side of Dean's hospital bed. "I spoke with your doctor and he told me that he was very clear when he explained that, because of your condition, you were instructed to take it easy."

"Doc, I was just playing a little ball," Dean complained.

"Basketball is too much for your body to handle. You may have thought the weather was cool enough for you to run up and down the basketball court under the sun, but that drains your energy. That is why you collapsed. You have to get some rest, Mr. West. No more strenuous exercise." He handed Dean a few papers and a pen. "Sign here and you can go."

Dean signed his release forms and threw his legs over the side of the bed.

"Man, what condition is the doctor talking about?" Colin asked.

"Man, I'm sick."

Colin looked down at Dean's shaking hands and knew that Dean was scared. "What's wrong with you?"

Then the white curtain opened up, and in rushed Olivia. "Honey, what happened?" She ran and wrapped her arms around Dean's neck. "Are you all right?"

"I'm fine." He gave Colin a look to keep quiet. "I think we were playing a little bit too hard. The doctor said I was dehydrated and exhausted. He recommended rest."

Olivia helped him down from off the bed. "Well, no more basketball for you."

They walked out of the emergency room together, leaving Colin to wonder what was wrong with his friend.

Chapter 17

Reverend Simms repeated a conversation he overheard between a pair of ladies right before the start of service.

"I betcha he's guilty," the one woman said while the other nodded her head in agreement. "All white people are prejudiced."

That woman's words bothered him. Still lost in a daze, Reverend Simms watched the ushers signal to one another that it was time to take collection.

Suddenly, he jumped up from his seat and spoke into the microphone, "Excuse me, before we take collection I would like to take a moment to address the situation with Judge West."

The ushers stopped what they were doing and stood against the far wall.

"The judge and I had a pleasant visit not too long ago, and a handful of you will be glad to know that despite his circumstances he is doing well."

"Amen!" one of the deacons shouted from the first pew.

"I'm sure everyone here has heard about the disturbing accusations against the judge, and I know a lot of people think we should turn our backs on him."

A few people in the audience mumbled, "Yes."

"I'm not standing before you to plead the judge's case, because that's not my job. I'm standing before you because I feel it necessary to remind the members of this church and of this community how much Judge West has done for us."

A lot of condemned souls looked down at the floor, and no one spoke a word.

"Jesus died not just for me and you, but also for the President of the United States. He died for the Taliban and he also died for the skinheads, Klan members and the Nazi party. You may think God only cares about the good people, but He cares about all people, and it doesn't matter what we've done in the past. Once we accept Christ, those sins are wiped clear from the slate."

Reverend Simms tried to look a few people in the eye, but they refused to look his way.

"The only person who can respond to the allegations being brought against Judge West is Judge West, but I thought now would be the perfect time to remind this community of the countless number of times the judge has come through to help us. He has been a pillar of this community. He's stood up for us so many times. Can't we stand behind him right now?"

The audience clapped their hands.

Then Reverend Simms motioned for Reverend Baxter, to join him in the front of the church.

"First Nazareth, it's a pleasure to be here with you again, and I wish it were under better circumstances. Listen, I don't know Judge West that well, but from the few times that we did speak I could tell he was a giving person. Reverend Simms asked me to come here today to tell you about the defense fund I've set up on behalf of Judge West. He is going to need the best representation, and I contributed the first five thousand dollars for the lawyer's retainer fee, but it's going to cost a whole lot more."

"Yes," Reverend Simms spoke loudly into the mic he held in his hand. "That is why I plan to donate this Sunday's offering and a percentage of each Sunday's offering until Judge West is released. First Nazareth, I'm asking you to dig down in your pockets and help us help one of own during his time of need."

Reverend Baxter and Simms watched as people pulled out bills and wrote out checks to put in that morning's offering.

"Reverends Baxter, it looks like every member of my congregation's heart has been open. Why don't we hold a benefit concert in the park on Germantown Avenue? That way, we can get the entire community involved."

Reverend Baxter smiled broadly. "That sounds wonderful, and if you need any assistance with it, please give me a call."

***

A week had gone by since Val had heard or seen from Jonah and Hope. She worried about them, but there wasn't much she could do. At the mission Val often volunteered to take out the trash. Up to four times a day she would check out the old, abandoned car for any sign of them, but the car remained empty, and it didn't look like they had been back there since she last saw them.

Val gave up all hope of ever seeing either of them again, until Jonah stormed into the mission yelling her name. She was in the middle of mopping the dining hall floor when Jonah charged in her direction. By the look on his face she knew something was seriously wrong. Hope was missing from her father's side.

"They took her," Jonah shouted. "My daughter's gone."

Val dropped the mop and pulled him over to the corner of the room.

Ms. Ward stared at them from the kitchen.

"What happened? Where's Hope?" Val talked very low in an attempt to try to calm Jonah down.

He talked so fast that Val couldn't understand a word he was saying. The more he talked, the louder he got, so she took him by the arm and led him outside so they could talk in private.

Jonah slammed his fist into the palm of his hand and screamed out in anger. "She's gone!" His reaction startled Val.

She watched him pace in front of her like a madman before trying again. "Why don't you relax and tell me what happened?"

Jonah stopped and allowed the cool spring air to caress his face and dry his tears before explaining. "Hope and I found an empty lot to sleep in. It had about six or seven abandoned cars surrounding it. The area looked almost like a junkyard. Hope and I were out late last night. She was tired and was getting cranky, so I figured it would be all right if we slept in one of those cars until morning. I planned to leave early enough so that no one would ever know we were there. I woke at dawn and Hope was still sleeping. I knew she was exhausted, so instead of waking her up, I figured I could run to the corner store with the last of that twenty dollars you put in my pocket and get us something to eat."

Val shifted her eyes to hide her guilt.

"I was gone less than twenty minutes. By the time I returned to the lot, she was gone."

"Did you search the area? Maybe she got up and went looking for you."

"No. The entire car was gone. When I returned, I saw a tow truck pulling the car down the street. I yelled to the driver, but he couldn't hear me. There was another tow truck loading up one of the other cars, and I told him that my daughter was in the back seat of that car. He called the other driver on his cell phone, and the guy did stop, checked the car and found Hope."

"Well, where is she at?"

"After he found her, he called the cops. The guy I was talking to said they were required to report any children found in the cars they towed. When I heard that, I got scared and ran." He pulled his hat off his head and threw it on the ground. "They're going to take my daughter, aren't they?"

"I don't know, but I'll do what I can to help you get her back. Stay right here."

Val went to Kyle's office and told him she had to leave because of a family emergency. Then she rushed out of the mission and to her car. She and Jonah left together and went back to her house to make a few phone calls.

"I don't understand why the driver didn't notice a little girl in the car." Val held her cell phone pressed against her ear and was searching in her purse for a pen.

"I can't blame him. He probably never knew she was in there. I told her that if anyone was to ever come up to the car and I wasn't around that she was to hide on the floor and not move until I got back."

"How often do you leave your daughter alone?"

"Not often, but there were times when I would have to steal the things we needed to survive, and I preferred not to do those kinds of things in front of her."

Val contacted the Philadelphia Police Department, and they transferred her to the Department of Family and Children Services. Now she was on hold.

Finally somebody picked up the line who could help her.

"Yes, I'm trying to locate a little girl who may have been placed in your custody earlier today. She was found in the back of an abandoned car," Val explained. "Sure I'll hold." Val rested against the kitchen island. "Yes, you do have her."

Jonah moved closer.

"Well, I'm representing the girl's father as legal counsel, and we would like to petition the court for an immediate custody hearing." Val wrote a few things down on the notepad in front of her. "Thank you. I'll be there tomorrow morning to file the appropriate papers." She disconnected the call.

"You're a lawyer?" he asked.

"Not exactly. I'm taking a break from law school."

"Well, what did they say?"

"We need to file a petition for custody with the Department of Family and Children Services. It's imperative that you find a job and a permanent place to live—today! The first thing the judge is going to want to know is why you were living in an abandoned car with a three-year-old child."

"You sound just like a lawyer," Jonah said.

Val sat on a kitchen stool next to Jonah and took hold of his hand. "Jonah, if there's anything you're not telling me about you and Hope, you have to tell me now."

He looked away, as if the truth could be seen through his eyes.

"If I don't know everything, then you're limiting the amount of help I can offer you and Hope."

Jonah saw sincerity in Val's eyes and knew he had no choice but to trust her. He placed his hands over his head. "I came here from New Orleans. After Katrina hit, we were one of the families who were rescued out of the Ninth Ward. We came to Philly because I was told I could get a job at one of the refineries. When we first arrived, the help the city provided was great. They helped me find a job, a place to live, and they even gave me money to help with daycare, since Hope was still an infant. Then the economy started to slump, and the refineries started cutting back. First, they cut my hours to part time, and then I was laid off indefinitely. I couldn't find another job. Unemployment ran out. The bills started to pile up. I couldn't pay my rent, and we were evicted. That's how we ended up on the streets."

"What about Hope's mother?"

"By the time we realized the storm was a category five, there wasn't anywhere for us to go. We were trapped. The floodwaters started rising, and we had to climb to the roof of my house for safety. It was horrible. Hope's mother held onto me, but the winds were so strong that I couldn't hold on to both her and the baby at the same time." Jonah put emphasis on his words to express how bad it was. "We were on the roof, and the water was around my waist. I held Hope above water and I held on to her mother for as long as I could, but I was losing all my strength. She shouted for me to not let her go, but the baby was crying and I had to either use both hands to save the baby or use both hands to save her. I chose the baby, and when I did the current swept her underwater. I searched for her for weeks. I prayed that she may have possibly survived, but it's been over two years and I still haven't heard anything. That is how I was left with Hope."

Tears formed in Val's eyes. She had seen the devastation of Katrina on television, but to hear an actual survivor tell his story was heartbreaking. She wiped away tears and realized Jonah wasn't a kidnapper. He was a hero. Val commended him for saving his daughter's life. She felt horrible for thinking the worst of him and wanted to help him out.

"Jonah, if you expect to get Hope back, then you'll need a permanent address. You can stay here until you get on your feet, and I'll call around to see if I can hook you up with a job someplace."

"Thanks, Val. I appreciate everything you've done for us so far."

"Don't thank me yet. The battle has just begun."

Chapter 18

"Are you ready?" Val glanced at her watch. It was getting late, and she wanted to make sure they arrived in court on time.

Jonah stood in the bathroom fumbling with his tie.

Val pushed his hands away and neatly fastened the tie. "Are you nervous?" Val could see balls of sweat forming on his forehead.

"No, I'm not nervous. Just anxious to see what the judge is going to say." Jonah brushed past her and descended the stairs.

She heard the back door open then close. He couldn't fool her. She knew he was worried about the hearing.

For days Jonah had scoured the city in search of a job, but like most major cities, Philly was experiencing a decline in the job market. Discouraged, Jonah felt like a failure. He knew how important it was for him to walk into this hearing employed. Being unemployed would prolong the process in getting Hope back.

In the car, Jonah was plagued with worry over Hope. This was the longest they had ever been separated. He prayed for God to keep her safe, but every time he opened the newspaper, there was another story of a child being abused, starved and treated inhumanely.

"God, if You keep her safe, I'll never do anything this stupid again."

When they stepped inside the courtroom doors, Jonah let the door close on her.

"Jonah!"

He looked at her unknowingly.

"You didn't hold the door for me."

"I'm sorry," he replied.

They grabbed two seats on the last row in the courtroom and waited for the hearing to begin.

"Are you hot?" she asked him.

Jonah wiped sweat off his forehead again.

"You've been sweating since we left the house," she replied. "It's probably nerves. Did I tell you how nice you look?"

Jonah smiled for the first time that morning.

Julian's suits were a bit long in the length for Jonah, but Val asked her tailor to hem the pants. Now the suit looked like it was made for him. It felt weird seeing him dressed in Julian's things, but it was for a good cause. Val shrugged off those bad feelings because this was for a good cause. Julian always said to be generous to others.

The closer it got to the eight o'clock hour, the more people piled into the courtroom. By the time a court official entered the room, it was standing room only. Every seat was full, forcing groups of people to line up against the walls.

The court official walked to the front of the room. She spoke loudly enough that she didn't need a microphone to address the crowd. "When I call your name, please gather your things and follow me through that door." She pointed to the door she entered through.

Because of her strong Russian accent it was difficult for Val to understand what the woman was saying. Everyone in the room must have felt the same way, because the room was silent.

Dressed in a dark blue pinstriped suit with matching wedges, the woman scanned her list until she came to her first name. "Rodriguez."

Two women seated in the center aisle excused themselves through the crowd and proceeded through the door.

Three hours later they were still sitting in the blazing courtroom. Val used her hand to fan herself. "I feel like I'm going to melt." She sat up when she saw the Russian woman come out of the room. "Please let her call our name."

"Gaines," she yelled then disappeared back behind closed doors.

"What's taking so long?"

"You know how the courts are. These things take time," Val reasoned.

After sitting there for most of the day Jonah's name was finally called. Inside the conference room sat a long cherry wood table. A library of books aligned the left wall, and a huge glass window magnified the Philly skyline. In the corner of the room sat a huge industrial fan that blew hot air across Val's face.

The court official escorted them in and offered them seats before exiting out the rear door.

Seated across the table from them was a man they assumed was the judge, from the official black judicial robe he wore. A woman sitting next to him, scribbled notes on a note pad. The beautiful crown of silver hair that covered her head made her look older than she was.

"I apologize for such a long wait. When I came into work this morning, I found out the air conditioning system malfunctioned overnight. It's just my luck that when the temperatures soar close to ninety degrees there's no air to keep me cool. The whole building has been suffering, but I figured it would be cooler to hold the hearings in here instead of the courtroom."

When the judge smiled, Val could feel the warmth from the sincerity in his voice fill the room. The more she looked at him, the more he reminded her of Santa Claus, because of his huge pot belly and long white beard.

The judge opened a manila folder and reviewed its contents. "I assume you're the father?" He posed his question toward Jonah. "Let me introduce you to Mrs. Chambers. She is the case manager in charge of Hope's case."

"Are you his lawyer?" the judge asked Val.

"No, my name is Valencia Benson. I'm just a friend here for support." She smiled broadly at the misinterpretation. It was flattering to be mistaken for a lawyer. To her that meant she looked the part; all that was missing was her degree.

"Mr. Reynolds, let's begin." The judge cleared his throat. "First, I'm curious about the circumstances that led you to take up residence inside an abandoned car with a small child." The judge's face turned serious.

Val could tell that Judge Cohen was a sweet man, but he was also serious when it came down to business.

Jonah repeated the same story he had told Val. He wrung his hands from nervousness and prayed that the judge would have mercy on him. He missed Hope so much.

"Mr. Reynolds, I understand that when citizens have to rely on assistance from the city that every once in a while some people may slip through the cracks and go unnoticed. Unfortunately, this had to happen to you. I'm sorry for everything you had to endure; however, I can't return Hope to your custody until I'm sure she will be properly taken care of. Now"—He folded his hands in front of him—"what are you going to do to turn this situation around?"

Jonah cleared his throat. "Your Honor. I'm temporarily staying at Ms. Benson's house until I can find a place of my own."

"What about a job?"

"I'm still looking, but it shouldn't be long before someone hires me."

"Young lady, are you prepared to help him take care of his daughter?" the judge asked Val.

"Yes, Your Honor."

"What is it that you do?"

"Last semester I was in law school, but I'm sitting this semester out because of personal reasons."

The judge was puzzled. "So you don't have a job?"

Val shook her head no.

"Your Honor, if it would help Jonah get his daughter back then I can get a job," Val offered.

"No, young lady. The sole responsibility lies on Jonah's shoulders."

He grabbed a pen and talked while he wrote some things down. "Mr. Reynolds, I don't know if the heat is affecting my judgment, but I'm going to give you a chance to right this wrong. First, you have to get a job. Then I'm going to have Mrs. Chambers set up an in-home study to check out your place to make sure it's suitable for a child. Once you submit three consecutive paystubs and you pass a home inspection, then Hope can go home with you."

Jonah smiled broadly.

"Mrs. Chambers will contact you to let you know when she'll be stopping by."

"Thanks, Your Honor."

"Don't thank me yet. Make me proud and get your daughter back."

As Jonah stood up to leave, Val posed a question toward the judge. "Your Honor, what about visits? Is it possible for Jonah to visit with Hope in the meantime?"

The judge looked to Mrs. Chambers for help with that question.

"I think I can best answer that question." She folded her hands in front of her. "Hope has already been placed in a foster home with a loving couple. Unfortunately, the couple frowns upon visits with members from the children's family, especially parents. They feel as though it disrupts the stable home they're trying to provide for the child, but I'm sure if I make a phone call they will allow you supervised visits."

"Supervised visits? With my own daughter?"

"Mr. Reynolds, don't forget we're doing you a favor. Either abide by our rules or suffer the consequences. It's up to you."

Val patted Jonah on his arm. "It'll be all right. Just go along with it."

"I apologize for getting out of line like that." He turned to Mrs. Chambers. "Anything you can do will be greatly appreciated."

"I'll give them a call in the morning," she responded before jotting a note down in her daily planner.

Chapter 19

Colin knocked twice on Reverend Simms's office door before rushing in. On the opposite side, Reverend Simms was in deep talk with Dean.

Colin had not spoken to Dean since he was released from the hospital. His calls went unanswered and his messages ignored, but Dean could no longer hide. Today was his wedding.

Reverend Simms greeted Colin with a firm handshake. "Now that the best man has arrived, I'm going to go make sure everything is on schedule in the sanctuary." Reverend Simms left the two of them alone.

"You look good." Colin playfully punched him in the arm. "You haven't been back out on those basketball courts, have you?"

"Man, please don't lecture me. I get enough of that from my doctor."

"That's his job, to keep you as healthy as possible." Colin pulled up a chair. "Are you going to confess and tell me what really went down last week? What put you in the hospital, and why don't you want to tell Olivia?"

Dean sighed. "I have cancer."

Colin's head dropped down in front of him. Dean's revelation was hard to swallow. He couldn't believe it. Colin got up and walked to the other side of the room.

"The doctors told me I could die if I didn't get any treatment, but those procedures are so exhausting. Afterwards, I feel sick and sluggish. I might as well be dead because I'm missing out on life."

"But if that's going to keep you alive, then I think it's worth it. Don't you?"

"Is it? Is it really worth it? How am I supposed to teach Bryce how to play baseball? Or make love to my wife when I can't even muster up the strength to get up out the bed?"

"I'd rather lie in a sick bed than my death bed."

Thirty seconds of silence passed before Colin spoke again.

"How long have you known?"

"For almost two years. I found out right after I started dating Olivia," Dean confessed. "When Olivia and Bryce walked into my life, I knew God had finally answered my prayers. She's not just a dream come true. She's my reality. If I acknowledged the cancer, it would put such a strain on our relationship that I would have to be totally dependent on Olivia. The Bible says the man is supposed to be the head of the household. I couldn't do that to her. I would allow nothing to interfere with fate bringing us to this day."

"And you still haven't told Olivia?"

"No."

"How can you claim to love her and not tell her the kind of life she's marrying into?"

Dean looked up with tears in his eyes. "Don't think I haven't thought about telling her, but I have to be sure she's marrying me because she loves me, not out of pity."

"Olivia loves you, and she deserves the truth." He grabbed Dean by his arm. "Man, you're making a big mistake. There's still time before the ceremony. I'm sure she'll understand."

A light rap at the door interrupted their conversation. "Fellows, it's almost time to begin. We better take our places." Reverend Simms stuck his head inside the room.

Colin and Dean looked at one another. Then Dean shrugged his shoulders. "I promise I'll talk with her after the ceremony."

Olivia stared at the heavy raindrops that fell outside the limousine window. She prayed the weatherman's forecast for torrential rains was wrong, but the way the rain was pouring from the sky, it didn't look like it was going to stop just for her wedding.

The limousine stopped right outside the church doors. Each one of her bridesmaids dashed out into the rain carrying dresses, shoes and makeup cases.

"Livie, be careful." Aunt Stephie held her umbrella open to protect the bride. "We don't want to get your hair wet."

Olivia carefully climbed out of the limo and stopped momentarily when she heard the church bells loudly ringing. The rain washed away any ill feelings she had about her wedding day being a washout. In her heart she knew the Lord was going to bless her union.

"Olivia!" Her aunt gave her a slight nudge. "Hurry, before we both get drenched by the rain."

They ran into the church foyer together.

Her aunt closed the umbrella and pointed down the long corridor. "This way to the dressing room."

Chaos was the only word Olivia could think of when she entered the dressing room. Val rushed past her holding the back of her neck, while Tressie chased behind her apologizing for burning her with the curling iron. Olivia chuckled as she watched Danyelle struggle to get her dress up over her wide hips.

"Now look at your sister. She is well aware that she inherited her big thighs from our side of the family. Why didn't she buy a girdle to wear underneath that dress?" Aunt Stephie rushed over to help Danyelle. "Olivia, go put your things down in the next room, and I'll be there in a minute to help with your hair and makeup."

The adjoining room was reserved especially for the bride. Olivia stepped into serenity. The light blue walls were soothing, and the scent of lavender reminded her of being in an enchanted garden. The room was so comforting that it made her want to pray. She had to take a moment to just give the Lord thanks. The moment she closed her eyes, she was disrupted by her aunt charging through the door, followed by Danyelle, Val and Tressie.

Olivia wasn't mad they were intruding on her time. This was another blessing from the Lord to be surrounded by so many people who loved her. They may have been loud and annoying at times, but He couldn't have chosen a better group of friends.

Val's cell phone rang from the other room and she rushed to answer it.

"Do you think Val has a new love in her life?" Danyelle said.

"Stop gossiping in the church." Aunt Stephie swatted her comb at her.

"I'm not gossiping. Tressie, how many times has Val's phone rung in the last fifteen minutes?" Danyelle asked.

"At least twelve," Tressie said, "and every time she answers, she whispers into the phone and turns away from us."

"I told you." Danyelle smiled at proving her point.

Olivia had to admit, she was curious about Val's mysterious behavior lately. She seemed to have moved past the stage of depression, but something else was occupying her time. Every time she called, Val claimed she couldn't talk. Then while everyone's back was turned, Val moved out of her parent's house. Aunt Stephie was hysterical. Her father was concerned. But Olivia was suspicious of her one-eighty degree change in behavior.

Val walked back in the room carrying a huge bouquet of calla lilies.

"Where did they come from?" Aunt Steph took a huge whiff.

"Me!"

Olivia looked around. Her gorgeous son stood in the doorway beaming with pride. Olivia called him over and gave him a huge hug.

"I hope you like them, Mommy."

"I love them, and you look so adorable in your mini tuxedo." She kissed Bryce on the cheek, leaving traces of her lipstick on his face.

"Dean told me to come and spy on you," her son confessed.

Everyone laughed.

Aunt Stephie took him by the hand and led him toward the exit. "Well, you go back and tell him he is gonna have to wait with everyone else." She turned back toward Olivia. "I'm going to walk him back around to where the fellas are. I'll be right back."

"You look beautiful." Val admired Olivia's makeup. "This will be our last time together with you as a single woman. I'm so happy for you."

The girls embraced with tears in their eyes.

"Val, you know it wouldn't be the same without you, but I hope none of this is going to be upsetting for you." Olivia turned back into her mothering mode.

"No." Val patted her hand. "Listen, I will always love Julian, but he is gone and I can't break down every time somebody else finds happiness." She looked around. "Here comes my mom. I'm going to allow her to help you finish getting dressed."

The organist started to play. On cue, Aunt Stephie sent the girls down the aisle one by one. Dressed in candy apple red gowns, each girl carried a unique look of elegance.

Tressie's sandy brown medium-length hair was neatly curled into a motif of spiral curls. Her slender frame and striking features made her look like a model walking the runway. Everyone admired her beauty.

Like a vision of loveliness floating on a cloud, Val made the way for the maid of honor. Her long tresses were pinned atop her head, and tiny strands of hair cascaded down her back.

Danyelle's transformation was stunning to the guests. Her entrance was grand. The entire church was blinded by her radiance. She never looked lovelier than she did that day. Her eyes twinkled from the bright lights.

Bryce had the most important job. He paved the way for his mom by strutting down the aisle, doing his own version of a pimp walk. He confidently walked up to Dean, slapped his hand and took his place next to him.

Suddenly the tune changed, and everyone stood. The doors at the back of the church swung wide open. Escorted by Val's father, Olivia stepped out surrounded by a reminiscent glow of innocence. Dressed in a cream gown and wearing the same wedding veil her mother wore, she marched down the aisle. Camera bulbs flashed throughout the church.

Olivia looked straight into Dean's eyes. It was the longest journey of her life. The trek down that aisle represented her walking away from life as a single person and stepping into a union with the man of her dreams. When she reached him, he took her hand in his. In her ear she could hear her mother's voice, "A godly man will appreciate and value you." In Dean she had found unconditional love. He unselfishly gave everything he had and never looked for anything in return. She knew he was a blessing.

Reverend Simms greeted the couple then instructed their guests to be seated. The ceremony began by him explaining the sanctity of marriage. Then he spoke those famous words, "If any person can show just cause why they may not be joined together, let them speak now or forever hold their peace."

Silence filled the church, and Reverend Simms proceeded as usual. As the reverend spoke, Dean reached out for Olivia's hand and squeezed it lightly.

"Dean, please face Olivia and repeat after me."

It was time for them to recite their vows.

"The couple has prepared their own vows, so I will let Dean recite his first." Reverend Simms stepped back.

Happiness covered Dean's face. He had been waiting for this moment since Olivia was in pigtails. He couldn't stop smiling, he was so excited. He took a deep breath.

Then Olivia watched as the smile slowly faded from his face and the joy in his eyes vanished. His eyes rolled up in his head, and he collapsed to the floor.

Olivia screamed in horror.

Colin rushed to his friend's aid. "He's not breathing." He checked for a pulse. "Somebody call an ambulance." He tilted Dean's head back and gave him mouth-to-mouth resuscitation. Olivia cried hysterically into her sister's bosom.

A crowd gathered around. Reverend Simms asked the crowd to stand back.

Ten minutes later the paramedics wheeled a stretcher in. The EMTs frantically tried to revive him. They worked on Dean until he started breathing on his own. Then they rushed him to the hospital.

At the hospital Colin stopped a nurse to ask for an update on Dean's condition. She wouldn't release any information but told him that the doctor would be out to speak with them shortly. Colin immediately took hold of Olivia's shaking hand, and they prayed.

Over an hour passed and they were still waiting on the doctor.

"Colin," her voice was flat and lacked any emotion, "what's wrong with Dean?"

Colin wanted to tell her the truth. He couldn't lie to her.

Tears rolled down her face. "Since the last episode when he passed out from exhaustion I've been making sure he's been getting enough rest and eating healthier." Olivia needed answers. "What's going on?"

"Excuse me." Colin and Olivia looked up.

"I'm Doctor Bell, Dean's physician. Are you his family?"

Colin nodded.

"Good! Could you follow me?" He led them to a small conference room, and they gathered around a table. He set a chart down on the table. "Dean was scheduled to have a very important procedure performed this morning and he never showed up."

"We were supposed to be getting married today," Olivia solemnly replied.

Dr. Bell noticed she was still dressed in her wedding gown. "I'm sorry. Did this happen at the church?"

"Yes, in the middle of the ceremony," Colin replied.

The doctor jotted more notes down in his file. "Now I understand why he skipped out on his appointment. After the procedure, he would be so drowsy, he wouldn't have been able to stand, let alone get married."

"What exactly is this procedure for?" Olivia directed her question toward the doctor. "Is Dean sick?"

Colin took her hand. "Livie, Dean has cancer."

She slowly shook her head.

"He told me minutes before the ceremony began. He didn't want to worry you."

Olivia stopped crying and looked at the doctor. "Is it terminal?"

The doctor slowly nodded.

She cried again, and Colin pulled her into his arms.

"He has a rare liver cancer. There is no cure. The only thing we can do is slow down its advancement. It had gone into remission for a while, but it came back. We ran tests today, and the results are not as bad as I suspected, but I still can't offer much hope."

Olivia looked down at the floor.

"He is slowly losing functionality of his liver. This is the calm before the storm. Dean needs to rest as much as possible. No more sports. No lifting anything heavy. He will need all his strength toward the end. I'm going to keep him here for a few days for observation. If his condition improves, I'll release him. Do you have any questions for me?"

"Can we see him now?" Olivia asked.

"Sure." The doctor pulled out one of his business cards. "If you think of anything you want to ask me later on, call me anytime." Then he escorted them to Dean's room.

Olivia gasped loudly when she walked in. The sight of him connected to so many machines and breathing into a facemask was much worse than she envisioned. Her light brown eyes filled with tears.

"God, why him?" she cried loudly.

Colin tried to console her, but she pulled away and stroked the side of Dean's face as he slept.

Olivia wondered why this was happening to them. They were the perfect couple. She had finally found the missing piece to make her life complete, and now she felt like God was punishing them. Or was God punishing her?

Olivia had never forgiven herself for breaking the vow she made to the Lord. Giving her virginity to Bryant was a mistake. A mistake she thought she had paid the price for when her son was kidnapped and nearly sold.

She laid her head down by his side and revisited Reverend Simms's speech about sacrifice. She sat up and wondered what Dean would do if she was the one lying in the hospital. Her heart spoke back to her. Dean would do everything humanly possible to make her happy, and she was going to do the same for him.

They sat with him for over an hour before Dean opened his eyes. He lifted his eyelids. This was the first time she could actually see how sick he was. It scared her to see him wither away right before her eyes.

"Let's get married," Olivia spit out. "Let's get married, today."

Dean looked at her strangely.

"We already have the marriage license, and Colin is here. He can perform the ceremony."

Dean shook his head. Then he pushed the breathing apparatus away from his face. "No," he said gasping for air, "you deserve a real wedding."

Olivia touched the side of his face. "What I deserve is to be married to you." She giggled. "Now will you lie back and let your future wife take care of things?" She smiled at him. "I have a wedding to prepare for."

"Partner, you better listen to her. I wouldn't go against any woman's wishes," Colin joked.

When Olivia saw the sparkle in Dean's eyes, she knew she was doing the right thing.

"Olivia, I'm going to run home and grab my Bible." Colin checked his watch. "Do you want me to call Danyelle?"

Dean waved his hand to refuse. "I don't want anyone to know about my illness," he whispered.

Olivia looked back at Colin. She really wanted her closest friends and family to witness them getting married, but she didn't want to go against her fiancé's wishes.

"No, that's okay. I can find somebody else to be a witness."

A half hour later, Colin returned to officiate his first wedding ceremony. One of the nurses on the floor agreed to be a witness, and within minutes Olivia and Dean became husband and wife.

Chapter 20

The transition between Val and Jonah moving in together wasn't as easy as they'd anticipated. It was Val who insisted Jonah stay with her until he was able to find a job and decent place for him and Hope, but it wasn't until late one night that she realized she was living in sin. Her parents would die if they knew she was living with a man who wasn't her husband. That's why she hadn't mentioned him to anyone, not even Olivia. Livie was her best friend, and they usually shared everything, but she wasn't ready to explain where Jonah came from.

Jonah respected Olivia and her house. That's why he tried to stay out of her way, but it was hard living with such a beautiful sista. He noticed that Val also kept her distance from him, but he thought it was because she wasn't interested in him. She never flirted with him, but her tight clothes, voluptuous curves and perky breasts seemed to address him every time he looked at her.

He was attracted to her but didn't think it was wise for him to try and get close to her. It was obvious by her home, car and clothes that she was definitely out of his league.

During the day Val spent a lot of her time at the mission fulfilling her obligation to the city. At night she would come home and spend hours on the computer trying to help Jonah find a job. Together they must have applied for over thirty oil refinery and construction jobs. Only two companies were interested in interviewing him.

As luck would have it, as Jonah was walking home from the store one evening, he happened to overhear two guys talking. The gentleman talking wore a security guard's uniform, and he was telling his friend that the hospital he was working at was looking to hire a janitor.

Jonah applied the next day and was hired on the spot.

After several weeks, Jonah had finally fulfilled the requirements the judge had set for him. Mrs. Chambers was expected to drop Hope off at any minute.

When they heard a knock at the door, Jonah charged down the stairs with the energy of a boy rising early on Christmas morning. "I'll get it!" He pulled open the front door, and when Hope saw her father, she broke away from Mrs. Chambers' grasp and leapt into Jonah's arms.

Val could hear Hope squeal with joy at being reunited with her father. She watched the two of them embrace from the kitchen. Hope wrapped her tiny arms around her father's neck and wouldn't let go. Jonah kept trying to pull her back to give her kisses, but she was too scared to let go.

Jonah carried her into the living room.

Mrs. Chambers closed the door behind them and followed. "Let me get a good look at you. It seems like a lifetime since I've last seen you." Mrs. Chambers set down a suitcase full of her things.

"Mrs. Chambers, would you like a seat?" Val offered as Mrs. Chambers admired her decorative living room. She and Jonah had spent most of the morning preparing for Hope's homecoming. The dining room table was full of gifts and a huge chocolate cake, all for Hope.

"No, thank you. It's obvious Hope was missed." She smiled broadly.

"Yes, we are excited to have her back home," Val replied.

"Mr. Reynolds, there are a few forms I need for you to sign, and then I'll be on my way." She pulled a manila folder out of her briefcase and set it down on the coffee table.

Hope hung on to her father so tight that he had a hard time signing the forms, but after some maneuvering he got it done.

"This is a beautiful home," Mrs. Chambers commented.

Val beamed with pride. It wasn't easy furnishing her entire house in less than three weeks, but she got it done. With the help of professional decorators, she selected color patterns and furniture and updated the entire house with the latest in kitchen appliances. The kitchen cabinets were now full of real plates and cups instead of Styrofoam. Pictures of Bryce, Olivia, Danyelle, Tressie and her parents hung throughout the house. It now felt like a real home.

"This is a great neighborhood to raise a child in. The schools are excellent, the streets are clean and there are lots of community events held for children Hope's age," Mrs. Chambers pointed out.

"I recognize I've been blessed." Jonah's gaze fell on Val.

When Val realized he was referring to her, she simply gave an uneasy smile and turned on the television for Hope.

"Well, it appears as though I have everything." Mrs. Chambers gathered the forms. "The background checks that were run on you and Val came back clean, I have three consecutive paychecks, plus references from your supervisor documenting how superior your work ethics are. The only thing I would like to see is where Hope will be sleeping. When I came the first time, the room was still under construction. In my report I documented that she had her own room, but I would like to see the finished project."

"Sure, follow me." Val led her up the back steps.

When she opened Hope's bedroom door, Mrs. Chambers looked impressed. Splashes of lavender paint covered every wall and small pictures of ballerina shoes filled the room. Hanging from walls were ballerina shoes, and sitting on the shelves were baby dolls all waiting to be claimed by Hope.

Jonah and Hope followed close behind them. When he stepped in the room, Hope screamed out and struggled to get down from her father's arms.

Hope's positive reaction put Val's mind at rest. She prayed that Hope would approve of the decorating choices she made.

They watched her run over to her bed and pick up a baby doll and cradle it in her arms.

"This room is fantastic," Mrs. Chambers said.

Jonah walked up beside Val. "I was wondering why every time I walked by this room the door was closed. I thought you were hiding something."

"I wanted it to be a surprise. I knew you had bought Hope a lot of different clothes and toys, but I wanted to do something special for her. Something that came from me."

"Val, you didn't have to go through all this trouble, but I thank you, and so does my daughter. Hope, why don't you come and give Val a hug and kiss for buying you all this stuff?"

Hope turned and looked at her father beckoning her over. She slowly walked toward Jonah.

Val bent down to give her a hug, and Hope reluctantly stood as still as a stone. Afterwards, she turned back toward her father and refused to look in Val's direction.

"She's shy," Jonah replied.

"Well, I'm convinced that I'm leaving Hope in a stable, loving home, but I must remind you that my home visits will continue. If at any time I feel anything suspicious, then your daughter will be immediately placed back in the custody of the state. Do you understand?"

Jonah happily nodded his head. "That was easier than I thought it would be," he whispered in Val's ear.

The following Saturday, Val watched Jonah and Hope watch cartoons together in her living room. She sighed heavily. It hurt that she couldn't establish the same kind of bond Jonah shared with Hope. She realized that he was her father, but Val had tried everything to get Hope to trust her. The little girl acted like she hated her. Jonah asked Val to be patient, but no matter how hard Val tried, Hope left her hopeless.

Hope soared through the air and landed on Jonah's back. He fell over and accidentally knocked over Val's brand-new crystal vase. It fell to the floor and shattered into pieces.

Hope and Jonah looked at the vase, then at Val. Their faces were full of fear. They knew they were in trouble.

"Val, I'm so sorry. We shouldn't have been playing in the house," Jonah said. "I'll replace it when I get paid on Friday."

"Don't worry about it." Val got up to pick up the broken pieces before anyone cut themselves. "I'm not used to having a child living with me. I should have bought cheap vases from the dollar store."

"I know you're probably tired of having us take up your space." Jonah helped her clean up. "It won't be long before I have enough money to move us out of here."

She touched his hand. "Jonah, I enjoy having the two of you here. If it weren't for you, I'd be living in this big house all alone."

They shared a smile.

Then an unexpected knock at the door pulled Val away. When she answered the door she was surprised to see Mrs. Chambers standing on the other side, accompanied by a police officer.

"Hello, Val, is Jonah here?"

Mrs. Chambers' official demeanor scared her. She could feel her heart pump faster. Uneasiness filled her stomach. "Jonah!" She hollered for him.

When Jonah reached the door and saw the cops, he instinctively ran back for his daughter.

Mrs. Chambers and the police officer barged past Val and into the living room.

"Jonah, don't make this any harder than it has to be," Mrs. Chambers tried to reason.

"Is there a problem?" Val could see something was wrong.

"Why don't you ask Jonah that question?" Mrs. Chambers kept her eyes on Jonah. "Someone has made a claim that Hope isn't really your daughter. Is that true?"

Jonah held back the tears and momentarily closed his eyes, as if his worst nightmare had come true.

"Hope will have to remain in our custody until the matter is resolved."

Val couldn't believe what she was hearing. This had to be a mistake.

Mrs. Chambers looked disappointed. "I'm sorry, but we have to take Hope back with us. We have a court order signed by the judge." She pulled out a slip of paper from her pocket and handed it to Val. Then she reached out for Hope.

Hope must have sensed that something was wrong because she screamed out.

Jonah stepped back from Mrs. Chambers and held onto his daughter even tighter.

Then the police intervened. "Sir, don't make this any harder than it already is. We could have you arrested and then take the child."

Val could see that the papers had been drawn up earlier that morning and signed by the judge. She walked over to Jonah and whispered, "Jonah!" She placed a loving hand on his arm and slowly shook her head.

Her eyes said there was nothing they could do. He had to give Hope up. He reluctantly loosened his grip.

Mrs. Chambers pulled Hope from him, and she kicked and screamed for her father. They quickly took her out of the house and put her in the police car that was waiting at the curb.

After they left, Jonah paced the living room floor until his anger couldn't be contained any longer and he slammed his fist into a nearby wall. He hit it so hard that he made a hole.

Val had never seen Jonah this angry before. She watched him for moment. The release of all that anger made him stagger over to the fireplace.

"I should have left when I had the chance," he cried. "I stayed too long, and now they've taken my daughter."

Val watched from a distance.

He knew she wanted answers to questions he prayed he would never have to acknowledge.

"Biologically, Hope is not my daughter."

Val listened closely.

"My best friend was a soldier in the army. He was deployed to Iraq, but never came home. He was a casualty of war, leaving behind a wife and baby. They adopted Hope a few months before he left. Once my friend was gone, his wife had nowhere to go. So I invited her to stay with me in New Orleans until she got on her feet."

"Is that who was lost in the storm?" Val asked.

"Yes. After we were rescued, I went to my momma's house in Baton Rouge. We stayed there a few weeks, until one afternoon the police came looking for us. They told my momma that they wanted to talk to me about Hope's parents. I thought the state had found out she didn't belong to me and was going to try and take her from me. I couldn't allow them to place her in foster care. I'm the only family Hope has. So I skipped town. We hid out like thieves, living from town to town, until I caught the bus here."

"I wish you would have told me all of this sooner," Val said.

"I was scared," he replied.

"Is that everything? You didn't leave anything out, did you?"

"No."

"These kind of legal technicalities are beyond my legal expertise, but I'll call a few of my professors and see if they can recommend a lawyer who specializes in family law." Val went to her home office.

West watched a kid who looked like he was fresh out of law school tussle with a mound of files and papers. "I don't understand," Judge West spoke up. "Didn't they tell you that I already have a lawyer?"

"Yes, a court appointed attorney, and I was hired by the pastor of your church. He insists he only wants what's best for you."

"Who are you again?"

"My name is Joseph Morris, and I work for Myers and Kittering law offices."

"Are you sure you're a lawyer and not a law clerk?"

This kid didn't look polished enough to handle his case. The judge already knew that his was a high profile case and that the lawyer who represented him would have to have experience on how the system worked.

"That's funny, sir." Joseph finally found what he was looking for. He pulled out a pen from the inside of his jacket pocket and sat across from the judge. "I may have just graduated from college, but I did graduate at the top of my class."

"Well, that's good to hear. Where did you go to school?"

"Ankara Law School."

"Where? I've never heard of it? Where's it at?"

"It's in Turkey."

"Are you referring to the country of Turkey?" Judge West laughed to himself. "This has got to be a joke. Are you licensed to practice law in Pennsylvania?"

"Yes, sir. I took the bar exam for Pennsylvania and passed. I'm not from Turkey. I am actually a United States citizen. I was born and raised in Nebraska."

"Why did you choose to go to school in Turkey?"

"I felt like I would do better studying abroad."

Judge West was now convinced that this guy was not ready to represent a client in court.

"And my pastor hired you on my behalf?"

The kid nodded.

Judge West was aware of the fact that Reverend Simms knew a lot of prominent experienced trial lawyers. It made him wonder why he chose this kid.

"Yes, when he came to my office he said he was referred by another pastor." He thought for a second. "A Reverend Baxter."

"Will this be your first case at the firm?" Judge West asked.

"Yes, sir, this will be my first case to ever present before a jury." Joseph pulled out a notepad. "Now, sir, can you please tell me exactly what happened, in your own words?"

Joseph looked harmless. Actually he reminded Judge West of an out-of-place country boy living all alone in the big city of Philadelphia.

"Before we begin, why don't you tell me about back home?" Judge West requested.

"Back home?"

"Yeah, tell me about Nebraska. Since we'll be working together, I want to know as much about you as I can, since you already know a lot about me."

The judge was searching for any sign that Joseph may be connected to the brotherhood.

West sat back in his chair and listened to Joseph ramble on about his strict Mormon upbringing. He was raised on a farm and was the first of eight siblings to leave home.

Once he was finished, West was convinced that this kid wasn't associated with the brotherhood.

"Okay, kid, that's enough talking about you." Judge West looked around. "Where is your tape recorder? Joseph, remember, whenever you meet with a client, you always want to record any conversations you have about details of the charges. It makes it easier for your secretary when it's time for her to transcribe everything."

"Oh, okay." He dug through his briefcase. "I have one of those right here." He set it down in front of them.

West got up to leave. He banged on the door for the guard to take him back to his cell.

"Where are you going?" Joseph questioned the judge as if he were on the stand.

"Listen, kid, go back to your office and call my pastor and tell him I'm all right. I don't need counsel. I'm going to get out of this because I didn't do anything wrong. Please tell Reverend Simms I fired you, and you are free to go."

Joseph looked shocked and disappointed. He couldn't believe he had just lost his first case before it even got started.

Chapter 21

Three days after the wedding, Dean was released from the hospital. Instead of moving into Olivia's small apartment, he suggested that she and Bryce move into his grandpa's Victorian-style home with him. Olivia was hesitant. She didn't want to intrude while Judge West was incarcerated, but Dean assured her it would be all right. Besides, Dean never expected his grandpa to walk freely again.

Their first week in the house, Olivia kept busy. Never one to complain, she cooked dinner, washed dishes, kept the house clean and made certain her husband abided by the doctor's stern instructions to get plenty of rest, take his meds every three hours and drink plenty of water.

Bryce adjusted to the change well. He loved going to a new school, living in a new house and especially having a backyard to play in. Olivia wished Kennedy and Clinton, her dogs, were more open to their new environment. This unfamiliar environment resulted in them going to the bathroom throughout the house. It was frustrating every time she found more dog doo-doo in inconspicuous places.

Thankful that Colin offered to take Bryce for a few days, Olivia planned to spend plenty of time alone with her husband. Dean was getting stronger every day, but he was still not physically able to consummate their marriage. So to compensate for the lack of intimacy in their marriage, Olivia did other things.

She lit scented candles in the bedroom and gave him a sponge bath every night. They would watch a movie or read a book together. Most nights they would simply sit up late at night and talk.

"Livie, when I go, I want to make sure you and Bryce are taken care of," Dean said.

Olivia lay against his chest. She turned to face him. "Let's not talk about the future. Instead, let's focus on the present."

"I've set up a trust fund for Bryce when he goes to college," Dean told her.

"Dean, it's good to know you're saving for our son's future, but you're going to be here to see him graduate from college, get married and even make us grandparents. You're not leaving me yet. You just got here."

He gave her a quick peck on the lips. "I hope you're right." Then he closed his eyes and drifted off to sleep.

A week later, Olivia sat in the living room folding laundry. Colin had just called her to let her know he was bringing Bryce home. She couldn't wait to see him. She hated being separated from her little boy.

When her cell phone rang she assumed it was Colin, until she looked at the caller ID and saw it was her sister. Olivia pushed the button to send the call straight to voice mail. Danyelle had been calling and leaving Olivia messages all week, each message sounding angrier.

Olivia understood why she was so upset. She had gotten married and hadn't bothered to call anyone to let them know. None of her family knew she was married, except for her son. It bothered her that the people closest to her couldn't be there when she got married, but she had to respect Dean's privacy. He still didn't want anyone to know about the cancer.

That's why it was taking her so long to return any calls. She was avoiding their questions. She didn't want to lie to them, but she couldn't tell them the truth.

Olivia folded the last of Bryce's clothes and put them away in his room. She looked in on Dean, who was sound asleep, and walked back into the living room. Then she walked toward the laundry room, took clothes out of the washer and headed out the back door to hang clothes on the line.

She whistled for Kennedy and Clinton to follow her. She thought it would be good for them to get some fresh air.

Taking a few white T-shirts out of the basket, she hung them by clothespins on the line. She failed to notice her sister standing right behind her.

"Why have you been ducking my calls?" Danyelle shouted in Olivia's ear.

Startled, Olivia looked around. When she realized who it was, she realized it was time to face the music. It was only a matter of time before Danyelle came looking for her.

"I was going to call you, but I've been busy."

"You left me a message telling me to leave Bryce over Aunt Stephie's. That was the day of the wedding. Since then I haven't heard from you. You couldn't even call and update me on Dean's condition? I would have thought he was dead if it hadn't been for the fact that Reverend Simms told everyone you two had gotten married at the hospital."

Olivia turned her eyes away and stepped farther away from her sister. Again, she started to hang up clothes, but Danyelle stopped her.

"What is going on with you?"

Olivia was an awful liar. The one thing she hated doing was keeping things from those she loved, but this was one secret she couldn't share with her sister.

"Livie, you owe me some kind of explanation. You can't ignore me."

"What do you want me to say?" Olivia shouted.

"I want you to explain why I had to find out through a third party that my sister was married,"

Danyelle screamed. "Tell me why you moved out of your apartment and didn't bother to tell me"—She pointed to herself—"Val"—She counted off on her fingers—"or Aunt Stephie. Why is this such a big secret?"

"It's not a secret. I told you I've been busy."

The two sounded like they were at a screaming match.

The sound of Olivia's back door opening caught both of their attention. Bryce stuck his small head out the screen door. "Hey, Mommy! I'm home."

"Hey, honey."

Bryce ran out to give her a hug. "Reverend Colin is looking for you. Hey, Auntie Danyelle." He ran back toward the house and yelled out to his mother just before he went inside. "Oh! Mommy, I forgot to tell you that Dean is calling for you."

"Okay, baby, tell him I'll be right there."

Olivia stepped forward, but Danyelle blocked her path.

"Is Dean here? If you won't tell me what's going on, then maybe he will."

Olivia dug her fingernails into Danyelle's arm. "Danyelle, I think you've overstayed your welcome." Olivia stared her sister in the eye. "Please leave. I won't have you bothering my husband."

Danyelle had never heard her sister sound so cold. Olivia tried her best to disguise the fear on her face as overprotectiveness, but Danyelle could see through her façade.

"Fine, but don't think we're finished." Danyelle marched off.

Colin peeked into the storage closet. Danyelle stood in the midst of church supplies. "You summoned me?" Colin stepped inside the closet with her. "I knew you'd come looking for me one day. I just didn't think it would be this soon." He took and kissed her hand.

She snatched it away. "Would you stop it? I called you down here for answers." She pulled a hanger from out of the closet and slid on one of the children's choir robes.

"Oh! Is that all? I thought you called me down here to smoke a blunt with you. I mean, this is where you go to sneak in a few puffs on those days when we have morning and afternoon services."

"Colin, we are not talking about me, we are talking about them." She picked up another robe from out of the pile left on the floor and tried to put it on its hanger, but she was so mad that the hanger slipped out of her hand and she ended up throwing the robe back on the ground.

"Why don't you calm down?" Then he pulled Danyelle out of the closet and pointed for her to sit in a nearby chair. "Why don't you tell me what the problem is?"

"It's my sister's marriage." Colin studied her facial expressions. He tried to figure out what was bothering her. "My sister is hiding something from me, and I need to know what it is."

"Have you tried talking with her?"

"She won't talk with me. I want to let it go, but something is nagging at my soul. I can't let it rest." He grabbed a hold of her hands. "I wish she would talk to me."

"She will when she's ready. Don't push. Give her some space."

"She's telling everyone that Dean passed out from exhaustion. Is that true?"

Colin stared into the eyes of the woman he loved. He was sworn to secrecy by Dean. "The doctor says that Dean was overexerting himself and that he needed plenty of rest."

"Well, I'm glad to hear that. I was beginning to think he had some kind of life-threatening disease," Danyelle replied.

Colin loved looking at her. He wished he could be this close to her all the time. He pulled her face closer to his. He wanted to kiss her. He stroked the side of her face.

"Ms. Danyelle," a child's voice screamed. Then the patter of little feet ran through the church hallways. A young boy came to a halt when he saw the adults so close. "Ooooh, Ms. Danyelle and Reverend Colin are in love," he shouted. He sprinted up to where they were sitting and dropped his robe in Danyelle's lap before disappearing out of the room.

Colin and Danyelle laughed at the little boy's reaction.

Danyelle stood on the front steps at Judge West's home. It was the Friday before Mother's Day, and she was ready to make amends with her sister. The last time she left, Danyelle was so angry she vowed to never return until Olivia called and apologized. That was two weeks ago, and she was still waiting on that call.

Danyelle had no idea how she ended up back at the judge's house. She had a strict itinerary set for the day. Her plans were to study for her finals, get some laundry done and meet Colin for dinner later that evening. Then as she drove to the cleaners she heard a commercial on the radio advertising the release of *Horton Hears a Who*. It was in the movie theaters, and Bryce had been bugging her to take him when it came out. She couldn't break a promise to her nephew. Before she knew what she was doing, she turned the car around and was pulling into Judge West's driveway.

She rang the doorbell. No answer. Danyelle placed her ear up against the door. She could hear music blaring in the background and Olivia hollering for Bryce. Danyelle tried the front door and it opened. She stepped into a maze of boxes. Again, she heard her sister screaming for Bryce to bring her a rag.

Danyelle stepped around and over huge boxes. They were piled so high on top of one another that Danyelle thought she would never find her way out. Fortunately, Olivia had a habit of talking to herself when no one was around and it led Danyelle straight to her. She found her sister on her knees scrubbing the inside of the oven. Through the sliding glass doors Danyelle could see Bryce in the backyard playing with Clinton and Kennedy.

Here was the perfect opportunity for them to make up while there was no one around to disrupt them. "I've come to make a truce."

Frightened by the sound of her sister's voice, Olivia lifted her head and banged it hard against the inside of the oven. She crawled out of the oven, rubbing the back of her head.

"I'm sorry. I overreacted the last time I was here."

Olivia heard the sincerity in her sister's voice. She was glad Danyelle had come by because she couldn't take another day of them not speaking. Olivia opened up her arms, and the two hugged.

"I'm sorry, too," Olivia said.

"I knew you missed me," Danyelle boasted. "Now where is my new brother-in-law? I would like to properly welcome him into the family."

"He and Colin are moving boxes from my place."

Danyelle smiled to herself when she heard Colin's name. Their relationship was still a secret, but she wondered how much longer they were going to be able to keep it up.

"They should be back any second."

"Well, can I take Bryce off your hands?" Danyelle didn't want to be there when Colin returned. "I promised him we would go to the movies to see *Horton Hears a Who* and it was released yesterday."

"I know. That's all he keeps talking about. I'll go get him for you." While Olivia was gone, Danyelle snooped in a few boxes. The boxes were full of things from Olivia's apartment.

She was still looking for a clue that would explain why Olivia and Dean married so quickly, but to keep the peace she decided to let the issue rest for the moment.

Hours after Danyelle left, Dean held the front door for Colin as he stumbled in with an armful of boxes. "Colin, do you need any help?" Olivia cleared boxes out of Colin's path so he wouldn't trip over anything. "I told him I could carry something, but he wouldn't let me." Dean sounded agitated.

"Thank you for telling my husband no," Olivia said. "He doesn't seem to understand that just because he's not laid up in the hospital or in bed that he's still sick."

"No problem, Livie. Where would you like these boxes?" Colin asked.

"You can set them down right here." Olivia pointed to the only open spot in front of her. "I might as well try to empty as many boxes as possible." She dug through and revealed a vast collection of paintings and prints. "I love Cidne Wallace's work. She immortalizes the attributes of every black woman so tastefully."

She placed the print to the side and searched the box again. "This painting used to belong to my daddy. It's called 'The Resurrection of Lazarus.' " Olivia held it up so the guys could get a good look at it. "It's a reprint done by Henry Tanner. He—"

Colin cut her off. "He was a prominent African American painter in the country who was raised in Philadelphia and his father was an A.M.E. minister. His mother escaped slavery through the Underground Railroad."

"You've heard of him." Olivia was glad someone loved art as much as she did.

"I studied his work while in college." Colin had never seen an actual reprint this close before. He studied how Tanner captured the realness of Lazarus wakening from death. "This is priceless."

"I've never seen any of these pictures hanging in your apartment," Dean added.

"No. There was never enough room for them with Bryce's pictures filling my walls. I kept them stored away. I promised myself that when I bought a house I would have enough room to display them all." Olivia admired the lovely images of black people being artistic. "These pictures have such a warm feeling; it will make this place really feel like home."

Dean walked over and kissed her on the forehead. "If that will make you happy, then I'm happy." Then he noticed how quiet it was. "Where's Bryce?"

"Oh, Danyelle was here."

Dean looked surprised.

"She came and took him to the movies." Olivia checked the time on her watch. "As a matter of fact I have to go pick him up from her apartment."

"Don't worry. I'll stay with Dean until you get back." Colin put her mind at ease.

"Thanks." She grabbed her purse and car keys.

"I'm not an invalid. I can be alone in the house."

"We know." She gave him a quick peck. "But I feel better knowing someone is here with you." She rushed out the door.

As Dean's eyes followed her vision he became dizzy. He reached out for Colin.

"Are you all right?" Colin led him to the couch and went to the kitchen to get him a glass of water.

"I'm okay. I think maybe my legs were getting a little tired."

"Man, I told you to take it easy." Colin sat on a nearby box. "Do you want me to call your doctor?"

Dean shook his head no. "Don't do that. It'll just upset Olivia. Plus, there's something I want to talk to you about now that Olivia is gone."

Colin listened closely. He was sure Dean was going to confide in him his last wishes in case anything were to happen to him.

"Remember the day I was rushed to the hospital and we were talking about my grandpa?"

Colin said yes.

"Well, I found out something that may change your mind at how you look at him as a man."

Colin waited for him to tell him more.

"I have to show you something." Dean got up. "I'll be right back." He left the room and went into one of the back rooms.

A few minutes later he walked back into the living room wearing the white-hooded Ku Klux Klan uniform. The only thing that could be seen was the whites of his eyes.

When Colin saw him he was startled and started to run for the door, but stopped when he noticed it was Dean underneath that getup. "Man, what are you doing?"

Dean pulled off the hood. "I thought if I tried it on, maybe I could figure out what would make my grandpa join such a hateful organization."

Colin looked at Dean and then at the white sheets and slowly shook his head.

Chapter 22

Val unbuckled her seatbelt and turned toward her passenger. "Are you ready?" It was Wednesday night, and her Bible study group was scheduled to meet that evening. The girls had gotten used to holding Bible study at one another's apartment, but Val specifically asked them to meet her at the church. She felt like she and Jonah both needed to dwell in the house of the Lord, with everything they had been going through.

"The last time I was in a church was the night before Katrina hit New Orleans. Our pastor brought a small portable radio into the sanctuary to keep us abreast of the storm's progress. The pews were packed. People were laid out on the floor and on the altar. It was barely enough room to stand. I guess everyone felt church was the safest place to be that night."

"There is no better person to turn to than Jesus in the midst of a storm," Val said.

They got out and walked into the church together, but there was no one there.

"Olivia." Val expected everyone to be waiting for her. Instead, the church was empty, but she knew they couldn't be far because she saw two cars parked outside. "Danyelle!" she hollered.

"Val, we're downstairs. We'll be there in a minute," Olivia yelled from the basement.

Val and Jonah sat on the pews nearest to them.

Seconds later Olivia climbed the back steps and stepped into the sanctuary dusting herself off. "Girl, I was downstairs looking for Sunday School workbooks for Bryce's class. You know Ms. Young can't ever find anything and she"—Olivia looked up from dusting off her clothes and stopped mid-sentence when she saw Jonah sitting next to Val.

Danyelle was so close behind her that she didn't notice her sister had stopped walking and ran straight into her.

"Girl, what is your problem?" Her eyes followed Olivia's gaze, and she too noticed Jonah.

Val giggled at their reaction. She knew they would be shocked to see her with a man. Val had never been with any other man except for Julian, so for her to bring someone to church with her meant he was something special.

"Where's Tressie?" Val asked.

"She's out of town on business again," Danyelle replied. "I think she had to go to Nebraska."

Val said okay and introduced everyone to Jonah. She wasn't the least bit surprised when Danyelle started to playfully tease her.

"So, Val, is this your new man?" Danyelle asked.

Olivia's face turned red from embarrassment. Sometimes her sister took things to the extreme. "Danyelle, would you stop it?"

"I betcha my sister didn't bother to call and tell you the latest newsflash," Danyelle instigated.

"What is she talking about?" Val hadn't really kept up with Olivia and what was going on with her and Dean.

"Does this have anything to do with the wedding? You and Dean are still getting married, right?"

Olivia smiled and tried to shrug off her questions. "We'll talk later." She cut her eyes in Jonah's direction. "When we're alone."

Now it was time for Danyelle to interrogate their guest. "Jonah? That's a biblical name. I like it. Do you know about Jonah in the Bible?"

"Yes, ma'am," Jonah replied.

"Listen to his country accent." She laughed loudly in his face. "You have to be from down South because nobody says, 'Yes, ma'am', from these parts," Danyelle mocked him.

"I'm from New Orleans," he boldly declared.

"What can you tell me about Jonah in the Bible?" Danyelle grilled him.

"Would you leave him alone?" Olivia scolded her sister. "He didn't come here to explain anything to you."

"Hush! I'm just trying to make conversation," Danyelle replied.

"No, it's fine. I don't mind answering her question." He turned in Danyelle's direction. "Jonah ran from God. He was running from being obedient to God, and whenever a person runs from God, they end up being eaten by a big fish."

Val could see that Danyelle was impressed.

"Well, this country boy does know his Bible," Danyelle replied. "So, Jonah, are you running from something?" Danyelle's face turned serious. "Perhaps from God?"

"Danyelle?" Olivia gave Danyelle a stern look, warning her to cut it out. "That's a personal question." She looked at Jonah. "You don't have to answer that."

"What? I just asked him a question."

"You don't know this man," Olivia pointed out. "What makes you think he's running from God?"

"Let's just say it's intuition," Danyelle said.

"I'm sorry," Olivia said to Jonah. "What may seem like odd behavior to you is normal for her."

"No. That's all right, I have nothing to hide." He looked Danyelle straight in the eye. "As a matter of fact, I'm not running from God, I'm running toward Him. I endured the disasters of Katrina, and that is only because I knew Jesus was right there with me as I hung on to my rooftop with one hand and my daughter in the other. When I left my home in New Orleans I wasn't running from God, I was following him. He brought me here to make a new friend." He glanced at Val.

Olivia knew Jonah's answer impressed Danyelle, because afterwards she stopped with the questions and opened the meeting in prayer.

Chapter 23

On Friday afternoon, Val, Jonah and Mr. Lawson, their lawyer, entered the courthouse together and took the elevator to the fifth floor. The moment they stepped off the elevators, a security guard greeted them. "Good afternoon. Could each of you please sign in?" He pointed to a lined piece of paper on the table.

Afterward, he searched the computer for their names. "Please follow me," he said to Mr. Lawson. "The judge has closed the hearing to the public to protect the child."

They made a left down another hallway.

"You are the last party. The hearing should begin as soon as you get in there." He stopped and allowed them to pass through a huge wood door. The security guard closed the door behind them and returned to his post.

Together they walked toward the defense table, and as Val proceeded down the center aisle, she could feel a pair of eyes watching her. When she looked up she abruptly stopped in her tracks. Sitting at the table across from theirs was Caitlyn and her lawyer.

When Caitlyn realized she had Val's attention, she gave a sly grin and whispered something into her lawyer's ear. The lawyer turned over his shoulder to look at Val, and the two began whispering again.

"Val, what's wrong?" Jonah came up behind her. "Is everything all right?" He was concerned.

Val couldn't take her eyes off Caitlyn.

He looked to where Val was staring. "Come on, let's not keep Mr. Lawson waiting."

The two of them grabbed a seat next to Mr. Lawson and waited for the judge to enter.

Val kept sneaking looks in Caitlyn's direction. She wondered what she was doing here.

When Judge Cohen walked into the courtroom, everyone stood. "You may all be seated," he announced. He sat down in his chair and picked up the papers set before him. When he saw Jonah's name, he dropped the papers back down on his desk. "Mr. Reynolds," he proclaimed, "what are you doing back in my courtroom? Did I make a mistake by returning Hope to your custody?"

"No, Your Honor." Jonah's eyes pleaded with Mr. Lawson to step in.

"Your Honor, there seems to be a question of the child's *maternity*," Mr. Lawson stressed the last word.

"Now, I'm confused. Can someone please tell me what is going on?" the judge asked out loud.

Caitlyn's lawyer stood up to speak, "Well, Your Honor, my client has reason to believe that Mr. Reynolds is not the child's biological father. This is the biological mother." He pointed to Caitlyn. "She gave the baby up for adoption, and since then both adoptive parents have died and she would now like to get her daughter back."

The judge turned toward Jonah, and he could see by the look in Jonah's eyes that there was some truth to Caitlyn's story.

"Well, I don't think I've ever had to rule on a case this complex," Judge Cohen commented.

"As you can see, I have provided a copy of Ms. Haas's financial records for the past three years. I have provided depositions from her friends and associates that can vouch for her character."

Caitlyn's overzealous lawyer tried to charm Judge Cohen with his flattering words. He mentioned a lot of prominent people in Seattle who were associates of Caitlyn's, but Judge Cohen seemed unmoved.

"Ms. Haas, where is Hope's father?" Judge Cohen asked.

"Well," Caitlyn cleared her throat before stealing a glance in Val's direction, "her father played for the NBA, but he was killed not too long ago in a plane crash."

"Julian Pennington?" the judge questioned.

Caitlyn affirmed by nodding her head yes.

Val sat up in her seat and stared at Caitlyn. She was sure she had heard her incorrectly. At first she thought this was another one of Caitlyn's sick jokes. A vicious lie she had concocted to hurt her.

Then the weight of Caitlyn's words started to affect Val in a negative way. Her mouth turned dry, and her stomach turned. The room spun around her. The well-ventilated courtroom was now suffocating, and Val felt like she couldn't breathe. She grabbed for her purse and rushed out the courtroom doors.

As she left, she could hear Jonah call out her name, but that didn't stop her. Val ran to her car and jumped into the driver's seat. She watched her hands shake. Her heart raced with fear. She noticed her doors were unlocked, and she slammed her hand down on the lock button.

Val was intimidated by Caitlyn's courtroom revelation. She didn't know why her lies would shake her to the core. There was no doubt in her mind how much Julian loved her, but Val felt like Caitlyn had won because she'd had his baby. From the parking lot she stared at the courthouse. She couldn't stay any longer because she wasn't emotionally prepared to face Caitlyn again.

She started her Mercedes and spun rubber to get out of the parking lot as fast as she could. Val drove through the streets of Philly erratically. The Mercedes cut off trucks, ran through red lights and barely yielded at stop signs. She wasn't sure where she was going. Her subconscious took over control of the car.

The car came to an abrupt stop in front of First Nazareth A.M.E. He had safely directed her to His house. The Lord's house.

She struggled to get out of her seatbelt and staggered up to the church doors. Inside, the church was empty. Val didn't wonder why no one was around. She knew He planned it this way. When she needed to talk with Him at one of her most vulnerable times in her life He made His altar available. She ran to the altar and prayed earnestly. The word that kept crying out from her soul was *"Why?"*

At that moment a lot of truths were revealed to her heart. Since Julian's accident, she hadn't prayed at all. Months had passed since the last time she came to the Lord with love in her heart or praise on her lips. In her heart she could hear God asking her, "Why?" Why hadn't He heard from her? He was delighted each time she called on Him, but lately He missed the sound of her voice. He wanted her to pour out her sorrows to Him.

Val knew what God wanted, and without hesitation she handed her troubles over to Him. Her soul immediately felt light. "Thank you, Jesus, for Your grace and Your mercy."

Val heard the reassuring sound of his voice telling her, "Everything is gonna be all right." With that thought she closed her eyes and envisioned God holding her tight in His arms. She simply laid her head on the altar—which in her mind was God's shoulder—and smiled, to herself.

Back inside the courtroom Caitlyn's lawyer was still trying to get the judge to side with his client. "Judge Cohen, as you can see from Caitlyn's references, she comes from a very good family. There is no doubt she can provide for the child financially. The child will attend the best schools and have all the advantages a child needs. We ask that the court stop wasting taxpayers' money by humoring Mr. Reynolds and his need to seek custody of a child he has no claims to. Ms. Haas would like to expedite the matter as quickly as possible so that she may be a mother to her daughter."

Offended by the lawyer's remarks, Judge Cohen became increasingly leery of the lawyer's true intentions as time moved on. The young experienced lawyer lacked respect for the court and spoke to the judge as if he were a peon.

"Ms. Haas, what was your reason for giving your daughter up in the first place?" the judge asked. Her lawyer sighed when he realized the judge had disregarded his remarks. "Your Honor, I'm not sure," she stuttered. "I guess I felt like I was too young to care for a baby."

"Is it safe to assume the father felt the same as you?" Judge Cohen dug deep for answers.

"No." Uncertain of what to do, she searched her lawyer's eyes for an answer. "He never knew he had a daughter."

Judge Cohen stopped writing and set his pen down in front of him. "You mean to tell me Julian Pennington never knew he had a daughter?"

Caitlyn halfheartedly shook her head no. "Your Honor," Caitlyn's lawyer tried to intercede on her behalf. "If you don't mind—"

"I do mind." He was tired of the lawyer's nonsense. Then he shifted the focus back to Caitlyn. "Why would you keep something like that a secret?" The judge sounded like a stern father reprimanding his child for doing wrong.

Caitlyn shrugged her shoulders in response.

Frustrated with the entire case, Judge Cohen sighed. "Ms. Haas, you carry very impressive references." He handed the bailiff a folder to give back to Caitlyn's lawyer. "You also come from a very good family, but none of that means much in my courtroom. I'm going to put in an immediate order for DNA testing. Ms. Haas, Hope and Mr. Reynolds will all have to be tested. It's only fair to Hope to know her true lineage. Once the results are in, they will be returned to my office. At that time I will contact all parties through their lawyers. We will meet back here, and I will not only read the results out loud, but also grant full custody to either Mr. Reynolds or Ms. Haas. In the meantime, I'm going to grant both you and Ms. Haas visitation to Hope at the group home where she is currently living." He picked up the gavel and slammed it hard against the sounding block.

Val slid her key into the lock that opened her front door. She entered, and from the kitchen she could hear Jonah talking with Mr. Lawson. The screen door slipped out of her hands and slammed shut, creating a noise so loud, she felt like an intruder in her own home.

Jonah jumped from his seat and rushed into the foyer. "Hey!" He opened up his arms wide and embraced her with so much love, she thought she was going to start crying again. "I was worried when I couldn't find you at the courthouse. I tried to reach you on your cell phone, but it kept going straight to voice mail."

"I'm sorry," she whispered. "I wasn't feeling well and I left to come home. But I thought maybe I just needed some fresh air, so I went out to the park."

Jonah looked at her strangely. "Are you feeling all right? I thought something else was wrong." Jonah pressed her for information.

"No." Val straightened out her clothes.

At the park, Val calculated the amount of time that had passed since Caitlyn and Julian were last together. She subtracted out nine months and ended up with a three-year-old child. Val added and subtracted months, weeks and years from every angle. It all turned out the same. There was a great possibility that Julian was Hope's father. If Hope really was Julian's child, that meant his seed had been living in her house, eating her food and sharing the same air as her.

Val closed her eyes and prayed this was all a dream. This couldn't be happening. Having to deal with Caitlyn was enough, but caring for Julian's daughter was too much.

"Val." Jonah touched her lightly to wake her from her thoughts.

"I'm fine." Val turned toward the kitchen and saw Mr. Lawson watching them. "Mr. Lawson, I apologize for leaving so suddenly at the courthouse. Sit down while I get you another cup of coffee, and you can tell me about the hearing."

Jonah watched Val strut past him and toward Mr. Lawson. He could sense that there was something wrong with her. What that was, he wasn't sure.

The following morning Val left the house when the sun was still down. She hadn't slept a wink all night. All she could think about was Caitlyn being Hope's biological mother.

After her talk with Mr. Lawson, Val volunteered to help in any way she could. That's why she was the first person in the law library that morning. She was determined to find any information to help Jonah keep Hope.

On her computer screen was a list of adoptive cases similar to Jonah's, but none denied the birth mother custody. In each case the child was always returned to the biological mother, except in instances of child abuse or neglect. She tapped a few keys and read through another list of cases. The database listed over three hundred cases, and she planned on going through every one.

After five hours of research, Val was tired. She couldn't take it any longer and needed help. Val sought assistance from the librarian. Mr. Lawson had warned her that this would be a hard case to win, but Val was determined to find at least one case of precedence. She put her trust in God and knew that with Him anything is possible.

Chapter 24

The fragrance of lavender-scented candles saturated the air, Will Downing's sultry voice adding a bit of spice to the evening and Olivia's sheer Calvin Klein dress was the finishing touch she needed to a perfectly planned rendezvous. This was the night she had been dreaming of since Dean's discharge from the hospital.

Over the past few weeks Dean had regained his strength. A good dose of rehab, rest, good cooking and lots of love from Olivia and Bryce were all contributing factors to his speedy recovery. He even felt strong enough to return back to work.

But tonight would be the night they would consummate their marriage. Olivia designated that night as their honeymoon, since they never got a chance to have one like most couples.

Olivia fanned her hands back and forth to dry her freshly painted nails while she waited for Dean to come home from work.

The timer on the stove alerted her to remove a pan of pasta shells stuffed with ricotta cheese and tomato sauce.

The enticing aroma swept past Olivia's nose and caused her stomach to growl. After taking the contents out of the pan, she neatly arranged the main course on a serving platter. She placed everything on the dining room table and took one final look. Olivia excitedly tapped her right foot on the rug. "It's perfect! This is a night he will never forget," she said out loud. Then she grabbed a wineglass full of sparkling cider and relaxed until Dean arrived.

Fifteen minutes later Dean walked in the door unaware of what his wife had planned for the evening. She greeted him in the living room. The first thing he noticed was how low-cut her dress was.

"What's going on? Did I forget something? I know your birthday isn't until October." Dean was worried.

Olivia led him to the dining room table set for two with the fine china that belonged to her mother. "I thought we deserved to spend a quiet evening alone."

"Where's Bryce?" He sat across from her at the table.

"He's staying the night with my sister."

Worry lines formed along Dean's forehead.

"It's okay. Bryce is at that age where he tells everything he sees. If Danyelle does anything I won't like, he will tell me."

Olivia served her husband as if he were king. She looked stunning, and the candlelight seemed to only enhance her beauty. Once again he thanked the Lord for sending him a wife who possessed every quality he ever desired in a woman.

"What did you do with Clinton and Kennedy?" Dean looked around for the pooches. They usually welcomed him home.

"I put them outside for the night. I know they're used to sleeping in the house, but it won't hurt for them to sleep outside for one night."

"I miss their daily routine of jumping up on me when I come home from work." He smiled.

The couple ate their dinner in silence. The only sound they heard came from the knives and forks hitting their plates.

Dean practically cleared his plate before he took a hold of Olivia's hands. "Livie, don't think I don't appreciate everything you do for me." Dean didn't let a day go by without telling Olivia how much he loved her, but tonight was different. She had gone through a lot of trouble to make this night special. The candlelit dinner and sensual atmosphere were something he would cherish for the rest of his days.

"Listen, I know I've asked you to do some things you wouldn't typically do, like marry me without your family and then keep secrets from them, but if it gets to be too much, you have to let me know. I wouldn't want you to carry a burden that's too heavy for you."

With tears in her eyes she said, "I love you."

After they finished eating, Dean volunteered to clear the dishes from the table.

While he was busy cleaning up, Olivia slipped into their bedroom to change clothes. She opened her top dresser drawer and pulled out the red-and-black negligee Tressie helped her pick out earlier that day.

Olivia walked out and found Dean sitting comfortably on the living room sofa waiting for her to return. She cleared her throat. The dazed look on Dean's face visibly said he was confused and didn't know what was going on. Embarrassed, Olivia's face turned red. She timidly forced herself to stand directly in front of him.

Dean never knew Olivia had such a voluptuous body. Her curvy hips and ample thighs shouted out to him. He wanted to reach out and touch her long vanilla legs that were unblemished. He couldn't believe anyone that alluring could be real because he was sure she was a dream.

"Olivia." Dean reached out to caress her waist, but when he touched her she jumped away. He realized she was nervous. "We don't have to do this." He didn't want her to feel obligated to be with him.

"Why? Are you not feeling well?" Olivia grew concerned.

"No, I feel fine. Better than I have in weeks. But if you're not comfortable, then I can wait. I want us both to want this."

She may have been a little scared, but she was ready to be with her husband. Olivia took a deep breath and closed her eyes and climbed on top of him. That was her way of saying she was ready.

Dean rubbed her thighs. He was sure he would enjoy the rest of the evening. She climbed off him and led him to their bedroom. The look in his eyes said he had been waiting for this moment for a long time.

Bubbles greeted them as they entered the room together. Dean stopped and thought he had entered into Fantasy Island. Their bedroom had been transformed into an enchanted garden.

Olivia hoped she was seducing Dean the right way. Tressie often shared intimate details of things she did to set the mood for her ex-boyfriend Payce. She had to give it to the girl. Tressie did some creative things with candles, feathers and rose petals; but Olivia wanted something different. That's when the idea of bubbles came to her. Bryce had a bubble machine that Olivia used to fill the room with bubbles. She decorated the room with a few plants. The final touch was the soft pink lightbulb that illuminated the room.

Olivia was pleased that every minor detail went as planned. She loved Dean, and it was important for their first night together to be unforgettable. She wanted to give him just her body, but also a part of her soul.

As they sat on the side of the bed. Olivia waited for him to touch her, but he never did. Instead, he avoided looking at her by staring at the far wall.

Dean hadn't been with a woman in such a long time, he was just as nervous as she was.

Once she realized he wasn't going to make the first move, she took his hands and wrapped them around her waist. Pulling him down on top of her, she kissed him passionately.

Instantly the intensity grew between them. His hands roamed her body, and within minutes they were both unclothed. Dean gently laid her down on the bed, and the two of them made love late into the night.

After hours of lovemaking, the newlyweds passed out in a loving embrace. With bed sheets twisted around their naked bodies, dreams of their night together filled their mind.

Hours later Olivia, never a sound sleeper, woke at the sound of something crackling in the distance. It wasn't a loud noise, but it was enough to wake her. She turned over and pulled the pillow over her head, hoping it would block out the sound. The disturbance continued. Then she was forced to get up and investigate.

She looked around the bedroom and then over at Dean. The darkness of the room gave it an eerie feel. For the first time since they had moved into the house she felt vulnerable and unsafe.

Throwing on her robe and slippers she went into Bryce's room out of habit. She became alarmed when she found his bed empty, until she remembered he was staying with Danyelle. She walked back into her bedroom and climbed back into bed. She leaned over to kiss Dean and hopefully wake him for another sex session when she saw a bright light glowing from outside their bedroom window. She got up slowly and tiptoed toward the window. When she looked outside she screamed.

"Dean!"

The high-pitched way she yelled his name scared him. He lifted his head and jumped up when he saw the distress on his wife's face.

She called his name again and waved him over so he could see what she saw. Olivia pulled the blinds up and watched a wooden cross burn on their front lawn.

Dean grabbed Olivia's hand, and they raced down the stairs. They had to get out of that house. He pulled open the front door and was ready to run out when he was stopped by the startling sight of Olivia's two shih tzus. The dogs had nooses tied around their necks and hung suspended from the rafters. Their fur had been burnt off, and blood dripped off their bodies.

Olivia screamed, and Dean ordered her back inside. She ran toward the phone and called the police.

Before Dean rushed back inside he saw the taillights of a pickup truck pull off a few feet away from the house.

Ten minutes later, the police and fire department had arrived and took statements. The firemen hosed down the burning cross and took it down.

Detective Craig Denali stared at the racial slurs that had been written on the front of the house in blood. Then he went to speak with Dean.

"Mr. West, I know this must be upsetting for you and your family. The police department is going to follow all leads to find out who is responsible for this, but I don't think this is just a random act of hate. I would bet my badge that Judge West's home was targeted on purpose."

Dean took a seat on the curb and watched the police take samples of blood from the house and place them in a small petri dish. He was afraid to tell anyone else his secret. He wasn't sure if he could trust the police to protect him and his family.

"I'm going to post a car out here to watch the house for the rest of the night," the detective said. "We have all units searching the area for any suspicious persons, but if you need anything, give us a call." He handed Dean his card and walked away.

Chapter 25

Val pressed both hands against her temples to try and stop the throbbing headache that had haunted her all morning and most of the afternoon. She popped two aspirins in her mouth and waited for relief. She couldn't believe how bad her head hurt. Val crossed the floor to the librarian's desk.

"Hi. Did you happen to find any of the information I was looking for?" Val hoped the librarian had some luck, because she was running out of options.

The librarian knelt down and placed a pile of books on the counter. "This is all we have in this library. Honey, if you don't find what you're looking for in here, then I doubt you'll ever find it."

Val pulled the pile of books closer to her, but the librarian stopped her.

"You don't look well. Your eyes are really red."

"I have a headache," Val told her.

"Is it hurting your eyes?"

"A little," Val replied.

"Why don't you go home? You've been the first person in this library every day for the past couple weeks, and you stay until it closes. I know lawyers like to burn the midnight oil, but everyone deserves a little rest." She pulled the books back toward her. "Now go! I'll save these books for you."

Val reluctantly went back to the table and gathered her things. She didn't want to leave, but the librarian had a point. If she went home and got some rest, she could return in the morning refreshed. A clear mind and fresh eyes may have been preventing her from finding the right precedence case.

As Val exited through the revolving doors, some college kid bumped into her. He almost knocked her to the ground. Val wouldn't have cared, if it wasn't for the fact that she got a huge whiff of the sandwich he was carrying. Her stomach growled from the pastrami and cheese on toasted roll. It was her favorite.

"That looks so good." Her gaze followed the boy and his sandwich until they disappeared out of sight.

Instead of heading toward the parking lot, Val strolled toward the nearest deli. She had to get a sandwich. On her way she passed by a children's boutique that happened to have a sign outside advertising their grand opening. From the sidewalk, dresses, skirts and tiny little patent leather shoes called her inside. Instantly, she fell in love with what the store had to offer.

An hour later Val emerged with both arms loaded with packages. She was now starving, but there was one more thing she had to get. She walked a few feet and entered the toy store. Hope had plenty of toys at the house, but Val had her heart set on something special for Julian's only daughter.

She walked straight to an aisle full of teddy bears, all wearing New York Knicks jerseys with Julian's number. After Julian died, the bears were sold throughout the city in remembrance of his life. She was glad the stuffed toys were still being stocked and even happier that she was able to find one so easily. She knelt down to grab a bear from off the bottom shelf, one that hadn't been touched. Then a pair of legs wearing white tights and a short purple skirt walked up to her.

"Do you need any help?" the stranger offered.

"No, actually I think I got what I came for." Val stood up and looked straight into Caitlyn's eyes and at her shopping cart full of toys.

Val was weary. She didn't trust Caitlyn.

Caitlyn stepped up closer to her and pointed her finger in her face. "Are you going to hit me? Go ahead. I want you to. I would love to tell the judge how Hope's father's girlfriend violated the restraining order I have against her."

Val ground her teeth together to remain calm. "Caitlyn, why are you here?"

Caitlyn sucked her teeth. "This is not about you. I came here to buy my daughter a few toys." Caitlyn looked at the bears sitting on the shelf. "It's obvious you also were shopping for my child. Val, let me give you a bit of advice—Don't bother. As soon as those test results come back, my daughter will be coming home with me. She won't need anything from you. I can provide all her needs, especially when I get back to Seattle."

"What do you think your family is going to say when you return home with a black daughter?" Val's patience was about to blow. "They will disown you and cut you off financially, and I'm sure you could never live with that," Val said.

Caitlyn gave her a smirk. "I hear jealousy in your voice. The same kind I heard when you found out Julian chose me over you. Are you jealous? Jealous of the fact that I had Julian's child and you didn't?"

Val was tired of talking and tried to walk around her, but Caitlyn stood in her path.

"No. You're going to listen to every word I have to say."

Val was surprised by her boldness.

"You should have seen your face when you walked into that courtroom and realized I was Hope's mother." Caitlyn laughed. "You know, I paid one thousand dollars for my plane ticket here, and my lawyer charges me seven hundred and fifty dollars an hour, but the look you gave when you found out Julian was the father was priceless." She laughed in Val's face. "The only thing that would have made that moment better was if Julian was here to tell you himself."

"Julian didn't know about Hope." Val sounded unsure of herself. "He would have never abandoned his child."

Caitlyn giggled, turned her back to Val and picked up a teddy bear from off the shelf. "No, Julian didn't know about the baby. I was going to tell him, but my family didn't think it was wise. Having his baby may have tarnished my family's name."

"What?" Val couldn't believe what she was hearing.

"My uncle didn't think Julian was good enough to be counted among the greats like Charles Barkley, Isaiah Thomas or Larry Bird. That's why he didn't have any problems trading him when Julian asked. When I found out I was pregnant, no one was more shocked than me. I knew that you and Julian were back together, and I was so far along that an abortion was not an option. So I settled for adoption."

"So why do you want her back now? How can you tear her away from the only father she has ever known?"

"Isn't it obvious? I love my daughter and I want her with me." Caitlyn's words sounded empty and uncaring. "When I take Hope back to Seattle with me, don't fret, because I plan to leave you with something to remember me by." Caitlyn's sincere smile turned to a smirk. "A broken heart— because, rest assured, I'll have a seat sitting next to me for that handsome Jonah."

Val rolled her eyes.

"Just like old times."

Val pulled her car into its regular space in the garage. She pushed the button to turn off her ignition and rested a minute before going inside. Laying her head back on the headrest, she closed her eyes to slow her adrenaline down. Caitlyn was the one person who always managed to bring out the worst in her. She sat for a second and prayed that the Lord would take over her spirit. After she finished, she took a deep breath and realized it had been a while since she'd last spoken with Olivia. They were way overdue for one of their heart-to-heart talks.

Val set her things down in the living room. The faint sound of a radio playing in the distance and the clanging sound of weights made her stop what she was doing and listen carefully. It sounded like it was coming from the basement. She slipped off her high-heeled shoes and attempted to go downstairs when the house phone rang.

Val picked up the kitchen extension. She was surprised. It was Julian's mother on the other end. "Hey, Val, it's Mrs. McCormick. I was just calling to find out how you were doing."

Val's heart nearly jumped out of her chest. It shouldn't have been a surprise to hear from the woman who would have been her mother-in-law. Julian's mother worried about her almost as much as her own mother, but her call was so unexpected. What if Jonah would have picked up the phone instead of her? How would she explain that one?

"I'm doing well. How about you?" Val had to cut this phone call short.

"I'm trying to keep busy. Mr. McCormick wants to go away on vacation, but I'm not sure I'm ready to leave home."

Val listened to Mrs. McCormick talk, but she was too deep in thought to comprehend a word she was saying. All she could think about was Hope. How would she explain to Julian's mother that she has a three-year-old granddaughter? She held the phone to her ear, wondering if she should tell her about Hope now or later.

"Mrs. McCormick," Val interrupted her mid-sentence. "Do you ever feel like Julian left a piece of himself here with us on earth?"

Silence filled the line, and it took Mrs. McCormick a moment to respond. She found it strange that Val would ask such a question. "Yes, I do."

Val was caught off-guard by her answer.

"I know I sound like a grieving mother, but I carry my son with me everywhere I go. Whether it be the supermarket, the park or work, I carry him in my heart."

That was not the response Val was looking for. Then she was reminded of Jonah by the sound of him rapping in the basement. Val quickly ditched her idea to tell Mrs. McCormick anything. First, she had to tell Jonah about Julian.

"Mrs. McCormick, I have to go, but I promise I'll call you later on in the week." Val hung up the phone and bolted down the steps to the finished basement.

When she reached the bottom step she was stunned at the sight of Jonah's bare chest glistening with sweat under the bright lights. He lay on a bench press lifting one hundred and seventy-five pounds. Val watched his bulging arm muscles flex. She watched for a moment before clearing her throat.

He looked up. "Hey, I didn't hear your car pull up. I hope you don't mind me using the weights. I found them pushed in the corner and I needed to work off some steam."

Val looked around at all the equipment laid out on the floor. They were Julian's weights. "I'm surprised to find you home."

Over the past couple weeks Jonah had stayed busy. He spent close to sixteen hours a day at work and at least four hours at the children's home with Hope. The remaining four hours of the day he used to sleep.

"Did you forget? We're supposed to meet with Mr. Lawson tonight. He wants to discuss details of the case with us tonight over dinner."

She threw her hand to her mouth. "It must have slipped my mind."

Just a minute ago she was all ready to tell Jonah everything about Julian, but something stopped her. She couldn't bring herself to do it. Her past relationship with Hope's biological father could complicate things, and she couldn't risk Jonah losing faith in her.

"I bought some clothes for Hope. You can take them to her the next time you visit," Val said.

"Thanks." He got up to load the bar down with more weights. "I'll take them tomorrow." He started pumping iron again.

Val was mesmerized by the sight of Jonah's muscular body. He noticed her watching him and stopped lifting. She couldn't pull her eyes away, and before she realized what was happening, Jonah stood directly in front of her. Her hands quivered and he pulled her lips toward him. He softly brushed his lips against hers. She savored his touch and she felt her heart flutter. She felt something for Jonah that was foreign. It was different than her love for Julian.

He pulled her closer by embracing her waist and kissed her a little deeper. She opened her mouth and allowed his tongue to enter. A soft moan released itself from her. She abruptly pulled away from him.

"I'm sorry," he apologized. "I shouldn't have . . . I thought that . . ."

"No, it's not your fault. I . . ." She looked away and thought about Julian. Guilt flooded her conscience. She scolded herself for being so weak and betraying her love for Julian. "I need to go get ready. We don't want to be late." She disappeared up the stairs.

A tall slender hostess escorted Jonah and Val to the table where Mr. Lawson was already seated and enjoying a huge lobster tail. He wore a bright red plastic bib that extended from his neck down to his huge protruding belly. When he saw Val and Jonah walking his way, he waved them over with one hand and used the other to take a swig of beer from his mug. Jonah pulled out a chair for Val and, once they were seated, placed their orders with the waitress.

"Folks, I'm sorry to be the bearer of bad news." Mr. Lawson didn't waste any time. He cracked open a lobster claw and gazed at the meat momentarily before shoving it in his mouth. "I've studied practically every adoption case in the state of Pennsylvania, Washington and Louisiana, and I can't find one that has not returned a child to its birth mother.

Jonah cupped his head in his hands and let out a low discouraging groan. Mr. Lawson had confirmed his worst fears. He was going to lose his daughter.

"The only instances I found where a birth mother was denied custody of their child was if the mother was a drug addict or lived the kind of life that would put the child in physical danger. I even went as far as to get a few people I know to look into the girl's past. She came back clean. A few parking tickets and they were settled by her family lawyer. She wasn't lying when she said that her family practically owned Seattle." Mr. Lawson looked toward Val. "Did you come across anything at the library that could possibly help us?"

Val's eyes offered him no hope.

Val knew in her heart that Caitlyn was an opportunist and gold-digger, but she doubted that Caitlyn had any skeletons in her closet worth uncovering. If she did, the Haas family would have them buried so deep, it would take decades to uncover them.

Mr. Lawson's cell phone rang loudly. He answered and quickly placed his hand over the mouthpiece. "I wanted to tell the both of you in person that I don't think there is anything else I can do for you." He threw his napkin down on the table. "But don't think I've given up. I'm going to work on this until the very end." He pointed toward the phone. "This is a close business associate of mine. I have to get going, but anything you order is on me. So enjoy."

Val and Jonah thanked him, and as Mr. Lawson walked away he spoke into the phone, "Reverend Baxter, what can I do for you?"

Once their meal arrived, Jonah and Val ate their dinner in silence. "Do you want to talk about what happened between us earlier today?" Jonah played with his food.

"No, not really." She pointed across the table. "Can you pass me the salt?"

He handed her the saltshaker. "Val, I feel something special whenever I'm near you, and I know you feel the same." He touched her hand. "You're the most beautiful, intelligent and generous woman I know, and it's rare to find a woman as pretty as you who isn't conceited, stuck-up or selfish."

She couldn't help but smile. She threw her napkin at him playfully.

"I'm just kidding, but can you do me a favor?"

She nodded her head yes.

"Would you go out with me and Hope this Saturday?"

"Are you sure?" Val was honored that he wanted to share his time with Hope. "I don't want to intrude on your time together."

He nodded his head. "The last time I visited with her she asked me"—he pointed to himself—"to ask you"—He pointed toward her—"to go out with us, and I told her I would."

Val eyed him suspiciously. "She did not say that."

"No." He laughed. "Those weren't her exact words, but we did talk about asking you to go out with us on Saturday. It's the first time social services are going to allow me to visit with her away from the home. I thought it would be fun if you came along. She's grown so much since the last time you've seen her. We figured that if we treated you to lunch that would be a start at thanking you for everything you've done for us."

Val pushed the broccoli around on her plate. Jonah's request warmed her heart. It felt good to be wanted by someone. "I would love to go out with the two of you on Saturday."

"Great. I know exactly where we'll go. I promise you will enjoy yourself. So it's a date. I'll pick you up at one o'clock sharp in your living room." They looked at one another and laughed heartily.

Chapter 26

Dean wanted to come to the jail alone. He wanted to confront his grandpa in private about the vandalism that happened at the house, but Colin thought it was a bad idea. He knew how upset Dean was and he didn't want things to get out of hand. So he offered to tag along to make sure things went smoothly.

"I appreciate you coming with me," Dean said after they sat down in the visiting room. "I'll do whatever I can to help you out." Colin gave him a brotherly hug before Judge West was escorted in.

"Congratulations!" the judge shouted. "I heard you and Olivia got married. I always said she was a good woman. I'm so glad you made it official. You made a good choice."

"How did you find out?" Dean wasn't going to tell him anything about the wedding.

"Reverend Simms told me. He still comes to visit at least once a week." Then he turned to Colin. "I guess your partner told you everything."

Colin nodded his head yes.

"Are you disappointed?"

Colin wasn't sure what to say. "Judge West, I love you. What you did in the past has nothing to do with right now. As far as I'm concerned, your slate is wiped clean with me." Colin turned toward Dean. "It's others who may not be as forgiving."

Judge West understood then spoke to his grandson. "I thought you were finished with me for good. What brings you back to this hellhole?"

"As if you don't know."

The judge looked at him confused.

"Your friends left a burning cross on our front lawn? What do your people want? Why are they harassing me and my family?"

The judge inhaled a few times, and when he was finally ready to talk, he had tears in his eyes. "At first I thought they just wanted payback against me because I had left the brotherhood, but after the letter I got the other day, now I know they want more."

He had Colin and Dean's full attention.

"The brotherhood accused me of abandoning them. They told me I was a thief, because I took their money for law school and they were never compensated for paying my way."

"So this is about money," Colin said.

"I wish it were that easy, but I think this is their way of warning me not to implicate any of them in the murder of that boy. If I try to cut a deal with the feds or cooperate with them in any way, they will reach out to hurt my family."

"Damn!" Dean slammed his fist down on the table. "I can't believe this could affect my family." He pointed in his grandpa's face. "Nothing better not happen to my wife or I'll kill you myself."

"Dean . . ." Judge West was at a loss for words.

"Judge, is there anything we can do to stop them?" Colin intervened.

"I did get a letter the other day and they offered to have all the charges against me dropped," Judge West said.

"They can't do that," Dean said. "The feds are the ones prosecuting you."

"Don't you understand? They *are* the government. I told you that they have connections everywhere. Don't underestimate the power of the brotherhood. A lot of liberals think that racism has ceased to exist, that it died off after the civil rights movement. That is far from the truth. Trust me, it's alive and well." He folded his arms in front of him. "Just because they don't lynch people from trees any longer doesn't mean that minorities in this country aren't still being lynched. Millions of narrow-minded people run this country. They come in all forms. It could be that lovely real estate agent who is so nice and has done everything she could to help you find the perfect house, but she only shows you the homes in the black neighborhoods because they don't want your kind living next door to them.

What about the school guidance counselor who insists that your child is not smart enough to keep up in the regular classes? Then your child is labeled as a special education case until graduation."

"What do they want you to do?" Colin asked.

"They've asked me to rejoin them. They want to reinstate my membership and have me do the work I was supposed to do when I left the brotherhood."

"Yo, man," Dean was talking to Colin, "I told you this was some sick stuff. So I guess this means you're going to rejoin them."

"If it means keeping you and your family safe, then I'll do what I have to do," Judge West replied.

"Man, I can't take any more of this." Dean tapped Colin on the arm. "I'll wait for you out in the car." He left the room.

"Colin, you have to understand I'm just trying to do what's right, so that no one gets hurt. I know what kind of power that organization has and what they can do. They'll kill him if I don't cooperate."

"Don't worry, Judge, I'll talk to him. But what about you? This has to be hard for you."

"I've been beating myself up over being so dumb."

"You were a kid. You didn't know any better. It's a good thing God doesn't hold us accountable for the things we did before we were covered with the blood." Colin could see how sad he was. He needed some reassuring words.

"Some days I feel so ashamed of what I did in the past that I can't even get out of bed. I cover my head with blankets to try and hide my disappointment from God."

"Let's pray!" Colin spoke a powerful prayer asking God to heal all hearts surrounding the matter.

Together they ended the prayer with, "Amen."

"What do you do now?" Colin stared into the old man's aging bloodshot eyes.

"Nothing. I wait for them to get in touch with me. That's when I'll tell them that I'll rejoin them." He looked Colin in the eye. "Please don't think less of me because of what I'm doing. I could never again believe in what they represent. I may have to do some unethical things to keep my family safe, but in my heart, I love all God's children." He looked away.

"I figure the first thing they'll want me to do is work on this bill the Black Caucus is trying to pass. They sent me newspaper clippings describing the bill in detail. Ultimately, the bill will reopen hundreds of closed murder cases that occurred during the civil rights area. In more than ninety-five percent of those cases no one was ever charged. Each case, no matter what the evidence suggested, was automatically classified as a suicide or accidental death." Judge West slowly shook his head. "I'll probably have to move back to Washington."

"But it would take more than your vote to kill the bill," Colin told him.

"They wouldn't want me to be a part of this for nothing. I'm sure they already have several members strategically in place to assist me. I'm just a small piece to the puzzle. I'm sure they have Charles Seale, Joel Watkins, Eddie Frist and Henry Sellers working for them."

"Who are they?" Colin wondered out loud.

"They were guys just like me. The brotherhood put them through law school, and I know that each of them have become very successful in Washington. I've followed each of their careers, and I can tell by the things that they've advocated against and for that they are still active members of the brotherhood. One guy is even a part of Congress. They have people throughout this country shaping it into what they feel it should be."

Colin looked at his watch. "Listen, Judge, I have to go, but I promise I'll be back to visit you some time next week." He got up, and the two hugged.

"Colin, can you keep an eye on my grandson? I can see how this ordeal is taking a toll on his health. He looks so thin."

Colin looked into his eyes and remembered that Judge West didn't know about Dean's illness. "Yes, sir. I'll do that." He then left out the door.

***

"Colin, what's wrong? You haven't said much since you picked me up." Danyelle and Colin held hands as they strolled along the Penn's Landing waterfront. He smiled before kissing her hand. "I'm just enjoying the evening with one beautiful lady." "Olivia told me you and Dean went to visit with Judge West this afternoon. How did it go?" she asked.

"It was nice."

His words were empty, and his face was so emotionless, Danyelle guessed that the visit was heavy on Colin's mind.

They walked a few more feet before Danyelle stopped and turned toward him. She grabbed both his hands. "You can tell me anything. I'm here for you whenever you need."

Colin's heart formed a smile. It felt so good to know that Danyelle did care about him, but he couldn't let her know that. "Why you being so nice to me?" He looked at her suspiciously. "This is not the same hard, cold girl that brushes me off every time I speak to her."

She pushed his hands away from her.

"The Danyelle I know would have hung up on me when I called."

"I'm worried about you."

Her words were full of sincere warmth that confirmed Colin's thoughts that she was the one for him.

"If that were true, then I wouldn't feel like you and I were secret lovers."

Danyelle's face turned guilty.

"No one knows how I feel about you, and you act like you want to keep it a secret from your family and friends when I'm ready to tell the whole world." He pulled her closer to him. "Can you put a little trust in me? I wasn't lying when I told you that I love you."

"I want to believe you, but it's hard for me to put one hundred percent of myself into what we have. I'm scared that if I start caring for you that I might lose sight of God's vision for my life. I know the Father will provide all my needs, but I can't afford to lose favor with Him. He's brought me so far. I finally have a prosperous outlook on life."

"Do you think I would get in the way of that?" Colin asked.

"Not intentionally, but it comes naturally for a woman to want to nurture her man. Right now I only have room for one man, and that's God."

Colin was disappointed, but he understood. "I would try and change your mind, but I'm not going to do that. You may not know it yet, but God has already told me that we belong together. So I'm going to pray on it, and one day you will be mine." He pulled the back of her hand up to his lips.

Chapter 27

Saturdays were generally hectic at the children's home, and this Saturday wasn't any different. Jonah opened the lobby door for Val.

Mrs. Chambers smiled when she saw the couple enter together. While balancing the phone in one ear, she turned to another staff member. "Can you please go get Hope Reynolds from the rec room? I remember seeing her in there watching cartoons."

The girl dashed off and Mrs. Chambers spoke to Jonah. "You are one of the more reliable parents. You haven't missed a Saturday," she said.

"I miss her," Jonah replied. Children screamed, phones rang and chaos was erupting in every direction.

"Jonah, I have to apologize again for not being able to get that overnight pass for you, but my supervisor wouldn't approve it because of the questions surrounding Hope's maternity."

"That's okay, Mrs. Chambers. I appreciate being able to spend the afternoon with her."

"She's excited. One of the aids was helping her get dressed this morning and she bragged about the new clothes you bought for her. Today she's wearing your favorite color."

"Yellow," Jonah said.

"Yes, but don't tell her I told you."

Whoever had Mrs. Chambers on hold returned back to her.

"Daddy!" Hope screamed and ran into her father's arms.

"Don't you look pretty? And you're wearing my favorite color."

She delightfully nodded her head up and down.

He turned toward Val. "Aren't you going to say hi to Ms. Val?"

She glanced at Val and hid her face in her father's neck.

Val knew Hope hadn't seen her in a while. She prayed their outing today would make her feel more comfortable around her.

Jonah signed Hope out, and they left.

"Where are we headed?" Val asked once they were in the car.

"Have you ever heard of the Please Touch Museum?" Jonah studied a few Internet printouts.

"Yes, Olivia takes her son there all the time. I've never been, but I heard it's a great place for kids." Val merged into traffic.

"It was listed as one of the city's best places for children. I figured Hope would like it. She likes to explore."

Val glanced at Hope in her rearview mirror. She sat quietly in her car seat checking out the new doll her father bought her. "I think you're right. She'll love it."

The Please Touch Museum was built especially for young children. It encourages youngsters to touch the displays while at the same time providing a playful learning experience. Both Jonah and Val felt like children. The trio browsed the aisle of the mini supermarket and later had tea with Alice in Wonderland.

During the course of the day Hope's attitude toward Val changed little. By the smiles on their faces, any stranger would assume they were a happy family. They laughed and played together, but when Val tried to get close to Hope, the little girl got stiff. Her body would tense up, she avoided even looking in Val's direction and would run to the safety of her father's arms.

Upset that she couldn't connect with Hope, Val stepped back and watched how Jonah interacted with his daughter.

He saw her watching them. He told Hope she could continue playing in the pool of balls just as long as he could see her. Then he went to rest next to Val.

He took a seat. "What's up?"

"Nothing. It's been a long day, and I'm getting tired. I don't want to ruin your time with Hope, so I think maybe I'll leave and allow you to spend some time alone with her."

"Listen, I told you it's going to take some time for Hope to trust you. I've seen how distant she is toward you. Stop being so anxious. She'll come around when you least expect it. Are you hungry?" Jonah didn't want her to leave. He grabbed Val's hand and wouldn't let it go. He called Hope over, and the three of them left. "Where shall we get something to eat?"

They stood outside the museum contemplating their next move.

"Why don't we let Hope pick?" Val suggested.

"Nope! Not this time. We invited you out. We always eat wherever Hope wants, and it's usually pizza."

Hope squeezed her father's hand.

"Okay." Val laughed. "I don't really like fast food. Let's see if we can find a restaurant close by where we can sit down and eat."

They turned to stroll down the surrounding streets when Val's body froze at the sound of her name. She would recognize that voice anywhere. She turned around and stood face to face with Julian's mom and stepfather.

"Hi!" Val sang.

Mrs. McCormick reached out to give Val a hug, then her eyes did a beeline straight to Jonah and Hope.

"I told my husband that was you." She smiled. "I would recognize those hips anywhere."

"What are you doing out here?" Val's body temperature was steadily rising.

"We were taking a walk in the park, and I think he's getting a little dehydrated because he started getting a little sluggish during that last mile." She reached out and patted her husband on the stomach. "We're going to the convenience store to get him a Gatorade."

"You two have to be careful out here. Summer is fast approaching. We don't want either of you to hurt yourselves."

There was an uncomfortable silence as everyone searched for something to say.

Mrs. McCormick knelt down in front of Hope. "You are such a pretty little girl."

Val couldn't believe Hope's reaction. She let go of Jonah's hand and leapt into Mrs. McCormick's arms.

"And friendly. Look, honey," she said to her husband. "Isn't she cute?"

He nodded his head yes.

"She doesn't do that with just anybody," Jonah said. "I'm her father, and this is my daughter Hope."

Val looked like she was in a daze. Jonah wondered why she hadn't introduced them to her friends.

"It's a pleasure to meet you."

They shook hands.

"Were you at the Please Touch Museum?" Mrs. McCormick asked.

"Yes, and I shopped at the supermarket and I got this." Hope held up the trinkets she bought at the museum store.

Val was stunned. She not only went to Mrs. McCormick, but she also talked to her. The little girl wouldn't even speak to her.

"She is adorable," Mrs. McCormick said. "Val, you have to bring them by the house for dinner."

"I would like that," Jonah replied.

Val smiled. "Sure, Mrs. McCormick. I'll give you a call." And she stepped backward, hinting it was time for them to leave.

Jonah held out his hand for Hope, they said their good-byes and left.

"You were unusually quiet at the restaurant." Val hadn't even noticed Jonah had gotten back in the car. "Did you see how she reacted to Mrs. McCormick? Hope doesn't even know her."

"I told you Hope is funny like that. Some people she takes to more readily than others. Plus, that lady reminded me of the grandmotherly type."

"How did it go when you took Hope inside?" Val wanted to change the subject.

"She cried and reached out for me. One of the staff members had to pull her away. We go through the same thing every week. It's hard leaving her behind. I hope Mr. Lawson finds a way for us to be together."

Val could hear how hard it was for Jonah to leave his daughter behind. She rubbed his back. "Listen, don't give up. Stay prayerful. I don't know what's in the Lord's plans, but I know He won't let you down."

Val backed out of the parking lot, and they headed home.

"Mr. and Mrs. McCormick seem like a really nice couple. Mrs. McCormick talked like she's known you for a long time," Jonah said.

Val kept her eyes straight ahead. She was not ready to have this conversation, but she knew this was the perfect opportunity for her to come clean.

"Why do I feel like there's tension in the air?" Jonah asked.

Val swallowed hard. "I was engaged to their son."

"Oh! Now I understand why you were acting so nervous," he replied. "You kept playing with your hands and shuffling your feet."

"I was not." She laughed.

"Well, I guess we won't be going there for dinner."

"I don't think so."

"Why didn't you tell me you were engaged?"

"There's not much to tell. Weddings are called off every day. I don't want to act like my broken engagement was something special."

"Yeah, but I'm sure it hurt. Is that whose clothes were packed away at the house?"

Val nodded her head yes.

"I don't know what happened, but I can see it was painful. I won't mention it again."

Val sighed. "I appreciate that."

When they entered the house Val laid her keys down on the kitchen table and went toward the stairs to take a hot shower and change clothes.

Jonah stopped her and walked up close to her. Their lips were inches apart.

"Thank you," he whispered.

Val could feel the intensity of the moment. When he looked at her she could feel her heart being drawn in his direction. Her palms perspired. She wiped them along her pants, and before she knew it, he pressed his lips to her and pulled her into his embrace. Val couldn't stop herself from wanting more kisses. She kissed him back, and her arms caressed his back. The kisses quickly rose in passion, and through his pants Val could feel his erection.

She pulled away from him. "We have to stop."

But Jonah didn't want to stop. "We don't have to." He tried grabbing at her.

"No." She backed away. "Good night, Jonah." Val turned and retreated to her bedroom.

Chapter 28

Colin swung his office keys in his left hand and snapped a beat with his right hand. He picked up his pace. He had to drop his things off at his office before his first class started. A quick glance at his watch showed he only had ten minutes before he would be late.

On his office door someone had posted a bright yellow note with his name scrawled across the front. He snatched it off and read it.

PLEASE SEE ME AFTER YOUR FIRST CLASS— REVEREND BAXTER. The urgent box in the far left-hand corner of the note was checked.

Enthusiasm grew. Colin had a good idea what the reverend wanted to see him about. It had to be about the Assistant Dean position he applied for weeks ago. It was about time Reverend Baxter appointed someone to that position.

With his spirits high, he opened the door and placed his briefcase down. He grabbed the books he would need, then dashed back out the door. On his way to class he couldn't help but smile.

Colin was friends with just about every candidate who applied for the position, but the difference between him and them was their true intentions for wanting the position. The thirty-thousand-dollar pay raise was a huge incentive for many, but Colin wasn't in it for the money. He loved to teach, and this new position would allow him to develop new programs, and enhance the Christian learning experience.

When Colin arrived to class, his students were waiting on him. He walked to the head of the classroom and handed out a pop quiz. His students sulked and moaned in response, but he whistled happily as he gave them thirty minutes to complete the test.

A half hour later, he instructed those who weren't finished to hand in their papers. Then he gave his students a rare treat—an early dismissal. Colin was anxious to get over to Baxter's office.

Colin set out on foot to Baxter's office. Although he had to travel over a mile, it didn't matter. His long legs got him there in no time.

He entered the building and walked the long corridor that led to Baxter's office. When he reached his destination he saw that Baxter's office door was partially ajar. He could hear voices inside. One was Baxter's, the other was unfamiliar to him. Out of respect, Colin didn't want to interrupt their conversation, so he stepped away from the door and chose to wait out in the hall.

A few feet away Colin was sure he heard the two men mention his name. He crept back toward the door and eavesdropped on their conversation. He was dying to know if he had gotten the job or not.

"So you're really going to offer Montgomery that Assistant Dean position?" the stranger asked.

"He is the most qualified. Plus, it looks good for the school. He would be the first African American in the history of the school to be appointed to such a high position, not to mention the increase in federal grant money from the government for promoting a minority." He laughed. "Of course, I've already arranged to have my cut taken off the top. The school wouldn't be getting these extra dollars if it weren't for my brilliant thinking."

"Make sure you keep that coon in check. You know how they get when they get a little bit of power. They start thinking they're in charge."

They chuckled together.

"Times certainly have changed. My ancestors were slave owners. They actually owned blacks, and now they have more rights than we do," Baxter replied.

Colin couldn't believe what he was hearing. Professor Baxter was someone he considered a friend. They had a good relationship. Colin never suspected the man was a racist. He had eaten at this man's dinner table, played golf with him and even got into serious debates about the different mysteries of the Bible. Colin was stunned.

"What happened with Eddie Frist?"

That name sounded familiar to Colin, but he couldn't remember where he had heard it before.

"The feds didn't even have enough evidence to hold him, but we're still working on Ernie West, and I can just about guarantee he'll side with us. He would rather die first than let anything happen to that black grandson."

"I still can't believe you're the one who found West after all these years."

"Neither can I. Imagine my surprise when I visited Montgomery's church and I saw him sitting out in the congregation. The only white face among a sea of blacks. I had to return a second time just to make sure it was him. But it was smart of him to hide out all these years in the black community. I would have never thought to find him there. I got a call from the former Grand Wizard, and he said that he would make sure I was generously rewarded at the banquet ceremony. Are you going?"

"Yup. I just received my invitation," the man replied. "Isn't it set for next week at the Claymont Country Club?

"Yes, the brotherhood is not only moving up in the world, but also out into the open." Baxter gave a hearty laugh.

Colin slumped against the brick wall. *How does he know Judge West?* Colin's mind was in a daze. He stumbled toward the men's room to splash some cold water on his face. He drenched his face three times before drying off with a towel. *What am I going to do?*

The door to the bathroom opened, and Reverend Baxter entered.

"Colin, I was just talking about you to a colleague of mine. I assume you got my note that's why you're here."

Colin gave him a blank stare.

"Is everything all right with you?"

Colin turned back toward the mirror. In it he could see both of their reflections, and for the first time Reverend Baxter did not look anything like the godly man he had grown to trust. Baxter's features transformed right before his eyes.

In the blink of an eye, the professor's pale skin turned a shade of dark red. His eyebrows arched up, and the pupils in his eyes lost their color. Colin could feel wickedness in the room.

He jumped back and tumbled over the trashcan. Everything, including him, fell to the ground.

Baxter went to help him up.

"No." Colin shielded himself from any help.

"Colin, you don't look too well."

"I-I have to go." Colin dashed out.

"Don't worry about the rest of your classes. I'll find someone to cover for you."

Baxter yelled out after him, but Colin never heard him. He was already out the door and over to the music arts building.

He rushed in and searched several classrooms before he found who he was looking for.

He charged into the classroom. He wrapped his fingers around Danyelle's arm and pushed her out of the room.

"Colin!" Danyelle shrieked. "What are you doing?"

He pulled Danyelle outside into the hallway. "I need to talk with you, and it's important." He paced in front of her, waving his hands like a madman.

She had never seen him act like this before. She stopped him and took his hand. "Tell me what's going on."

He sighed heavily. It was strange how, at a time when he had just heard the worst news possible, all he could think about was how much he loved Danyelle. He moved one of her golden brown micro braids away from her face and caressed her cheek. He didn't think it was possible to love another human being as much as he loved her.

This was all for her. The advantages this new position would bring him would be meaningless without Danyelle. He thought about what he would have to give up if he turned the position down and resigned from teaching. He couldn't work for a man like that. The biggest disappointment he would have to endure would be postponing his future with Danyelle.

That meant he would have to look for another job, and he was sure he would have to take a significant pay cut.

He thought he needed to talk to Danyelle, but he changed his mind. He needed to talk with God.

"Colin, are you going to tell me what's on your mind?" Danyelle asked again.

"Nothing is wrong with me. I was just having a bad day, and seeing your pretty face just made it a whole lot better. Now since I've already interrupted your class, why don't we go down to the cafeteria and grab something to eat?"

Although Danyelle wasn't totally convinced of his answer, she decided to let it go. She knew he would talk to her when he was ready. Until then she would wait.

Chapter 29

The risqué scene that erupted between Jonah and Val left them afraid to be alone together. For days the two tried to avoid all contact, but it was hard. They stopped talking, eating meals together, and they barely spoke to one another.

It was weird for Val. The kiss, the passion and desire that raced through her body when Jonah touched her were something she wasn't expecting. It was like she had been drugged with a poison that she couldn't control. She was so ashamed of her lustful desires that she repented daily. Her feelings frightened her so much that she locked herself in her bedroom and only came out when Jonah wasn't at home.

Jonah also had a bunch of feelings that left him confused. His behavior the other night was so unexpected. He had never acted like that before. It's not like he had never been with a woman before, but holding Val and caressing her soft body made him insane. He would have laid her down on the spot.

Now he regretted his actions. Things were so different between them. Val put so much distance between them, he didn't know if he would ever get close to her again.

Jonah stood outside of Val's bedroom door all ready to go spend the afternoon with his daughter. He'd promised Hope he would pick her up early, but he didn't want to leave without Val. They had so much fun together the week before, he wanted to do it all over again.

Jonah stared at her closed bedroom door, contemplating his next move. Should he knock and ask her to go, or should he go alone? He checked his watch. If he didn't get going he was going to miss the next bus. He turned to leave and glanced back over his shoulder one last time before racing out the front door.

Val stood on the opposite side of the door with her ear pressed up against the door. Jonah usually spent his Saturdays with Hope, and Val had been up for hours waiting for him to leave the house. She was still hiding from him, but today she had plans. Olivia had invited her over for lunch. Val couldn't wait to see her. She needed somebody to talk to.

Val waited another twenty minutes before driving over to Judge West's home.

"Where is my godson?" Val dropped her purse and car keys down on the coffee table. Then she looked around strangely. "Why are all your things here?" She pointed to an African mask hanging on the far wall. "And why did you ask me to meet you here instead of at your apartment?"

Olivia gave her a sly smile. "Sit down." Olivia pointed to the seat next to her on the couch.

Olivia finally confessed that she and Dean had been married for weeks.

Val thought Olivia was joking with her, until she looked down at the wedding band on her left hand.

"Why didn't anyone call to tell me?" Val pulled Olivia's hand up closer to her face so she could get a good look at her ring.

"Because you never answer the phone. Besides, I asked everyone to try and keep it quiet. I wanted to tell you myself."

"Have I been that consumed in my own life that I haven't had time to hear about my cousin's wedding?" Val felt guilty for only thinking about herself for the past few weeks.

Olivia patted her hand. "It's not your fault. We've all been busy."

"So when Dean passed out at the church, what brought that on? You never got around to telling me the details."

Olivia wasn't sure how to respond. Val was the first person to come straight out and ask her about Dean's condition. Her usual response to anyone who asked about her husband's health was, "He's doing fine."

That simple answer wouldn't go over well with Val. She was expecting a logical doctor explanation.

"Stress," Olivia blurted out. "It was just stress, and the doctor gave him a clean bill of health."

Satisfied with Olivia's response, Val got to the point of her visit. "Livie, I also have some surprising news to share with you."

Olivia waited with bated breath. She was sure this had something to do with Jonah.

"Jonah and I have been doing more than spending time together."

"I figured you two were getting serious. You should have seen the way he looked at you when we were at the church. Danyelle couldn't believe you would ever get over Julian and she—"

Val cut her off mid-sentence. "We are living together."

"Did I hear you correctly? You and Jonah are living together? As in living in the same house—under the same roof?" Olivia pressed the back of her hand against Val's forehead. "Are you sick?"

This wasn't the kind of response Val was expecting.

"You moved in with him?"

"No. He moved in with me."

Olivia knew Val was acting a little strange lately, but this was insane.

"We're staying at the house Julian and I bought just before the accident."

"Okay, now I'm worried. You're doing things that you normally wouldn't do. This relationship is moving way too fast. How well do you know this man to ask him to move in with you? It's only been"—She thought back—"a few weeks," she shouted.

"Olivia, calm down!" Val pleaded.

"Don't you remember what happened to me when I allowed a man to move in I hardly knew?" Olivia reminded her.

"Let me explain!"

Val gave Olivia a quick recap of how she met Jonah and Hope, her confrontations with Caitlyn, and then she unveiled the biggest secret.

"Hope is Julian and Caitlyn's little girl."

After she was finished, Olivia was speechless.

"Wow! That's an amazing story. It's weird how God works. What are the chances of you taking Julian's daughter into your home?"

"I had the same thoughts. I wish God could tell me how this is going to end. I would hate for Caitlyn to get custody of Hope."

"How do you feel about Julian having a daughter?" Olivia asked.

"I can't help but love her. Even if I wanted to hate her, I couldn't. I must admit it felt strange when I first found out she was Julian's child, but I never felt any resentment toward her. I see her as a blessing. Julian's gone, but he still managed to leave a part of himself behind." Val's eyes danced with joy as she talked about Hope. "Livie, you should see her. She's adorable, but I'm not sure she likes me. She's very cold and withdrawn when I'm around."

"How do you know for sure she's Julian's child?"

"Every time I look at her I see glimpses of him," Val replied. "I know that I shouldn't take Caitlyn's word on anything, but I guess the only way we'll know for sure is to get Mrs. McCormick to take a DNA test."

"What did she say when you told her she has a grandchild?"

Val took her tongue and wet her lips, then avoided the question by looking down at her watch.

"You didn't tell her?" Olivia was livid.

"I was going to, but if I did that, then I would have to tell Jonah about Julian, and I'm still trying to figure out how to do that."

Olivia opened her mouth to complain, but Val held up her hand.

"I'm scared. I'm not sure how he is going to react once he finds out I was engaged to Hope's biological father. He may think I was trying to trick him or take Hope away from him. I need to make sure he understands how much I care about him and it has nothing to do with Hope. He doesn't trust too many people these days, and I happen to be one of the few he does trust."

"Oh! So you care about Jonah. Is something going on between the two of you?"

Again Val put her head down. She was guilty.

"I knew it!" Olivia jumped up from her seat. "It was so obvious when you brought him to church." Olivia danced around.

"Don't get so excited. My life isn't as grand as yours. You might be mad at me after I tell you how I've been acting."

Val then told her about the kiss they shared and how she had been avoiding him.

"Why are you hiding from the man?" Olivia placed her hands on her hips with attitude.

"I think I'm falling in love with him."

"It's okay to have feelings for another man so soon after Julian. He wouldn't want you to be by yourself. You're too beautiful for that, but I am concerned about your living arrangements."

"Don't worry about that. I'm not going to do anything I don't want to do," Val said.

"That's what worries me. Once that lust settles in, it's so much easier to give in than stand up for your beliefs." Olivia sighed. "Girl, whatever you do, don't give in. If Jonah is as real as he portrayed himself to be when he was at Bible study, then he'll wait. Plus, I know you wouldn't fall in love with just anybody."

Her eyes followed Jonah up the steps and into the building. She was ready to give the performance of a lifetime.

When Jonah emerged from the group home with Hope in his arms, Caitlyn jumped out of her car and ran over to them.

"Hey, Jonah!" Caitlyn waved. "And there's my little girl."

Hope frowned her face when Caitlyn pinched her cheeks.

"I thought today was my Saturday." She threw Jonah an innocent look. "No, I'm pretty sure it's *my* Saturday, but I could be wrong. Let me go back inside and check with Mrs. Chambers."

He turned to go back inside, but Caitlyn stopped him.

"There's no need to do that." Caitlyn was the master of manipulation. "You already signed her out, so you two go ahead and enjoy your time together. I'm a little disappointed that we won't be able to fly the kites I bought, but we can do that next Saturday."

Caitlyn faked disappointment and sulked as she turned away.

"Why don't you join us?" Jonah didn't want her to feel left out. Jonah hated to see any woman upset. Besides, he knew how he would feel if he couldn't spend any time with Hope. "There's no reason why we can't spend time with her together."

Caitlyn played like she didn't want to intrude, but a little prodding from Jonah and she easily gave in.

They climbed into her car and headed toward the park.

Hope, Jonah and Caitlyn looked like a family together at the park. Hope jumped for joy at the different kites her father flew in the air.

Later, they walked over to the playground and allowed Hope to play in the sandbox while Jonah and Caitlyn talked.

"How many kites did you buy?" Jonah's arms were tired. "Every time I thought we were finally done, you pulled another one out your bag."

Caitlyn laughed. "I bought one of every kind at the toy store."

Jonah giggled to himself.

"I know you're probably thinking I'm trying to buy Hope's affection, but that's not true. Material things are the only way I know how to show someone that I care. That's how I was raised. I know nothing else."

Jonah felt sorry for her. "Hope and I were homeless for almost six months. For her last birthday, I bought her a lollipop. That was the only thing I could afford. I felt like a failure. But to her it was the best present in the world. She wrapped her arms around my neck and planted a huge kiss on my cheek. Then she told me I was the best daddy ever." The pleasant memory left a smile on his face.

"You really love her, don't you?" Caitlyn could hear in his voice how much he loved her.

They watched Hope play with another little girl in the sandbox.

"You can come visit her when we move back to Seattle."

Jonah twisted his head in Caitlyn's direction at warp speed. "How can you be so sure you're going to win this case?" He stormed away, regretting that he'd invited her along.

"I didn't mean to upset you." She walked up behind him. "But I know she's my child."

"I'll do anything. Please don't take her from me. She needs me," Jonah pleaded.

"What about me? Don't you think I want what's best for my daughter? A little girl needs her mother. There are things that only a mother can teach her child."

"We were fine," Jonah said more to himself than to her. "Me, her and Val."

Hearing Val's name made Caitlyn's blood boil. "Do you think I would allow Val to be a mother to my child?" Caitlyn spat. "That will never happen. She may have gotten Hope's father, but she will never get Hope."

Caitlyn stomped off toward the sandbox.

A moment passed before Jonah realized what she said, and he ran to catch her. He spun her around to face him. "What did you mean by Val had Hope's father?"

"Julian. She took Julian from me. They were planning to get married, but his plane crashed and . . ."

Astonishment covered Jonah's face. It was apparent he wasn't aware of Val's relationship with Julian. He walked a few feet away from her.

"She didn't tell you about Julian?"

"She . . ." he stuttered. "She told me she was engaged, but she didn't say to whom."

A fury of excitement danced around inside of Caitlyn. She couldn't believe her luck. There's nothing like the taste of sweet revenge. She had waited a long time for this day, and she didn't even have to arrange for this to happen.

"I'm not surprised she kept who she really was a secret. If it weren't for her, I think Julian and I would have stayed together, and I would have never put Hope up for adoption."

"Can you tell me what happened?" Jonah had to know their history.

Right before Caitlyn began her story, Hope ran over to tell her father she was hungry.

"Why don't we go get something to eat and then take Hope back to the children's home?" Caitlyn suggested. "Afterward, I'll answer any questions you have for me."

Three hours later, Jonah and Caitlyn sat on the sofa in her hotel suite.

"Julian and I were in love." This was the story Caitlyn had concocted in her mind. "As a matter of fact, I'm still in love with him. Julian started his career playing for the Seattle Supersonics. We met at a mixer that my uncle, who happens to own the team, threw for the entire basketball organization. We were hot and heavy from the start." She stood up and walked over to the bar to pour herself a drink. "There was nothing tame, innocent or endearing about our courtship. From our first night together, we both knew we were meant to be together; except there was one problem."

"Val?"

"Yes." Caitlyn took a sip from her glass. "They were already engaged, but it wasn't going to last. They were having their share of problems. So we kept our relationship hidden from her, until the tabloids took a picture of us together in Aspen. Our picture was plastered on every newsstand in the country.

"Once our relationship was out in the open, Julian asked Val to move out of the house. When she moved out, I moved in. The morning I found out I was pregnant, Val came back to the house and physically attacked me."

Jonah gave her a strange look.

"Yes, she pushed me to the ground, jumped on top of me and slammed my head into the floor until it bled." Fake tears poured from her eyes. "I was terrified. Luckily, Julian had come home early and pulled her off me."

"That sounds nothing like the Val I know," Jonah replied.

"Then you really don't know her. My lawyers issued a restraining order against her a few months ago because she attacked me again! At the cemetery! That girl is crazy."

Jonah couldn't believe they were talking about the same woman. "So what happened between you and Julian?"

"We were happy, but all that changed when the league found out he was using steroids during the regular season. Our life was turned upside down. He lost everything: his endorsements, his teammates turned against him, and there were rumors going around that the organization was trying to trade him. He was humiliated, and after the league temporarily suspended him, he fell into a depressed state."

Caitlyn sat back down next to him. "Determined to stand by my man, I told him that my love for him couldn't be swayed. Then my uncle came by the house to let him know he had been traded to New York. He was furious, and that's when he turned on me. He thought I knew about the trade and accused me of deceiving him. I know he was just upset, but what he said hurt," she cried. "He threw me out the house and moved back to the East Coast. I never saw him again. That's why he didn't know about the baby. I never got a chance to tell him, and he wouldn't take any of my calls. I wish I did get a chance to tell him because maybe, if I did, we could have been a family. I would have never given Hope away, and he would never have been on that plane."

Caitlyn played the wounded actress well. The tears flowed freely. Everything she told Jonah was a lie, but he believed every word of it.

"I'm sorry. It sounds like you've been through a lot."

"That's why I say you can't trust Val." Caitlyn dried her tears with the back of her hand. "I suspect she had something to do with the NBA finding out about Julian's steroid use."

"Why would she do that?" Jonah couldn't believe she would be that vengeful.

"Val was so angry when she left Seattle, I think she would have shot us both if someone had given her a pistol." She sat up straight. "After Julian left Seattle, I moved back in with my parents. I overheard my uncle telling my father that the request to have Julian's urine tested came straight from the NBA offices in New York. It's rare that they would do something like that.

"Who else would tip off the NBA? I know it was her. That's why I say be careful. She is a very conniving person."

Jonah had so many thoughts going through his mind. The biggest question he kept asking himself was, Why did Val keep her fiancé's identity a secret from him? He didn't want to believe that she was responsible for the downfall of her fiancé, but if she could ruin the man she loved, what would she do to him? Jonah wasn't sure what he should do. He had confided in her some personal aspects of his life. *Would she use that against me?* He needed time to think.

"Do you mind if I sleep here tonight?" Jonah looked like he was about to cry. "I mean, I'll sleep out here on the couch, but I don't think I want to go back to Val's tonight."

"Sure, that's no problem. I'll go get you some extra blankets from out the bedroom." On her way out of the room Caitlyn thought to herself, *Once again I win, and this time Val won't get a second chance to take what's rightfully mine.*

Val felt rejuvenated after her visit with Olivia. Spending time with her cousin had always been therapeutic for her. She entered her house and called out for Jonah. It was quiet. "He must still be out with Hope."

She kicked off her sneakers at the door and turned to her favorite channel, Lifetime. While watching television, she decided to take Olivia's advice and tell Jonah about her and Julian.

Lately, God had been speaking to her heart about being honest, but she kept pushing the Lord out of her head. Today, He put Olivia in her face to tell her what she already knew. It was time to come clean. She had waited long enough. *Besides, what's the worst that could happen?*

Stretched out on her fluffy couch pillows, she drifted off to sleep.

When she awoke it was morning and the television was still on. The women from the sitcom *The Golden Girls* were gathered in their living room talking. She got up and turned the television off. "I must have been tired. I didn't even hear Jonah come in last night."

She climbed the stairs and went straight to his bedroom. She knocked on the door. When he didn't answer, she knocked again, but still no answer. She slowly cracked open the door and called out his name. Stepping inside his bedroom, she saw that his bed hadn't been slept in.

The worst entered her mind. There was a lot of crime in Philadelphia. She prayed nothing happened to him. He could have been shot, robbed or mugged. Anything was possible living in the city.

She raced back down the stairs to find her cell phone. If he called and she didn't answer, she was sure he would have left a message. When she reached the kitchen, she heard the back door swing open. It was Jonah.

She ran and wrapped her arms around him. "I'm so glad you're all right. I was worried when I couldn't find you."

Jonah gave her the cold shoulder and merely brushed past her. He started up the stairs.

Val followed. "Jonah, there is something really important I need to speak with you about."

Jonah glanced over his shoulder and gave her an ugly look, but he didn't stop his stride.

"Jonah! I'm trying to talk to you."

When he walked into his room he grabbed a handful of clothes and stuffed them in his duffel bag. Then he gathered his sneakers and work clothes.

"Jonah, what's going on? Why are you packing your things?" Val was confused.

"I can't live here any longer," he shouted at her.

She stepped back. He was angry, but she had no idea why. "Jonah, what's wrong? You can talk to me about anything."

"Why don't we talk about how you were engaged to Hope's biological father?" His unsuspecting words were hurled in her face.

How did he find out? "Jonah, I was going to tell you, but—"

He charged toward her and pointed in her face. "If you were going to tell me, then why did I have to hear it from Caitlyn? Stop with the lies. What were you trying to do? Play me for a fool? Were you going to set me up and try to take my daughter from me? Tell me, what was the game?"

"Jonah, I," she hesitated, "I wanted to tell you, but when we first met I was trying to erase all memories of Julian from my life. Then came the revelation about Hope's true paternity. It took me a few days to believe it was true."

"That's why you left the courtroom in such a hurry that morning."

Val confirmed his suspicions.

"And now. What's your excuse for not saying anything after all these weeks of being together? I've been confiding in you, trusting you, inviting you to spend time with me and my daughter."

Val wanted to tell him that she was scared, but at the moment he didn't look like he would be sympathetic to her needs. She had never seen him this angry.

He raced back down the stairs.

Val stood in the middle of his bedroom, her heart beating out of control. An overwhelmingly frightening feeling took over her body. She knew that if she allowed Jonah to leave her house, she would never see him again. She chased after him.

"Where are you going?" she cried. "You can't leave me."

"I'm going to go stay with Caitlyn."

Val's face turned to horror.

"It looks like she's the only person who can be honest with me."

Flashbacks of when Julian betrayed her to be with Caitlyn played out right before her eyes. "Jonah, I don't know what's going on, but I do know that she can not be trusted."

"That's funny, because she said the same thing about you. Besides, she made me an offer I can't refuse. We already know that once the DNA results come back that Caitlyn is going to get full custody of Hope. So she has graciously invited me to move back to Seattle with her, so that I could be close to Hope. I'll be living with her."

"Is that where you stayed last night?"

Jonah rolled his eyes. "Not that it's any of your business." He stressed his words. "But if you must know, I did stay the night with her last night." He picked up a few of Hope's toys from out of the living room.

She couldn't believe he had fallen for Caitlyn's tricks. Still in a daze, she heard a knock at the door.

When she answered, Caitlyn stood on her back step with a taunting smile on her lips.

"Hi! Is Jonah around?"

Caitlyn's innocent, sweet voice was a disguise. She tried to sound completely harmless, but Val was on to her. Val slammed the door in her face and walked away.

Jonah witnessed everything. He practically knocked over Val to open the door.

"Don't be mad with her." he said to Val. "She just did what was right."

Jonah apologized for Val's rude behavior. "It's okay."

Then Caitlyn whispered, "I told you she was violent." She took the bags he held in his hand. "I'll take these out to the car."

"Okay! I'll just be a few more minutes. I need to double-check to make sure I have everything." Jonah jogged back up the stairs.

When he did, Val caught up with Caitlyn out by the car.

"Whatever you're planning, it's not going to work."

"It looks like it already did. This must feel like déjà vu to you, losing yet another man to me." She pointed to herself. "Don't worry. This time you won't be getting him back." She turned and walked away.

"That's what you think. Game on."

Caitlyn and Jonah pulled off in the car. "Are you all right?" she asked.

"Yeah! I'm fine. I feel like I was living with the enemy. It's scary because I had no idea she could be so nasty."

"Jonah, I think you made the right decision to get away from her. At any time she could have gotten Julian's family to come and take Hope away from you and there is nothing you could have done about it." Caitlyn hit the gas pedal to beat the red light. "Thankfully, his family has no chance of taking her from me. From now on, you and I will be Hope's parents. Why don't we get married?"

Jonah stared at her strangely. "Let's do it. We'll get married, and then you can legally adopt Hope and we can be a family." Jonah was hesitant to go along with Caitlyn's suggestion, but he spoke without thinking.

"Okay, let's do it."

"Great. When I get back to the hotel, I'll call my lawyer and have him call the judge. The sooner Hope is in our custody, the sooner we can go back to Seattle."

Chapter 30

Frustrated, Colin sat with his head in his hands. He spent the past few hours combing through every religious book in his home library. There had to be one book that would tell him how to dispel the strong feelings of hate he experienced every time he ran into Baxter at the college. He rubbed his tired, red eyes and looked down at the concordance flipped open on his desk. His computer screen listed several scriptures that talked about hate.

"Matthew 5:44—Love your enemies and pray for those who persecute you."

He stared at the scripture and repeated it in his mind. "God, I've never had to pray for anyone who hated me because of the color of my skin."

The question, Why? burned inside Colin's soul. Why did hate seep into his body and spread like the plague? It ran through his veins like a fresh, rolling stream. It was so strong that it frightened him.

Then Satan kept putting thoughts of revenge in his head. Images of Baxter being tied to a tree while Colin flogged him repeatedly with a bamboo whip flashed in his mind. He smiled when he envisioned Baxter crying out to the Most High God as he ripped open his flesh.

This evil was consuming him.

Colin picked up the phone to see how his friend was doing.

"The cancer came out of remission." Olivia looked over her shoulder to check on her husband resting comfortably on the sofa. "We just came from the hospital, and of course they wanted to keep Dean overnight, but he refused."

"Did the doctors say what happened?" Colin couldn't take any more bad news. "I thought they had it under control with the radiation and chemotherapy."

"His body is not responding to the treatments. He waited too long. The joints of his arms and legs are swollen and in pain. He can barely walk. What scares me the most is his difficulty in breathing. Colin, he's getting sicker." Olivia tried to hold back the tears. She didn't want to cry in front of Dean.

"Who's that you're talking to on the phone?" Dean heard his wife whispering. He hoped she wasn't talking about him to one of her friends.

"It's Colin." She brought the phone closer to him. "Do you want to speak with him?"

He took the phone from her. "Hey, man, what's up?" Dean sounded tired.

"Man, I didn't mean to call and interrupt your rest," Colin apologized.

"No. It's fine. This is just a minor setback. What's on your mind?"

Colin called to find out when was the last time Dean spoke with Judge West, but under the current circumstances, Colin decided not to worry his friend with something he could handle on his own.

"Man, I called to wish you a speedy recovery. I'm going to try and make it over there one day this week so you can cheat me in a game of chess."

Dean laughed. "I look forward to it."

Judge West knelt down beside his bunk with his hands cupped before him. He had repeated the same ritual for the past twenty years. Being locked away in a jail cell hadn't changed anything. He would still give thanks to the Lord, because whatever this trial and whatever the reason, he knew there was a purpose.

Two FBI agents walked toward his cell, both wearing dark blue suits with plain matching ties. Their wing-tipped shoes tapped hard against the concrete floor as they moved closer to West's cell.

One gentleman cleared his throat to acknowledge their arrival.

West didn't budge as he continued to pray.

The man cleared his throat again, except a little louder. Still no response from West.

He opened his mouth to bark at West, but the other agent stopped him and shook his head no. He was respectful of God and understood that every man deserves time to commune with God.

They waited until West lifted up from off his knees.

He turned to face his guests. "What can I do for you gentlemen?"

"We heard what you told your grandson and that preacher during that last time they came to visit. You were never given permission to release that much information. What you told them was confidential."

"I'm tired of being a puppet for the federal government. I've done everything you've asked, and you couldn't even keep my family safe. I'm tired of it all. I'm going to reactivate my membership with the brotherhood." Judge West picked up his Bible and shook it at the two agents. "If Christ willingly gave His life for me, I can't see how I wouldn't give up mine for my flesh and blood." He pointed his finger at them. "I hope you're not here to change my mind because, if so, you're wasting your time." The judge gave them a stern stare as if to dare them to say anything.

The tallest agent walked up to the cell and stuck his hand out to give West a handshake.

"Welcome back to the brotherhood."

The judge gazed at his outstretched hand a moment. He looked into the agent's eyes. He should have known the brotherhood would send someone to make certain he was telling the truth.

"What's the matter, aren't you going to shake my hand?" A sly grin formed on the agent's face. "That's all right. I was told to expect your unfriendly demeanor." He pulled his hand back. "Now that we know you're on board, when I get back to the office I'll make a few calls, and you'll be out of here in no time."

The agents looked at one another and in soldier-like synchronization marched away.

"Wait a minute," West screamed. "I have some questions for you."

The agents ignored his cries and kept on stepping until they were outside the jail and back in their car.

Chapter 31

Val cultivated the soil then dug a five-inch hole. This was her first attempt at trying to make her front yard look professionally landscaped like her neighbors' yards. Her house was the only one on the block that looked like a barren desert. Every garden tool she bought from Home Depot lay scattered around her.

She grabbed another flower bulb from the three dozen she had bought earlier that day and set it down in the small hole. She covered it with soil. She wiped the sweat from the bridge of her nose. It was high noon, and the summer heat was quickly approaching.

"I've only planted one and I'm already tired, hungry and thirsty." She laughed at her efforts at manual labor. She knew she should have gone with her original plans to call a gardener.

The reason she'd decided to do it herself was to get Jonah off her mind. She missed him. He had only been gone for a few days, and the house seemed so quiet without him. She often daydreamed that he would come back, but her mind kept telling her he was gone for good.

Mr. Lawson called the house early that morning to let her know the court clerk called his office. They were scheduled to meet in the Judge Cohen's courtroom Friday afternoon. She told Mr. Lawson he could contact Jonah at work. As for herself, she didn't think she would be attending the hearing. She no longer had anything to do with the case.

"Excuse me."

Startled, Val looked up at the owner of green eyes and sandy blonde hair.

"I was told Jonah Reynolds lives here." Even in his casual blue Dockers, off-white polo shirt and loafers, he was still good-looking.

Val stood to her feet and brushed her hands off before offering her hand to him. "He's not here right now. Is there something I can help you with?" Val wasn't sure if this guy was from the courts or social services, but she guessed it had something to do with Hope.

"My name is Cole Haas, and I have a very important matter that I would like to discuss with him."

Val's attitude quickly changed from friendly to untrusting. For some reason, she didn't trust this guy.

"It's concerning his daughter . . . Hope."

Her leery looks made him continue talking.

"Are you his wife?"

"No, I'm just a close friend. I'm Valencia Benson."

"I knew you looked familiar. I remember seeing you at a few of the Sonics parties held by my uncle. You were dating Julian Pennington."

She slowly nodded her head and finally realized who he was.

"You're part of the Haas family." Her voice turned threatening. Then she felt frightened. She thought Caitlyn had sent him to harm her. "If you're here to harass me, I'm calling the cops."

She turned to run into the house, but before she got far, Cole grabbed her arm.

Val swiftly put to use her self-defense moves she learned in college. She gripped his wrist and twisted it so far that she flipped his entire body over her. He hit the ground hard.

"Please, don't hurt me," he yelled. "I'm not here to cause you any trouble."

"Then what do you want?" Val had her sneaker lodged in the crease of Cole's neck.

"I want to help Jonah get his daughter back."

"Why would you do something like that?" Val was convinced he was lying.

"Please." Cole could barely talk. "If you let me up, I'll explain everything."

It took a few seconds before Val decided to give the man a chance to plead his case. She released her foot from his throat and allowed him to get up from the ground.

He tried to brush off the abuse he had just incurred. Then he sat on her front steps and chuckled to himself.

Val switched to her professional legal persona. "Mr. Haas, I'm sorry, but I fail to see any amusement in anything that's happening right now."

"I'm sorry for laughing"—He rubbed his neck—"but I forgot that my sister and you share a turbulent past. You've experienced firsthand how manipulative and conniving Caitlyn can be." Then he turned serious. "Val, I'm here to save you from any further trouble from my sister."

"You're a few days late. Hurricane Caitlyn has already blown through here and left behind massive destruction."

Cole dropped his head in front of him, disappointed. "It's not too late. We can still stop her," he said.

"I'm telling you it's too late." Val looked out. "She's beaten me this time."

"You may not feel that way after I tell you what I know."

Val turned toward him with a glimmer of *hope* in her eyes.

"The reason I'm here is because our grandfather passed away a few months ago. He was the founder of our family empire. Every Haas I know is an entrepreneur. We own a newspaper, a basketball team, hotels. Anything you can think of, someone in my family owns at least a piece of it."

Val sighed loudly. "I already know how rich your family is. Can you get to the point?"

"Okay, I'm getting to that," he fussed. "Anyway, like I said, every Haas I know is an entrepreneur, except for my lazy sister. Caitlyn has never worked a day in her life. My parents had her so spoiled that I believe she really thinks there's a money tree in my family's backyard.

"About a year ago my parents cut her off from all financial support. They told her it was time for her to grow up and get a job. Vowing to never speak to my parents or anyone in my family again, my lowly sister departed the Emerald City in search of her own fortune. Then we heard she started dating some baseball player out in California. That didn't last long. So I suppose she was broke again. Then my grandfather passed away. She missed the funeral, but managed to make it back to Seattle for the reading of the will. My entire family was aware that Grandfather was going to leave his fortune to the oldest grandchild, which is me."

Val signaled her hand to tell him to wrap his long story up.

"Okay, listen to this. There was a clause in the will that none of us knew about until after his death. It stated that if a great-grandchild was born before his death then the oldest great-grandchild would receive the inheritance."

"Cole!" she screamed. "What does that have to do with Jonah and Hope?"

"Think about it. Hope is Caitlyn's daughter. The first and oldest great-grandchild." Cole had to practically spell it out for Val to understand. "That little girl is set to inherit billions of dollars. That's why it's so important for Caitlyn to get custody of Hope. If she does, then she will be in control of all that money."

"It never crossed my mind that Caitlyn was doing all this for money, but it doesn't surprise me. We have to tell Jonah," Val said.

"Great. When will he arrive?"

When Cole asked that question, Val remembered that Jonah wouldn't be coming home. That was when she explained how Caitlyn had gotten Jonah to move in with her.

"It's time for us to ring the alarm." Cole was eager to expose his sister. "If we go and tell him everything, everyone will win. Jonah can have Hope, and my sister will get nothing."

"I don't think your sister is just going to hand Hope over that easily. She has the courts on her side. It makes no difference if she has an ulterior motive for wanting Hope back. The courts only look at if she's the child's biological mother. It's only a matter of time before she's granted full custody," Val replied.

Cole slammed his hand into his fist. "She can't get away with this. There has got to be something we can do to stop her."

"Why are you doing this?" Just because Cole was helping her didn't mean she had to trust him. "Are you doing this for Hope's sake? Because she deserves to be in a good home with a family who loves her. Or is it because, if Caitlyn returns to Seattle with Hope, then you lose your inheritance?"

He turned his eyes away in guilt.

"You're going to have a hell of a time getting into heaven. Your love of money is greater than your love of God."

"God has nothing to do with my money," he brazenly replied. "Listen, I will gladly set aside a trust that will take care of the baby for the rest of her life, but I need that money. I've been planning for this my entire life."

Val was disgusted with him.

He pulled a business card out from his pocket along with a pen. He scribbled his hotel number on the back.

"Listen, I have a plan that I think would get us each what we want. Me, the money. You, Jonah and the kid." He placed the card in her hand and walked away.

"Good morning," Cole mumbled into the phone. One eye opened wide enough to peek at the alarm clock on his nightstand.

"Good afternoon," Val replied. "By the sound of your voice it sounds like you had a very good night."

"Better than you think." He turned over and jumped when he saw a bush of red hair lying on his pillow. Thinking it was a wig, he grabbed the hair to throw it across the room.

"Ouch!" A woman screamed and shoved him away from her. Then she pulled the covers back over her head.

"Sorry about that." Cole flung his legs over the side of the bed and rubbed his head.

"I hope that's a woman lying next to you and not a man." Val giggled.

Cole looked behind him and lifted the covers to make sure it was a woman. "Yes. It's definitely a woman." He strained his eyes to get a good look at his houseguest's naked body. She had to be the stripper he gave most of his money to last night at the gentlemen's club. He couldn't remember much, but he was sure he had one drink too many. "Val, I'm surprised you put my number to use."

All night long Val weighed the pros and cons of getting involved with Caitlyn's brother. A bad omen hovered over her back, telling her it wasn't good to get into bed with any member of the Haas family. She wanted to trust her conscience, but Cole's offer to remove Caitlyn from their lives forever kept drawing her back in.

By the time sunlight cut through the darkness, Val was still undecided.

She convinced herself that it wouldn't hurt to call Cole and hear what he had to say. She twisted the telephone cord around her finger, something she only did when she was nervous.

"Meet me in the lobby of your hotel in twenty minutes."

"For what? What's wrong with us talking on the phone?" he protested, but she had already hung up the phone. He was talking to a dial tone.

Twenty minutes later Val impatiently waited in the lounge area. She lifted a bottle of mineral water to quench her thirst and impatiently drummed her perfectly manicured fingernails against her chair. "What's taking him so long?"

She watched another busload of tourists crowd around the check-in counter, before Cole finally joined her. He showed up wearing gray sweatpants, slippers and a hotel robe.

"Sorry it took me so long. I had some unfinished business to take care of."

The elevator doors opened, and out stepped Cole's overnight guest. She frantically waved her hands good-bye and flashed the money he paid for her services.

"I don't understand why we couldn't talk over the phone," he dryly replied.

"I didn't want you to say anything incriminating over the phone."

"Oh! So you think I'm planning on breaking the law?" He pulled out a pack of Marlboro cigarettes from his pocket. "Do you mind if I smoke?" He tapped the pack a few times to pull a cigarette out.

"As a matter of fact, I do." Val immediately snatched it out of his hands. "I don't know how they do it in Seattle, but you can't smoke in public places here."

"Darling, I didn't come all the way to go to jail. If I did that, I'd never get my money. I'm smarter than that."

Cole raised his hand to get the attention of one of the waitresses from the hotel's bar. He ordered a gin and tonic.

It didn't take her long to return with his drink. She gently set it on the table, and he tossed her a twenty-dollar bill, which accidentally fell to the floor. Instead of him picking it up for her, he arrogantly turned his back to her and faced Val.

The bar maid stooped to the ground, picked it up and threw him a dirty look before switching away.

"Why are we here?" Cole stirred the drink in his hand.

"I slept on what you said, and it's no secret I don't like your sister. And even though Jonah and I aren't speaking, I still can't stand by and watch Caitlyn take Hope away from him."

"I'm glad to hear you say that. But once I tell you my plans, you can't back out on me. There's no turning back from this point forward."

Val fully understood.

"We need to get started as soon as possible. I'm going to run upstairs and change my clothes. When I get back we'll take a short ride and I'll fill you in on what I have planned for my sister."

A half hour later they drove out of the city limits and into the suburbs. As they rode, Cole did everything, except reveal his master plan. He called his accountant, his lawyer and a number of other people.

After his last call, Val spoke up, "Do any of those people you spoke with have anything to do with your plans?"

He shook his head no.

"Then why am I here?" She threw up her hands toward the high school they sat in front of.

"Be patient."

Val wished she had gone with her first instinct and stayed home.

Minutes later they heard the final school bell ring, dismissing classes for the day. Teenagers came rushing out the doors. Dozens of kids boarded school buses, while others walked home in hordes.

One kid walked past the car with arms the size of boulders. His muscles bulged under the T-shirt that represented his school's colors.

"What are they feeding these kids that they look like that?" Val pointed.

At that point Cole jumped out of the car. "Hey, kid! Wait up."

The kid stopped and turned around just as Val followed Cole out of the car.

"Aren't you Max Ferretti?"

The kid moved his book bag off his right shoulder to his left then nodded his head yes.

"You're the captain of the wrestling team, right?"

The kid smiled a little at the recognition. He figured Cole was a fan who saw his picture in the paper.

"Great! I've been wanting to meet you." Cole held out his hand, and the two shook hands. "You know, I think we have a mutual friend."

"Who?" Max's smile was so wide that Cole could see his tonsils.

"My sister. Caitlyn. Caitlyn Haas."

Max's smiled faded, and his eyes dropped. "Don't worry, I'm not here to get you in any trouble, I just want to talk with you."

Max nervously took a step backwards.

"When's the last time you heard from my sister?"

Hesitant to reply, Max kicked around some pebbles on the ground. He glanced at Val suspiciously.

"Man, that's my . . . my wife."

Val gave Cole a strange look.

"It's okay to talk in front of her. She won't say anything," Cole reassured him.

"It's been a while." Max's face turned red.

"Don't lie. I believe the last time she was here was last week, and I also know what it was she supplied you with. You are one of her favorite customers. She talks about you all the time."

Max gave an uncomfortable grin.

"I'm sure it's almost time for you to replenish your prescription."

Max shrugged his shoulders. "I guess."

"Listen, kid, Caitlyn tells me everything. I know how she's been hooking you up with steroids and how you've been giving them to the entire wrestling team."

When he said *steroids,* Val swung her head around. She couldn't believe what she was witnessing.

"I've read how your team is now ranked number one in the state."

"Mister, what do you want?"

"I need you to do me a favor," Cole said.

Max shook his head no. "I don't know. I think I'd rather just be left alone."

When Max tried to turn and leave, Cole put his arm around Max in a friendly way. "Kid, I would hate to have to go to the principal and suggest he give you and your teammates a piss test, because we both know what the outcome would be."

Val couldn't believe Cole would go as far as to threaten a high school kid to get to Caitlyn. "Cole!"

Val was going to put a stop to this and demand he take her home.

"What do you need me to do?" Max looked like he had been blocked into a corner and had no choice but to cooperate.

Max called Caitlyn, after Cole had already coached him on exactly what he needed him to say.

"Hey, Caitlyn! It's Max"—He paused—"I was wondering if you could hook me up. I'm really in desperate need of some juice." He listened to Caitlyn and watched Cole. "Listen, I have practice tomorrow, so I can't meet you at our usual place. Can you meet me inside the coach's office on the second floor of the school?" He wiped sweat off his forehead. "No. The coach will be with us. During practice I'll tell my coach I need to run to my locker. That way, I won't raise no questions by running outside to meet you. Okay, I'll see you tomorrow at four o'clock." Max disconnected the call.

"Good job." Cole patted Max on the back and gave him a hundred-dollar bill for his trouble. "Remember, this is between you and me."

Cole opened the passenger side door for Val to get in.

"I can't believe Caitlyn is selling steroids to high school kids."

"That's the only way she can make any money. I told you she was flat broke." Cole walked around to his side of the car and got in.

"Why did you arrange for them to meet in the coach's office? Aren't you scared they'll get caught?"

"He won't be the one meeting her—I will. When I confront my sister I want to make sure she has no way of escaping. That's why we had to make sure the meeting place was inside the school. That was the only place the kid could guarantee we could be alone with her. He knows the layout of the school a whole lot better than I do."

Cole stopped in front of Val's house to drop her off.

She placed her hand on the handle, but before she got out she had to ask him something that had been bugging her since they left the school. "Do you think Caitlyn had something to do with Julian taking those steroids?"

Cole looked at her. "I really can't say for sure, but it's a good possibility."

Chapter 32

"Dean, are you sure you feel up to this? I told you I don't mind doing this alone." Colin turned off the car's engine. Today was the day he would expose Baxter for who he really was.

For days Colin had been dodging Baxter, still unsure of what to do. He prayed and fasted, but he was running out of time. Sooner or later he would either have to accept Baxter's offer and work side by side with a racist, or resign and start his career all over again at another university.

"What? And have you meet with one of Satan's helpers alone? Naw, I couldn't do that." He opened the passenger side door. "You know me my man. I always got your back."

They gave one another a pound.

"Make sure you stay out the way, just in case I have to start knocking somebody out. I can't allow you to get a scratch, or Olivia will kill me," he joked.

Both men, dressed in black tuxedos, walked up the front steps that led to the prestigious Claymont Country Club.

This club had a reputation of catering exclusively to rich white men. The structure was built several hundred feet above sea level on top of one the steepest mountains in Pennsylvania. Tourists would come from miles away to get a look at the white porcelain and gold palace that towered over the city.

When they entered the lobby entrance, the light buzz from several conversations being held among its members ceased. It was hard for Colin and Dean not to notice that the focus in the room had turned to them.

Dean turned and whispered in Colin's ear, "Why do I feel like I just walked into a Klan meeting?"

"Maybe because we did," Colin shot back.

"Gentlemen." A tall, uptight man with perfect posture and a thick British accent snuck up on them from behind. "Can I help you?"

Although the man was so tall that he towered over Colin and Dean, he still managed to keep his nose in the air, to plainly show they weren't welcome.

"Yes." Colin forced a cheery smile on his face and greeted the man with just as much enthusiasm. "Yes, I'm Reverend Colin Montgomery, and this is a friend of mine, Mr. West. Could you direct us to the awards banquet? We were invited by Reverend Baxter."

A look of confusion filled the man's face. "Reverend Doctor Baxter?" the man stuttered.

"Yes, that's right. Is there a problem?" Colin spoke with confidence. He refused to allow the man to think he was lying.

"Do you have your tickets?"

Dean stared in disbelief. He had never seen a man act so pompous before.

"He told me I wouldn't need a ticket and for me to just walk in."

The man looked uncertain of Colin's story. Reverend Baxter explicitly instructed him to not allow anyone in without tickets.

"Wait here."

They watched as the man called a waiter over and whispered in his ear. They glanced back over their shoulders at Colin and Dean before disappearing behind a pair of closed doors.

As expected, Colin and Dean were ignored by all the guests mulling around in the lobby area. People turned their heads and acted as if they didn't even exist.

"I never thought I would experience the same blatant racism that went on in the sixties," Dean said as they watched two janitors wipe down the glass door handles they entered through.

Seconds later Reverend Baxter charged through the doors. His eyes scanned the room. When he saw Colin and Dean, his face turned white with horror. He took quick long strides until he reached them. "Montgomery, what are you doing here?" Baxter seemed confused.

"Sir, I heard about your banquet, and since we've been missing one another at the school, I figured I would come here to speak with you in person."

"Reverend." Baxter stopped a moment to acknowledge Dean. "Now is not a good time." He placed his arms around Colin and Dean and pushed them toward the exit. "How about we meet first thing Monday morning in my office?"

Colin laughed. "Professor, I feel like you're embarrassed of me."

"No, that can't be true. Why would Reverend Baxter be ashamed of his new assistant dean?" Dean's words were dripping with sarcasm.

"You're going to accept the position?" Baxter was delighted at the news before he remembered something. "How did you know I was going to offer you the position?"

"Remember when you left that note for me to stop by your office? I overheard you talking with your friend."

Baxter looked confused. He wasn't exactly sure what Colin was referring to.

"Now that I've accepted the position, I just want to know, am I going to get a piece of that hefty finder's fee from the affirmative action dollars that will be pouring into the school?"

Clarity unveiled itself on Baxter's face. "Colin, I think you misunderstood my conversation," Baxter tried to explain.

"No, I don't think I did. You're part of an extreme racist group that has terrorized minorities for years." Colin's voice was steadily rising. He was so angry that Dean thought Colin was going to hit him.

"Let me show you something." Baxter led them through a pair of double doors.

Colin and Dean looked bewildered when they looked out at the tables full of people of various nationalities. There were blacks, Orientals, and Mexicans in the room. Everyone was dressed in beautiful ball gowns and talking and drinking amongst themselves as if they were a huge family.

"Excuse me," a black man spoke into the microphone at the podium. "This is a part of the program where we present our financial contributions to our young people."

The crowd applauded and cheered.

"I would like to begin by extending well-wishes to our recent high school graduates, and I want to be the first to contribute to our children's future."

The man pulled out five white envelopes from out his tuxedo pocket and handed one to each one of the children sitting at the head table. There were three white boys, a white girl and one black male boy. Then one by one everyone got up from their tables to give the graduates gifts.

Baxter leaned over toward Colin. "Each one of those envelopes contains at least five thousand.

We take care of our own, and it has nothing to do with color, and guess what? The largest contribution we have is coming from your church."

Colin looked at him strangely.

"What does First Nazareth have to do with this?"

"Remember all that money we collected for Judge West's defense fund? Unfortunately, it never made it to the lawyer's hands. I helped Simms in choosing a lawyer, and I made sure I found the cheapest, most inadequate lawyer in the city. We paid him a small fee, and the rest went in my pocket and toward our children's future."

Then Baxter gestured for them to follow him into an adjacent room. This time Colin was the one with a confused look on his face.

"What's the matter, Montgomery? I told you that you misunderstood my conversation. I'm not a racist, but I do actively support the uplifting of my race, the superior race, in controlling this county."

"So what lies have you told the minorities in that room? Because I can't believe they support the uplifting of the superior race!" Dean shouted.

"Every person out there is a living example of the theory 'a person should not be judged by the color of their skin.' Mexicans shouldn't be allowed any special privileges because they're immigrants. America is a country that does not discriminate. Every citizen of this country is given the chance to get a good quality education and the opportunity to work hard." He pointed at Colin. "Just like you did. You told me that you put yourself through college with no grants and no help from the government. You're successful and smart. The perfect example for your people. That's why I want you to not only accept my invitation, but to also accept membership into our organization."

"You can't be for real. You really expect for him to join a racist extremist group?" Dean was in shock.

"We are no different than the NAACP. They support the education and the rights of their own. We accept all nationalities, but we actively oppose affirmative action. We want the Blacks and Hispanics to have their own companies and own neighborhoods. I don't believe in blood mixing; it messes with the purity of our race."

Dean rolled his eyes at him.

"You can hate us, but without people like us your grandfather would never had gotten to where he is today. We paid for his law degree. The millions of dollars that are donated each year allow us to strengthen our bond, expand our network and help kids like the ones being celebrated outside this room."

"This is insane," Dean cursed. "Why would he join a group of people whose primary goal is to destroy everything he's worked so hard for? Like the community centers, free healthcare, and most importantly a better quality education taught in the ghettos."

"If you join us, you'll have a slew of banks ready and willing to give you money for any business venture, community project, idea or proposal you desire. And don't forget about the amount of money you'll be making. Colin, we wouldn't simply look at you as a black member, but someone who chose a better quality of life."

"A better quality of life?" Colin repeated.

"Yes. This is to your benefit. I'm giving you the opportunity to live a whole lot better than your ancestors."

Baxter walked closer to the window and pulled back the curtains to display the country club's breathtaking mountain view.

The scene reminded Colin of the Biblical story when Satan offered Jesus the kingdoms of the world if he would only bow down and worship him.

"Think about it. The amount of money you'll be making as Assistant Dean will afford you any luxury you desire."

"How much money do you think will be collected at this banquet to support your organization?" Colin asked.

"I can guarantee we'll collect close to a million dollars," Baxter said.

"Colin, you can't seriously be considering this guy's proposal." Dean never thought Colin would betray his own people for a couple dollars.

Colin considered Baxter's offer a moment before speaking up. "What about Ernie West? If you can guarantee the release of Judge West, then I'll join you."

Dean pulled at his friend's arm. "Man, you don't have to do this."

Baxter smiled to himself. He had already been informed that Ernie had agreed to reactivate his membership and was set to be released. "I don't think that'll be a problem. Shall I introduce you to the group?" Baxter extended his open arms toward the banquet hall.

The three walked out together and toward the front of the stage.

The emcee for the evening was just about to wrap things up and wish everyone a safe drive home when Baxter walked up behind him and took over the mic. "Ladies and gentlemen, I know you are in a hurry to get out of here, but I had to take this moment to introduce a good friend of mine." He beckoned for Colin to come closer.

Colin went to step on stage when Dean stopped him one last time. "Man, you don't have to do this. My grandfather's not worth it."

"It'll be all right," Colin said before joining Baxter on stage.

"This man not only works with me, but he's also a pastor. Please welcome Reverend Colin Montgomery."

The crowd gave a round of applause.

"And today he's decided to become a part of our organization."

The crowd gave another round of applause, and Colin humbly waved back to the crowd.

Then suddenly the applause was cut short by the raid of dozens of FBI agents storming into the room. They surrounded the place with their guns drawn and told everyone to put their hands up.

Several agents ran onto the stage and pushed Baxter against the wall. Then they searched his body.

"Officer, I'm not sure if you know who I am, but if you get in touch with Federal Agent Charlie Watkins, I'm sure this misunderstanding can be cleared up."

"Sorry, Baxter. Watkins was arrested earlier today. We've known for a while that he's been a part of your organization, and he now has a long list of corruption charges to face." The officer turned Baxter around to face him.

"Dean." Judge West climbed through the chaos in the room.

"Grandpa, what are you doing here?" He was surprised to see him.

"Your grandfather has been working with us from the beginning," a female agent explained to Dean. "The only reason we took him into custody was for his safety. We've been watching this sector of the brotherhood for quite some time. We had no idea one of our own agents was working with them until a few months ago. That agent tipped them off that we were bugging their offices. That's when they fed us bogus information and tried to pin that thirty-year-old murder of that kid on Judge West. We decided to go ahead and arrest Judge West and make it as public as possible. That allowed us more time to further gather enough evidence to convict them."

"I should have never doubted you." Dean felt like a fool for the nasty way he'd treated his grandpa.

"It's all right, son. I understand how you must have felt, but that's why I couldn't tell you the truth. It was all confidential."

"We could have never wrapped this case up without your grandfather's help," the female agent added. "We've worked with him in the past as an informant, so we knew he wasn't responsible."

"Ernie West. You're a traitor!" Baxter screamed. "When I get out of jail, watch out, because your family will pay for your sins."

Baxter struggled with the two agents who were trying to lead him out of the building. Baxter fought to get at Judge West. He finally got one hand loose and grabbed one agent's gun from the holster.

Baxter fired shots into the crowd. Everyone ran for cover. Judge West ducked and narrowly escaped the first shot, but the second shot hit Dean straight in the neck. Dean's body fell to the ground hard.

Judge West hollered, "Dean!" He put his hand over the gaping hole as blood poured out. "Hold on!" As the blood stained the carpet and Judge West's clothes, a faint smile formed on Dean's lips.

An eager and hungry rookie agent, looking to prove himself, pulled out his gun and fired at Baxter. He was shot twice in the torso. He also fell to the ground bleeding.

"Somebody call the ambulance," Judge West hollered. Dean's eyes fluttered as if they were going to close. "Don't you do it! Don't you dare die on me!" the judge screamed.

Within minutes the paramedics arrived, and as they lifted Dean onto a stretcher, another ambulance arrived for Baxter. They were both rushed off to the hospital.

Colin had this feeling of déjà vu. Once again Dean was being rushed to the hospital, and again he had the responsibility of calling Olivia. He had to tell her to meet them at the hospital.

By the time Colin and Judge West arrived, Olivia was already there. She told them that Dean had been taken straight into surgery. When she saw Judge West had been released, a fury of uncontrollable tears fell from her eyes. He wrapped his arms around her with enough faith for the both of them that everything would turn out okay.

Thirty minutes later they sat in the waiting room still waiting for an update from the doctors.

"What happened?" Olivia asked Colin.

Colin brought Olivia up to speed on everything that had happened up to the shooting, and just as he finished, Baxter's wife walked into the waiting room.

Her eyes met the attention of Colin, Olivia and the judge, but she didn't want to cause any trouble, so she stayed on the opposite side of the room. In silence she tried to focus on the sitcom that played on the television.

A nurse came in shortly after to inform her that Baxter was in surgery.

When the nurse left, Mrs. Baxter couldn't contain her grief any longer. She had no friends or family around to console her. She cried to herself and tried to stifle her cries by pushing tissues up to her mouth.

Olivia heard her cries, and with compassion in her heart she got up and walked over to Mrs. Baxter. She sat down wrapped her arms around

Mrs. Baxter's shoulder. The two women cried together for all the hurt that had been generated between them.

The ladies sat holding hands in silence for over two hours before two surgeons came out.

The one surgeon spoke to Mrs. Baxter. "Your husband is in stable condition."

She breathed a sigh of relief.

"He is a very sick man. The bullets damaged his lungs. He needs an organ transplant."

"Okay. Well, how long will that take?" she asked.

"Mrs. Baxter, we don't have a set of lungs available for him at the time. We'll have to put him on a waiting list, and if a set of lungs become available that have the same blood compatibility as your husband then we can do the exchange. We're going to transfer him to the intensive care unit, and we'll pray that he won't have to wait long for a donor, because the longer we wait, the less his chances are of making it through this successfully."

Mrs. Baxter nodded her head in understanding.

The other doctor turned to Olivia. "A lot of your husband's major arteries were hit, but he is in critical condition. He could still make it."

Olivia immediately held out her hands for everyone around her to join hands. Judge West, Colin, Olivia and Mrs. Baxter prayed together for the Lord to save their loved ones.

"Excuse me." A nurse interrupted them. "If you would like, the doctors said you could visit with your husbands, but please not for long, because they both need their rest."

The two women followed the nurse to the intensive care unit.

Olivia entered Dean's room. She couldn't help but cry. A teardrop fell from her eye and landed on his cheek. He looked so peaceful. She wished he would wake up so she could look in his eyes. Olivia leaned over and kissed Dean, hoping her kiss would waken her prince, but he remained asleep.

When the nurse came in to tell her that visiting time was almost over, Olivia whispered in Dean's ear, "I love you."

Olivia left the intensive care unit, and behind her she could hear the nurse in the next room over say that her visit was over.

Mrs. Baxter stood next to her husband with tears in her eyes. As she stood over him he opened his eyes and whispered, "Don't let me die."

Mrs. Baxter broke down in tears. She couldn't allow her husband to leave her. She needed him. He was her provider and her mate. What would she and the children do without him in their lives? Mrs. Baxter left the room and went to speak with a nurse about his condition.

"Nurse, do you think my husband is going to make it?" she asked.

"Ma'am, I really can't answer that question, but it's still early. The sooner we get an organ donor, the better his chances are." The nurse went back to checking patient charts.

"Thank you." Mrs. Baxter moved toward the exit doors when she saw Dean lying in his room. "Excuse me, nurse. Can I visit with him? I'll only be a minute."

Earlier, that evening the nurse saw Mrs. Baxter with Olivia together praying and holding hands, so she thought it would be okay. "Sure, but don't stay too long."

"I won't." Mrs. Baxter walked into the room and stared at Dean's chest as it heaved up and down from the breathing apparatus. Being in the hospital she realized she was surrounded by death. Her husband could die, Dean could die. She couldn't take it much longer.

She turned around to rush out and ran into Dean's nurse. A bunch of papers went falling to the floor, and so did Dean's chart. Mrs. Baxter tried to help her pick up her things, but in the process she got a good look at Dean's chart and noticed that Dean's blood type was O Negative, the same as her husband's.

The following morning Mrs. Baxter sent her young children off to school and sat at her computer. She typed in the word *euthanasia*.

The Internet listed thousands of pages of information about euthanasia. Mrs. Baxter wrote down all the information she was looking for and headed back to the hospital.

Once visiting hours began Mrs. Baxter sat with her husband, who was still drifting in and out of consciousness, until it was time for her to go.

Before she left she noticed that Olivia hadn't made it to the hospital yet to see Dean, so she slipped into his room. Mrs. Baxter set her pocketbook down and walked up to Dean's bed. When she did, his eyes unexpectedly opened, startling her. She jumped back when she realized he was watching her. That is when she pulled out the hypodermic needle she stole from her drug-addicted brother and injected a lethal amount of barbiturates into Dean's IV bag. His eyes grew big, but he was unable to speak. He grunted a bit but not enough to alert anyone to what she was doing.

"Sorry, Dean, but if I had to choose between you and my husband, then I will always choose my husband."

She quickly exited because she knew that he would be dead within fifteen minutes. On her way out the door she ran into Olivia, Colin and Judge West.

"Hello, Mrs. Baxter, how is your husband?"

Mrs. Baxter seemed jittery and nervous.

"Are you all right? Is it your husband?"

"I'm fine." Mrs. Baxter was in a rush to get as far away as she could from Olivia and the scene of the crime. "I need to go pray. I'm going to the hospital chapel." Mrs. Baxter raced toward the elevator doors.

Olivia worried about her. She wasn't too fond of Mr. Baxter, but she liked his wife. As they marched toward Dean's room they heard the monitors start sounding off. A bunch of nurses pushed past them and raced into his room. Another nurse escorted Olivia, Colin and the judge out of the intensive care unit.

Olivia was hysterical. "What's happening?"

Colin held her for a while, before a doctor came out to give them an update on Dean's condition.

"Mrs. West, your husband has suffered a setback. At the present moment the only thing keeping him alive is a life support machine."

Olivia closed her eye to block out the reality of what the doctor was telling her. Colin pulled her closer to him and she laid her head on his shoulder.

"Medically, there is nothing more we can do for your husband."

"So what?" Olivia screamed. "You're just going to give up and let my husband die?"

Colin walked up beside Olivia and pulled her toward him. "Livie, what the doctor is trying to tell you is that Dean is already braindead. The machine is pumping life into him. It's up to you to decide when we should disconnect the machines."

Olivia couldn't believe they were leaving the decision up to her of whether or not to kill her husband.

"This is too much. I need to go pray." Olivia moved toward the elevator doors.

Colin and the judge followed her. "No." She held out her hand to stop them. "I need to go alone."

Colin looked at the judge, unsure if he should honor her request. Judge West nodded his head to allow her to go by herself.

Mrs. Baxter knelt at the small altar with her head bowed and anguish in her heart. She couldn't believe she was so desperate to save her husband that she tried to kill somebody. That morning when she thought of the plan, it seemed so easy and so right, but after she did it she knew she had done the wrong thing. For the past thirty minutes she prayed that the poison she'd used wasn't enough to do any damage. That's when she heard someone come in and kneel next to her. When she looked to her left, Olivia was next to her.

"He's gone," Olivia cried. "The only thing keeping Dean alive is a life support machine."

"Don't cry." Mrs. Baxter tried to make her feel better, even though she was the cause of her pain.

"Mrs. Baxter, they want me to tell them it's okay to pull the plug. I'm not so sure I can do that. I hate to sound selfish, but I don't want him to go. If I have to spend the rest of my life visiting him in the hospital, then that's what I'll do."

"Olivia, I hate to tell you this, but what you see upstairs lying in that bed isn't Dean. It's just a shell of the man you married. If you keep him alive on that machine, you'll never hear him say the words *I love you* again. You'll never see him open his eyes. You'll never be able to do the things that young couples like you do."

Olivia cried harder. "I don't want to let go."

"I know, honey, but sometimes we have to do things that we don't want to do," Mrs. Baxter said.

Olivia got up from the altar. "I guess it's time for me to say my last good-byes to Dean."

Before Olivia could walk out the door, Mrs. Baxter stopped her. "Olivia, I hate to ask you this, but I need to ask you for the biggest favor."

Olivia waited for Mrs. Baxter to continue.

"Since you decided to take Dean off of life support, could you wait and tell the doctors that you want to harvest Dean's organs? My husband could use Dean's lungs."

Olivia was stunned by her request. She couldn't believe Mrs. Baxter would ask such a thing. Her husband was the reason Olivia had to make such a decision, and now Mrs. Baxter wanted her to save her husband's life.

"You want me to save the man who killed my husband?" Olivia asked in disbelief. She stormed towards the door, but Mrs. Baxter stepped in her path.

"I know you're upset, but I wouldn't ask this if it weren't a matter of life and death. My husband could die if he doesn't receive a lung soon."

"How do you know Dean and your husband are even compatible?" Olivia was furious. "I don't," Mrs. Baxter lied, "but we could ask the nurses to check, and if they are I would forever be indebted to you."

Although Olivia was upset, she couldn't deny Mrs. Baxter's request. "I can't promise anything. I'll think about it and let you know."

When Olivia walked out of the chapel, Mrs. Baxter prayed that Olivia would have mercy on her and her husband.

By the time Mrs. Baxter returned to the intensive care unit she saw a group of doctors and nurses surrounding Dean, and Olivia stood at the nurses station crying. "Olivia." She gently touched her shoulder. "Are you okay?" "Yes." She wiped a few tears away from her cheeks. "I told the nurses what I wanted to do. They're getting the paperwork for me to sign."

"Thank you, Olivia. What you're doing is so brave."

"It's more than brave."

Mrs. Baxter and Olivia looked up at the same time to find Judge West and Colin standing behind them.

"Yes, it is more than brave," Mrs. Baxter agreed.

"Olivia, I hate to intrude on the promise that you made to Mrs. Baxter, but I must insist that she compensate you for your loss."

"Compensate?" Mrs. Baxter shouted.

"Yes," the judge said. "Listen, I used to be a part of the brotherhood and I'm fully aware that they take care of their own. You and your husband are sitting on a lot of money, while my granddaughter has just lost her husband and has a little boy to take care of."

"So, this is about money?" Mrs. Baxter assumed.

"Judge West, you don't have to do this." Olivia tried to keep the peace. "I really don't want any money from them."

"It's not about you wanting it. It's about you needing it. You have a husband to bury and a little boy to take care of."

"All right." Mrs. Baxter pulled out her checkbook. "What do you want? A couple thousand dollars? Enough to pay for funeral arrangements?"

"We want half a million dollars," Colin blurted out.

Mrs. Baxter slowly looked up from her checkbook and turned her head in amazement.

"Lady, don't act like you don't have it. We just left a banquet where the brotherhood received millions of dollars."

"Yes, but that money isn't ours." Mrs. Baxter cried.

"And I know for a fact that your husband stole thousand of dollars from the church in contributions for the judge's defense fund. You have the money, and if you don't, then call your friends and borrow it."

"It's not that easy."

"But it was easy and brave for Olivia to give up her husband's organs to save your husband's life."

Mrs. Baxter swung her eyes from Colin to Judge West. "Fine. I'll get you the money, but it's gonna take me a while."

"The longer you wait, the longer it will be before my granddaughter signs any papers to save the good Reverend Baxter."

"Excuse me." The nurse came in with a clipboard. "Mrs. West, if I can get your signature, then we can go ahead and harvest your husband's organs."

Judge West took the clipboard out of the nurse's hands. "We need to make sure she reads these over thoroughly before she signs anything."

"Of course," the nurse replied before walking away.

Mrs. Baxter realized the longer she procrastinated, the greater her chances of losing her husband. "I'll make a few phone calls." Mrs. Baxter left the intensive care unit to gather the money she needed.

Within thirty minutes she returned. "I'll have the money to you by the end of business today, but you have to promise me that you will never tell my husband where he received the organs from."

"Why?" Judge West questioned. "Because Dean is a black man?"

The judge already knew the answer. He handed Olivia the clipboard. "Now you can sign."

Olivia signed the forms and went to go search for the nurse.

Chapter 33

The whistle blew and the coach yelled, "Max, what's wrong with you? You never allow your opponent to lock your leg. That's why he pinned you. That's a basic move. What's wrong with you today?"

The guy released Max from off the mat and they both got up. "Sorry, Coach." He glanced up at the clock through the corner of his eye. "Can I go to my locker?"

The coach thought his request was odd. "You have to go now?"

Max nodded his head yes.

Frustrated, the coach exhaled before letting him go. "Don't be all day, or I'll have you running laps for the remainder of practice."

Max jogged out of the gymnasium and around to the side entrance to let Val and Cole in.

"Your sister is already up there," he said to Cole. "I told her I had to go collect the money from the guys."

They took long strides through the corridor. Val and Cole did a slow jog trying to keep up with him.

"Listen, you can't be long. If you get caught inside the school, there are going to be a lot of questions." He stopped at the end of the hallway and pointed to the last classroom on the right. "I left her in there."

Again, Cole gave him another hundred-dollar bill. "Thanks, and I promise after today, you will never hear from us again."

Max took the bill. "I got to get back to practice before my coach comes looking for me." Max took off back down the hall and down the stairs.

"Are you sure you're going to be all right?" Cole wanted to be sure Val was okay with the change he made to the original plan. On the way over to the school he thought it would be better if she confronted Caitlyn. Their volatile relationship could be essential in provoking Caitlyn into confessing. "If you need any help I'll be right outside the door listening. You have the tape recorder on you, right?"

Val pulled it out.

"Instigate. Start something. Push her buttons. She'll get so mad, she'll end up telling on herself. My sister doesn't handle pressure well. Get her to confess about the steroids. Once we have her on tape, we'll threaten her to either leave Hope or go to jail." Cole pushed the button to record and slipped it in Val's pocket.

Val took a deep breath before taking the short journey down the hall toward the coach's office. When she stepped inside, Caitlyn spun around.

"What are you doing here?" Caitlyn stuttered. Her eyes blinked rapidly. She couldn't believe Val had found her. "Did you follow me?"

"I'm the one who requested this meeting," Val said.

"I don't know what this is about"—She gave Val a high and mighty look as if she didn't belong—"but I'm leaving." She tried to walk away, but Val wouldn't allow her to pass.

"Sorry." Val folded her arms. "I can't let you do that."

Caitlyn laughed. "What?" She took a step back. "Do you want your man back?" She swung her blonde hair over her shoulder. "Well, you can't have him."

"How do you think he'll react once he finds out you're a drug dealer?"

Caitlyn acted as if she didn't know what Val was talking about.

"I know all about the steroids you've been selling to those kids, and I would bet my life that you had something to do with Julian and the scandal surrounding his steroid use."

"You have no proof."

"No, I don't, but those same kids who bought the drugs from you are the same ones who told me everything. They would give you up before they sacrifice themselves." Val was trying her hardest to goad her into a confession. "Caitlyn, it's over.

Let's go down to the authorities and you can turn yourself in."

Desperation filled Caitlyn's eyes. She felt trapped. A letter opener lying on the desk called out to her. She wrapped her bony fingers tightly around the handle and held it like a weapon. "Move!" she demanded.

Val was careful not to make any sudden moves. She wasn't scared, but she knew Caitlyn wouldn't hesitate to stab her and say it was in self-defense. After all, Caitlyn was the one with the restraining order.

"Now!" Caitlyn screamed.

Val couldn't figure out a way to get that letter opener away from her without getting stabbed, so she slowly slid away from the door.

The first chance Caitlyn got she attempted to dash past Val, but Val rammed her tiny body into the blackboard. The two struggled over the letter opener and they fell back against the desk. Papers, books and pens fell to the floor. Caitlyn landed on top of Val. Caitlyn had the upper hand and used all her strength to push the sharp object into Val's heart, but Val wouldn't let her win. She fought back.

"Cole!" Val screamed.

Seconds later, he rushed into the office and lifted Caitlyn up off of Val. Caitlyn didn't hesitate to go after her brother. She jabbed toward his gut, and he easily took the weapon right out of her hands. Caitlyn was no match for her brother.

Realizing she was outnumbered and without protection, she ran out of the room and down the back stairwell.

Val and Cole rushed after her.

"What do we do now?" Val tried to catch her breath.

He pointed in the opposite direction using the letter opener. "You go that way and get the car." He gave her his car keys. "She won't try anything, but we have to keep a close eye on her. I'm going to make sure Max is all right."

They went their separate ways. Val took off one way, and Cole raced off in the opposite direction.

Cole pushed open the heavy steel door that led to the stairwell and sped through. As he crossed over the threshold he wasn't aware that his sister was standing on the other side.

Once he passed through, Caitlyn stuck out her foot. Cole stumbled and flipped head first down the stairs. His body tumbled over itself until he stopped on the landing in-between floors. The letter opener she tried to stab him with was now lodged in his side. Blood poured out of the wound. Caitlyn glared down on her brother from the floor above.

"Help me." Blood spilled from the corner of Cole's mouth.

Caitlyn stepped down the stairs one at a time. "Help you? What would you like me to do?" She pulled out her cell phone. "Do you want me to call 9-1-1?" She pushed the number nine on her phone. Her brother watched with wide eyes wondering why she was being so slow.

Then she hit the one. She looked at her brother, gave a wicked grin and slammed her cell phone shut.

"What are you doing?" he whispered in agony.

"I'm helping you. The same way you helped me." She stooped down next to him and gazed into his eyes. "How could you team up with Val? You know she's the enemy." Caitlyn took off one of her high-heeled shoes and hammered the letter opener deeper into his side. He cried out in pain. His breathing became labored and more blood gushed out of his mouth, then his head dropped down front of him.

"Big brother, you always said I would be nothing. Watch how I capitalize off your demise. You have no idea how many times I've prayed to be the oldest grandchild." She kissed Cole lightly on the side of his cheek. "Who says that prayer doesn't work?" She stood straight up and brushed herself off. Then she sang, "I'm rich!" as she descended the stairwell.

Val sat in the car waiting for either Cole or Caitlyn to emerge from the school. Ten minutes passed. Then another five. Suddenly, a shiver crept through her body, leaving her with a gut-wrenching feeling that something was wrong. She got out of the car and ran back into the building. Careful not to get caught aimlessly wandering the halls, Val ducked into the same stairwell she last saw Cole enter. She climbed a few stairs that led her straight to Cole. His body sprawled out across the landing. She ran to his side. "Cole!" She shook him and lifted his hand, but it went limp. Pressing her fingers to his neck she couldn't find a pulse.

Unsure of what to do Val got up and tried to drag his body, but he was too heavy. She didn't want to leave him, but then she heard voices coming their way and she had no choice. She dashed up the stairs and exited the school through a different exit and drove away as fast as she could.

Val slammed the back door behind her. She charged into her kitchen and pulled down the expensive bottle of vintage cognac from the top shelf. Her hands shook as she twisted the cap and broke open the seal. Skipping ice, she poured herself a drink and swallowed the brown liquor whole. The burning sensation hurt her throat and made her yell. After she inhaled deeply to cool her throat she took another drink.

"I know Caitlyn had something to do with her brother's accident." Val paced her kitchen floor. Different scenarios charged through her mind. The most logical explanation was that his sister pushed him down the stairs. Now Val regretted not going with him.

She thought about Jonah. He needed to know about what Caitlyn did. She picked up the phone and placed it back down, realizing he didn't have a cell phone. She had no way of getting in touch with him. It was too late for her to call him at work.

Double vision took over. Two identical cognac bottles moved around her kitchen table. She rubbed her eyes and held out her hand to steady herself. Her head felt woozy. The alcohol was taking control. Val became paranoid and started hearing strange noises in the house. She stumbled around the house, checking to make sure all her doors and windows were locked. *Caitlyn is a lunatic. She could be on her way over here to finish me off.*

Val poured herself another drink. The aroma drifted past her nose. "Oh! This stuff is strong." Drunk, she staggered into the living room before passing out.

The following morning, Val was jolted out of a sound sleep by the telephone ringing loudly in her ear. She clutched her head to try and stop the pain, but every time the phone rang, the throbbing beat a little bit harder. She had to stop the pain.

The cordless phone sat on her coffee table. She answered.

"Val, it's Mr. Lawson."

"Uh-huh." Her mouth wasn't fully functioning yet.

"Where's Jonah? The judge has called us into court for late this afternoon."

"This afternoon?" Val sat straight up.

"Yes, the courts just alerted my office. The judge has called an emergency meeting. I need you and Jonah down at the courthouse at three o'clock. Don't be late."

Val looked at the clock. It wasn't even ten o'clock yet. "Mr. Lawson, Jonah's not here. Maybe you can catch him at work."

"All right. I'll give him a call and I'll you see at the courthouse."

Chapter 34

Jonah mopped the corridor floor just off the main hospital entrance. This was one part of the hospi-tal that didn't get a lot of traffic. It was times like this, when he was all alone at work, that he talked with God. "Father, I know a lot of times I stray so far away from You that it may seem like I don't even know who You are, but here I am again. Like the prodigal son, I've come home and I'm begging for Your help."

"Fortunately, God doesn't condemn us for our transgressions."

Jonah turned around and found Mrs. McCormick standing a few feet away.

"Isn't it a blessing to have a Father who doesn't hold a grudge?"

She walked up closer. "I hope I'm not intruding, but I remember meeting you and your daughter with Val in front of the museum. I was on my way to visit with a few members from my church and I thought you looked familiar."

He quickly remembered her face.

"I didn't know you worked at the hospital."

"I haven't been working here for long," Jonah replied.

"Well, can you tell me how Val is doing? I haven't heard from her since I saw the two of you together."

"I really haven't seen too much of her lately."

"Oh!" Mrs. McCormick sounded disappointed. "I hope everything is all right between the two of you."

Jonah rubbed his face, unsure of what to say.

"When I saw the three of you at the museum together, that was the first in a long time I saw Val with a genuine smile on her face. I could tell she was happy. I don't know if she told you, but at one point Val was engaged to my son."

"Yes, she told me." He dipped the mop he was holding back in the bucket. "I'm sorry about your loss."

"Don't be. My son did more in his lifetime than most people who live to be sixty years old. He went to college, played in the NBA, and most importantly he knew what it felt like to be loved."

She noticed Jonah's eyes fall to the floor. She placed her hand on his shoulder. "Val is such a remarkable woman. She reminds me of myself. That girl will do whatever necessary to protect those she loves. She's a good person to have in your corner. You know, when I saw you with her I was surprised, but I'm glad to see she found such a nice young man to hang out with. I'm not going to say it doesn't feel a little odd to see her with someone besides my son, but you look like you have a good head on your shoulders and you have that beautiful little girl. Val is like a daughter to me, and I want to see her happy, and it looks like you make her happy."

Jonah smiled a bit.

"See, I knew I could get you to smile."

Mrs. McCormick waved good-bye, and Jonah thought about what she said about Val. He had to admit that since Val walked into his life, she had been a steady rock, always there when he needed her most. She saved him from the beating, gave him clothes, food, a roof over his head, not to mention the lawyer she hired on his behalf.

He slammed the mop down on the floor and it broke. "How could I be so stupid?"

"Reynolds." He turned around to face his supervisor. "A Mr. Lawson called and left this number for you to call him back. He said it was important." He handed Jonah the slip and walked away.

Val arrived at the courthouse early. Instead of going straight inside, she chose to sit on the benches outside the courthouse. She didn't want to miss either Jonah or Mr. Lawson when they arrived. She was still unsure of how Jonah would react when he saw her, but she had to speak with him.

Val pulled her sunglasses down over her eyes. The excruciating headache from her hangover prompted her to pull out a bottle of aspirin.

"Do you have a headache?" Caitlyn stood over Val. "Does your head hurt because you feel responsible for my brother's death, or is it because you in some way feel responsible for Jonah losing Hope?"

"What happened to Cole?" Val pushed the aspirin bottle back down into her purse.

"How would I know?" Caitlyn acted innocent. She pulled a cigarette out of her purse and lit it up. She blew cigarette smoke out her mouth and walked closer to Val. "Stay out of my way. Hooking up with my brother was the biggest mistake you could have ever made. If you're not careful, you could take an accidental fall." She chuckled.

Val pointed her finger in Caitlyn's face and squared her lips to rattle off a list of four-letter words when Jonah walked up.

"Caitlyn?" He was happy to see Val, but he didn't want to talk with her in front of Caitlyn. "I got a call from my lawyer that you requested this hearing. What is this about?" He took her by the elbow and guided her away from Val so they could talk in private. "You were gone all day yesterday. When I got up this morning you were already gone. We need to talk."

"Jonah," Mr. Lawson interrupted, "the hearing is about to begin, and I need to speak with you and Val."

Jonah looked torn. It was important for him to speak with Caitlyn. He was having second thoughts about them getting married. He prayed that wasn't the reason she initiated this meeting.

Mr. Lawson gestured for Jonah and Val to follow him. Caitlyn and her lawyers followed behind them.

"Do either of you have any idea what this is about?" Mr. Lawson asked. "It must be important for the judge to grant an emergency hearing."

Jonah mulled over telling them about him and Caitlyn getting married.

"Well, it doesn't matter now because we're about to find out." He nodded toward the judge entering the courtroom.

Everyone stood to their feet, and the judge didn't procrastinate on starting the proceedings. "Ms. Haas, I would like for us to get straight to the point, since you insisted I cut my lunch short in order to get you on my calendar this afternoon."

Caitlyn stood to her feet, "Your Honor, I know that you were about to rule on the custody case for my daughter, but after much consideration I have decided to withdraw my request."

Judge Cohen was surprised. "What made you change your mind?"

"Jonah is an awesome father. He is so good to my daughter. He is both a mother and father to Hope, and right now I'm not ready to be the kind of mother she needs. Plus, with the news that I received this morning concerning my brother, I feel like now is not the time."

"Ms. Haas, I heard about your brother's accident, and I'm sorry to hear about his passing."

She nodded her head thank you.

"So, if it pleases the court and Jonah agrees, I would like to sign away my parental rights, and I will not stand in the way of him officially adopting Hope."

"Is this arrangement all right with you?"

Jonah was in a daze and didn't realize the judge was talking to him.

"Mr. Reynolds, is this a good deal for you?"

Jonah stood to his feet. "Yes, Your Honor."

"Good. I will have Mrs. Chambers contact you about getting the adoption process started. Just to inform everyone, the blood test results came back. Hope is undeniably Ms. Haas's daughter, and I would have ruled in her favor."

Caitlyn acknowledged his remarks by a nod of her head. Judge Cohen adjourned court and slammed his gavel down.

"Well, this is definitely a miracle." Mr. Lawson patted Jonah on his back. "Somebody must have been praying for you."

Jonah looked over at Val. "I've been meaning to call you. I really need to—"

Caitlyn interrupted them by calling out to him.

He got up from his seat. "Stay right here. I'll be right back." He went to her with open arms. "Caitlyn, I really appreciate this. You won't regret this decision."

"I know I won't." She gave him another hug, and from over his shoulder she winked her eye at Val.

Then Mr. Lawson called Jonah. While Jonah finished up his business with Mr. Lawson, Caitlyn sashayed over to the table where Val was sitting.

"I can tell by the confused look on your face that you're surprised at what happened here today."

"I guess I am."

"Let me take you out of your suspense. Now that my brother is dead, I'm rich. The inheritance that was entitled for my brother is now mine."

"So you no longer need Hope." Val was repulsed by the mere sight of Caitlyn.

"Exactly." She pulled her coat tightly around herself and left.

Anger boiled through Val's veins. She was furious that Caitlyn would again get away with the wrong she had done. Val was ready to tell the whole world how Caitlyn was responsible for her brother's death. She would love nothing more than to see her rot behind bars, but then her eyes rested on Jonah. He was finally happy. He and Hope would finally be reunited forever, and if she told what she knew that could jeopardize his happiness.

For now she would have to swallow her pride and allow Caitlyn to bask in her triumph. Val prayed that today would be the last time she ever laid eyes on Caitlyn. Hopefully, she would be walking out of their lives forever.

Jonah shook hands with Mr. Lawson before returning back to Val. "Mr. Lawson said if I wait here they'll bring Hope to me."

"Are you still upset with me?" Val asked.

"No. I apologize for acting like a fool." He took her hand in his. "I overreacted, and I wouldn't blame you if you didn't accept my apology." Then he bent down and kissed her lightly on the lips.

"I think I can accept your apology." She smiled.

Later that evening Hope, Jonah and Val stood on Mrs. McCormick's doorstep. "Are you sure you're ready to do this?" She held her finger inches away from Mrs. McCormick's doorbell.

"Yes, I think it's time for Mrs. McCormick to meet her granddaughter." Jonah kissed Hope on the cheek, then turned and also gave Val a kiss.

She nervously pushed the doorbell. This reminded her of the first time Julian brought her home to meet his parents.

When Mrs. McCormick answered the door, she was so happy to see Val, Jonah and Hope together that she insisted they stay for dinner. Mrs. McCormick loved to cook and she made enough to feed the entire neighborhood.

After she served dessert and everyone was chatting around the table, Jonah gave a subtle nod to Val that he was ready to tell them.

"Mr. and Mrs. McCormick, we have some startling news to tell you and we don't want you to get alarmed."

Mrs. McCormick braced herself for the worst.

"Hope." She nodded toward the little girl who was licking the vanilla ice cream from her fingers. "She's adopted."

Mrs. McCormick laughed. "Oh! Is that all? Val, that isn't startling news." Relief showed over her face.

"Yes, but"—Val suddenly wished she didn't have to tell her this—"what you don't know is that Hope is your grandchild."

Mrs. McCormick looked at her strangely.

"I know this may be hard for you to understand, but Julian might have fathered a child before he died."

Speechless, Mrs. McCormick dropped the butter knife she was holding on her plate. She looked toward her husband then she looked at Hope. The little girl was so absorbed in eating her ice cream, she had no idea what was going on around her. Mrs. McCormick got up and walked around to Hope's chair. When Hope saw her, she smiled at her grandmother before pushing another spoonful of ice cream in her mouth.

"This is my grandbaby?" Mrs. McCormick ran her fingers over Hope's hair. "She's really Julian's daughter? How could this be?"

After Val explained Caitlyn's pregnancy and the DNA tests that were performed by the courts, Mrs. McCormick cried tears of joy and hugged her grandchild close to her.

"You don't know how badly I've wanted a grand-daughter. I loved Julian and I always will, but to have a second chance with his daughter is a blessing. The Lord took my son, but He kept his promise to give me a grandchild." Then she got up and hugged Jonah. "Thank you! Thank you so much for taking care of this child and enduring everything you had to go through. You had to risk your life, and I love you for that." Tears fell from her eyes. "And I want you to know that I would never try to take her away from you. Since Val recommended we do a DNA test I will contact my lawyer sometime this week, but I would never try to disrupt Hope's life with you."

Hope's new grandparents wasted no time in spoiling Hope. They started making plans for Disney World and private school.

With so much movement in the house and everyone making such a big fuss over Hope, Val slipped away into the living room for a moment by herself.

It was hard being back in Julian's parents' house. Memories filled the room. Mrs. McCormick still had the room full of his pictures. She remembered the day they got engaged. Julian asked her to marry him in the same spot she was standing in.

"Are you happy?" Jonah scared her.

"Very. No more secrets and no more lies."

"You how know important it is for me to give Hope a family," Jonah said, "and with her grandparents being a part of her life, the only thing missing is a mother."

Val closed her eyes a moment, and when she opened them again he was down on one knee.

"Marry me?" Jonah popped the question.

Val was unsure how to react. They were in her ex-fiancé's parents' house.

"Valencia."

The sound of her name brought back memories of Julian. He was the only one who called her Valencia. She looked around the room, and it was Hope calling out for her.

Hope walked over to Val and opened up her arms for a hug.

"I told you she would warm up to you," Jonah reminded her.

Val picked her up and hugged her so tight that she cried.

Chapter 35

Five days following Baxter's successful lung transplant, Colin returned to the hospital to visit with his former boss. When Colin walked in, Baxter was asleep. Colin stood for a moment and watched as the breathing apparatus pumped life into his lungs. Baxter's chest rose up and down. Colin couldn't believe a part of his friend now lived inside Baxter. He reached out his hand to touch Baxter's chest. He just wanted to feel a small piece of his friend again, but before his hand settled, Baxter's eyes flung open.

Baxter looked petrified. Colin pulled his hand back and waited to see what Baxter would do.

Baxter moved the mask from his face. He had a little trouble breathing, but he talked rather well. "How is West's grandson?"

"He's dead," Colin told him. "Good. At least something positive came out of this." Baxter seemed to relax better at the sound of that news.

Colin chuckled. He didn't question God when He took Dean home to be with Him, but he often wondered why God would leave Baxter on earth with them. "It's good to know you're pleased with the outcome, but just because Dean is dead doesn't mean parts of him won't live on." Baxter looked at him strangely. "What do you mean by that?" Colin gave him a sly grin and walked out of the room.

Olivia spread every outstanding bill she had over the kitchen counter. She studied the balance of each credit card statement, her car payment and her monthly utility bills. She gathered everything into one pile and prayed over it.

She refused to worry because she knew God would make a way when she had none. Her daily prayers went up and God knew the petitions of her heart. Dean was a great provider when he was alive, and she thanked the Lord every day for their union, but she knew God wouldn't leave her wavering in the wind. It wasn't easy to let go and let God, but ultimately she had no choice. Olivia was sure she was living in the center of God's will.

One worry she didn't have to burden herself with was a mortgage or rent payment. Judge West opened his home to Bryce and Olivia for as long as they needed. Living rent-free would help her in paying off her bills. But, as soon as she was financially able, Olivia wanted to look for a house of her own. This place held too many memories of Dean.

Olivia took a sip from her coffee mug before realizing how late it was getting. Dean's lawyer had set up a meeting for her to finalize his estate. She finished off her cup and did a little cleaning before leaving.

The huge gold-plated revolving doors were much heavier than they looked. Olivia pushed her way into the office building and stopped in the middle of the floor. "You look lost. Can I be of any assistance to you this afternoon?" A friendly overweight security guard grinned at her.

"Yes, I'm looking for Mr. Sexton's office."

"He's located on the seventh floor. Walk around to the elevators on the far right side of the building, and the doors will open right in front of his office."

"Thank you."

Olivia maneuvered around the maze of office workers and mail carriers as they raced to and from their destination. She found the elevators with ease and boarded along with a crowd of people. The elevator stopped at every floor, making the duration of the ride longer than expected.

Finally it reached Mr. Sexton's floor. She got off the elevator and walked straight into the law office of Marcus Sexton. Marcus was a close college buddy of Dean's, and after Dean passed she'd learned that he was handling most of Dean's business matters.

She introduced herself to the receptionist, and within seconds Marcus came out into the lobby to greet her. "Olivia, I'm so glad you could make it."

They shook hands, and he escorted her down a narrow hallway. They entered his plush office, and he offered her a seat.

"How are you making out?" He sat down behind his desk.

She sighed deeply. "Every day I think it gets a little easier, but it's still hard to believe that my husband is gone. I still don't think my son understands that Dean isn't coming back."

"I understand. I miss him myself. A few times I had to catch myself from picking up the phone and dialing his office." He grabbed a huge manila envelope and pulled out a copy of Dean's will. "I guess we should get started. It's not really that difficult. He left you everything. You are the sole beneficiary of Dean's estate. Today, I'm going to take the time and go over everything with you. If you have any questions, don't hesitate to ask. I'm here to assist you." He laughed to himself. "Dean gave me strict instructions to treat you special."

Olivia smiled.

"He also told me not to hit on you."

Olivia gave him an amused look.

"Don't worry, I'm not going to hit on you. You're pretty, but I'm married." He flashed his wedding ring.

He pulled out some forms and placed them down in front of Olivia. "Before I give you any checks, you must sign for them." He pointed to a few lines on the paper.

Olivia squinted. "These are a lot of forms."

"Well, this one is from Dean's pension plan." He pointed to the first form. "I took the liberty of rolling his pension into an IRA in your name so that you wouldn't be penalized."

Olivia picked up a check that was written out for over seventy-five thousand dollars and set it back down. "At least I don't have to worry about retirement," she commented.

"This is also a pension fund that he had from his second job." Marcus pulled out a second packet and had her sign in various spaces. The check for that pension was close to eighteen thousand dollars. "I'll also roll that over into an IRA account for you if you want."

"I had no idea Dean had so much money put away for retirement."

"Yeah, he often called me for legal advice. Fortunately, we both learned how to save a dollar when we were in college." Marcus chuckled. "These next four documents are from different stocks and investment clubs Dean was involved in. He was sure you would need the money, so he asked me to cash these out for you."

Olivia signed for all four checks, and he handed her checks that totaled close to a million dollars.

"This is all mine?" Olivia stared at the dollar amounts. She never saw a check with so many zeros. Each check was written out for no less than two hundred thousand dollars. Her eyes began to get blurry, so she rubbed them and sat back in her chair.

"Let me get you some water." Marcus ran out of his office and returned with a cold bottle of spring water.

"Dean never mentioned he was into the stock market," Olivia said.

Marcus opened the water bottle before handing it to her. "He didn't participate that much. I encouraged him to invest, and fortunately he invested at the right time. His stocks doubled in a few short years."

Marcus could tell Olivia was not expecting to receive this kind of money. "The last check is from his life insurance policy. He had three policies that equaled over two hundred thousand dollars each. Two of the checks are made out to you, and the third he wanted put into a trust fund for your son."

Olivia cried. She couldn't believe Dean was providing for her even after his death. Marcus handed Olivia a few tissues to wipe her face.

"I'm sorry, I wasn't expecting all this," she cried.

Olivia knew that Dean was gone, but she never felt more alone than she did at that moment. More than anything in the world she wished her husband was still alive. Having all this money and not being able to share it with the one she loved broke her heart. She wished she could tell him one more time how much she loved him.

"Thank you, Marcus." Olivia put her signature on the last of the forms.

"There were a few more checks, but that went toward Dean's medical expenses and the funeral. Believe me when I say you and your son were Dean's first priority. He said his soul would be at ease knowing you were well taken care of." Marcus sounded so sincere.

Olivia held out her hand. "I appreciate all your help." They shook hands.

When she stood to her knees she felt a little weak. The room spun, and she quickly held on to the chair until she was able to regain her balance.

"Are you all right?" Marcus asked.

"I'm fine," she reassured him.

"Olivia, spend your money wisely, and if you need any legal or financial advice you can call me day or night."

She smiled warmly before closing the door behind her.

"Thank you, Dean," Olivia whispered in the elevator. "You always did have my best interests at heart."

Chapter 36

Four months later

Today was opening day for the Dean West Elementary School. Olivia gave a generous donation to the school, which helped expedite the opening for next school year. Colin and Judge West worked hard to make sure their dream of opening a good, safe school for their children was a reality. Standing in front of the school steps were the mayor, along with numerous other government officials. Even the governor of Pennsylvania had made it to the ceremony. Lots of people stood out in the audience anxious for them to open a school that cares about their children getting a good education.

Val held Hope's hand as they listened to the different speeches being given by several city dignitaries when Jonah approached her with a copy of the *USA Today* newspaper.

"Look at this," he said.

Val took the paper in her hand. The front page displayed a picture of Caitlyn being hauled into the Seattle police headquarters. Val quickly skimmed through the article to discover Caitlyn had been arrested for her third drunk driving offense. Currently her lawyers were working overtime to avoid her from doing any jail time.

"I guess money can't buy everything," Val whispered.

"I guess not," Jonah replied. "It's a blessing she did what she did and gave full custody of Hope over to me."

"Yes, I have to agree, Caitlyn made the right decision."

Jonah hugged Val tightly around her waist and planted a wet kiss on her cheek.

After Caitlyn left town, Val had told Jonah everything about Cole and the inheritance. The couple cleared up any misunderstandings they had and made a vow to never keep any secrets from one another again.

Right beneath the article about Caitlyn there was a small article that reported Reverend Baxter was sentenced to fifteen years in jail for the murder of Judge West's grandson.

Val tossed the paper in the trash.

"Parents," Judge West announced, "I promise you that this will be a school that will reach high. We will strive high in expectations, and we will not let your children down."

Everyone cheered. Judge West and the mayor cut the ribbon strings together, and everyone was welcomed into the school to get a grand tour.

Olivia, Bryce and Danyelle stood on the far end of the stage together.

"Dean would have been so proud." Tears poured out of Olivia's eyes.

"Yes, he would have," Danyelle replied.

Chapter 37

The Wedding

It was a splendid fall day for a wedding. First Nazareth looked more like heaven than a church. The entire interior of the church had been covered in white. The pews were decorated with white sheets. Huge long white centerpieces sat in each windowsill adorned with red long-stemmed roses.

Tressie looked around. She had never seen the church look lovelier. She was a bit jealous, but at the same time happy for her friend. She wished that she was the one getting married, but she knew her turn would come one day.

Val took Jonah's hand in hers. The couple snapped pictures of Hope as she stood at the front of the church dressed in a simple yellow-and-white flower girl's dress. Hope saw them, smiled and waved back. She and Val were quickly becoming close friends. They did things a mother and daughter would do together.

After Jonah had proposed, Val took her time giving him an answer. As a matter of fact, he was still waiting. Once he realized she was stalling for time, he told her it was no rush. He would wait until she was ready to say yes.

Grateful for his patience, Val took that extra time to go back to school, get to know Hope better and make sure they had God situated right in the center of their relationship.

The bride looked radiant in her gown. After searching endlessly for the perfect dress, she had decided to wear her mother's gown.

"Do you, Danyelle Benson," Reverend Simms began, "take Colin Montgomery to be your lawfully wedded husband?"

The look of love in their eyes was obvious.

"Yes," she replied.

It came as a complete surprise to everyone when Danyelle announced that she was getting married. No one even knew they were dating.

Colin repeated his wedding vows, and before they knew it, Reverend Simms was pronouncing them husband and wife.

"You may now kiss the bride."

Colin lifted her veil and sealed a kiss on her lips that would last a lifetime.

About the Author

Jersey girl Dynah Zale was born and raised in Deptford, New Jersey. She graduated with an Associate's Degree from Camden County College and then moved to Atlanta, Georgia to complete her studies at Spellman College. Her move to Atlanta was short-lived, and she soon returned back to her home state, where she currently resides.

Dynah's love for books and the admiration she holds for the writings of Terry McMillan, Connie

Briscoe, and Victoria Christopher Murray are what encouraged her to embark on her own professional writing career.

She hopes her unique writing style combined with an inspirational flair will not only tell a story, but deliver a message; a message of hope to the hopeless and tranquility to all troubled hearts.